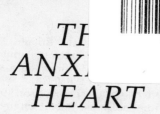

THE
ANXI...
HEART

Denise Robertson

Constable · London

First published in Great Britain 1992
by Constable and Company Limited
3 The Lanchesters, 162 Fulham Palace Road
London W6 9ER
Copyright © Denise Robertson 1992
The right of Denise Robertson to be
identified as the author of this work
has been asserted by her in accordance
with the Copyright, Designs and Patents Act 1988
ISBN 0 09 470980 7
Set in Linotron Palatino by
CentraCet, Cambridge
Printed in Great Britain by
St Edmundsbury Press Limited
Bury St Edmunds, Suffolk

A CIP catalogue record for this book
is available from the British Library

1

It had rained throughout the night, drumming noisily on roofs and window-panes, but the rain ceased with dawn and gave way to a watery sunlight. In Grimshaw Road the pavement steamed gently for a little while, the litter gurgled briefly in the gutters and then lay still, and the terrier in the end house nosed aside the lace curtains to look out at a new day.

Julie Baxter, the first-floor tenant in No. 13, shot out a thin, bare arm to grasp the alarm clock as it began to ring. She depressed the button and raised herself up in the bed, bare-breasted and shivering, listening in case the noise had wakened the baby. There was silence and for a moment she contemplated snuggling down again into the warm. But only for a moment. She had a lot to do!

Her clothes lay discarded beside the bed and she reached for an oversized sweater, pulling it over her head and lifting free her long, fair hair. She relaxed a little in the comfort of the wool and turned to the boy lying beside her. Her mouth softened at the sight of him. He was seven days younger than she and they had been friends since their first day at Infants' School. Last night she had held him in her arms while he sweated and groaned above her, all the while remembering when he had been a flower monitor and she had had to keep him right.

Now she put out a hand and shoved at his shoulder. He groaned and tried to roll away but she was adamant.

'Come on, Link. Up.'

'What time is it?' His voice was thick with sleep.

'Half-past six . . . and keep your voice down or you'll wake the bairns.'

5

This time his groan was one of outrage. 'Have a heart, Julie, man. It's the middle of the bleeding night.'

She was out of bed now, stepping into pants and jeans, tucking her hair behind her ears.

'It might be the middle of the night for you but some bastard's had Nana Foster's milk the last two mornings and he's not getting it again. Apart from which, I want you out of here before the bairns are up. I've told you that before. I don't want them finding men here in the mornings. It's not right.'

Link sighed and slid further beneath the bedclothes but they both knew she would have her way. She always did. As she left the bedroom he swung his legs to the floor and sat shivering on the side of the bed, trying to remember where he had left his jeans.

In the living-room-kitchen Julie drew aside the curtains and looked out on the rain-washed street. On the sill her window-box showed green but there were no flowers left now that it was November. She liked flowers. She turned on the tap and filled the kettle, then switched on Radio One.

While the kettle boiled and music throbbed she fetched paper and pencil and sat at the kitchen table to compose a note. She frowned, seeking the right words, and then wrote busily. When it was done she grinned and went back to the bedroom door. Link was under the covers again.

'Get a move on!' Her tone was hostile now.

The body in the bed stirred. 'OK, OK,' he sighed. Mornings were not his best time.

Julie turned back into the living-room, her eye taking in the poster of Sting on one wall, Kim Wilde on another, both in erotic poses. Between them a print of the Madonna, knee-deep in lilies, looked incongruous but tranquil. Julie's face showed satisfaction. She was getting the room nice. She moved to touch the frame of the Madonna into line and then opened the door to the landing of the terrace house.

There was silence. No throaty cough from Nana Foster below, no sobbing from deserted wife Yvonne above. The buggers swore blind they never slept, Julie thought, but they were like bloody logs in the mornings. It would be up to her to safeguard the milk.

It stood on the outside step, full-cream for Nana and Yvonne, semi-skimmed for her. They were killing themselves with cholesterol but she couldn't worry about everything. She lifted all the milk inside and laid the note in its place. 'TOO LATE,' it said in hasty capitals. 'HA BLOODY HA.' As she went upstairs Julie felt a frisson of satisfaction. Life was one continuous battle and it was nice to win a skirmish now and again.

There was still no sign of life in the bedroom, only a mound beneath the covers. She seized the blankets and tugged. 'Up!'

Link was curled like a baby, naked except for his striped socks.

'Up! I'm not moving till you're out of here.' It had been a mistake to let him stay the night. He was never content with an inch, it had to be a sodding mile. 'Up, Link, or it's the jug of cold water!'

She stood mercilessly while he stumbled into his clothes. In spite of last night's love-making he tried to hide his nakedness from her but she stayed put, stony-faced. She had turned her back before and he had been into the bed again in a flash.

When he was into jeans and T-shirt he fished in his back pocket for a comb and turned anxiously to the mirror.

'It's all right, Link, your hair's still there,' Julie said. The blond thatch was his pride and joy, part of his rock-star dream. She left him to his toilet and went back to the kettle.

When he came into the living-room she thrust a mug of tea at him. 'Get this down and then scram. Jason'll be up in a minute.'

He sipped the tea, wincing at its temperature, but when he spoke his voice was hopeful. 'Shall I come round later on?'

Julie tried to keep the distaste out of her voice. Men were a turn-off in the mornings. 'No. Bye-bye.'

Link was wiping the tea from his mouth as she pushed him on to the landing and shut the door on him. She wanted tonight to herself. And besides, there was Billy to be dealt with. Delinquent little Billy from downstairs, who would get them all into trouble before he was finished.

It was The Happy Mondays on the radio now and she began to gyrate to the beat of the music. With luck she still had a few minutes before the children woke. She moved well and she knew it, thrusting out her hips and rotating on her long, thin legs. She felt her spirits rise until she heard Yvonne moving overhead, her feet dragging as she went about her morning chores. She would have to dry Yvonne's tears again today and tell her her missing husband would come back sooner or later, and then there would be Nana to sort and, if she had time, the DHSS to be cajoled and threatened. And Billy. Always Billy. She ceased to swing and moved to the window to look out at the lack-lustre window-box.

If only there was a flower. One. One bright splash of colour to shout defiance to the glowering sky.

She went back to the table but her mug of tea had gone cold and the pot was stewed. She rested her chin in her hands and thought of the coming winter. November, December, January . . . not a sign of a flower before March.

Above her the pulley was loaded with drying clothes, Jason's at one end, the baby's in the middle, her spare bra and several pairs of nylon briefs at the other. The briefs were bright colours – reds and pinks, mostly, shirred at the edge with lacy elastic. Julie's eyes narrowed. She had two more pairs, three if you counted what she stood up in. And they didn't take a minute to rinse through if you ran short.

She stood up and pulled two red briefs from the pulley, twisting each one into a fat rosette. A moment later, impaled on forks, they bloomed in the window-box, scarlet blossoms, exotic among the sooty greenery. She shut the window, boiled up the kettle and scalded a celebratory tea bag. There was always a way to cheer yourself up if you looked for it.

On the other side of the city, in Eastgate, where roads were wide and tree-lined, Graham Iley was also preoccupied with underwear, this time boxer shorts. There had to be a clean pair somewhere. But the drawers were filled with sports wear and odd socks, and in the end he had to rescue last night's discarded pair with their 'Cherchez la femme' slogan and step into them with a grimace of distaste.

Dirty dishes stood on the draining-board in the kitchen and a film of dust covered his music-centre. Dust was death to good sound. He would have to do something . . . something concrete . . . about the state of the place. Good resolutions were useless.

He moved an empty wine bottle from the bench to the waste-bin and looked in vain for bread to put into the toaster. Charlie had offered to wash up last night but he had turned her down. Once they did the domestic bit your days were numbered.

Graham had a sudden vision of marriage to Charlotte. It mightn't be too bad. But not yet. There would have to be help of some sort in the mean time, that was all. A Jeeves! He retrieved a T-shirt and shorts from the dryer and pushed them into his squash bag. There was only one clean sports sock and he found its mate still in the laundry basket, stiff and stinking.

He rinsed it in the kitchen sink and put it into the tumble-dryer while he ate onion-rye bread and sliced cheese in place of non-existent butter, watching the eight o'clock news on the kitchen TV until it was time to retrieve the sock. It was still wet but if he didn't leave now he'd be caught in the rush-hour traffic, and he had an early appearance before the Bench. He put the sock in the plastic side-pocket of his bag and collected his racquets. He was still hungry but when he looked there was only the remains of last night's lasagne and a strawberry *fromage frais* in the fridge.

He spooned the pink fluff into his mouth while he watched the BBC sports desk, and topped it off with a kiwi fruit, skin and all. It stung his mouth and he had a sudden longing for the sort of breakfast his mother had always made, creamy porridge, crispy bacon and toast in a rack with butter and preserves.

Julie seated Jason at the kitchen table and put the baby in his high-chair. It was twenty-five to nine. Ten minutes for

9

breakfast and five to the school yard. They could just do it. She sliced the top off Jason's egg for him and cut a slice from the granary loaf.

'I want proper bread,' Jason said flatly. He meant sliced white but Julie tried to look uncomprehending.

'This is proper bread, only it's brown.'

'It's got flies in it.'

Julie bit her lip and prayed for patience. He was too young to be told about bowel cancer.

'They're not flies,' she said evenly, 'they're grains. Grains is good for you. This is granary bread and it costs more so it's better for you. And eat up your nice chucky egg or your arms and legs'll snap.'

Jason gave her a look of disdain and prepared to leave the table.

'All right,' Julie said desperately. 'Eat the egg and you can have one slice of white . . . but you're having polyunsaturated on it.'

The five-year-old brows were down now. 'I want butter.'

She felt her nails dig into her palms. 'I know what you want, mate, and it's got nothing to do with cows! Look, eat your egg and I'll take you down the library after school.'

'Bet you don't.'

'I will. I want a book meself.'

She watched Jason fondly as he ate, all the while spooning cereal into the baby's mouth. Dollops of it fell on to the rusted tray of the high-chair and she wiped them off instantly with a dishcloth.

'There now, two good boys,' she said when they were done. She wrapped them both up in case it rained but when they reached the lobby sun was streaming in through the fanlight. Nana's milk was still outside her door, which meant she and Billy were probably still in bed.

Julie dragged the pushchair from under the stairs and fastened the baby into his harness.

'Come on,' Jason said, tugging at the door.

'Wait on. I'll just gave Nana a knock.' Billy was already in trouble for truancy – they couldn't afford another black mark. Julie hammered on the door until she heard movement and protestation behind it. 'It's ten to nine. Get him up and out of there, lazy little sod.' She dropped her voice on the last word and turned back to the pushchair. Most people didn't worry about swearing nowadays but she didn't like it in front of kids. You had to have some standards.

Outside Grimshaw Street was full of kids, the odd mother sprinkled amongst them. Jason saw a bosom friend and ran ahead to join him. Julie watched his legs, sturdy inside the corduroy trousers. He had good limbs, like his dad. She felt her face soften and schooled it instantly. It didn't do to get cocky. That was when things went wrong.

She would have kissed him at the school gate but he wriggled away, ruffling his black hair where she had stroked it.

'Eat your dinner, mind.' He turned at her shouted admonition and put out his tongue. Little bugger! Julie was smiling as she turned the pushchair and made for home. The baby had succeeded in getting the strap of the harness into his mouth and was sucking vigorously, and she started to go through her pockets for his dummy.

'Don't do that, pet.'

He smiled up at her but went on sucking. His eyes were as blue as Jason's were brown. But then his dad had been fair as a lily while Jason's dad had been dark and sallow. For a moment Julie tried to remember either man's face but they eluded her. She felt a faint mist of rain on her face and, abandoning the search for the dummy, began to run for home.

She didn't stop running until she reached the door and was bundling the pushchair over the step.

'Is that you, Julie?' Yvonne's face peered over the stairs and as Julie looked up she saw that the paint was peeling from the underside of the banister, leaving raw wounds of mahogany. 'God, this place is a dump,' she thought and shook rain from her hair.

'Yes, it's me.'

'Are you coming up?' Yvonne's voice had the usual sob in it and Julie sighed.

'In a minute. I want to pop into Nana's first. Put the kettle on and I'll be up.'

She unstrapped Damien and lifted him on to her hip, then she bent to retrieve the pint of silver top she had saved earlier. She tried Nana's door handle and felt it give. At least they were up.

'It's me, Nana.' Inside the flat the air was thick with smoke. 'My God, what are you doing in here? Curing herring?'

Nana Foster sat by the fire, snug in a man's cardigan, her bare legs in unzipped carpet slippers. Around her the room was buried in clutter, every chair, every corner, every flat surface. 'God,' Julie said, wafting the air with her hand, 'it's like a smoke-chamber.'

'Billy had a fry-up for his breakfast,' Nana said defensively. She loved Julie but feared her tongue. Once launched into a lecture she was almost unstoppable and Nana was not in the mood for censure, not this early in the day.

'Take Damien,' Julie said, depositing the baby and flapping the air with a dubious tea-towel. 'Honestly, Nana. I've saved your milk for you but I don't know why I bother. You've been in that chair all night smoking, haven't you? And don't bother to perjure yourself . . . I can hear your arteries hardening.' She had reached the window and wrestled with the rusted catch. 'That's better.'

Inside her cardigan Nana shivered. 'That's right, see me off. I might as well be gone.' She shifted the baby into a more comfortable position and heaved a sigh but Julie only smiled as she filled the kettle and put the pint of milk in the bowl of water that served as a fridge.

'I hope your Billy's gone to school?'

'Yes,' Nana said tartly. 'As usual, he has.'

'As usual! My God, you can lie like a trooper.'

'He does go when he can. He can't help it if his trousers let him down. D'you want him to go bare-arsed?'

'Bare-arsed, bare-faced . . . as long as he gets there. And are you going to get this place cleaned up?'

'I might, as soon as I've pulled meself together.'

'As soon as you've picked your trebles for Sandown, you mean.' The paper lay open at the racing page, mute testimony to the truth of Julie's remark. 'You spend your mornings picking winners, your afternoons watching them lose and your evenings totting up your losses.' She had fetched a carpet-sweeper from the kitchen and began work on the ash-strewn carpet. 'Mind your feet.'

Nana obligingly lifted both feet, slightly clinging with one hand to the arms of her chair, hefting the baby theatrically in the other arm, as though they were both about to be devoured.

'I said "mind them",' Julie repeated harshly, pushing at the slippered feet with the sweeper. 'Up! Honestly, a Buddha would be more use. "Find me a flat near a nice, white-haired old lady," I said. "The grandmother type" . . . and they put me beside a geriatric delinquent like you.' She swept vigorously back and forth, cutting swathes through the dust and ash on the faded carpet. 'You'd sit like this for a fortnight if I stopped calling.'

'I'm not well,' Nana said, her eye edging towards the paper. 'I could do with some peace.'

'No chance,' Julie said brutally. 'Not till I see you on your feet. I've warned you Hunchfront's due again and if she finds this place a tip she'll have you. The Pied Piper had nothing on Social Services. They'll slap a care order on your Billy and that'll be that. You've never been down the Magistrates' Court, have you?'

Nana's eye slit up. 'I could do with a nice little stretch in Durham. Prison food'll be better than what I get here.'

'Go on, make a joke of it,' Julie said. 'But they won't put you in gaol, they'll put your Billy in a hostel.'

At last she had scored. All Nana had left was her grandson, Billy, whom she had reared since her only daughter went off with a soldier. She could not imagine life without him. Who would lay her bets, to name but one essential?

'All right, anything for a quiet life.' Nana looked down at Damien, placidly sucking the neck of his cardigan. 'I'm glad to see you've got him in a bit of wool. They don't dress babies properly nowadays, it's all those gro-bags. Go back to your mammy, pet, and let me get on.' Freed from the baby she heaved herself to her feet and pushed up her sleeves for action.

As Julie left the flat she could hear the sound of running water and clattering breakfast dishes. So far, so good. She parked the pushchair under the stairs and went up two flights to Yvonne's flat.

In contrast to Nana Foster's it was clean and tidy, filled

13

with pleasant modern furniture, but Yvonne, plump and in her late thirties, looked downcast. Before her marriage she had been a well-paid shorthand typist. Now she was a deserted wife and the transition had been painful.

'I like your hair like that,' Julie said positively. 'It's better than a centre parting.' She put the baby down on the shag-pile hearth-rug and sank into a chair.

'Does it make my face look thinner?' Yvonne asked anxiously, fingering her sideswept hair. Her cheeks bulged comfortably above her tense mouth and the buttons of her shirt strained over a runaway bosom.

'Yeah, a bit,' Julie said.

'I'm getting fatter, Julie.' Yvonne sounded desperate. 'I can't fasten this shirt . . . not properly. And I can't stop nibbling. I'm living on me nerves.'

'That's funny,' Julie said. 'I thought you were living on mine. Still, your hair's nice. I'll have to get some Hiltone when I get the Family Allowance. Me roots need touching up.'

Yvonne had scalded the coffee in flowered mugs. Now they sat opposite one another in deep Dralon chairs and drank.

'I'd give you a biscuit but I've got none.' Yvonne's eyes flicked guiltily to an empty packet on the coffee-table.

'It's OK. I don't like biscuits early on,' Julie said point-edly. Yvonne had been known to polish off a packet of custard creams for breakfast. Now she hurried to get off the touchy subject of food.

'Has Billy gone to school this morning?'

'Well, he wasn't downstairs when I was there. Not that that means anything. He usually hangs round the bus shelter when he's swagging off.'

'I'm sure I heard him come in after one,' Yvonne said.

Julie nodded. 'It figures.'

'Do you think we'll have trouble like that with our kids?' Yvonne asked, her eyes filling at the thought. She picked up the empty biscuit packet and searched it with hope of finding some crumbs. It was picked clean, and a tear rolled down her cheek.

'Oh God, it's not Happy Hour again, is it?' Julie said with deliberate harshness.

14

'I know, I know . . . I am trying.' Yvonne blew her nose on a tissue and reached for a cigarette butt from the mantelpiece. 'It's just that I've got so many worries.'

'Hasn't he paid up?' There was a clutch of opened bills on the mantelpiece under the Constable print in its gilded frame.

'No, and I've had the red notice for the electricity. I'll die if I get cut off. Apart from that, we need groceries and Andrea has a school trip coming up. And it's six days to the next Giro.'

Julie sipped and pondered. 'Got anything you can flog?'

'Not unless there's a mad rush for fondue sets. I got rid of a lot when the house had to go – I knew there wouldn't be much room here. Now I'm down to basics. And if they go . . .' The tears came silently, running down the plump cheeks to splash the over-full shirt.

'How long have you been on Social?' Julie's brow was furrowed in thought.

'Fifteen months . . . ever since Trevor went off to Spain. It's him being out of the country that makes it so difficult about the money.'

'Have you ever tried for bedding?' Julie asked.

'What do you mean?'

Julie sighed and sought for words. 'You go down the Social and say you're skint and you haven't got enough bedding and the kids are freezing and you're all in one bed under a blanket and they come and look and give you a Giro. You have to pay it back, a grant's like gold nowadays. Still . . .'

'That's no good. I've got plenty of everything . . . sheets, blankets, the lot.'

Julie's eyes closed in momentary anguish. 'Listen,' she said patiently when they opened again. 'You wrap up what you've got and bring them to my place. Just leave enough to look realistic. Then take the money they give you and get your bedding back. Everybody does it.'

Yvonne was looking both hopeful and dubious. 'I don't know if I dare. I mean, is it right?'

'No. It's wrong, but it's survival. I wouldn't fiddle if I didn't have to. They don't give you enough to exist on, never mind live, so you have to fiddle.'

15

'I know, but it doesn't seem right.' Yvonne was twisting her fingers together, her wedding ring biting into her newly plump ring-finger. Julie looked at her, feeling her patience evaporate.

'All right,' she said, getting to her feet. 'But you've got two kids and rent arrears and a husband who thinks he's El Cordobes. We have to play things by ear, people like you and me. We can't afford scruples.'

'Maybe I could get a job?' Yvonne said, brightening. 'I could do thirty words a minute once.'

'Good idea,' Julie said. She was about to add that Yvonne would have to smarten up first when she saw that, for once, her eyes were dry. A pity to spoil it.

The memory of his mother's cooking persisted all the way into town and up to Graham's office, where he hung the damp sock on a radiator and appealed to his secretary for coffee. She was a mother of three and brought him biscuits as well.

He telephoned Charlotte while he ate and drank, hoping for the sound of her voice and sympathy. He got one but not the other. 'Poor you. Now ring off and don't ring again. I've got meetings all morning and if I don't get my head down this afternoon I can't make Etta's tonight. Pick me up at quarter to, and don't forget a bottle.'

'Love me?' he asked, biting into the last shortcake.

'Possibly. It depends. Tell you tonight. Now ring off. I haven't even opened my mail yet.'

He put down the phone and sat still for a moment, thinking of Charlotte, remembering the feel of her in his arms last night, warm and naked, her legs entwined with his, her hair against his mouth, the hollow of her spine going on forever. It had been awful when she insisted on getting up and going home. If they married they need never be apart again. She was always hinting at it – but then that was what women did, wore you down.

His trance was broken by the taste of kiwi fruit, hot and sour in his throat. Oh God, he'd be belching all day if he wasn't careful. He took Alka-Seltzer from his desk drawer and went to get some water.

His appearance in court was brief, and by twelve he was free to go in search of lunch.

The salad bar was full and he had to push his way up to the bar. 'A half of Carlsberg and a ham salad in brown, please.' There was no one he knew in sight, though a red-haired girl in a business suit met his eye and held it. Very nice, but not at lunch time. Besides, there was Charlotte. He was half in love with Charlotte. Mustn't stray!

He carried glass and plate to an ivy-twined pillar, balanced them on the narrow ledge that served as a table-top, eased his hip on to a red-topped stool and pulled his *Independent* from his pocket. There were pages and pages of foreign news and he flicked over them guiltily. You ought to think globally but sometimes it wasn't easy. Instead he thought about court this morning. He had been persuasive and his client had got off lightly, which was good. He looked up as someone loomed over him.

'Graham?' The newcomer was sober-suited and bearing a pint and a pie.

'Jack . . . long time no see.' Graham folded his paper and moved his plate to make room. Jack Longman had been a good prop forward in his time, before he went to foreign parts.

'You still making an honest living?' Jack asked, levering himself on to a stool and loosening his jacket. There was a trace of a belly now and a jowl around his chin.

'I'm still with Dutton and Close . . . litigation mostly. You were off to Barbados the last time I saw you. Didn't it work out?'

'Very well . . . what a life! Sun, sea and sand. Lots of jollies . . . and thereby hangs a tale. I had to do the honourable thing, so here I am, back in Britain with a barely detached and an unbelievable mortgage. I've gone back to liquidations. It was that or tax – what a choice! The kid's super, though . . . I've got a picture somewhere.' Jack put down his glass and began to search his wallet.

It happened to everyone, Graham thought. Even the best. The rest of the crowd were dropping off two by two. In the end he'd be left out, unable to compare house prices and birth weights and the pros and cons of private education. That was all you talked about once you got hitched.

17

It was all right now, while they all still got together for rugger in winter and cricket in summer. But that couldn't go on forever. Already he sometimes felt shattered on Saturday nights. The thought of age creeping up on him was depressing. He would have to find other diversions, that was all. Perhaps Charlie would move in with him? He remembered the clutter he'd left behind and panicked for a moment. She would never stand for that. Maybe he should advertise – a nice motherly woman could do wonders. He certainly wasn't ready for the bonds of marriage. Not yet.

'Let me get you another half,' he said to Jack and threaded his way back to the bar as a sheaf of baby pictures appeared and were spread among the plates and glasses.

It was drizzling again as Julie and the children came home from the library. Jason had two books zipped inside his anorak and Julie had Robin Day's memoirs and a psychology textbook under the plastic cover of Damien's pushchair. As she hurried along she looked at the book's cover. *Understanding the Human Mind* it said, the letters superimposed on a human brain divided into sections. The librarian had recommended it as 'comprehensive' but was it comprehensible? That was her new buzz-word and she repeated it under her breath, enjoying the sound.

They were passing the bus shelter where Billy hung out and she peered in. It was empty but daubed with graffiti and littered with cigarette ends and sweet-wrappers from the shop across the road. If he wasn't there where was he, the little sod? Not in school, that would be too much to hope for.

Tommo's van was parked outside the house in Grimshaw Street when she rounded the corner. Up above the window-box bloomed, looking entirely natural at a distance, and Julie was smiling as she negotiated the step and pulled the pushchair into the hall.

Tommo was coming down the stairs, a trio of eggs in one upturned hand. His face lit up at the sight of her. 'I thought you were out.'

'I was,' Julie said, unbuckling Damien's harness. 'But I'm back now. Want a cuppa?' She liked Tommo a lot, and pitied him too. He was getting on, thirty at least, but still living with his mother who sounded a right bitch. And being a tallyman was a mug's game nowadays, when hardly anyone paid.

'Telly,' Jason said imperiously when they got upstairs. 'Telly now.'

'I'll give you "now",' Julie said but she switched it on just the same as he settled on an armchair.

'I brought these eggs for you and the bairns,' Tommo said, following her into the kitchen. 'They were warm when I got them out of the nest-box.'

'Ta.' Julie had plugged in the kettle and was assembling cups. 'Had a busy day?'

'Tuesday's always busy. It's Family Allowance day, and if I don't get in quick they'll have it spent. And I had to feed the hens this morning – mother's not too bright.' The splash of colour in the window-box caught his eye. 'What've you got there?'

'Rare blooms, Tommo. Knickeranii.'

He went to the window and peered, putting a cautious hand through the opening to feel. When he turned back he looked bemused.

'They're briefs,' Julie said encouragingly. And then, as he looked blank, 'Panties.'

'You'll be locked up one day.' Tommo's tone was admiring. 'Why didn't you say? I could've got you some artificials from the market. Asters, peonies . . . they've got the lot.'

'They wouldn't be the same, Tommo – those are originals out there. Bleeding Picassos . . . Besides, I couldn't afford them.'

'I didn't mean you to pay for them.' Tommo's face was crinkled with the desire to please and Julie decided to be firm.

'I couldn't've taken them, Tommo. You know how I feel about taking things.'

'But I like giving you things, Julie. I . . . well . . .' His words petered out and she hurried to change the subject.

'Nana's expecting Hunchfront to call any day now.'

'The social worker?' He was trying not to laugh aloud as Julie's hand mimed an ample bosom. 'She is a big woman. Still, Nana's not worried, is she?'

19

'Not half as much as she should be. Billy's always swagging off school, and Yvonne swears he slinks out at night.'

In the corner the baby had found a corner of the carpet and was sucking vigorously. Julie scooped him into her arms and deposited him back in the centre of the room. Jason looked up briefly from the television and then settled down again. Tommo had pursed his lips.

'Not good.'

'Too right, not good. He goes down the bus shelter – glue, booze, nicking, they're up to the lot there. It just needs to get to Social Services and they'll have him!'

'It might be the best thing.' As soon as the words had left his lips Tommo regretted them. He had heard Julie on the subject of social workers before.

'She's his gran, Tommo. She's looked after him since he was born, practically, and now that he's coming to an age where he could do a bit for her, they're going to take him. Well, over my dead body!'

'Can she cope? Lads of that age are a handful.'

'Lads of any age are a handful, I know that from our Jason.'

'Didn't you think about that before you had kids?' Tommo asked the question carefully but Julie didn't take offence.

'I never thought about anything before I had our Jason. Except getting a lad and getting away from school. Honest, I'd rather've done Borstal than stopped on there. "You could get Grade 1 CSEs, Julie," they used to say. "So what?" I said. I mean, CSEs weren't revelant . . . relverant . . . anyway, I wasn't stopping. I couldn't have, anyway, because I was pregnant. And then, when our Jason was born . . . well, he was that canny. I like kids.'

'Did you never think about getting married?' He was still trying to sound nonchalant but his concern showed through.

'Didn't get the chance, did I? Gary's mother had him in the Army so quick his feet didn't touch. And then he got into trouble, and the Army put him out. Last I heard he was navvying in Wales.' She twisted her legs under her on the settee and pulled her skirt over her knees.

'Is that why you don't get maintenance?'

'I wasn't going to claim off Gary! Not after he went away. He could've told his mam to get lost, couldn't he? No, I've got my pride. The Social went on and on about making the father pay. "Father?" I said. "What father?" They couldn't decide whether I was backward or the Virgin Mary, so in the end they gave up. They must've forgotten about him now 'cos they never ask about him, but I can still remember him. He had a good body . . . you know, nicely formed like our Jason. Our Damien's more stocky.'

'Gary wasn't Damien's dad, then?' Tommo asked. He had been told Julie's story in half a dozen spiteful versions but he hoped the truth might be more palatable.

'No. Dave, Damien's dad, was just passing through. He put the new pipes in Bower's Brewery and me in the club while he was at it. I can't remember much about him, except he was posh and we went out once and had broccoli. I love broccoli, it's like little green feather-dusters. I'd have it every day if it wasn't 48p a bunch.'

'You're a funny lot in this building,' Tommo said, a little embarrassed at Julie's frankness. He had drained his cup and held it out for a refill.

'How d'you make that out?'

'Well, there's three of you. Yvonne upstairs spends most of her time crying.'

'I know . . . her bladder's too near her eyes. Still, she has been left to cope with two kids on her own.'

'You have two kids to cope with and you don't cry about it. And Nana downstairs . . . credit where it's due, she's always good for a laugh.'

'She's a card, all right, but she's getting old, Tommo. If that little sod Billy doesn't watch it they'll have him off to a hostel and Nana'll be on her own.'

'It's no concern of yours,' Tommo said firmly. 'You've got enough troubles. And I shouldn't be sitting here as though I had corn growing.' He drained his cup again and got to his feet.

'Talking of work . . .' Julie was looking up at him almost coquettishly and he knew she was going to ask a favour. 'How does Nana's debt stand?'

'It stands still! She pays about one week in four. Why?'

21

'Billy needs some trousers. He's only got one pair, so if they're out of use he stops off school. If you could get him some jeans, cheap, he'd have a spare pair.'

'I'll see what I can do.' Tommo wanted to reach out and stroke Julie's thin arms but he hadn't the nerve. She was little more than half his age, or at least it felt that way. He turned to the door. 'I hope you'll remind Nana she owes for them, though. She tends to forget little details like debt.'

'Talking of debt,' Julie waved a hand towards the window, 'those blooms aren't half showing up my nets. I need some new ones, the frilly kind with the lift in the middle.'

'Jardinières?' Tommo looked at Julie's long, bare, goose-pimpled thighs. 'I could see more sense in you getting some warm clothes.'

There was genuine surprise in her voice. 'I've got heaps of warm clothes!'

'OK,' he said. 'I'll drop a few nets off and you can take your pick. Hope the kids enjoy the eggs . . . and get one yourself.'

'OK, dad. And don't forget Billy's jeans.'

Julie's smile was melting and Tommo felt once more the urge to reach out. But it might spoil things, and half a loaf was better than no bread at all. He contented himself with smiling and went off down the stairs.

When he was gone Julie set about the tea, wrestling with Jason over what he would and would not eat, spooning up the baby's spillage, her mind running ahead to the moment when she could get them down and open her books. It wasn't a prime night for telly, which was all to the good. TV was all right but it sapped your initiative.

She was in the middle of washing up when she heard whistling outside the window. Billy Foster was crossing the street towards the house, spiky head at a jaunty angle, jacket flapping above the patched jeans and huge orange boots. She took a quick glance at her children. They'd be all right for a minute or two. The next moment she was down the stairs, in time to meet Billy as he came in through the front door.

'I want you,' she said. He would have walked past her to his own door but she stood squarely in front of him. He was big as her and could have escaped but instead he stood his ground, looking insolently at a point over her head.

'What were you up to last night? Don't lie, because you were seen.' Billy didn't answer, not even when she put out a hand to shake his arm. 'All right, play dumb. But you cross these doors tonight and I'll massacre you.'

He shrugged off her hand and she let him go.

She was nearly back at her own door when Yvonne's head appeared above.

'What happened?' she asked, in a conspiratorial whisper that echoed around the stairwell.

'I told him.'

'Did he take any notice?' Yvonne asked mournfully.

'I doubt it.' There were ominous sniffs from above. 'And don't start crying again, Yvonne. I'm not sure we've got a damp course.'

'I'm just sorry for his gran. I wish I could help . . .'

Julie was almost through her door. 'Cheer up. I'll fettle him. Don't give it another thought,' she said airily, but she was far from sure of her ability to sort Billy out.

She drew the baby on to her knee and cuddled him close. A clown was blowing bubbles on the box. She felt her mouth upturn and lifted her legs on to the chair. She would just have a few minutes off . . . she'd always liked clowns.

She had washed both children and put the baby down when she heard the tap at her door. There was no one there when she opened it but a bunch of broccoli lay on the threshold. She picked it up and carried it to the table where *Understanding the Human Mind* lay, still unopened. She looked at the broccoli, fresh and green with lots of thin stalks, just the way she liked it, then laid it down beside the book. 'It's funny,' she said aloud to no one in particular. 'But the human mind is a strange organ which stops you fancying the one decent feller around who fancies you and gets you tied up with all the odds and sods and layabouts who intrude into your cosmic space. In other words, Julie Baxter, you need a psychiatrist.' After a moment she raised her eyes heavenwards. 'And if you send one, God, let him look like Sting!'

*

Julie had put Jason to bed, fetched him two drinks and threatened him with a good hiding if he didn't shut up, when she heard the noise in the hall. It would be Billy, making his exit! But when she reached the landing it was Link who was trying to negotiate the stairs. In his arms he held a video-recorder and several tapes, two bottles and a gaily coloured box which seemed to contain a toy.

'What are you doing here?'

'I've brought a video for you,' Link said hopefully. 'And a toy for the kids that I got down the market . . . and some Cherry Bs. I know you like Cherry Bs.'

'Go away, Link.'

'Come on, man, Julie,' he said, still struggling upwards. 'This lot's heavy.'

'Tough,' Julie said, preparing to go back inside. 'I told you not to come round.'

'I was at a loose end.' His head had appeared above stair-level now and their eyes met.

'You're always at a loose end, that's your trouble. And you haven't carted that video through the streets, have you?'

Link was on the landing now, leaning against the banister to get back his breath. 'Yeah.'

'You're asking for it. You'll get a custodial next time.'

'You don't get custodials for nicking . . .' She had trapped him and he tried to retrieve himself. 'Anyway, I didn't nick it, so no sweat. Let's in, Julie.' His voice became coaxing. 'I've got *Suburban Erotica*.'

'I don't care if you've got *Suburban Ex-otica*, Link. You are not getting in this place tonight.'

He had slid to the floor and was making himself comfortable with his back to the wall. 'Come on. I won't give you any hassle.'

'No, you won't, my son, because I've got enough hassle without you. You may not have noticed it, Link, but there's a war going on here. Social Services are the Alien Invaders, I'm an urban guerrilla and poor Nana'll be a human sacrifice if we're not careful.'

'She'll be all right!' Link sounded complacent and it annoyed Julie. In a moment she was back over her threshold, the door was shut and she was calling her goodbyes

24

through it. She added an afterthought, 'Make sure the law's not around when you carry that video out. I don't want any trouble.'

'Please, Julie!'

''Night, Link.' She made a show of shooting the bolt, leaving him to stagger back down the stairs with his burdens.

She had meant to return to her book but she couldn't settle. Instead she went to check on her sleeping children, smoothing hair from foreheads, moving sheets and blankets from small, relaxed mouths, finally putting Jason's library book on his side table and putting out his light.

She went into her bedroom, intending to get undressed. Instead she crossed to the window and looked out on the darkening street. Now that she had got rid of Link she felt suddenly flat. She could ask Yvonne to look out for the bairns and go in search of him but if she did she would regret it. He was just another problem, one more child to care for. She felt tears threaten and blinked them away. There was too much to do for tears and she never understood why she sometimes wanted to cry. Not when it was just a waste of time.

She went downstairs, first making sure that Link was not lurking, and tried Nana's door. It was open and she went in. The old lady was asleep in her chair by the fire, a burning cigarette in the ashtray, an empty glass slack in her hand. Julie removed it gently, and put it on the cluttered table, and stubbed out the cigarette. The door to Billy's bedroom was ajar and when she looked in it was empty. So he was already out somewhere, getting into trouble. Still, there was nothing to be done about it now. She took a last look round and tiptoed from the room.

Upstairs, in her own flat, she filled a hot-water bottle and carried it and her book to her bed, grateful that tonight she would sleep alone.

2

It was cold, Julie thought as she accompanied Jason to school. She watched him go in, trying not to look too proud, and then hurried to the corner shop. She had been awake since five trying to think of a way to sort Nana, fix Billy and get Yvonne off her back. Getting a copy of last night's paper was the first move.

She glanced at the bus shelter as she passed, but it was mercifully empty. Perhaps Billy had deigned to go to school today.

The Asian shop-owner hovered over her once he had provided the paper, seeming oblivious of his wife's resentful eyes from her perch behind the till. Julie scanned the shelf of health foods, occasionally examining a label for the dreaded E numbers.

'Do you get much trouble from that lot that hang around the bus shelter at nights?' she asked as she browsed. The shopkeeper's eyes rolled heavenwards in the dark and handsome face.

'Oh I should say so. Noise . . . abuse . . . I fear for my windows. A zoo, I tell you. A zoo! But now they are doing *wicked* things.' His voice dropped as he put up a hand to mime glue-sniffing and then reeled, goggle-eyed. 'They will kill themselves. My wife says, "Good riddings to bad rubbish," but I tell her they are still children. I myself am not selling glue ever! I tell the police, but they just drive past in their posh cars. It is not good enough.'

Julie nodded glumly, her worst suspicions confirmed. She reached for a silver-wrapped bar. 'This nutty crunch . . . it's not full of sugar, is it?'

'Absolutely not . . . no sugar. Well, perhaps a little sugar. But very much fibre . . . very healthy.'

While Julie deliberated he offered the baby a sesame-seed bar but his eyes were on Julie rather than the child. 'And this is for a good boy,' he said as Julie replaced the nutty crunch.

Across the shop his wife's eyes were signalling storm and when they got to the till she gave him a rapid burst in their mother tongue. Julie couldn't translate but she got the message. Outside she peeled the paper back and let Damien suck.

'He's going to suffer for that, pet. She doesn't like him giving samples. He's not bad looking, either . . . a bit like Richard Gere.' She looked up to find the wife's eyes fixed on her through the window as she released the brake and moved off with a final word to the baby. 'I hope you enjoy that, pet. I think it's begrudged.'

All the same, he should keep his eyes at home. He had a good-looking wife, a bit like the Madonna with that coiled hair and the smooth brown skin. Julie put up a hand to her own skin, tight and dry since her morning wash. Asian women were lucky.

She went straight up to Yvonne's flat. The door opened to her touch and she went through to the kitchen.

Yvonne was sitting at the kitchen table, still in her dressing-gown, clutching a cup of tea and staring glumly into space. Her hair hung to her shoulders except for two rollers, one either side of her centre parting. So she had returned to the old style: that was a bad sign. Julie passed a hand before her friend's eyes and, receiving no response, poured herself a mug of tea from the pot on the draining-board.

'Good night?'

'I never slept a wink, Julie. Two, half-past, three, half-past three . . . I heard them all.' Julie had listened to Yvonne's tales of insomnia before and would have disregarded them if Yvonne had not mentioned Billy.

'He was out again, that Billy. I saw him go, and I watched till well after midnight and there wasn't a sign of him coming back. Do you think we should tell the authorities before he gets into trouble?'

'The authorities *is* trouble, Yvonne, I keep telling you that. Never tell them anything unless you have to. No, I'll fettle Billy. If I miss him at four o'clock I'll catch him later on.'

Yvonne pushed her mug from her and leaned her elbows on the table. 'What'll I do if John turns out like that? And Trevor all those miles away.'

Julie dodged the prospect of a second delinquent in the building amd moved on to Yvonne's favourite subject, the absent Trevor.

'How did he come to wind up in Spain?' She had heard the story before but telling it always energized Yvonne.

Now her eyes filled with tears but there was a touch of relish in the way she launched into her tale.

'We took the kids on a package holiday. I thought it was just like Blackpool but Trevor was in there, snapping his fingers and shouting *Olè* . . . the bullfights fascinated him. Then six months later one of his friends went out to open a fish-and-chip shop in Benidorm and Trevor just upped and went with him. Threw up a good job just like that, a trained draughtsman.'

'Did you know he was going?'

'Just the day before . . . when it was too late. "I'll send for you," he said.' The tears were flowing freely now and Julie put out a comforting hand.

'He might. Maybe he's just getting established . . .' She had said the wrong thing.

'Established?' Yvonne wiped her eyes. 'I'll establish him when I catch up with him. He's dumped me, Julie, *and* his kids. Surplus to requirements, that's what we are. I wouldn't have him back, anyway.' She was lying and they both knew it but at least she had cheered up.

They went back to their tea until Julie remembered the paper.

'I've got last night's local here. Remember what you said about a job?' She was opening up the tabloid at the Classified section and spreading it on the table.

'Do you know how long it is since I worked?' Yvonne said dubiously. 'Twelve years. For twelve years I've been a skivvy. A handmaiden, Julie. And more!' Her voice was full of innuendo and Julie tried hard to school her face.

28

'More, Yvonne? What do you mean?'

'You know. At his beck and call. On tap. And all for seven and six.'

'It's £25 now, I think.'

'Well, you know what I mean!'

'Are we talking sex here, Yvonne?'

Yvonne's rollered head dipped and waved in assent.

'Straight sex?' Julie asked. Yvonne was suddenly uneasy, sensing she was being taken out of her depth.

'Straight?' Julie persisted.

'Well, I'm sure it was just the normal relationship . . . well, I thought it was normal.' Yvonne was definitely flustered.

'Ah,' Julie said wisely, 'but there's the problem. Where does normality end and the psycho-bestial begin?' She had made up the word in an instant but it sounded good.

'He wasn't like that, Julie. Always a gentleman, that was Trevor.' Mentioning Trevor's good points was a mistake. Yvonne wiped her eyes with the sleeve of her chenille dressing-gown as the tears brimmed again.

'Wrap up, Yvonne. Here's a good job.' Julie shook out the paper and read aloud. '*Smart, attractive assistant wanted for fast-food outlet. Approximately 16 hours a week.*'

'Fast-food outlet?' Yvonne said dubiously. They both arrived at the answer at the same time. 'Fish-and-chips,' Yvonne said and went back to crying at the thought of Trevor battering in Spain.

'Here's something else,' Julie said, peering closer. '*Wanted, household help for bachelor household. Usual duties, light cooking. Good remuneration for right applicant.*' This is it, Yvonne. This is definitely it.'

'What about the Social?' Yvonne said. 'They'll only keep it off me benefit.'

'Yes,' Julie said patiently. 'If you're fool enough to declare it they'll do just that. Only you won't declare it, will you?'

'What if he's a DHSS man?' Yvonne said, and then dramatically, 'What if it's a trap?'

'If he's a bachelor he won't be a DHSS man,' Julie said. 'They're all androids. And if it's a trap we'll have him up for false pretences so you can go to gaol together.'

When she left the flat Yvonne had promised to get washed and look through her wardrobe for something to wear to an interview. 'But it won't work out, Julie, you'll see. Things never work out for me.'

Julie had washed up the breakfast dishes and was hoovering the floor when Tommo arrived, his arms full of window nets. He put them down on the couch, moving aside her library book. '*Understanding the Human Mind* — that sounds heavy?' He turned it over to read the back cover.

'It's OK actually, as far as I've got. Thanks for the broccoli, by the way, but you shouldn't've bothered.'

'I like bothering.' He tapped the book. 'You've got a brain, you know, Julie. You should be making use of it.'

Julie's eyes rolled skywards. 'The other day it was why didn't I get married; now it's why aren't I still at school.' She liked what he was saying but wanted him to stop just the same.

He was not prepared to let it go. 'I don't like waste. A pretty girl like you, clever, nice habits . . .' He gestured around the tidy room. 'You should be married, not fending for yourself.' There was no mistaking his meaning and Julie tried to fob him off.

'Oh yes, marriage is great! Mendelssohn going *up* the aisle and "Who's Sorry Now?" coming down. I saw plenty with me mam and dad . . . her with her nose in Mills and Boon and him out the back with his shit-machines.'

'His what?'

'His pigeons . . . that's all they're good for, making muck. Never had a word for me mam unless it was a grumble, but he'd sit for hours chatting up his birds. "Eeh, mind you're a bonny bird. By, you're bonny." If I wanted him to notice me I had to make on I was moulting.'

'It can't have been as bad as all that,' Tommo said.

'It was, you know. There was nine of us. Nine. I think they used the rhythm method, and you can't always find a band at bedtime.' Tommo was suddenly stiff with embarrassment but Julie didn't notice. 'Not that it's a joke. Me mam just keep soldiering on but she's worn out.'

Tommo nodded but he was anxious to change the subject. 'Will you get some reading in tonight?'

30

'Yeah, once I get the bairns to bed.'

'You have no life, Julie.' There was sympathy in his voice and irritation too.

'It's not so bad. At least I get a bit of peace, that's more than I got at home. It's lonely sometimes . . . I talk to meself a bit . . . but one way and another I like it.'

'One night, if you got Yvonne to watch the kids, we could go out somewhere? Go for a meal. We might get some broccoli.' When he smiled he was almost handsome, Julie thought. But not her type.

'I'd like that . . . getting all duded up and everything. And broccoli. We'll see.' She was putting him off and they both knew it.

Tommo got to his feet. 'Cheerio then. I'll pick the rest of those nets up tomorrow, when I bring the jeans.'

When he had gone Julie sat on for a while, trying to work out why she felt disconsolate. But there was work to be done. She fetched her purse and carried Damien downstairs and out to the call-box to ring about Yvonne's job.

She put 60p into the slot in case the call lasted. It would be humiliating to be cut off, or have to fumble for change, and she didn't want to create a bad impression. It would be difficult enough to explain why she was phoning on Yvonne's behalf without further complication.

She held the folded newspaper up to memorize the number and then dialled. She had expected a man to answer but it was a woman.

'Dutton and Close.'

'I'm ringing about an advert. For a cleaner.' Had she misdialled?

'Oh yes, you want Mr Iley. Hold the line.'

A moment later he was there, his voice deep and pleasant and perhaps a little uncertain.

'Graham Iley. Are you calling about the cleaning job?'

Suddenly Julie couldn't go into an explanation about Yvonne's inability to face even a phone call. Instead she tried to sound older and speak nicely, like Yvonne on her best behaviour, though it wasn't easy with Damien a dead weight on her hip. 'Yes. The advert in the *Echo*. I thought it might suit.'

At the other end of the line Graham Iley shifted uneasily

in his seat. It had seemed a good idea at the time, but now he was not so sure. Perhaps he should have left it . . . perhaps, even now, it was not too late? He could say the job was filled and apologize for wasting the caller's time. But the voice on the other end sounded young and vulnerable trying hard to be brisk and mature. He felt better able to cope with someone like that and began to discuss details.

They arranged to meet at six tomorrow, at the flat, and Graham rang off. If she wasn't suitable he would say he had others to see and would contact her later. If she *would* do, she could start right away.

As he went back to his file he thought of crisply ironed shirts with no crumpled tags to irritate the neck, of casseroles waiting to be lifted from the oven, of well-stocked cupboards and helpful messages by the phone. Even a whisky clinking with ice when he came from the shower. A sparkling loo and neatly folded sports gear on demand. It could work out very well . . . very well indeed.

They spent a fruitless afternoon looking through Yvonne's wardrobe for an interview outfit. What would do wouldn't fit and what would fit was hardly suitable. In the end Yvonne cried until the tears ran down between her fingers and into the baggy cuffs of her cardigan.

'Better?' Julie said resignedly, when tears gave way to sniffing. 'Now let's start again.' In the end they fixed up a navy skirt that could not be zipped up but could be pinned to stop it from falling down. A double-breasted navy and white striped blouse had its buttons moved until it was single breasted and the lot was topped off with a loose red jacket. 'You'll do,' Julie said and went back downstairs to her flat.

For a while she sat beside Jason, watching *Blue Peter*. She had watched it herself when she was a kid – a lifetime ago. Sometimes, when she thought about things, she felt a sudden inexplicable need to cry. But it was daft crying for nothing. You never knew where it could lead to. Instead she pressed her fingertips against closed lids until her eyeballs tingled and the urge to weep departed.

'I want to make one of those, mam.' She blinked to see

that Jason was looking at her trustingly and she glanced from him to the screen, where an enterprising novelty was being knocked up from household left-overs. 'That . . . that on the telly. I need a tube and some crêpe paper and paints and glue . . .'

He had paints but that was all. Julie felt a spasm of hatred for the blond girl on the screen, talking as though everybody's house was filled with tubes and glue. They weren't. Sometimes there weren't even important things like food and heat. Not even any bloody bog-paper sometimes, never mind its cardboard centre. She was seized with misery, with a sense of failure, but she had coped with this before.

'Hold on.' She got to her feet and went through to the lavatory, took the roll of tissue from its holder and began to wrench at the inner tube.

In the end she had to unroll it, marvelling at the mound of soft pink paper that rose almost to her knees.

'There now,' she said, in triumph, when she got back to the living-room. 'What else did you need?'

It wasn't often that she minded being poor. Only now, when it was for the bairns, did it sting. 'Someone should have told me it would be like this,' she thought as she searched for flour and water to make paste instead of glue.

She tore up a bag that had held brown rice, as the nearest she could get to crêpe paper, and sat Jason down at the table to begin his task. His head, when she stroked it, was soft to her touch with only the faintest hint of bristle to show he was five years old. She had to do right by him, by both of them. That was the trouble with fucking, it was so easy. It was the consequences that were difficult.

She had felt clever when she was pregnant, clever and powerful. Not at first – then she had simply been afraid. But afterwards the sense of power had grown. She wouldn't really mind being pregnant again, feeling creative and mysterious, almost holy. But there wasn't a suitable man around. Only Link, and he would be a disaster. Julie's mouth curved at the thought of Link as a family man. He would get sympathetic labour pains in the first month and take to his bed, and afterwards he would never be off her neck. That was why she let him into her bed occasionally.

33

He was such a bairn that she pitied him and making love was almost all she could do for him.

She watched Jason's fingers, fumbling sometimes, at others incredibly deft, and while she watched she tried to imagine what life might have been like with his father there.

'Ask your dad.' That was what the other mothers in the street said. 'Ask your dad.' Anything to get the kids off their backs. When Jason first left babyhood it had been like a knife in Julie, the knowledge that there was no one for him to refer to, no strong male figure to hoist him up to the skies or carry him running along the wall like the blackie from No. 3 did. But lately she had realized that she worked a lot harder at motherhood because she was all her kids had.

She felt extra tender towards them at bedtime, consenting to read a story and play 'Round and round the garden' with Damien till his eyes drooped and he fell asleep.

Jason was harder. She had just settled with her book when the first call came.

'Mam!'

She paid no attention and it came again, louder.

'Mam!'

'I'm not listening,' she said, trying to concentrate on a chapter headed 'Teenage Turbulence'. God, if it got worse when they got older she would probably crack!

'I want a drink, mam.'

'You've had a drink.'

'I want another.'

'No chance.' She turned a page and concentrated hard.

'Please.'

'No. And if you wake our Damien you know what you'll get.'

'What?'

In the end Julie put orange in a glass and watered it as pale as she dared. Fruit drinks made him pee the bed, but it was all she had.

'Here you are. This is all you're getting and it's only because you made that nice . . .' She hesitated and pointed to the *Blue Peter* artefact on the bedside table. 'Now, night-night and no more shouting, or else.'

'Or else what?'

'You know.' They were grinning in mutual affection as she reached to switch off the light. 'God bless.'

She was almost through 'Teenage Turbulence' when she heard a noise below. She glanced at the clock: it would be Billy slipping out. Eight o'clock was his time, with Nana comfortably asleep over the telly and the coast clear. But when she reached the banister it was Link again, making his way up the stairs.

'You're not coming in, Link. I'm reading.'

He had taken out his comb and was attending to his hair. 'I like books,' he said amiably.

'You wouldn't like this book.'

He followed her into the flat. He wore a tartan waistcoat over his denim shirt and his backside showed through a split in his denims. He looked at her book. 'What's it called? I might like it.'

'It isn't a comic, Link. It's called *Understanding the Human Mind*.'

He blanched a little but tried to sound erudite. 'Oh yeah. Interesting.'

Julie had returned to the printed page. 'It says here that ours is a lost generation. In 1980, in Japan, they picked up 50,000 teenage runaways.'

'What had they gone to Japan for?' Link asked, his mouth open in wonder.

'They hadn't gone to Japan,' Julie said patiently. 'They lived there.'

'I thought you said they'd run away. Oh, I see what you mean,' Link said.

'One million ran away in the United States in 1981,' Julie continued.

'I wouldn't run away if I lived in the States. I could do things with my life if I lived there. They've got the readies . . . holding down two jobs and everything.' He sounded wistful.

'You can't hold down one job.' Julie's tone was scornful.

'That's the recession,' Link said firmly.

'Get off! You got sacked from the Parks Department for kipping in the shrubbery and you lost your YOPS job at the bread factory 'cos you wouldn't take your ear-ring out.

35

"Inability to settle on an occupational identity" – that's what you've got.'

'Don't blame me, blame the Job Centre . . . they're the ones not finding me a job.'

'They're not likely to, are they? Considering what you're registered as. In case you haven't noticed, we live in urban sprawl. There's not a lot of work about for shepherds.'

'I wanted to register as a musician but she wouldn't let me. Not without I was in the Musicians' Union, and you can't get in that if you don't get gigs. So I said "shepherd" just to nark her, and she wrote it down. I wouldn't mind being a shepherd . . . having a dog and a crook and everything.'

He had embarked on a little daydream but Julie was reading on.

'There's another bit about you in here. "The psychic life of a man is determined by his aim. All man's activities are determined, modified and directed by his aim. All functions of the psychic organ are a force directed towards a goal."'

Link looked as though he thought this might be vaguely pornographic and shifted uneasily on the settee.

'What's that got to do with me, then?' he said at last.

'Well, like it says, your psychic life is determined by your aim . . . in other words all your mental energy's directed towards idling about, getting a treble up and landing in my bed. But not tonight, Josephine.'

'Come on, Julie,' Link wheedled. 'And then we can read a bit more. It sounds like a good book. And I *have* got an aim . . . we're going to do a demo disc when we can afford a studio. Let's stop?'

'Link, to be serious, you have more chance tonight of winding up with Hilda Margaret Thatcher.' Julie read on. '"An easily recognized type is the person who has stopped his or her mental development somewhere in adolescence."'

'That's not me!' Now Link was stung. 'Let me stay, and I'll show you whose development's stopped.'

'I'm going to bed, darling. I need to be up in the morning if you don't.'

'Please, Julie . . .'

36

"Night Link.'

He knew he was beaten and went quietly.

Julie had wanted to read but now that he was gone the book had lost its charm. She put it aside and turned up the volume of the TV. There was an advert on and the voice-over was persuasive. 'This is a happy family group . . . but where would they be if one of them went out of the picture?' The man faded from the screen, leaving the woman and children alone, and then the virtues of insurance were extolled. Julie stood up and switched off.

There was a tiny flutter of panic in her chest but she had had it before and knew the cure. She checked on the sleeping children and then turned on Radio One. When all else failed there was always the beat. She began to gyrate, slowly at first, and then faster and faster until abandonment was complete.

3

'Ta,' Yvonne said as Julie planted a small loaf, a tin of corned beef, a packet of custard creams and a red net of onions down on the table. 'I'll pay you back.'

'You will, sunshine.' Julie's voice was firm. 'But only if you lay your hands on some cash, so I hope you're ready for tonight.'

'Tonight,' Yvonne said uneasily.

'Yes, tonight. Your interview, remember? Don't say I've set it all up and you're chickening out?'

'I'm not sure it's the job for me, Julie. I mean, working for a bachelor – I'm not sure Trevor would like it.'

'Trevor's not going to know about it, Yvonne.' Julie's patience was wearing thin and Yvonne's eyes flickered to the groceries on the table. Julie was quite capable of taking them back if she was thwarted.

'I'm going, Julie. I never said I wasn't going, I only meant I had doubts. Anyhow . . .' She brightened visibly. 'I might not be what he's looking for. And then there's the wage to be considered.'

'Take a bit of advice,' Julie said. 'Ask what the minimum is and say you'll do it for half.'

It took Yvonne a minute or two to digest this. 'They say you shouldn't do that, Julie. I've heard MPs on about it.'

'The only honest man to go to Parliament was Guy Fawkes, Yvonne. Forget what they say. Get the job first, do it well, and then ask for a rise. After all, you haven't worked for years, you've *never* been a cleaner . . . you can't go in there making demands.'

Yvonne had risen to scald tea as the kettle boiled. 'I ran a home for twelve years, I've brought up two children, and

38

I am . . . was . . . a wife. I'm not exactly inexperienced.' She reached for the custard creams and broke the seal. 'I expect he only wants basic things like hoovering and ironing, anyway.' She dipped her biscuit into her tea and then, when it threatened to disintegrate, looped it hastily into her mouth, making a sucking noise as she did so. Julie winced but made no comment until the performance was repeated.

'Do you know what that sounds like, Yvonne? The assault on Pearl Harbor! Those biscuits were for the bairns, you said, or I wouldn't have brought them.'

'I know,' Yvonne said guiltily, refastening the packet. 'I've got to stop nibbling.' But as Julie picked up Damien and walked to the door she could hear the stealthy rustle of paper.

'Yvonne!' she said accusingly, halting by the door.

'Don't blame me,' Yvonne said, abandoning caution to snatch a custard cream from the bag. 'Blame men. All over you one minute, over the horizon the next.' She was eating the biscuit hastily, in case Julie decided to wrest it from her. 'Not that it's not my fault, I suppose, for picking Trevor in the first place.'

Julie sighed. 'It's no one's fault, Yvonne. We've all got 20/20 hindsight when it comes to men. Still . . .' She crossed back to the table and confiscated the biscuits. 'I'll just take these into protective custody till tea-time. Now wash your face and cheer up, and then press your skirt for six o'clock. I'll be up in plenty of time to see to the kids. If you come back with a job you'll get some pride in yourself . . .' Yvonne continued to look despondent. 'And I might let you have a biscuit,' Julie said and left.

She rested the baby on her hip while she fished for her key but as she put it into the lock of her door she heard the outer door downstairs open and close.

Looking over the banister, half-expecting to see Tommo's upturned face, she saw instead the dreaded Hunchfront, briefcase in hand, fist upraised to knock on Nana's door. Julie's heart sank. God only knew what things were like in there. She must create a diversion and give Nana some time.

'I'm sorry,' she called, beginning to descend the flight. 'Mrs Foster's out.'

Up close Hunchfront was even more formidable. 'But I like her blouse,' Julie thought, looking at maroon silk neatly pinned underneath a carefully made-up face.

'I see,' the social worker said. She drew a folder from her briefcase and leafed through the pages. 'Well, I'm afraid I must see her today. And I have my senior case-worker with me. He's just parking the car.'

'I'm sorry,' Julie said again, trying to edge between Hunchfront and Nana's door. 'You could try tomorrow.' The social worker's perfectly lipsticked mouth formed an O of contemplation.

'No,' she said at last. 'We'll come back in a few minutes. She may be back. If you see her, tell her I called.'

Julie nodded and tried to look obliging, all the while terrified that Nana's cough would rattle behind the door. Hunchfront refastened her case and opened the outer door. 'It must be today,' she said firmly. 'I want Mr Sproxton to see her while he's here.'

Julie waited until the click of Hunchfront's footsteps died away then she moved forward and dropped the latch on the outer door. As she did so the flat door opened and Nana's face peered through the crack.

'Has she gone?'

'Only temporarily. She's coming back, and she's got the Boss with her.' She pushed past Nana and looked round the disordered flat.

'You'll have to clean up this place and do something about your clothes . . . they look like they've been shot on to you from guns.'

'I won't have to put me brassière on, will I?' Nana asked anxiously, clutching her cardigan to her chest.

'No,' Julie said, reaching for the carpet-sweeper. 'There isn't time for major reconstruction. Just change your pinny and do your hair. And don't drop any more fag ends! If she finds this place a tip she'll say Billy's living in a health hazard. Any reason'll do.' As she scooped up a pile of old newspapers and looked round for somewhere to stow them Julie thought of the tyranny of officialdom. You could never get away from it. She moved towards Nana's bedroom, oblivious of the old lady's swift intake of breath, and pushed open the door.

The unmade bed was covered with an assortment of discarded clothes but Julie's eyes were fixed on something on the floor.

'What's that in there?'

'What?' Nana said, coming to stand beside her.

'That!' Julie said, pointing. 'It's a potty!'

'So what?' Nana said, a bit shamefaced. 'Never seen a jerry before?'

'But you've got a perfectly good bathroom,' Julie said. 'Avocado tiles and a low-level flush.'

'I don't like coming down once I've gone up,' Nana said firmly.

'Up?' Julie was clutching her hands to her cheeks. 'Up? It's all on the flat, this place.'

'Well, you know what I mean. We always had a jerry at the old place. It's warmer.'

Julie threw the papers on to the heaped-up bed. 'Give me strength! Well, get it emptied and out of sight.' She was going back into the living-room when she heard a sound. She stopped and looked around suspiciously.

'Where's Billy?'

'He's at school,' Nana said but her eyes had flicked instinctively towards the other bedroom.

'Oh yes?' Julie said, advancing and throwing open the door. Inside the room Billy sat on the bed, a grey jersey over striped pyjamas, his bare feet thrust into unlaced training shoes. 'At school, is he?' Julie said. 'And which classroom is this – the Biology Lab?'

'He couldn't go,' Nana said. 'His jeans are in the wash.'

Julie was about to wreak vengeance on the truant when there was a sharp knock on the door.

'Oh, my God,' Nana said, swaying slightly. 'It's them again. What are we going to do?' She looked suddenly old and defeated and the 'I told you so' died on Julie's lips.

'Get in the bedroom,' she said. 'And keep quiet, both of you.' She looked around at the dereliction. There was nothing to be done with it. They mustn't be allowed in. For a moment she contemplated lying low herself but Damien was already moving restlessly on the floor, where she had

41

placed him. She picked him up and went to the door, squaring her shoulders as she went.

She opened the door just enough to squeeze through and closed it behind her. The large and glamorous Miss Hays loomed over her but Mr Sproxton was mercifully small and looked kindly.

'I'm sorry, but Mrs Foster's still out. I was just checking her oven for her. She's got Billy's meal in.'

'She knew I was coming today,' the woman said to her supervisor. 'I sent her a letter.'

So Nana *had* known, Julie thought and pledged retribution. Aloud she said, 'Yes . . . she told me to say she was sorry but this is her day for night classes.'

'At eleven in the morning?' Hunchfront said.

'Well, further education . . .' Julie answered. 'I call it night classes but that's just me getting it wrong.'

Mr Sproxton was looking decidedly interested. 'You didn't tell me Mrs Foster was studying, Miss Hays. Very commendable.' He turned to Julie. 'What's her subject?'

Julie thought rapidly, and then, remembering the jerry, inspiration came. 'Pottery.'

'You didn't mention that earlier,' Hunchfront said suspiciously.

'Didn't I?' Julie said artlessly. 'Honestly, sometimes I think I'll forget my own name . . .'

Mr Sproxton was nodding sympathetically and chucking Damien under the chin.

'Splendid,' he said. 'Such good therapy, pottery. I've thrown a pot or two in my time.' He turned to Hunchfront. 'I think we can leave this for today, Miss Hays.' And then to Julie, 'Perhaps you'll tell Mrs Foster we called?'

'Yes,' Hunchfront said. 'Tell her I'll be back.' Her eyes locked with Julie's and each took the other's measure.

'Yes,' Julie said slowly. 'I'll make sure I tell her to expect you.'

'Bitch,' she said, when the door shut behind them. All the same, it was Vigilantes 1 Aliens nil.

'I'm glad you were free for lunch,' Graham said, settling Charlotte into her seat. 'I wanted to see you about tonight.'

'Tonight?' Charlotte was running her hands through her gleaming hair.

'The interview,' Graham said desperately. 'The cleaning woman.' He handed her a menu and opened his own. 'I suppose you couldn't come round and give moral support?'

'No,' Charlotte said firmly. 'See to your own domestic arrangements.' She folded the menu and put it down. 'Grilled sole and the French beans and for God's sake get things into proportion. This is a cleaner you're engaging. She's hardly likely to have a Ph D. Check her references, offer her £2.50 an hour and the run of the fridge, and then give her a list of duties. Even you should manage that.' She sounded annoyed and Graham wondered why.

He ordered two sole and two French beans and a carafe of house white. He didn't like fish much but he wasn't in the mood for further hassle. Charlotte was wearing a sludge-coloured suit over a green shirt which exactly matched her eyes. She was clever with clothes. He found himself looking furtively from side to side to see if other people were appreciating how good she looked, but they were all engaged in animated conversation, and besides Charlotte had intruded a new and uncomfortable thought.

'References?' he asked.

She looked at his disconcerted face. 'Well, you have thought of that, haven't you?' It seemed she was going to erupt but instead she reached out and patted his hand. 'Oh darling, you can be *green* sometimes. She could be fresh out of Holloway, whoever she is. Didn't you think?'

'No,' he said. 'I mean, if it was for a proper job . . . but tidying the flat . . .?'

'She's going to have the run of your home!' Charlotte said.

Graham shrugged. 'There's not a lot to pinch, is there? I mean, it's hardly Fort Knox. Besides – ' he couldn't resist a grin – 'she'd be hard put to find anything to lift in that chaos.'

'TV, CD player, video, two radios that I can think of . . . those cuff-links that your grandfather left you, the carriage-clock in the hall, not to mention the Rattray Cup which is silver and which you have to give back when your year's up. And I bet you're under-insured.'

The last vestige of delightful anticipation left Graham's mind. He would have to put the woman off, that was all. If he had one big purge and got the place up to scratch he could get up half an hour earlier each day and sort the place out himself. Yes, that was the best thing to do. He went back to contemplation of Charlotte's eyes and the interesting dark division between her breasts that just showed between the green revers.

Julie raked the spoon around Damien's mouth to remove the last of the mashed carrot and licked the spoon before she began to feed him the creamed banana. He liked the sweet gooey taste and smacked his lips.

'Yes,' she said. 'Nice. Now eat it all up and then we'll go upstairs and sort Aunty Yvonne.'

On the floor above Yvonne was spreading a slice of bread and marge with golden syrup. She licked the knife and then folded the bread in half and began to chew. Outside the window Grimshaw Street was red-brick and shabby. In Windermere Close she had had a garden with laburnum and flowering cherry and a little apple tree that had just begun to bear fruit when she left. It had taken them five years to get the house and five months to lose it. She pushed the last crust into her mouth and reached for another slice.

Any minute now Julie would be up to coax and push her into a too-tight blouse and skirt and force her out to a job she didn't want and probably couldn't do properly. She bit down on the sweet bread but suddenly it was too sweet and she gagged on the pulp. She closed her eyes, remembering the laburnum and the apple blossom the day she had left. The day she had packed up twelve years of marriage, on her own because Trevor was sunning it in Spain. There had been rubbish burning beside the compost heap and on an impulse she had carried Trevor's thermal vests out into the garden and fed them to the bonfire one by one.

She heard the downstairs door close and then Julie's purposeful step on the stair. She might stay until it was time to go and there would be no chance of another bite on the sly. In a panic Yvonne crammed the bread and syrup into her mouth and masticated madly so that she could present herself to Julie and claim she hadn't had a thing to eat all day.

'I don't think I can do it, Julie,' she said desperately when Julie entered the room. She didn't want the job. It wasn't that she was lazy or not up to it, it was simply that becoming the breadwinner herself would be to acknowledge the fact that Trevor might not be coming back. She saw Julie's eyes gleam with sympathy but only for a moment. She put the baby down on the floor and pulled John's toy-box within his reach.

'Now see here, Yvonne . . .' She was looking for something non-toxic in the toy-box and Yvonne seized her chance.

'I'm not up to it, Julie. Healthwise, I mean. I've got really run down lately with all the worry and the trauma.' She sniffed loudly and groped for a handkerchief, watching Julie through narrowed lids to see if she was having any effect. 'I think I need a doctor.'

Julie jammed a ball into Damien's hands and sat back. 'You need a job, Yvonne. A, to get you out of the house; B, to get you to smarten yourself up; and C, to pay me back for the corned beef and onions.'

'I'll have me Giro soon,' Yvonne countered. Julie shook her head.

'Three more days, Yvonne. We could all be dead of malnutrition by then.'

'Well, even if I get the job I won't get paid before the weekend,' Yvonne said smugly.

'No,' Julie said. 'But if you've got wages coming you can tick on with Ali. He'll let you if I ask him.'

'*She* won't,' Yvonne said, alarmed. 'She wouldn't give credit to Mother Teresa.'

'When I go in there I talk to the butcher, not the block,' Julie said firmly. She sniffed suddenly. 'Something smells in here.' She gazed around her and then advanced on a jar of wilting button chrysanths. 'It's these. The water's rotten.'

Yvonne had always had flowers in the old house. Now she bought a bunch when she could and hung on to them

45

until they withered on the stem. Julie carried the offending vase out to the kitchen and then came back to sit down, a fatuous grin on her face.

'It takes you back, that smell of mouldy water. I used to be the flower monitor when we were in the Juniors. "Strip the leaves, Julie. Hammer the stems. No, not like that, silly girl." Everyone was always trying to bring the biggest bloom. "My dad's asters are bigger than yours." "Call them chrysanths? They're more like Bachelor's Buttons." I did it for a year, and then Link took over so I still had to do it.'

'You never go on at him about not working!' Yvonne said defensively. 'And he's never worked. I paid stamps for eight years.'

'I do get on to him, Yvonne but let's face it, he hasn't got much chance of a job. He's caught in a Grange Hill time-warp. And it's not all his fault.' She removed a miniature hammer from Damien and, when he cried, lifted him on to her knee.

'He never had a choice, Link I mean. It was down the dole or down the Social for him. For all of our class. When we were little he was always on about how he was going down the pit. By the time he was old enough the pit was gone. So he followed me when I moved into the town and there was still no work and now he's playing his drums and waiting to be discovered.'

'He'll get a shock one of these days,' Yvonne said in a voice of bitter experience.

'Well, unless it's 10,000 volts he won't even notice it. Now, shall we sort your hair out ready for your big moment?' Julie saw rebellion spring up in Yvonne's eyes and hastened to quell it. 'Nana says the reason Link fails interviews is 'cos his hair looks like a lavvy-brush. Yours is more like one of those long, droopy mops. Still, if you've got some scissors . . .'

The threat was enough to make Yvonne submit to washing her hair and having it set on rollers. When Julie left to collect Jason from school Yvonne was raking through her make-up box and the neatly pressed skirt and blouse were hanging on the kitchen door. She looked up as Julie left. 'I hope we've thought of everything. My mind keeps wandering.'

'Don't worry,' Julie said kindly. 'It's too weak to get far.'

She had met up with Jason and was walking home when it began to rain, fine needles at first and then big splashy drops. She put up the hood of the pushchair and gathered Jason inside her coat. 'Hang on to mammy's legs,' she said, 'and then we can run.'

He clutched her jeans and did his best but it was impossible to synchronize their steps. It was hard to see the way ahead as rain collected in her hair and trickled into her eyes and she was uncomfortably aware of water running in and out of her worn trainers and squelching all the while.

She was almost ready to abandon the effort and take refuge in a doorway when Tommo's van drew up alongside. In a minute he was out of the driving seat and unlocking the back doors to lift in Jason and settle him among the boxes and bales.

'Into the front seat,' he said, taking Damien from the pushchair and pushing it into the van. 'Right,' he said, when they were all safe inside and the rain shut out. 'You all right back there, son?' He handed Julie a new tea-towel, pulled from a bale. 'You look half-drowned. Good thing I happened along when I did. I was coming to your place anyway. I've got those jeans for Nana's Billy.'

There was a bunch of broccoli on the dashboard and Julie knew it was for her.

'You're a godsend, Tommo,' she said, reaching back to wipe Jason's face and then doing the baby's and her own, towelling her wet hair so that it ceased to drip. The windows of the van had steamed up and Tommo put out a hand to wipe them clear. His fingers were short and blunt with nice nails. Nice hands. They had been firm but gentle when they bundled her into the van.

For a moment, while the wipers swished outside and she steamed gently, she indulged in a little daydream of always going home with Tommo, lighting the rooms and drawing chairs to the fire, fetching his food and watching him dandle the baby on his knee like a family man. But it was only a dream, dispelled when they drew up at the house and had to dash through the rain once more.

Tommo carried the baby in for her and then went back for the jeans and the broccoli, and by the time he was upstairs she had tea made and a buttered tea-cake cut into four. They sat at the kitchen table, beginning to dry out and feeling euphoric about it.

'Have you got many more calls?' Julie asked and knew, when he shook his head, that he had been waiting at the school on purpose. She would have to discourage him, she thought, when he had combed his wet hair and gone out to the van again. There was no future in it and if she wasn't careful he would think there might be.

When she had settled the baby in his high-chair she carried the jeans down to Nana's flat. She was almost at the bottom of the stairs when she heard Yvonne above her on the landing.

'Are you coming up, Julie?' There was no sign of Yvonne being made-up or dressed for her interview, and the rollers were still in her hair.

'I am coming up, Yvonne, but you should be further on than that. Have you given the kids their tea? Time's ticking on.'

'Don't frighten me, Julie. I can feel me nerve going without you making it worse.' As if in sympathy the battered picture of Beachy Head that adorned the staircase wall suddenly tilted sideways.

'See,' Yvonne said as Julie disappeared, 'I knew this was a mistake.'

Julie pushed at Nana's door but to her surprise it was locked. She rang the bell, leaning on it till she heard Nana protesting behind the door.

'Do you want me?' she said, when she opened it.

'No, I'm testing doorbells,' Julie said, pushing past her. The evening paper was lying open on Nana's chair and she looked at it scornfully. 'Checking your losers?'

'No, I'm not, Miss Cleversides,' Nana said, picking up the paper and flourishing it to show it was open at the announcements. 'Hatches, matches and despatches, that's what I'm checking. I fancy a nice funeral . . . not Catholic, they ring that many bells you can't hear yourself speak.

48

Harry Birkbeck's gone. They never got on, that family, so there might be a good dust-up . . .'

'I don't believe you,' Julie said. 'You're the living, breathing incarnation of Dracula.'

'No, I'm not. He drinks blood, I like Guinness – not that you'll've brought any.'

Julie held out the jeans. 'How about these for your Billy? I greeded them off Tommo but you'll have to pay.'

'Very nice,' Nana said, eyeing them. 'How much?'

'Thirteen ninety-nine,' Julie said. 'Make your mind up 'cos I've got to get up and sort Yvonne out. She's going after a job.'

Nana cackled and subsided into her chair. 'She'll never hold a job down.'

'She bloody well will,' Julie said. 'I want her out of this house, making money and building a life for herself. If I get her out working and you off the booze and your Billy in Borstal where he should be, I can put my feet up.'

Nana scowled. 'You're wasting your time trying to make something of that Yvonne. You can't get feathers off a monkey. What kind of job is it?'

'Cleaning.' Julie looked around the disordered living-room. 'You know, that lost art you practised once upon a time.'

Nana decided to ignore the jibe. 'Aye, well, that's the one job she might hold down seeing as she's a hoover fanatic. Morning, noon and night she brays hell out of those floorboards.'

Julie looked down at the ash-strewn floor but refrained from comment. You could only accomplish so much in one day.

Graham had left the office early to render his flat presentable. There had only been one applicant, so it wouldn't do, after all, to put her off. He switched on the kettle for coffee and then looked around him. Where to start? There was a pile of washing he had lifted from the dryer and put aside to iron. Some of it had been there a long time. A very long time. He carried it through to the bedroom and tumbled it into the bottom of his wardrobe. No point in frightening her. If he took her on he could infiltrate it into the ironing, a few items each week until it was gone.

He felt quite smug as he shut the wardrobe door until he suddenly realized that she might look in the wardrobe and see what he'd done. She might look elsewhere, as well. She was bound to be curious.

He panicked then, rushing from drawer to drawer, retrieving condoms and personal letters and erotica that he had meant to throw out years ago. There were his bank statements, too – not exactly private but not for public consumption, either. The woman might talk, was probably an inexhaustible gossip. He suddenly remembered the photos of Charlotte, topless on the beach in the summer. They would have go to somewhere other than his dressing-table.

Graham looked around the bedroom, suddenly seized with distaste at the whole idea of someone else, anyone else, intruding into his life. He had put in the ad on a whim. Now, weighing it up . . . Marjorie at the office, of course, knew all there was to know about him, but that was professionally. This woman was going to handle his smalls! No, it wouldn't work. He went through to the kitchen to scald his coffee, half determined to call the whole thing off.

He was seeking an acceptable form of words until he went to the fridge for something to eat and found the carton of coleslaw complete with fur collar and wicked bits of green mould. If he hung on to his privacy salmonella would get him. He bolted the hot coffee and took a duster to the hall table and the stereo. It would be up to him to set standards. He glanced at the clock and saw he had plenty of time to change the towels in the bathroom and clean the loo in case she said she wanted a leak. But the bedroom would have to be out of bounds, for the time being at least.

'Stand still, Yvonne,' Julie said, gripping both sides of the skirt to strain them close enough to pin.

'I am standing still but you keep pulling me over,' Yvonne complained. 'God,' she went on bitterly, 'men get away with murder. I bet no one's putting Trevor through the mill like this.'

'Maybe he doesn't look like a bale of hay,' Julie said through clenched teeth. She had brought the edges of the zip close but couldn't work out how to keep them there until she got the pin in.

'No,' Yvonne said, 'I bet he looks marvellous . . . swanning around in the sun all day, sipping Tequila Sunsets. It isn't fair.'

'It isn't fair,' Julie agreed, kneeling down to get a better grip, 'but it isn't a fair world.'

'Nobody tells you that,' Yvonne said, gesturing towards the TV set. 'If you listened to that thing you'd think the only thing you had to do to save your marriage was bung an Oxo cube in your gravy!'

'You may be right, Yvonne, but this isn't going to work.' Julie let go the sides of the skirt and they sprang apart, leaving a wide expanse of peach nylon.

'Well, I can't suck me breath in any more, Julie. I'm shattered.'

Julie was moving to the attack once more, speaking in a robot voice. 'We have the technology, Yvonne. We can rebuild you.'

Yvonne ignored the wisecrack. 'How'm I going to get there?' she asked. 'It's a good half-hour's bus ride and I haven't got a penny. Not a penny. I've got a pile of bills over there an inch thick.'

'You should do what Link does with bills,' Julie said. She had managed to get the two sides into one grip and was opening the pin against her teeth. 'He leaves bills under his pillow for the tooth fairy, and it seems to work!'

'What about the bus fare?' Yvonne insisted.

'Got it!' Julie said as the pin went home. 'I'll lend you the bus fare. Add it to the corned beef.'

'Shall we have a cup of tea?' Yvonne said, glancing at the clock. Suddenly there was the sound of her children on the stair and her face brightened. John was in first, fair and rosy-cheeked, his face set in a stubborn scowl. 'Don't listen to what she says,' he said, nodding towards his sister, smaller and brown-haired, at seven three years his junior.

'Now what's wrong?' Yvonne said, picking up his flung down anorak.

'He's her favourite,' Julie thought and smiled at Andrea, who was attempting to outline her brother's crimes. They fell upon the cupboards, rooting for biscuits, grumbling at the lack of them, settling at last for bread and syrup and then squabbling over which channel to watch on TV.

'You see that?' Yvonne said when she and Julie were settled with tea. 'They're always hungry, always raking the cupboards. And what can I feed them? Stodge! Anything to fill them up. Give your kids a healthy diet? I'm too busy filling a bottomless pit to worry about values.' Her mouth quivered and Julie leaped in.

'All the more reason for taking a job.' She looked at the clock. 'You should leave here in a quarter of an hour. You don't want to be late on your first visit.'

Yvonne's eyes rolled upwards, as though looking for deliverance, but she didn't mention the job again as they chatted about their children until it was time for Julie to go.

She was half-way down the stairs when Yvonne called her back. She was clutching the red jacket to her and her face was anguished. 'I can't do it, Julie. I should never have let you ring up. I've tried and tried but I can't face it, and it's no good you going on about it. Apart from anything else, who'd be here to see to the bairns every day?'

'I will,' Julie said swiftly. 'I'll see them in from school and I'll keep them off each other till you get back. Besides, you can probably set your own hours so you'd be here, anyway.'

Inside Yvonne irritation grew. She was scared of going out to work but there was something else – a principle to be preserved. Julie was half her age; furthermore she was not even respectably wed. She couldn't be allowed to dictate to a married woman, who might have come down in the world but still had some rights.

'You go, if it's such a good idea,' she said. 'You go and I'll watch *your* kids.'

She had not expected Julie to take up the challenge but she had reckoned without Julie's principles. Never ask anyone to do something you wouldn't do yourself. Besides, there had been that deep voice on the phone. 'All right,'

Julie said. 'If you haven't got the bottle, I *will* go!' She lifted her chin and stalked into her own flat.

Making up her face and combing her wardrobe for a decent outfit prevented any last-minutes nerves. She would have liked to change her knickers but one pair on, two in the wash and two in the window-box didn't allow it. She took Damien upstairs to Yvonne and adjured Jason to shout for Aunty Yvonne if he needed her. A swift last look in the mirror and she was on her way, almost before she had really given thought to what she was doing.

Julie found Chilworth Terrace without difficulty and pressed the third-floor bell. It was ages before there was any response and she felt her mouth go dry. What if he asked comprehensive questions? Could she give comprehensible answers? She knew how to dust and hoover, but her laundry techniques left a lot to be desired. And the advert had mentioned cooking. If he wanted anything fancy she would have to fall back on the library, that was all. You could find anything in the library, from home-brewing to fruit-bat farming.

The door opened suddenly and she lifted her eyes to meet the householder's gaze. 'I've come about the cleaning job,' she said, suddenly conscious of having on too much make-up and a too-tight, too-short skirt. This man was class . . . tall, lovely neat hair, thick eyelashes and a touch of stubble that made him look a bit like Don Johnson but chunkier.

'You'd better come in,' he said and stepped back to let her pass. She was aware of a faint odour of perhaps aftershave – something subtle, anyway – and then he was ushering her into a big room with black furniture and deep leather armchairs.

Julie had never applied for a job before but she knew when to go into the attack. 'About this job,' she said. 'In my last job I got £3 an hour . . .'

Twenty minutes later she was on her way back to the bus, her feet hardly touching the pavement. He had agreed the hourly rate without a flicker, agreed to the hours she suggested, and heaved a sigh of relief when she said she could start the day after tomorrow. He had asked vaguely about experience and references, and she had successfully waffled through it. He didn't think she was up to it, that much was plain, but he was desperate. Well, she would show him. Fifteen hours a week at £3: £45! And when she had tapped her nose and said it would have to be under the counter he had nodded straight away.

She decided to give Yvonne £15 for watching Damien. She would take Jason to school every day and collect him most days, so no sweat there. All in all, it would work out very well. It would be easier to do the work herself than keep Yvonne up to the mark and, besides, she needed a change. She would buy a decent skirt with her first week's pay and keep herself nice. It wasn't the career she would have chosen, but it would do for a start.

She was still euphoric when she got home but the sight of Link ensconced in her chair was a turn-off. He had *Understanding the Human Mind* open in his hand.

'I've been reading your book,' he said. 'It isn't up to much.'

Julie stepped out of her shoes and rubbed her toes where the patent leather had chafed. 'Bit beyond you?' she enquired sweetly.

'No,' Link said, closing the book and moving to rub her feet between his palms. At first the pain was intense and then the pleasure exquisite.

'Don't think this is getting you anywhere, Link,' she said, casting a glance towards Jason, thumb in mouth on the settee. 'As soon as I've got a blood supply again, you're off home.'

'Let's stay, Julie. I want to talk. Seriously talk.'

'You're not going to propose again, are you?' she asked wearily.

'You could do worse than me,' he said. 'Anyway, you could at least consider it.'

'I do,' she said drily. 'I've got it all worked out, to the smallest detail . . . for instance, twin beds.'

'Yeah?' he said doubtfully.

'Yes,' Julie said firmly. 'Twin beds. Mine in Newcastle and yours in Stoke-on-Trent.'

Link drew back, annoyed. 'That's right, make a joke of

it, when I'm trying to be serious. You'll be sorry when I get a job and I've got a good thing going.' He was sitting cross-legged now, miming his drum-playing, his hands performing paradiddles and triplets, his head nodding furiously to the beat.

'I'll tell you what,' Julie said, suddenly benign. 'Ask me again when you grow up. In the mean time, go up and fetch the bairn from Yvonne's and tell her I'll see her later. And just deliver the bairn, Link – don't come back in, because I've got my night all planned.' She was starting a new job the day after tomorrow and she meant to tie up some loose ends before she did.

It was Yvonne who brought Damien, Link behind her. 'So long, Link,' Julie said, arming him back through the door and closing it.

'Well?' Yvonne asked, round-eyed.

'Well what? I took it, if that's what you mean.'

'How much?' Yvonne said.

'Don't be so subtle, Yvonne. Just ask straight out.'

'Well, I only meant was it going to be worth it,' Yvonne said. She put Damien into his high-chair and buckled the harness.

'Oh, I think it'll be worth it,' Julie said slowly. She felt a strange excitement but it was overlaid by apprehension. What if it all went wrong?

She felt better once she got rid of Yvonne, who was delighted at the thought of an extra £15 a week for babysitting. 'You're sure I shouldn't tell the Social?' Yvonne asked as she went through the door and received a thump from Julie in answer.

Damien went down at once, Jason after a token defiance. That done, Julie changed into jeans and T-shirt and pulled her big sweater over her head. It was seven-forty-five. Any moment now, if he stayed true to form, Billy would exit from the bottom flat. She went into the loo, to find it still adorned with the tattered remnants of the tissue she had unrolled the night before.

'God,' she said aloud, treading the pink loops, trying to disentangle her feet, 'I feel like a labrador in an Andrex advert. Sometimes,' she said bitterly, as she unzipped her jeans, 'Sometimes I wish people on telly would think of the consequences of their words. "Take two toilet rolls and ten quid's worth of crêpe paper, stick it down with superglue, add a few sequins" . . . where from?' She gave the chain a vicious tug and went to wash her hands.

Her face, in the mirror above the hand-basin, was flushed and bright-eyed. If she kept the job, if it didn't evaporate like so many other goods things had done, they would have extras. Treats. Everything would be easier. But she mustn't get too excited. Right now Graham Iley was probably writing to tell her he'd changed his mind.

In the kitchen she boiled a kettle and filled her hot-water bottle. It would be cold on the landing. She went back into her bedroom and put an extra T-shirt under her sweater, and socks inside her trainers. A moment later, clutching the bottle, she was back on the landing, peering down into the empty hall and then sliding down until she was sitting with her back to the wall, her ear cocked for the slightest sound below.

She did not have long to wait. There was a click and then the squeak from Nana's front door. Silently she got to her feet and tiptoed down the stairs. Billy was backing out into the hall, drawing the door gently to behind him. He shut it with exquisite care, letting his breath out in a slow sigh as he did so. When he turned she was there, their eyes a foot apart, her akimboed arms blocking his way.

'Hallo, Willie Winkie. And where d'you think you're going? Upstairs and downstairs, and through my lady's chamber?'

'Get lost,' Billy said, but he made no move to push her aside.

'I know where you're off to – to pal up with that crap in the bus shelter. You won't be told, will you? You're begging to get lifted.'

Billy threw back his head and smirked. 'Yes, go on . . . laugh. But who'll watch out for your Nana when you're off on your little custodial? Tell me that!' She put out a hand and pushed him. 'Well, I'm going to best you . . .'

This time he laughed out loud. 'You and whose army?' he said.

'I don't need an army, mate.'

This was the moment of truth. Billy's eyes flicked to one

56

side and the other, estimating his chances of flight. He was as big as Julie, and heavier. If it came to a physical contest . . . But her eyes held his and after a moment he conceded defeat.

'OK,' he said. 'There's other nights.'

He was right, and Julie felt a twinge of despair.

'Never mind other nights,' she said. 'One day at a time. Now back inside, and remember I'm up there, waiting.'

She stood until he was back in the flat, and then turned towards the stairs. She noticed Nana's milk bottle, not out on the step where it would be collected but abandoned outside the flat door and thick with curds. With a sigh she picked it up and carried it upstairs to wash and put out with her own.

She got washed and cleaned her teeth and shrugged into the brushed-cotton nightie she wore when she slept alone, and then pulled her sweater on again. She had two bottles of her own, already rinsed, and she carried the three bottles out to the landing for the trip downstairs. She was about to take the first step down when she heard the door below opening and peeped to see Billy making a second cautious exit.

She set the bottles down with a crack and sped down the stairs.

'Bloody hell, if you had your head under your arm I'd think you were haunting the place. I said "not tonight" and I meant it!'

This time she pushed him into the flat, hearing the steady rattle of Nana's snoring, smelling the smoke and the odour of kippers, seeing the unclad bulb hanging from the ceiling so that the whole room looked bleak and depressing. No wonder the poor little sod wanted out of it. All the same . . . 'Take your jeans off,' she said. 'Now! Get them off or I'll rip them off.'

When they were down to his ankles she sorted through the mess on the sofa until she found the spare pair. 'Right,' she said, folding both pairs over her arm, 'you'll get these back in the morning.'

'Sod you,' Billy said with venom, but he looked oddly vulnerable without his jeans and she took no offence.

'I'll talk to your Nan in the morning and we'll sort

something out. Something – I don't know what, but for now you stay put.' There had been a moment when she might almost have given in but then she had remembered Hunchfront and what happened when the SS targeted a house.

Safely out in the hall she sank on to the bottom stair, hardly able to believe she had won. Yvonne's head appeared above her.

'Is everything all right?'

'There has been what you might call a little local difficulty,' Julie said. She raised her arm to display the jeans. 'But I've fettled him. He can't go out bare-arsed or he'll be arrested. His brain may be below the age of criminal responsibility but his backside's not.'

'So it's all right?'

'Yes,' Julie said.

'I'm so glad,' Yvonne said and her eyes filled with tears.

'Go to bed, Yvonne. Panic over,' Julie said wearily and began to mount the stairs. One way and another it had been a hell of a day!

4

Julie woke at daybreak and forced herself to stay awake. She must make sure Billy got to school this morning. Besides, she could hear Yvonne pacing above, bedroom to kitchen, kitchen to bedroom, kitchen again and then the sound of running water as she filled the kettle. The alarm clock said six-thirty-five. Soon the milkman would come, then the postie, and then the workers filtering to the bus-stop in twos or threes. '*I've* got a job,' she thought and felt astonished.

At seven o'clock she got out of bed and made tea, carrying it to the window so she could look out on Grim-shaw Street. She liked it in the early morning. It looked somehow refined, as though the night had cleaned and gentled it. By tea-time it would be its normal, scruffy, busy self but in the early mornings it had definite possibilities. She tried to imagine how it had been in the old days, when there had been just one family to each house and a maid in the attic. How lovely it must have been to have space, so you could move from room to room when you wanted to get away. She had lived all her life in the middle of an ant-heap – one ant-heap or another, it didn't seem to make much difference.

She sipped her tea as the West Indian came out of the door of No. 3. He looked up at the sky as he emerged, as though giving thanks for a new day. He was always cheerful, she had to give him that. He turned as his girlfriend came out on the step behind him, still in her nightie with bendy curlers all over her head. She was a bonny girl usually, always smart. Now she put her arms around her boyfriend's neck and reached to kiss him. They clung together for a moment, for all the world as though he were going to Siberia, never mind the council yard where he worked. Julie felt suddenly depressed at the thought of the other girl's day, looking after her bairns, getting in her shopping, looking up at the clock all the time to see how long before he came home.

Still Julie thought, she wasn't alone, like some people. She put aside dangerous thoughts and began to plan her day.

Damien wakened first. Julie heard him chuckling to himself and smiled with satisfaction at the sound. He was a *good* bairn, better than she deserved. She took him in a finger of brown bread and polyunsaturated, and checked on Jason, sleeping on his back with his mouth open as though his dreams had surprised him. He had his best pyjamas on, pale blue with a Ghostbusters logo. He looked healthy and cared-for, and she felt her spirits rise. It was going to be all right. There had been a time after she fell with Damien, when she had wondered how much more she could take. But she had coped. You always did in the end.

She left Damien cooing in his cot and carried the two pairs of jeans down to Nana's flat. While she waited for the door to open she considered the possibility that Billy had gone out again minus trousers and been arrested for indecency, but he was there, on the other side of the door, snarling, 'What do you want?'

'And *ciao* to you too, *amigo*,' she answered, and pushed past him into the room. Nana stood by the fire lighting a tab with a spill of rolled-up paper. As she straightened there was the sound of breaking wind, and behind Julie Billy groaned.

'Is that you farting?' Julie asked disapprovingly.

'No, me vest exploded,' Nana said, blowing out a column of smoke and looking up at the mantel clock. 'What time's this, then?' Her eyes fell on the jeans. 'What've you got there?'

'Your Billy's trousers . . . both pairs. I had to grab them off him last night to stop him taking off. I've warned you and warned you, but you don't listen.' She turned to see the effect of her words on the villain of the piece but he

60

had melted away and the door of his bedroom closed with a thud.

'I don't know,' Nana said, sitting down and belching. She didn't sound unduly perturbed and Julie sat down opposite her, ready to exhort.

'I don't know,' Nana said again, before Julie could speak. 'When they're babies you never think of this, do you? You think of little arms and silky heads and how they'll love you when they're all grown up.'

Julie shifted uncomfortably. This wasn't what she had expected. Indifference, maybe; resistance, possibly. But this was verging on the philosophical.

'It's just a phase,' she said comfortingly. 'All the same, you've got to watch him . . .'

'Watch him?' Nana said. 'What's the point of watching him? He's had it – a snowman's got more future than our Billy.' She sighed again. 'You feel powerful when you've fallen for a bairn, don't you? When I was carrying his mam I thought I could stop traffic. And then when she was toddling and I had our Leslie, I thought I was the bee's knees. I thought everybody should get out of my way, I was that important. Power? There's no power like a mother's power; you rule the universe. And then five minutes later they start giving you lip, and the next minute they're gone. Our Mollie's God knows where and I haven't seen our Leslie since the Jubilee.'

Julie's nerve was weakening and she was about to reassure Nana that all was well when she saw the old lady's eyes flick momentarily towards her and away.

'She's winding me up,' Julie thought. 'Before I can start in on her about Billy she's playing the sympathy card!'

'All right,' she said aloud, 'that's enough Helen Steiner Rice for the moment, thank you. I kept Billy in last night, now you get him to school. And if you want motivation, mind on that he won't be much use to you if he's off on one of Willie Whitelaw's short, sharp shocks. You're getting old, Nana. You want to watch out you're not left on your own, because I won't be able to see to you.'

Nana's eyes blazed. 'Wait till you're asked, miss, that's what I say. I wouldn't expect any sympathy from you. You can't get blood out of a stone.'

Julie stood up and addressed the mirror. 'Talk to your-self, Julie, you'll get a better level of conversation. I said get Billy to school for your own sake, Nana and I can't say more.'

She left the flat and ran back upstairs but Nana's words, however little meant, had rattled her. You did feel powerful when you had kids: for most women it was the nearest they ever got to being important. And then, when kids grew up, they did cast you off – like the sloughed-off skin she had seen in Chester zoo once, grey and lifeless and left behind while its former inhabitant slithered gleaming away.

Graham felt positively cheerful as he got ready for work. The funny little girl had seemed capable enough in spite of the tarty exterior. She had mentioned children but there had been no wedding ring – only bare little fingers with cruelly bitten nails. Was £3 an hour enough? His conscience smote him suddenly as he tried to compute his own hourly rate. He billed clients for £50 an hour of which something like £15 an hour came to him. Of course he had worked damned hard for his qualification, so perhaps it was OK. Anyway, if she was good he could always up the ante.

Charlotte was coming round tonight and it would be the last time he would have to scour the bog and the bath beforehand: that on its own was worth £20. He picked up Charlotte's photograph from the bedside table and looked at it solemnly. Nice eyes, nice teeth, wonderful hair. In bed she was the best he had had, powerful yet submissive, the way a woman should be. She had teased him about the new cleaner last night, asking how she could trust him with a serving wench. But he could be alone on a desert island with Julie . . . she had insisted he use her Christian name . . . he could be alone with her for twenty years and not feel even the urge. Some men actually sought out . . . he searched for the female equivalent of 'a bit of rough' but couldn't find it . . . anyway, they did; but he had never been like that. You had to have standards, and a good background meant a lot to him.

Still, the girl had looked pleasant and she'd be useful.

Graham took a last look round the flat and imagined it as it would look tomorrow, somehow warmer and more welcoming. Of course, she might turn out to be a disaster and have to go at the end of the week. But she had had a nice, cocky little face in spite of the stick-like arms and legs, and he had a feeling she was going to do. Pleased with the pun he let himself out into the hall and pressed the bell for the lift with a jubilant forefinger.

Julie had hoped to see Tommo on her way to or from the school and he was there, drawing up at the kerb, leaning from the van window to cluck at Damien and then smile at Julie herself. 'Need a lift?' he asked. She shook her head.

'No, ta. But I need a favour.' Out of the corner of her eye she could see a bunch of broccoli on the passenger seat. She liked the vegetable but there were limits.

'Shall I come round?' Tommo asked and her heart sank at his look of pleasure when she nodded her head.

'I need a club,' she said when they were safe in the flat with the kettle on and Damien ensconced in the lobster pot. 'I've landed meself a job . . . well, it was supposed to be for Yvonne but I wound up taking it on.'

Tommo looked less than enthusiastic and Julie's words dried.

'How are you going to manage?' he asked. 'I thought you had more than enough on your plate already, what with the kids and that lot.' His eyes flicked up to Yvonne and down to Nana.

'It's only fifteen hours a week,' she said carefully. She needed Tommo; no chance to say 'get lost'. 'The thing is, Tommo,' she said confidingly, 'it's a nice job. Easy. Just a bit of dusting and hoovering. But it's in Eastgate . . .' She widened her eyes in implication.

'Posh,' he said.

'Very posh. So you see I need something to wear, a suit or a nice skirt and blouse. I know I'm spent up, but if I could have a £10 order . . .?'

'You won't get much for a tenner,' he said slowly and she knew it was going to be all right.

He gave her a £25 order to spend at any one of the major

stores. 'And don't come back and say it went on the kids,' he said sternly. 'Look out for number one.' His voice had thickened with affection and Julie felt at once both pleased and apprehensive. He was a nice bloke. He probably had a little nest-egg, and a pension, and insurance policies, and everything that made for a safe life. Some girl would be lucky one day. She poured his tea and tried to imagine him in bed, but the image of him without collar and tie would not come. As for the down-belows . . .!

'Now what's amusing you?' he asked, and she had to dive for the kettle and fuss with the milk and sugar.

'What's she like, then?' he said, dunking his biscuit.

'Who?' Suddenly Julie realized he meant her new employer. Instinct made her fudge the issue a little. 'Oh, who am I working for, you mean? Well, I'm not sure really. I saw a bloke, but who else lives there I don't know.'

'Maybe he's on his own?' Tommo said.

'Yeah,' Julie said. 'He looked a bit lost. Maybe his wife's walked out.'

'That's the way of it, I'm afraid,' Tommo said. 'Women might've been the weaker sex once but it's all changed. They'd divorce you soon as look at you nowadays.'

Julie chuckled. 'He was guilty of unreasonable behaviour, your honour; he tried to get on the wedding photographs.'

'We're laughing,' Tommo said, 'but it's not far off the truth.' His face clouded. 'Not that there haven't always been dominant women . . .'

'Boadicea,' Julie said. 'Maggie Thatcher,' but they both knew he was thinking of his mother.

'Well,' he said, getting to his feet. 'You get yourself something nice. Don't stint. If it's a bit over the odds, tell them to hold it for you and I'll see to it.'

'Ta,' Julie said, seeing him to the door. She would have liked to reach out and pat his arm, just to show gratitude, but it wouldn't be fair to encourage him.

When he had gone she sat down with her refilled cup and tried to imagine marriage to Tommo. A nice house with a garden. He was handy about the house, she knew that. Some hens scratting in a wire enclosure, and neat rows of veggies. He would grow broccoli for her, row after row of it. 'My God,' she said, leaping up suddenly. A large blob of water had splashed down into her cup and she looked up in time to get a stream between her eyes.

She was across the room and at the door in a second, ready to sprint upstairs, but when she flung open the door Nana stood on the threshold. She looked past Julie to where the water was now cascading.

'What's that, a burst pipe?'

'No,' Julie said sarcastically. 'The ceiling's crying.' She was swift up the stairs but Nana's riposte was swifter.

'It's caught the smit off her, then.'

'Yvonne!' Julie called, hammering on the door. There was no reply, only the sound of Nana labouring up the stairs behind her. Julie tried the handle. 'It's locked,' she said.

'Oh my God, we'll all be drowned.' Nana's face was suddenly animated. 'I knew she'd be trouble the minute she arrived. No wonder he's taken off to Spain – he's got a bit about him.'

'Yvonne must've left a tap on,' Julie said, putting her shoulder to the door. It was solid and immovable.

'Get the pollis,' Nana said, already moving towards the stairs.

'No!' Julie's tone was desperate. 'We don't want them here.'

'We've got nothing to hide,' Nana said. 'What've *we* done?'

Julie pushed the door again. 'You don't need to've *done* anything. They can fit you up better than Moss Bros.'

'Well, I'm not staying here to be drowned.' Nana began to descend.

'Don't you dare tell the pollis,' Julie warned. Their eyes locked, until Yvonne's startled face appeared below them.

'What's the matter?' she said, the words ending in a wail.

'You've left a bloody tap on, lady.' Nana was triumphant now that fear of death by water had been removed. 'There'll be a nice little bill for damage. Three floors, not to mention the wear and tear at my age . . .'

Yvonne was crying now, fumbling in her bag for her keys but unable to see for tears.

'Sometimes,' Julie told the old lady, 'sometimes, I hate you.'

'Ooh, don't mince words,' Nana said. She began to go down again but was unable to resist a parting shot. 'At least you can't blame our poor little Billy for this. That'll disappoint you.' She descended a stair or two and spoke again, but Yvonne had found the key and she and Julie were too preoccupied with the flood to care.

The source of the disaster was the tap to the bathroom basin, where Yvonne had been steeping tights.

'I was only rinsing them through,' she said, looking at the sodden carpet. 'And then the kids needed coppers for school so I went for change.' She fished a box of matches from her pocket and looked from them to the waterlogged carpet. 'And I didn't even need them!'

Julie stayed until most of the water was scooped or squeegied into buckets.

'Before you go,' Yvonne said, brightening, 'let's have something to perk us up. I know it's early in the morning but we need warming up.'

She produced a miniature Christmas cracker which opened to reveal a small bottle of cream sherry. She poured it into two glasses, measuring carefully to ensure fair play. 'I've been keeping this for two years,' she said, wringing out the cuff of her cardigan which was sending unwelcome trickles up her arm. 'Now . . .' She raised her glass. 'Let's drown our sorrows.'

Julie shook her head. 'With our luck, Yvonne, they'll be amphibious.'

Back in her own flat she prepared Damien's dinner of corned beef and mashed potato, and made herself a cheese toastie. Her feet and hands were glowing now but the bottoms of her jeans were still wet and sent little messages of cold whenever she moved her legs.

The baby's eyelids drooped even as she fed him the last spoonful, and she carried him into the bedroom and settled him in his cot. She felt strangely elated thinking of tomorrow and her job, but first there was the new outfit to be bought. Yvonne had promised to look after Damien as soon as she had put her own flat to rights, and to collect Jason from school. Julie looked at the clock. With any luck she could be in town by two o'clock, leaving her three hours to shop.

In fact it was three o'clock by the time she reached the shopping centre. She knew what she wanted, could see herself in her mind's eye moving about Graham Iley's flat in a navy skirt, navy-and-white striped blouse, navy tights and court shoes and a touch of colour somewhere, a red scarf at the neck perhaps or some big red earrings. Twenty-five pounds wouldn't do it all but she could make a start.

She wandered from shop to shop but the things she could afford looked shoddy, with shiny materials and skimpy seams. In the end she sought out the better boutiques, fingering things that were far beyond her price-range, occasionally trying something on, luxuriating in the feel of silk and wool and ample folds.

She took refuge in a McDonald's, buying a doughnut and a carton of coffee to assuage her feeling of misery. But when she boarded the bus home, empty-handed, it was full of office girls, beautifully dressed and made up with swinging shiny hair, clutching seat-backs and handrails with pink- or red-tipped fingers. 'I could've been like that,' Julie thought, 'if I'd done their bloody CSEs or a commercial course.' She leaned her head against the window, her imagination running away with her as she thought of college and a cap and gown and letters after her name like a pedigree. Instead she had let Gary take her up a back lane and get her pregnant.

She tried to block out the pains of deprivation by thinking of Jason and Damien, waiting at home. They would be pleased to see her, their faces would light up at the sight of her. That was more important than clothes or hair-dos. She pulled her skirt over her knees to hide where the side slit was frayed and curled her fingers into the palms of her hands to dismiss their unmanicured state. When she started work . . . it would be different then. She laid her cheek against the window again and gazed out at the road that carried her back to Grimshaw Street.

Damien was asleep when she got home and Jason too preoccupied to lift his eyes from the TV.

'I gave them fish fingers and soldiers,' Yvonne said, already making for the door. 'I'll have to see to my lot

67

now.' She looked harassed and Julie put aside her own miseries for a moment.

'Got anything in for their tea?'

'Beans,' Yvonne said.

'Besides beans?'

'Some tartare sauce,' Yvonne said desperately, 'and half a malt loaf and a packet of meringue shells.'

Julie gave her a tin of frankfurters and a packet of chocolate bourbons. 'I know you're not keen on them, Yvonne, so the kids might stand a chance.' She reached for an apple, one of three. 'Take this for yourself, and cheer up. Everything been all right downstairs?'

'I haven't heard anything,' Yvonne said, 'so at least there's been peace. Ta for the eats. I'll pay you back.' She turned in the doorway. 'Did you get what you wanted?'

'Not today,' Julie said. 'But there's always another time.' She would wear her grey denim skirt tomorrow, the one with the zips, and her blue chambray shirt. It wasn't right, but at least it was clean. Besides, she told herself as she washed the tea dishes, she wouldn't even see Graham Iley so there was nothing spoiling.

She went down to check on Nana when the dishes were done. No news was not necessarily good news where Billy was concerned.

She found the old lady reading the evening paper. 'Looking for another funeral?' Julie said, moving a brush and crumb tray from a chair and sitting down.

'No,' Nana said complacently, 'I didn't enjoy that one. Poor turn-out and no invites back. No, I'm reading the court report. Him across the road's up again.'

'The doley in No. 4?' Julie said curiously. 'He's a layabout and no mistake.'

'Well, it says here he wants fourteen other offences taking into consideration, so you can hardly say he's sitting back and doing nothing,' Nana said. 'Still, I blame the courts. You watch, he'll only get promotion . . . I've seen it before.'

'Probation?' Julie suggested.

'That's what I said, cleversides. They get away with murder nowadays.' Nana laid the open paper down on her knee. 'I mind when Grimshaw Street was a real nice road.'

She plucked at her cardigan sleeves, pulling them down over her wrists. 'Respectable people, kept themselves nice. Now,' she looked up at Julie and cackled, 'we've got all sorts. All living on the Social. It'll come to a sticky end one day, madam, you watch. Everyone taking out of the kitty, no one putting in. The money'll run out one day and we'll all be scratting.' She picked up the paper again and shook it out, and Julie knew there was something lethal coming. 'This job of yours, good pay is it?'

'It's OK,' Julie said. The balance of power was definitely in Nana's favour now and they both knew it.

'You'll be coming off Social, then?' Nana said, peering intently at the paper.

'I might,' Julie answered but both women knew that the answer was no. The money she would earn meant the difference between existing and living, but there was no way it could replace her benefit.

She made her goodbyes and went back up stairs. She was going into her own flat when she heard the outer door open and when she looked over the banister Tommo stood in the hall, shaking drops of water from his brown head. He looked up and saw her.

'Did you get fitted up in the town?' he asked. He had a bunch of broccoli in his hand and a bag of clementines. 'I bought these for the bairns,' he said sheepishly, mounting towards her.

At first Julie was irritated. She wanted to spend the evening in planning and preparing for the morning, her first day at work. Then she was glad he was there – someone to share a pot of tea with, someone to tell her she was wonderful and repair the damage Nana had inflicted upon her self-esteem. But her pleasure was short-lived.

'I can't stop,' he said. 'Mother's not too clever today, so I'll have to get home.' He smiled at her and patted her arm as he turned on the stair. 'Good luck tomorrow. I'll call in to see how it went.'

When the children were safely in bed Julie trimmed the broccoli and put it into boiling water, but she felt no stirring of her taste-buds at the sight, not even when she had decanted the cooked broccoli on to a plate and topped it with a big lump of polyunsaturated. Why was it you only wanted things when you couldn't have them?

She sat cross-legged on the sofa, dipping the green spears in the watery butter and munching morosely. The clock said eight o'clock but it felt like eleven. She licked her fingers at last and put the plate aside, knowing she ought to sort out what she was going to wear next day, what they were all going to eat and what Yvonne would need to take care of Damien. But a terrible lethargy had overtaken her: she didn't want to do anything. On the other hand she didn't want to sit still. She flicked through the TV channels but there was nothing to hold her attention – a documentary on prisons, two comics acting out weak sketches, an agony aunt delving into divorce, and a crime thriller that seemed to be shot entirely in a dark back street.

Julie switched off the telly and was about to switch on the radio when she heard the clatter of a milk bottle and then a muttered oath below her window. She looked out to see Billy, hands thrust into pockets, head down against the wind, slouching across the pavement and into the road. If she ran downstairs she could probably catch him and bring him back, but she couldn't be bothered. She watched him cross the road, passing into the light from the street-lamp and out of it and then merging with the shadows that led to the corner and the bus shelter. She felt a sudden, terrible longing to see Tommo's van turn into the street and chug to her front door, but even as she imagined him climbing from the driving seat, mounting the stairs, moving to take her in his arms, she knew it was not what she wanted at all.

She cried a little, letting the tears flow, seeing them reflected in the window-pane, until she twitched the curtains back into place. Crying was stupid. She went into the bathroom and sluiced her face and then began to get ready for bed. She would have liked a bath but there was no hot water and she couldn't afford to feed the meter. She made do with a wash-down and cleaned her teeth. She felt old suddenly, and when she peered into the mirror she was sure that her face had aged. She had almost forgotten about her new job and the feller with the posh flat. It seemed like a dream, somehow, a TV commercial that would end with a bitter punch-line.

She put out the bathroom light and went to her bedroom in search of comfort, pulling on socks and struggling into her sweater, well knowing the advantages of warmth when you had the blues. She could feel her monthly moving around somewhere and she checked that she had two tampons left in a box in her top drawer. That was another bloody wicked expense and not a bit of help from the Social.

She was turning back the covers when she heard the knock at the door. 'Who is it?' she called through the panel, knowing full well it would be Link.

'Me, Julie. I've come round to show you something. Let's in.'

'Not tonight, sunshine.' She felt a sudden energy now there was something to oppose.

'Aw, come on, man. I've only trailed round for your sake.' She heard something rattle on the other side of the door. 'Come on, see what I've got. I only bought it for you.'

Julie was curious now but unwilling to give him access. 'What is it? You can tell me.'

'I can't.' Again the rattle. 'You've got to see for yourself.'

'If I let you in, will you go in five minutes?'

'God's honour.'

Julie opened the door to see Link standing there, a large, gaudy box-game in his hand. 'It's Cluedo,' he said.

'I'm not playing that!'

'One game, Jules. Just one game and then I'll go.'

They sat in front of the fire, frugally on one bar, and set out the game.

'Who do you want to be?' Link asked generously, already shaking the dice.

'Colonel Mustard. Have you had some supper?'

When he shook his head Julie fetched bread and sliced cheese and a jar of pickle, together with one plate and a knife and a bottle of red pop.

'Just one game, mind,' she said, but knew she would let him stay. Tonight was not a night to sleep alone.

5

Julie woke Link early and stood over him till he was dressed and at the kitchen table. While she poured tea he whistled softly under his breath and mimed playing his drums.

'Get this down and scram,' she said shortly, regretting her soft-heartedness of the night before, remembering only how it felt to have sex with someone who roused you not at all. 'It's got to stop,' she told herself while he went through his triplets and paradiddles but in her heart she knew it would happen again. Perhaps it was meant to be, that they should lean on one another for the rest of their lives as they had done amid the smell of sweat and chalk that was school?

'I could hang around today,' Link offered, pushing his mug forward. 'I'm at a loose end.'

'Well, tie a knot in yourself and hop it, Link. I've got a full day ahead of me and I want shot of you.'

His hands stilled and he leaned forward to look directly at her. 'Why are you nasty sometimes, Julie? I mean, why be like that?'

'Like what?' He had taken her by surprise.

'Sharp. Sarky. Sometimes you pretend you're joking but underneath you're not.'

'I have to be like that,' she said, trying to sound reasonable. She moved to the cupboard and began to assemble Jason's breakfast. 'I mean, you laugh or you cry! If I thought about being here on me own with two dependent kids, I'd crack. So . . . I wisecrack and I can manage.' She leaned forward until their eyes were only inches apart. 'Now that I've bared my soul, Link – ' He nodded expectantly. ' – will you go willingly or . . .?'

He rose reluctantly. 'If you're in one of those moods I won't stop.' He walked towards the door and she willed herself not to be conciliatory. As he left the flat she heard Jason's feet on the lino in the passage and turned to greet her son.

Lying awake in the early hours she had pictured the scene at the breakfast table, she indulgent, Jason compliant, both of them making plans for her first week's wages. But as usual fantasy and reality had little in common.

'I want a nana,' he said, swinging himself on to a chair and placing his hands flat on the table.

'I haven't got a banana, darling.' His fingers were short and stubby and yet strong. Nice little hands. She felt a quiver of pleasure.

'I want one.'

Irritation crept into her voice. 'I haven't got any nanas, Jason. Read my lips: no B-A-N-A-N-A-S. Apples yes, oranges yes, bananas no.'

Jason heaved a heavy sigh and leaned his head on his fist.

'He's a theatrical little bugger,' she thought, glowing with pride. 'Well?' she said aloud. 'Don't just sit there waiting, Jason. There's no bananas. Do you want a boiled egg or some orange with bread and butter? Or you can have rice crispies. And hurry up, before Damien wakes up.'

Jason opted reluctantly for rice crispies and began to fool about with the milk and sugar. Julie sat, holding her mug of tea in both hands, willing herself not to take the bait. She was going to have a nice couple of hours before she went to the new job. She had put a fifty-pence piece in the meter for hot water so she could get a bath, then get dressed. He was not going to wind her up – not now. She wanted to look nice. Graham had said he would leave a note but you never knew. He could turn up . . . and anyway there might be callers. You had to look the part. She raised her mug to drain it and caught sight of the damp patch on the ceiling. There would be hell to pay when the rent man saw it. Poor Yvonne, slapped with a repair bill.

'What are you doing at school today?' she asked, trying

to make conversation like they always said you should with your kids.

'Dunno.' The rise and fall of Jason's shoulders was more expressive than his words.

'You must know. What did the teacher say?' In her day teachers had always issued dire warnings about tomorrow. But he was shaking his head and squirming away from the table.

'Are you going to do spellings?' Jason rolled his eyes and shook his head. 'Well, sums then?' This time he groaned. Julie's fingers itched to box his ears but she resisted. 'I bet you're going to make something?'

'No,' he said, taking her by surprise.

'How do you know you're not?'

This time he put his hands over his ears and screwed his eyes shut. Oh well, at least she'd tried.

Graham Iley had also woken early, suddenly convinced that there would be nothing for the girl to do when she arrived. There wasn't enough work here to occupy someone every day. Whatever had possessed him to think there was?

He contemplated the bathroom while he showered. Today even that looked pristine. She could do the washing, of course, except that no one had touched his underclothes since his mother and that was years ago. Thinking of his underpants he felt suddenly vulnerable. Still, she had children so she wasn't the kid she seemed. She was probably very capable and would turn the flat into paradise. If he ever shacked up with Charlotte they could keep her on afterwards. For the next few minutes he thought of nothing but 'afterwards', living together versus the marriage bit. They would have to marry if there was ever a kid involved. He had seen too many men dropped by their lovers and deprived of all paternal rights. If he had a son he would make bloody sure he had care and control.

At least two guys he'd been at school with had been caught like that – and then there was poor Dudley at the club, who had married at eighteen and been deserted at twenty. His wife had gone off with an Australian tree-

74

surgeon, taking the two children with her, and now Dudley saw them every second year, which was all he could afford. No, if you were going to make a commitment it had to be watertight and you had to think it through beforehand. Some time he would have to really weigh marriage to Charlotte, make a list of the pros and cons and study it.

He made a list for Julie while he ate toast and marmalade and it looked quite respectable when it was done.

His bedroom was still a disaster area, the only uncluttered place the bedside table where Charlotte presided in Polaroid, smiling into the wind when they were sailing and mercifully fully clothed. Graham looked at the clock and then at the disorder. It would take an hour to make any impact and he had to leave in five minutes. He added a footnote to the list: *'No need to bother about the bedroom today. I have some work in there I'd like left undisturbed.'* He brought some old rugger-club minutes from the desk and scattered them around as though he was in the business of collating information. That should hold her. He shut the door of the bedroom with a thud. On an afterthought he fetched the tin of Scotch shortbread he had bought for his aunt's birthday and left it on the kitchen table for the new cleaner's elevenses. You had to make an effort nowadays, otherwise they moved on to greener pastures. He added a £20 note and a footnote about something on account and then left the rest to fate.

Julie carried Damien on to the landing when she was ready and drew the door to behind her. She had made a great effort to look smart and was pleased with the result. She had tied a patterned chiffon scarf under the collar of her shirt and pinned silver cartwheels in her ears. She looked smart but not gaudy, or so she hoped. She was about to carry the baby up to Yvonne's when she heard Nana's voice in the hall below.

'Are you off, then?' Nana asked when she peered over the banister.

'Yes, I'm just taking Damien up to Yvonne. She's going to watch him for me.'

'You're not leaving him with her?' Nana's tone was

scandalized. 'She cannat keep herself out of trouble, let alone a babby.'

Julie looked apprehensively at the upper landing. If Yvonne was lurking and heard this there would be another crying match. She descended halfway towards Nana and lowered her voice.

'Don't be spiteful, Nana. You know Yvonne's good with children. Her two aren't a scrap of bother . . . and she's looking forward to having Damien. She's lonely.'

'I'm not surprised. Her man probably had to run for his life before she drowned him. I knew what she was the day she moved in – straight in, without washing her paintings. I had her mark then.'

'I've heard of the pot calling the kettle,' Julie said drily. 'When did you last wash your paintings . . . for the Coronation?'

'Oh, your tongue's sharp, miss. You'll cut yourself on it one of these days. Still, you'll not be told. Take him up there if you're determined. Just don't cry to me when he's down the hospital.' Nana had gathered her cardigan round her and folded her arms.

'She's jealous,' Julie thought and tried to soothe. 'I would've asked you but I know you've got your hands full. And Yvonne's got a big gap in her life.'

'Aye,' Nana said, a little mollified. 'Well, if the match is in Barcelona and the tab's in Newcastle you won't get much of a smoke.'

'I didn't mean that,' Julie said. 'We don't all think of sex all the time.'

She had played into Nana's hands. 'So that's how you got two bairns, is it? Your mind wasn't on the job?' Nana was completely satisfied now that she had scored. 'Well, go on. Get up there and give her the poor little babby to keep her occupied, while you go gadding off.'

'Give me strength,' Julie said but the worm of guilt had gained entry now. Should she be leaving Damien at all? Was Yvonne capable? Was the extra money worth it? After she'd paid her bus fares and paid Yvonne she'd have less than £30 left . . . and her children were precious, the most – the only – precious things she had.

Her doubts were stilled when Yvonne opened her door.

'Come on then, pet. I've been dying for you coming.' Damien went to her outstretched arms without a backward glance and Julie felt her eyes prick.

'I know how you feel,' Yvonne said, suddenly, putting out a comforting hand. 'I can remember the first time I left John. It was like the end of the world. But it has to come sooner or later, so off you go.' She grinned. 'It's my first day earning, too, you know.'

Julie shook her head in wonderment. 'That's the first time I've seen you smile, Yvonne. You usually look about as happy as a Japanese in a Volkswagen. You're not bad looking when the sun comes out. You should try it more often.'

'You wait,' Yvonne said as Julie kissed Damien and made her way to the stairhead. 'You wait till you've been through the mill with a man. Try smiling when you've been dumped.' But Julie was half-way down the stairs and seemed not to hear.

Yvonne carried Damien into her living-room and contemplated him solemnly.

'Well,' she said at last, shifting him to her other arm. 'Let's see if I've lost the knack.'

Julie checked her bag twice on the bus ride, making sure the key Graham had given her was still there. She was having doubts about the enterprise again. What did he expect? She could keep house after a fashion but most of it she had just picked up from experience, bitter experience some of it, especially where washing was concerned. What if she turned his underpants blue, or something disintegrated? She had never handled an automatic washer. And his cooker had looked like something from *Space Odyssey*.

The thought of cooking for him terrified her. She could always rub things through by hand if the washer was beyond her, but cooking . . . well, there was no way round it. She took a deep breath outside his door and then inserted the key. 'Geronimo,' she said under her breath and stepped over the threshold.

The flat was smaller than she remembered from her interview and without Graham Iley's long limbs sprawled everywhere it seemed somehow tidier. She looked around the wood-panelled hall. That would take polish, and the

77

mirror was dull and in need of a clean. She moved towards the kitchen door, seeing the note and the money laid out on the kitchen table. He wanted a chop and veg for his tea, and there was a £20 sub for her. She picked it up and held it between thumb and forefinger. It was the first money she had ever earned. 'I'm twenty-one years old,' she thought, 'and this is my first job.'

She put her handbag and jacket on a chair and went through to the living-room, seeing it clearly for the first time. There were books everywhere and a complicated stereo system surrounded by CD tapes. 'My God,' she thought, 'how the other half lives.' The mantelpiece held three silver cups and she picked one up, resolving to clean them if he had silver polish in his cupboards. 'Rattray Cup', it said, and underneath was a list of names beginning in 1967 and ending with Graham Iley 1988 and then again in 1989. She might have known he'd be athletic from the length of his legs.

A letter-rack on the end of the mantelpiece was crammed with letters and what looked like invitations. She was dying to pluck out one deckle-edged card with a crown on the top, but he would be sure to notice if she poked and pried.

The room fascinated her. It was a bit like *Dynasty* . . . deep leather chairs and a dark-blue carpet with a silky sheen. She bent down and fingered it. Not nylon. Nylon carpets were sticky to the touch and collected muck. This was wool . . . or maybe even silk? She scuffed it with her shoe, making silver marks that died instantly when she reversed her tread.

She looked up suddenly to see herself reflected in the mirror above the mantelpiece. It was six foot long if it was an inch, bigger even than she had seen in a shop. She laughed suddenly, seeing herself reflected in the empty room, for all the world like a model. She sucked in her teeth and arched her back, narrowing her eyes and running a hand through her hair. My God, she looked half-way decent for a change. She jutted out her other hip and turned her head. Even better. For a moment she was tempted to add the finishing touch and put on some music, but the stereo had more knobs than Concorde so she

78

contented herself with humming 'Big Spender' and strutting across the mirror and out of sight and then back once more.

Now it was time to work. She went into the kitchen and rolled up her sleeves, peering at the note as she did so. He wanted his store cupboard checked and gaps rectified, and there was shopping money in a brown jar beside the microwave. She located the jar and lifted the lid. Pound coins and big silver and half full. She could take a coin and he would be none the wiser. Julie put back the lid and read the note again. He didn't want the bedroom touched. She looked through the kitchen doorway and saw that the door to his bedroom was tight shut.

She pictured the room – a big bed, king-size, with a duvet. Stripes or geometrics; nothing flowery. A nice suite in teak, or maybe pine, and a lovely carpet in toning colours. The first time she got a chance to buy a brand-new carpet she would get it to tone. Her mother had always believed in contrasts but if a room was too busy it got on your nerves.

She looked around for something to do to break the ice. A plate, cup and saucer stood on the draining-board. She could boil water and wash them up. But when she ran the tap the water was already red-hot. Hot water, and him out! She ran a bowlful and steeped her hands along with the crockery, lost in contemplation of such utter luxury.

Graham listened dutifully to his client's tale of mistaken identity but his mind kept wandering. The cleaner would be there now, moving around, fingering his possessions, even lifting an item or two if she was that way inclined. He ran an uneasy finger around his collar and the woman on the other side of his desk noticed and faltered. 'Go on,' he urged. 'I'm listening. This collar's just a bit tight.'

He had shut the bedroom door firmly to keep her out . . . not that that would stop her if she was nosy. He looked at his watch. Twelve o'clock. She'd had an hour or more by now.

If she'd turned up, of course. Graham felt suddenly hopeful. She was only a kid, after all, and kids were always applying for jobs and then vanishing. They'd had it happen in the office before now, never mind with cleaners. She had probably never intended to take the job . . . in which case she had a key to his flat! His skin prickled with fear suddenly, not at the thought of theft or mayhem but at the certainty of what Charlotte would say about his failure to take up the girl's references. He looked up and found his client's eyes fixed on him.

'Well,' he said expansively, 'I think I've got everything I need. I'll see you on the 8th, then, and we'll ask Mr Rackstraw to opt for the Crown Court. Try not to worry . . .' He was pushing back his seat, resisting the urge to sprint for the door and his car and the road home.

It took him twenty minutes to reach his flat and thirty seconds to get upstairs. He found Julie in the kitchen, unpacking a string bag of provisions.

'I found your note,' she said. 'I've got your chop and some lovely broccoli.' Her smile was begging approval, and Graham felt suddenly ashamed of his former doubts.

'I just looked in to make sure you'd been able to find everything.' He waved a hand around him. 'Sort it out to suit yourself,' he said generously.

She was smiling again and he felt suddenly uplifted at the sight. 'There isn't a cup of coffee, is there?' he said, and edged his hip on to the kitchen table.

She made him a coffee and cut thick slices from a freshly baked loaf to spread with butter, and some Marmite also produced from the string bag.

'I took £4 from the jar,' she said, 'like you told me. There's 74p change.' It was there in her rough little hand and Graham felt a sudden glow of pride in his ability to judge character.

'That's fine,' he said solemnly. 'Just dip into it whenever you need.' He felt an urge to do something for her, give her a present or a bonus or something to show he was glad she was there. 'You said you had kids?' he ventured, and when she nodded – 'How old?'

She didn't look old enough to have a five-year-old, and women from her kind of background were supposed to age before their time. How old would she be? Twenty-five, if the kid was five? No one had kids before twenty . . . well, say eighteen. That would make her twenty-three. He held out his cup for a refill and thought about how nice it would be to come in to a home-cooked meal tonight.

'I've got a little Dinky car somewhere . . . you could have it for one of your boys.'

Julie caught the half-past two bus from the stop at the end of his street. She had cooked his meal and left it neatly composed on a plate to go in the microwave when he got home. She had put a load through the washer without anything changing colour, and had hoovered and dusted everywhere except the forbidden bedroom. She might see that tomorrow, but not unless he gave permission. She had felt better after Graham's lunch-time visit but very definitely on probation, half-expecting a hidden-camera eye to be observing her every move.

She leaned her head against the window of the bus and closed her eyes. It had been nice, once she got used to it, moving round that spacious flat where nothing was faded or greasy or worn. There had been five tablets of soap in his bathroom and a rack full of towels. He used disposable razors, and Paco Rabanne. She had seen it in the bathroom and caught an elusive whiff of it when he had been in the kitchen, just enough to set your nostrils twitching. She had given Link some Brut for Christmas and people had had to move off him for a week, by which time the bottle was empty.

She wondered how much she should tell Link about the way Graham Iley lived. Would it spur him on or defeat him? Link could do something with himself one day, if they ever found out what.

The bus pulled up at her stop and she called in at the Paki shop to spend some of her first day's pay. There was no sign of the owner but his wife was there at the till, looking daggers from under her centre parting. 'Nice day,' Julie said and received a look of pure hatred in return. When she came back to the till with her wire basket the woman lifted out each item disdainfully and prodded the till with a stiff, red-tipped index finger.

'Ta,' Julie said, pocketing her change. She moved to the

81

door and turned. 'Keep smiling,' she said, dead pan, and left the shop.

Nana's door was open a crack. 'Is that you?' she called as Julie came through the outer door.

'No, it's me,' Julie answered.

'Never mind the comedy,' Nana said, folding her arms across her chest. 'You want to get yourself upstairs and get that bairn before she turns him funny. She's been in and out of here with that pushchair like a bloody yo-yo. Singing to herself and talking gibberish . . .' She pronounced it with a hard G but Julie knew what she meant. 'Where's the itsy-bitsy-witsy baby-boy, den? Where's the chukky-wukky little love-lamb?' Nana reverted to her own voice. 'Where's the psychiatric social worker, that's what I want to know. Her they took away across the road had more sense in her little finger than that one upstairs's got in her whole body. No wonder he's gone to Spain. Don't call it desertion, call it self-protection.'

'You're jealous,' Julie said.

'That's it, blame me. But when she's taken off with your bairn and Scotland Yard's looking for her don't think I'll keep my mouth shut. She's gone broody. I've seen it before.'

Julie ran upstairs and let herself into the flat. She felt suddenly excited at the thought of making tea for the bairns. She had bought a tin of tuna and some brown rice. Jason loved a curry. Everybody was going to be happy. At least Nana hadn't said Yvonne was crying. Drooling yes, crying no.

She was about to run upstairs and claim her child when Tommo appeared in the doorway. 'How did it go?' he said. 'Although I don't need to ask, do I? You're beaming.'

'It went all right, Tommo. I was a bit scared at first and then I just got stuck in. He was ever so nice . . .'

'Was there any woman?' Tommo was trying to sound laid-back but as usual when he was roused, his cheeks glowed.

'No. He's on his own,' Julie said and saw Tommo's face fall. 'He'll be out at work usually,' she said to comfort him. 'He just popped back today to see if I was coping.'

His shoulders drooped a little and she knew he wasn't

82

going to be awkward. 'You could cope with anything,' he said, admiringly.

'You can come again,' she answered. 'Now, I'll make you a cup of tea if you like but I've got to get the kid first. Yvonne'll be on her knees by now.'

'I don't think so,' he said. 'I saw her with the pushchair in Rosamond Street and she was practically skipping.' He went to the door. 'I'd love a cuppa but I've got to go. I just wanted to make sure you were OK.' He paused with his hand on the door. 'If Yvonne felt like doing overtime we could go out for a drink . . . or a meal? A bit of a celebration.'

Julie sighed. 'I'm whacked, Tommo. Another night . . . but tonight I just want to get the kids back and get into me nightie and switch the box on and sit and sit and sit.'

'Yes,' Tommo said. 'Yes, I can understand that. Well, some other time.'

Julie heard him go down the stairs with mixed feelings. She could have gone out for one drink. Nana would've watched the bairns – that would have stopped her feeling bitter and twisted. All the same, she wanted a night in. She had a lot to think about.

She was half-way to the door when she heard Link's unmistakable step on the landing.

'I can't stop now, Link. I'm on me way to get the bairns.'

'Wait on,' Link said, propelling her back into the room. 'I've got trouble. Real trouble, this time.'

'What?' Julie asked, intrigued in spite of herself.

'Restart,' he said as though announcing Armageddon. 'They want me down there a week on Friday.'

'Is that all?' She put hands on hips and looked at him scornfully. 'In five years you've worked a total of two months and three weeks. So now they're sending for you to sort you out and fix you up with a job. What else do you expect? You can't live at the taxpayer's expense forever, Link.'

'You do,' he said, stung by her lack of sympathy.

'That's different – I'm bringing up the next generation. Besides which, I work now.'

It was Link's turn to be scornful. 'Part-time . . . and you won't declare it. Come on, admit it: you're not going to tell

83

them.' He sucked in his breath. 'You're part of the black economy, working and claiming!' The thought of her greater sin was making him visibly increase in stature.

Julie looked at him sternly. 'Link, I have a difficult choice to make.'

His eyes widened. 'How d'you mean, Julie?'

'Do I kill you quick or do I kill you slowly?' She stamped her foot and advanced, pushing him before her out on to the landing.

'That's right,' he said bitterly as he descended the stairs. 'I come because I'm in trouble and you turn me away. Typical.'

She leaned over the banister. 'Tell them you want a job with Tuesdays off.' Link made the mistake of looking puzzled. 'That's the day you sign on, remember?'

She was still laughing as she let herself into the upstairs flat, where Yvonne sat with a sleeping Damien on her knee. At the sight of Julie her arms tightened around him.

'He's been a little angel today. I think he likes it up here.'

It took twenty minutes to prise Damien from Yvonne and point out that he would be back in eighteen hours.

'You forget how canny they are when they're little,' Yvonne said, the tears already starting. 'When my two were that age I didn't have a care in the world.' Her sobs were stilled by the sight of two pound coins.

'There's a sub,' Julie said. 'Don't spend it all at once.'

She collected Jason from school and made the tea, then took her time putting the children to bed, taking pains with their teeth and listening to their every word. Jason played with the new Dinky car and she played crashes with him while Damien roared with delight. She read Jason his Ninja Turtle book from cover to cover and then made up an extra adventure, only curtailing it when his eyelids drooped.

When they were both asleep she washed herself down and put on her nightie.

Alone in her bedroom she sat in front of the dressing-table and thought about the day. She had liked the big flat with its mirrors and tied-back curtains. She leaned her elbows on the dressing-table and looked at herself in the mirror as he must have seen her. It wasn't a bad face but it wasn't distinctive. He would want something striking in a woman, something that other men would envy. For some reason she thought of the Paki wife. She was beautiful in a cruel kind of way. She would turn heads.

Julie reached over and pulled the bedspread towards her. It was pink lace from the Oxfam shop, mended in places, but one of her prized possessions. She draped it around her head and tried to look disdainful. It was no good. There was a bottle of toilet water on her dressing-table, covered with a knitted black poodle cover. She uncapped it and dabbed some behind her ears and on her throat. Better! She picked up a lipstick and put a red dot on her forehead. That was definitely exotic. She gazed at herself for a while and then let the bedspread fall to the floor. She felt suddenly flat and a little ridiculous, and it wasn't a pleasant feeling. Defiantly, she reached for a lipstick and outlined her mouth then took a kohl pencil and drew a tear, clown-like, beneath her left eye. Finally she took a tissue and rubbed her face until it stung. She was worse than Jason, playing on with paint.

She moved to the window and lifted the curtain. It had begun to rain and Grimshaw Street was shining once more, its bad points softened by darkness. She smiled, remembering Graham Iley perched on the kitchen table, wolfing bread and butter. It would be up to her to see he was fed. She would go through his cupboards and fix them up properly and make sure he got plenty of wholefood.

She let the curtain fall back into place and went to kneel by her bed. It was ages since she had said her prayers but it was like riding a bike – the minute you assumed the position it all came back.

'Good?' Charlotte asked.

Graham was still gasping but he slid a hand across her belly and patted it, feeling the soft fuzz of pubic hair and the sharp projection of her hip-bone.

'Very good.'

Charlotte giggled. 'I felt strange when I came into this place tonight.'

'Oh?' He had recovered enough to pull up the sheet and turn towards her.

'It was so tidy out there. And it smelled like a brothel.'

'Yes, she's a bit heavy-handed with the air-freshener.'

'Air-freshener? I thought it was nerve gas.' She put out a hand to his now flaccid penis and stroked it gently. 'Poor Graham, you're just putty in the hands of women, aren't you?'

'Mush,' he agreed complacently. The bedside clock said eleven-fifteen. That meant Charlotte would stay, and he wouldn't have to drag himself out of bed and see her down to her car. 'Actually, she's quite nice . . . just a kid. She must've been at school when she had her first baby.'

'The teenage pregnancy figure is astronomic,' Charlotte said absently. She wriggled up on the pillow and looked at the clock. 'I ought to go.'

'Stay.' Graham moved down and nuzzled her breast.

'Only if you desist. I need some sleep.'

He rolled away instantly. 'I'll be good.'

'OK,' Charlotte said, 'but I want to be up early. I must go home before I go in to the office.' Her voice was already drowsy. 'Do you think she'll do?' she asked, reaching a hand to punch her pillow into shape.

'I think so. She's quite a capable little thing. Quaint.'

'Nice-looking?'

'Yes. A bit tarty . . . long legs and big eyes.'

'I thought you were going to say big boobs,' Charlotte said drowsily.

'No, she's quite flat-chested actually.'

'You've noticed!' Charlotte said, pretending outrage and wide awake now.

'Just in passing. I was merely being observant.' He was turning towards her, his left hand moving to cup her breast, his other arm sliding behind her head.

'I said no more.'

'Just a little bit.' As his mouth closed on Charlotte's mouth he reminded himself to clear all signs of Charlotte's occupation before he let the funny little thing in to clean the bedroom.

6

Nothing stirred in Grimshaw Street. Even the courting cats
had ceased to howl with daylight. Then the milkman
appeared at one end and the postman at the other. They
met half-way and exchanged moans about overwork and
under-pay. The milkman left the customary two pints of
silver top and two pints of semi-skimmed at No. 13 and the
postman left one letter, addressed to Mrs Yvonne Lister.

He came down the step, hefted his bag to his other
shoulder and went off whistling Andrew Lloyd Webber. A
moment later an eldritch shriek rang out from inside No.
13. It startled the milkman but the postman was too busy
crying for Argentina and went on his way.

Inside the house the scream had more effect. Julie
appeared on the landing, pulling down her sweater to
cover her naked thighs, a piece of wholemeal toast in one
hand, a comb in the other. She looked upwards towards
the top landing and then, as Nana's door opened, down
into the hall.

Nana stood in the doorway, fully clothed but rubbing
sleep from her eyes. 'My God, what was that?' she said,
heaving her bosom into a more comfortable position. Julie
swallowed the last bit of toast and began to mount the
stairs. At that moment Yvonne appeared above them, her
head a mass of brush rollers above her long white nightie
so that she looked like the Statue of Liberty, except that
she flourished not a torch but an opened letter.

'He loves me,' she said, waving the letter and beating
her breast with her other hand.

'Is that all?' Julie said. 'I thought it was at least rape and
pillage.'

87

Yvonne shook her head. 'You don't understand, Julie. Trevor's coming home, after all these lonely, barren, empty, loveless . . .'

Nana's face appeared above the banister. 'He's not coming back here, is he? Bringing all them nasty diseases with him? He might've caught anything out there, it's swarming. You want to watch he doesn't give you a dose . . .'

'Don't be crude, Nana,' Julie said.

'Well, someone's got to bring her down to earth,' Nana said righteously.

'No one could,' Yvonne said dramatically. 'Not today. Now I know dreams come true, prayers are answered . . .'

'. . . and chickens come home to roost,' Nana said darkly and turned to descend.

'What does she mean?' Yvonne asked, momentarily disconcerted.

'Probably nothing,' Julie said. 'I've given up looking for meaning in anything that's said in this house. All the same, Yvonne, I've warned you about letting yourself go. If Trevor does come back, he has a chance not to recognize you.'

Yvonne's tears were instant. 'He used to say I looked like Marilyn Monroe,' she said, lifting a sleeve to her eye.

'Well, now you look like a group of her,' Julie said unkindly.

Yvonne clutched the banister. 'Don't frighten me, Julie, I need to keep my nerve. Still, I suppose I could do with some smartening up.'

From below Nana's cackle split the air. 'The state you're in you better ask British Shipbuilders to take you in for a refit.'

Yvonne's tears ceased. 'She is a coarse old woman, Julie – not even you can deny that.'

But Julie's patience had snapped. 'I'm not denying anything, Yvonne. I'm going to finish my breakfast. If you're serious about sprucing yourself up we'll talk about it later.'

Yvonne nodded and turned to her own door. 'I've got motivation now. You'll see, I'll blossom.'

Julie raised eyes to heaven and went down a flight.

Nana was lurking on the half-landing. 'I meant what I

said: she's a bloody fool if she takes him back. And he can't move in up there, four of them in two bedrooms, if you don't count the attic.'

'If you help me get her into shape and Trevor takes her back, we could be rid of her,' Julie suggested, *sotto voce*.

'In that case I will help!' Nana said. 'I never liked her, not from the day she moved in . . .'

'. . . without cleaning her paintings,' Julie finished.

'Well, count me in if you're sorting her out,' Nana said. 'We'll go for the burn.' She opened her door and then turned, on an afterthought. 'Mind you, she'll never make Page Three.'

Julie was boiling eggs when Tommo's knock came at the door.

'Am I too early? It's just that I won't get a chance later – I've got a bit of business on – and I wanted to see how things were going.' He smiled a fatuous smile and Julie felt her lips twitch.

'Come in and sit down. I'm just brewing up, to have a cup before I wake the bairns. This has a chance to be the last bit of peace I get today.'

'Have you taken too much on?' he asked anxiously, but Julie rolled her eyes upwards in the direction of Yvonne's flat. 'Trevor's apparently coming home, and Yvonne wants a make-over.'

Tommo chuckled above his mug. 'She doesn't want much. What does she expect you to do, turn her into Cinderella?'

'A pumpkin'd be easier,' Julie said. 'She must've put two stone on since she moved in here. Still, I will give her a hand.'

'She's not a bad-looking lass, really,' Tommo said. 'She's got nice blue eyes, I only noticed that lately.'

'That's because they're usually red,' Julie said. She pulled at her sweater, aware suddenly of the long expanse of naked thigh. She would have put her jeans on but now she was caught. It would affect him more if she got up and moved to the bedroom. 'More tea?' she said.

He pushed forward his cup. 'Ta. You know I mentioned a bit of business?' Julie nodded. 'Well, actually, I'm thinking of striking out on me own.'

89

This time she was interested. 'Tallying?'

Tommo pursed his lips. 'Yes and no. I'm sick of tallying. It's changing, Julie. I started in it when I was eighteen – that's twelve years ago, more or less. It wasn't a bad game then. Nice lines, moderate prices . . . you had your regulars and, by and large, they paid you. Now everyone dodges. Well, almost everyone. The lines are Third World rubbish, they're knackered at the first wash . . . and the office are on to me day and night to push loans.'

Julie pulled a face. 'I don't like loans. They're round your neck forever.'

Tommo took a sip of tea. 'It stinks. Loans, I mean. Someone gets in trouble . . . they need money in a hurry. So they take out a loan – £50 or £100. They pay forty per cent, thirty if they're good customers. So right off they owe £140. They sign to pay it off over 100 weeks, only they're still in shtuck, so when they've paid £20 or £30 off they come back for more. "I want £50," they say, and then I have to say, "But you still owe £100." They beg and plead, and then I have to say – have to say, Julie, I'm under orders – "Well, you can take out £150 and pay the first £100 back." Poor mugs, they bite every time. They take out the £150 and the office slaps the interest on, which is another £50, making £200 in all. I hand them £50. *Fifty pounds* they get, Julie, but they owe £200. And the worst thing is, they know and I know that in a few weeks' time we'll go through the whole process again, and they'll get in deeper and deeper.'

'It's not your fault,' Julie said comfortingly.

'Isn't it?' She had never seen Tommo bitter before and she didn't like it. 'I'm not so sure. I put the paperwork through, I show them where to sign. I warn them, after a fashion . . . but not half enough. Anyway, I want out. I can't just pack it in, not with mother and everything, but I want to start something . . . a sideline. If it builds, well . . .' He raised his eyebrows and grinned. 'I'll be laughing.'

'And some other poor bugger'll be ripping off the punters,' Julie thought but didn't say so. She was interested in what Tommo was saying: she'd once been in the situation he described herself until she saw the light and lived through a horrendous six months to get out of it. So she wanted to listen to him but it was becoming increasingly

90

difficult to concentrate, since she also wanted to be alone to get her chores out of the way, to plan ahead to the time when she would reach Graham Iley's flat and begin her day's work. She was going to tong her hair before she went and put on her parrot earrings . . . or perhaps the plain gold-coloured studs with the tiny crystal drop. He didn't look the parrot type.

Graham had breakfasted on the last of yesterday's loaf, still crusty and fresh, and the last of the butter. There had been a large tub of sunflower-oil margarine in the fridge but no new butter. He would have to speak to Julie about that. All the same, it was working well. He had forgotten the bliss of a clean kitchen, an unscummed bathroom basin, of matching socks neatly rolled together, bone dry. If Charlotte came round tonight he would greet her calmly with a glass of wine, not breathless from a last-minute tussle with squalor. Yes, it was working out very well indeed.

By ten-thirty he had cleared his desk and was able to give his coffee and biscuits undivided attention. When the last crumb was eaten he wondered who he could ring, and then remembered the club's Autumn Draw.

'Neil? Yes . . . I was just wondering if you'd had any luck?' They had agreed on an Autumn Draw as the best means of raising funds for the Rugby Club, and Neil was Scrounger-in-Chief. This time he had excelled himself. Booze had been promised in plenty, four meals for two had been offered by various restaurants, and, wonder of wonders, there was a weekend for two in Paris.

'Not a top-flight hotel, I'm afraid, but passable. I tried that new travel agency in the Market Square. It's got a manageress, and they're always better for freebies. She had a cancellation, so she checked it out with her head office, and they bit. It's for the weekend of 6th and 7th December, so whoever wins it will have to be quick off the mark. If you win you can take the lovely Charlotte. Two hot nights of passion off the Champs – that can't be bad.'

Graham changed the conversation: he didn't like joking about Charlotte as though she were some bimbo. He was serious about her, after all – or he would be, eventually. 'What did Bruce say about the printing?'

'He said we'd have it by next week. *Gratis*, as usual . . . but not to expect it next time. They're feeling the pinch, as we all are. Ginny's in the club again, by the way. Bruce is pleased, says it's bound to be a boy this time. That's what Audrey told me last year! Still, you never know. You want to get a move on, old chap – there's only you and Eric left. You'll be too old for the fathers' race by the time you get your offspring to Ardsley House.'

Bruce had gone to Ardsley House, too. They had all gone to Ardsley House, come to think of it . . . except Christopher Ojuku, and he was fresh off a banana-boat. Graham leaned back in his chair, remembering Ardsley House . . . six years from five to eleven. He'd been happy there . . . and there *had* been a fathers' race, though the old man had never won it, blaming the gammy knee he'd got doing National Service. Was he ready for the fathers' race?

He had a sudden mental picture of Julie, all eyes and knees above Minnie Mouse shoes. She was at least seven years his junior, probably more, and already a mother twice over. If she could manage parenthood, with her background, he and Charlotte could walk it. He felt quite satisfied until he thought of Charlotte rampant in the pursuit of another client, another sale. He might be ready for Ardsley House but he couldn't see Charlotte in the mothers' egg and spoon, not by any stretch of the imagination.

Julie had tried to get rid of Link but failed. Every time she showed him the door he brought up a fresh topic of interest. He was on to football now, and the sweep he intended to run. 'If there's fifty people in at 50p a week, that's twenty-five quid. Say it goes four weeks till someone has ten goals . . . that's a hundred quid!'

'Where will you get fifty people?' Julie queried.

'Easy,' Link boasted. 'The lads in the betting shop'll see the lot off, no problem. You can go in, though, and Yvonne, if she wants.'

'Thanks,' Julie said. 'I can hardly wait.'

She went into the bedroom and began to get changed. Link appeared in the doorway.

'Do you mind?' she said. He put a hand up to cover his eyes.

'I'm not looking. Anyway, I'm not interested.' He sounded unbelievably nonchalant. Julie pulled her skirt up and tucked in her shirt. She had starched it lightly, which had brought the faded blue-and-white stripes up nicely. She turned sideways to the mirror and then sideways again. She looked all right. A bit subdued, maybe, but it didn't do to overdo things. She reached for her spotted ruffle and swept her hair into it. Better!

'So shall I put you in?' Link asked, widening his fingers to peer at her.

'Yes,' she said, absently, leaning forward to lick her finger and remove a trace of lipstick from the corner of her mouth.

'How many for?'

'How many what, Link?'

'Entries, Julie. Entries!'

It was too much. Julie swept up her jacket and bag with one hand and Link with the other and decanted them all on to the landing. 'You go down,' she said, pointing. 'I go up. Put me down, and if I don't win you're barred.'

'And cheap at the price,' she thought as she ran up the stairs to see Yvonne, knowing all the while that she didn't mean it. Link was as much a part of her life as breathing and a damned sight more trouble!

She was half-way up the flight when she both heard and felt Yvonne's presence. She heard her voice saying, 'One, two, three, four,' and she felt the stairs tremble as Yvonne leaped up and down in time to her chant.

'What on earth are you doing?'

Yvonne was dressed in washed-up ski pants and bowling shirt. Her feet were bare and her hair was bound back with a kamikaze-type headband.

'I'm limbering up,' she panted.

'Limbering up?' Julie enquired. The ornaments on the sideboard were juddering and chinking as Yvonne pounded the carpet. 'OK,' she said authoritatively, as

Yvonne's movements slowed and her breath rasped harshly. 'Take a breath.'

Yvonne didn't need telling twice. She fell into the chair, gasping for air like a stranded whale. 'It's not going to work, Julie, is it? I've never been athletic, I'm more a bookish person.'

'Yes,' Julie said, thoughtfully, looking at Yvonne. 'About thirty-two volumes of the *Encyclopaedia Britannica*.'

'I'm just going to ignore that.' Yvonne snuggled up in the chair and wiped her cheeks with the back of her hand. 'You can't help your sense of humour. But I've got to lose some weight. I thought I could do it with exercise but it's no good . . . when Trevor got back I'd be too worn out to appreciate him.'

'It's him appreciating you I'm worried about,' Julie said.

'Well, I can't jump about any more. I'll have to try something else.' Yvonne heaved herself out of the chair and made for the mantelpiece. As she did so the back seam of the ski pants split and she put back a hand to assess the damage. 'Oh well,' she said philosophically, 'I've had them a long time.' She ferreted among the bills on the mantelpiece. 'I cut this out the other day . . . it's fate, really. Exercise and diet are all very well but they take too long. And it's not as though I was fat all over.' She sucked in her cheeks and pulled in her tummy, causing the seam over her backside to unwind gently a further two inches. 'What I need is spot reduction. It's in this advert. They wrap your worst bits in bandages soaked in herbs and when they take them off you've lost pounds.'

Julie's eyes skimmed the advert. 'If that's all there is to it, I've got a bayleaf downstairs.'

'Go on, be clever,' Yvonne said. 'The one chance I've got of an uplift, and you pour scorn on it.'

Julie sighed theatrically. 'I'm not going to argue about whether or not this Wondaslim works, Yvonne. I'm simply going to draw your attention to the price: £50. You haven't got fifty pence.'

Yvonne was saved from an answer by the sight of Link appearing in her doorway. 'I forgot something.'

Julie gave him a withering look and turned back to

94

Yvonne. 'You've got to cut your food down. When you feel hungry think about other things.'

'Such as?'

'Well . . . the soaps. Politics. Anything. What's your favourite bit of music?'

Yvonne pondered. 'Right at this moment?' She put her head on one side and then broke into the jingle from the flake advert. *'Only the crumbliest, flakiest chocolate tastes like chocolate never tasted before.'*

'Quite,' Julie said.

They sat morosely for a while, Link taking the opportunity to establish himself on a chair, apparently forgetting he had come back for a reason. Suddenly he looked up. 'Listen, Yvonne, why don't you get an exercise bike?'

'Hah!' Julie said derisively. Yvonne turned reproachful eyes on her.

'I don't know if it would work, Link.'

'You just sit and pedal,' Link said. 'And I know where there's one going cheap.'

Julie was propelled into action, flapping her arms, chicken-like, in warning. 'Cheep, cheep! Stolen goods!'

'It's not,' Link said, stung. 'It belongs to a friend of mine.'

'Cheep! Cheep!' Julie repeated. 'Friendly stolen goods!'

'Lay off, man,' Link said, 'this is serious. Go on, Yvonne, give it a try.'

As Julie left, Link and Yvonne were deep in plans to acquire and use the bike. Nana was in the lower hall and she looked past Julie to the floor above.

'Is that flat of hers open plan . . . because if it's not it will be by the time she's finished leaping about.' She moved closer. 'I saw those bairns of hers yesterday talking to them lezzies next door.' The Lesbians in the next-door house were a constant thorn in Nana's flesh, inoffensive though their behaviour might be.

'What were they doing to the kids, Nana? Feeding them poisoned apples?'

'Quite possibly,' Nana said stoically. 'You laugh, but it goes against nature. Cocks and hens . . . that's what the Bible says.'

Julie's patience was wearing thin. 'Which Bible do you

read, Nana? The Jackie Collins version? 'Cos mine says "Blessed are the peacemakers," and that idea is foreign to your thinking. Now if you'll excuse me . . .' She paused as the banister trembled suddenly. From above there now sounded two voices: 'One, two, three, four . . .' and two pairs of feet pounding the floor.

'She'll bring this house down,' Nana said apprehensively. 'It went right through the Blitz but she'll do what Goering couldn't, mark my words!'

'Well, as long as she does it while me and my bairns are out,' Julie said. She had only one thought in mind now, to get to work and find in Graham Iley's quiet flat the peace denied her in her own.

7

Julie watched from her window as Billy Foster hurried from the door towards the main road. He was only half-dressed, tucking in his shirt as he went and halting his hurried stride to bend and hitch the heel of his shoe into place.

'Now where are you going this early?' Julie thought. Normally the little sod wouldn't get out of his bed, but this morning he was out at eight o'clock. Funny, funny. But there was nothing she could do about it. She let the curtain fall back into place.

She moved into the bathroom and skewered her hair on to the top of her head with the clips she kept on the bathroom ledge. In the mirror she looked bright-eyed and healthy. She leaned forward on the basin, fluttering her eyelashes and arching her lips. She didn't look bad, all things considered. She had the curse and her mastitis was playing her up. She put a thumb up into her left armpit and spread her fingers over her breast, frowning as they touched the tender spot. The first time she had felt it she had run all the way to the doctor's, terrified that she would die and the bairns would be left. Now she accepted it as just one more drawback to being a female and she examined her breasts regularly, like they'd showed her at the clinic.

She opened her eyes wide again, assessing her face. What did Graham Iley see when he looked at her? Sometimes he treated her like a lady, at other times like a mate. But at least he didn't depend on her, well not in any major way. He liked his fresh loaf and his ironed shirts, but he didn't ask her to make decisions and when he left her notes they set out exactly what he wanted. She loved that

97

moment when she saw what she had to do clearly laid out for her.

Sometimes she sat down in his leather chair just for a minute, fitting her feet into the faint scuff marks where his feet must rest. She felt at home in his flat now, almost proprietary towards it – but still he had not asked her to clean the bedroom, and she was curious about that. Would it have a double bed? King-sized, even? Or a narrow single with a striped duvet and a hard pillow?

She rocked back on her heels and began to get washed, wincing at the cold water. When she got sorted out a bit, before the winter came, she was going to put more money in the meter and have a bit of comfort. But however hard she tried to think of practical matters her thoughts kept returning to the bed and its occupant.

He would be nice to sleep with . . . well all men were nice at first, making a fuss, trying to pretend it wasn't all they wanted. And then they got mechanical about it, wham, bam, and thank you ma'am . . . if they thought on. After that, in her experience, they got a bit bored with the whole idea . . . not that any of her affairs had lasted that long.

She patted her face dry and soaped the flannel, ready to begin on her underarms and breasts. She had never really regretted anything before, regarding regret as a waste of time. Now, though, she sometimes wondered . . . if Graham knew, if she told him, would he mind that there had been so many others? She had a sudden moment of panic as she wondered if she could remember how many. She couldn't have forgotten, surely? They had never been earth-shattering affairs, not even with Gary, Jason's dad, but surely she could remember each one?

She sat down on the edge of the bath, ticking them off. You didn't count adolescent fumbles . . . so Gary had been the first, then she had been pregnant with Jason. After that Leslie Maudsley, and Fenner, and Link of course, although that hardly counted, and then there had been Dave, the pipe-fitter, and she had been pregnant again. And since then . . .

She hadn't been a slag. She stood up suddenly, anxiety plucking at her throat and belly. There were all those words

98

they used about women, easy lays and slags and cock-ticers. She reached for her toothbrush and squeezed paste on to it with a shaking hand. Well, even if she had been, she wasn't now. She had changed with the bairns . . . for the bairns . . . because of the bairns. And because she had more sense now. Link would have to go: they could still be friends but none of the other. It had always made her uneasy, anyway, seeming almost incestuous considering the way she felt about him.

Yes, things were different now. She recapped the tooth-paste and went back to the flannel, feeling the cold water strike her warm flesh, glorying in the discomfort because it made her clean.

On the floor above Yvonne too was doing some soul-searching. She had breakfasted on two pieces of Ryvita, eaten dry with a cup of sugarless tea. Now she watched her son and daughter scoop raspberry jam on to slices of damp white bread already thickened with butter. She felt a flash of resentment that passed even as it came. They were lovely kids and still growing.

'What are you doing at school today?' she said. There was no response.

'Something nice?' She raised her voice a little but all she got were two sets of shoulders raised in a shrug.

'Andrea?' This time Yvonne put a hint of a sob in her voice. She could always rely on Andrea to crack first. She knew it was wrong to use moral blackmail but sometimes you got desperate. It was wrong to target her daughter but, if she was honest, easier: somehow it seemed unfair to pressurize a boy. But even as Andrea struggled to provide details, Yvonne's mind was questioning its own reasoning. There was something wrong in what she'd just thought, but what was it?

She was still puzzling as she stood on the landing to wave them off to school. 'See you tonight. Don't fight with each other. Or anyone else,' she called, suddenly reminded of the wolf-pack in the school yard. When Trevor came back they would get away from here. Increasingly it was a jungle, with standards dropping everywhere. She went back into her living-room intent on clearing the table and getting off to a good start, but when she put her hand on the teapot it was still warm. One more cup could do no harm. She sat down and poured, and then, almost automatically, reached for a knife and the jar of jam. It tasted sweet on her tongue, the feel of the blade against her lips somehow titillating.

But it was disgusting to eat out of a jar, off a knife. She fished inside the plastic bread-wrapper and found the rejected crust. Everyone knew crusts were less fattening . . . and much chewier. She spread the butter thinly but was generous with the jam. She ate with relish, pausing between mouthfuls to swill lukewarm tea. When the crust was eaten she spread another slice. She had busted her diet for one day, so she might as well get hunger out of her system and clear the decks for tomorrow, when her transformation would really begin.

She was only half-way through the third slice when she heard Julie's step on the stair. She couldn't be back from the school already? But she was, bursting through the door, Damien in her arms, setting him down on the floor and raking the table with eyes like gun-barrels.

'My God, and you were going to transform yourself for Trevor! What into, Yvonne? A sperm whale?'

'It isn't mine,' Yvonne said, feeling the hastily swallowed bread move painfully along her gullet. 'This is the bairns' breakfast. They've only just gone.'

'It's a quarter-past nine, Yvonne, so don't perjure yourself. What's the tea like? And stop quivering: I'm not going to go on at you. It's none of my business if you don't care enough about your marriage to give up bread and jam.'

Yvonne had been about to offer a fresh brew. Now, hurt, she poured a cup of cold, yellow tea. 'I do care, Julie. Even after everything I care. As far as I'm concerned marriages are made in heaven.'

'So is thunder and lightning,' Julie said, tasting the tea and screwing up her face in distaste. 'Anyway, let it drop. Did you hear if Billy went out last night?'

'I heard something . . . you know I never sleep. It'd be him, unless . . .' She dropped her eyes, unwilling to suggest nocturnal visitors. She liked Julie and most of the time enjoyed her company, but there were standards. No matter what Trevor had done, she herself had standards.

She was a married woman; no one could take that away from you, not even an erring husband.

She looked up, afraid that Julie might have read her thoughts, but Julie was intent on persuading the baby to relinquish an old training-shoe of John's. Seeing her bend to her child Yvonne felt a stab of remorse. Who was she to judge Julie, without knowing what had influenced her? She had never imagined herself winding up in a tenement with a stack of debt, wolfing bread and jam in her dressing-gown. Life was the culprit; she and Julie were merely victims.

'I'll make you some fresh tea,' she said and stood up to pull the edges of her dressing-gown together and fill the kettle.

'I asked about Billy,' Julie said, 'because he was out of here this morning at the crack of dawn. Now, that's not like the lazy little bastard, so I wondered if it was because of something that happened last night.'

'Well,' Yvonne mused, 'there was something, but whether or not it was him . . .' She put the lid on the kettle and plugged it in.

Twenty minutes later Julie made her farewells to Damien and clattered down the stairs. She wanted to catch the quarter-to bus, but Nana barred her way.

'You've been up there again, hobnobbing,' she said, smiling thinly. 'I'm glad you've got time for losers. You'll be sorry when you find Yvonne's round your neck for the rest of your life.'

Julie smiled in what she hoped was an enigmatic way . . . until she saw a movement behind Nana in the flat's doorway.

'What's *he* doing there?'

'Who?' Nana looked round and scanned the now vacant doorway. When she turned back her face was blank with innocence. Too blank.

'Billy,' Julie said shortly. 'Your little turd of a grandson who is swagging off more often than he goes to school.' She put up a hand to her mouth, trying to stem angry words but it didn't work. 'It's not that I give a damn whether or not he gets an education – as far as I'm concerned he can stay as pig-ignorant as he likes. But what

101

I will not have . . . *will* not, Nana . . . is him attracting attention. Because if he does that we'll all suffer.' She nodded her head to emphasize her point and then grabbed for the front door. 'I'm off now – and for the love of God, get him to school. He was out early enough this morning, so what's stopping him now?'

'I'm sure I don't know what you're on about,' Nana said, moving back into the doorway in case Julie took it into her head to go searching. 'He went off to school this morning as bright as a button.'

'He went out all right – I saw him. But he's in there behind you now, and we both know it.'

'He's in that school,' Nana blustered. 'You can go down there and check.' She spat on her fingers and drew them across her chest. 'Strike me dead if he's not.'

Julie had to acknowledge defeat. 'OK, Nana,' she said, opening the front door. 'He *is* at school. And I know where Fantasy Island is – it's Grimshaw Street, Daunton, Tyne and Wear.'

Graham was at the brasserie first and managed to secure a corner table. Charlotte liked to sit in the corner when they came to Reno's, so that she could watch the other tables. 'Eternally hoping to see X lunching with Y's husband,' Graham had suggested once. 'Precisely,' she had said and grinned.

Now he watched her walking towards him, moving easily through the crowded tables. She was so *confident*! He stood up to greet her, wondering if every man in the place was looking on and envying him.

'Sorry I'm late.' Her eyes were green as glass, and when she put up her cheek to be kissed he could see the mascara coating her fair lashes. He liked to see evidence of feminine tricks. Once he had called on her unexpectedly, blundering into her bathroom to find her waxing her legs. It had made him feel unbelievably randy, and now he only had to see the Louis Marcel Wax adverts in magazines to feel horny again.

They pored over the menu, debating whether or not to have starters. 'I've got some news,' Charlotte said, when they had ordered and were sipping Perrier with ice and lemon. 'Alison has finally named the day.'

Graham liked Charlotte's sister, Alison. 'Good,' he said. He waited to see if his neck prickled at the mention of weddings but in fact he felt remarkably calm.

Charlotte was putting a long thin hand on his arm, and he saw a Biro stain on her middle finger. When she took clients round, she carried a clipboard and a pen. He had seen her once, in the garden of a vacant property in Louvaine Gardens, using her pen to point out features to a couple who had later bought for 150 thou. If they married, she would keep on her job. She was almost a partner, after all.

'Now,' she said, breaking into his reverie with a tug at his sleeve, 'tell me about the new factotum?'

'She's fine,' Graham answered.

'Is that all?'

'What do you mean . . . I mean, she's doing a good job.'

'No flaws as yet?'

'If you mean has she robbed me, the answer's no. She cooks, she shops, she cleans. I can find socks, and my shirts have the full complement of buttons. As far as I'm concerned she's . . . well, anyway, I feel sorry for her.'

The waiter was putting their lasagne in front of them, and Charlotte waited until he was gone.

'Sorry for her? I knew there'd be something. Come on, tell me.'

'She's a single parent. Two kids.'

'You never said she was divorced. You made her sound like an adolescent.'

'She's not divorced – she's not married.'

'You mean she's an unmarried mother? How old *is* she?'

He chewed for a minute, wrinkling his brow. 'Difficult. I mean, she could be eighteen or twenty-four. In that area. She's very protective of her kids, talks about them a lot and that sort of thing. I gave her that little red Dinky car I kept in the desk drawer, and you'd've thought it was a full-size Porsche. The kids are boys, obviously.'

'Why obviously? Girls play with cars.' Charlotte was teasing him about being sexist, but he could tell she was irritated by something else. Perhaps he should keep off the

subject of Julie? She was another woman, after all. Impossible to explain to Charlie that she was as safe as houses –
he wouldn't fancy Julie in a million years. It was partly a
class thing, if he was honest, but also a physical thing. He
didn't particularly like small women, they made him feel
clumsy out of bed and too dominant in it. Charlotte was
his equal everywhere, and he liked that.

'Tell me more about Alison,' he said, to change the
subject.

'The wedding's on 7 December. At home, obviously. St
Chad's. All the trimmings. I'm bridesmaid and you'll be
expected to dress up, too . . . in fact, you're probably going
to be an usher.'

'Do I get privileges with the bridesmaid?' he asked.

'Not under my mother's roof,' Charlotte said, pushing
aside her plate. 'It's a converted vicarage, remember.
Besides . . .' She toyed with her knife and fork. 'As far as
the parents are concerned I am still *virgo* very *intacta*. So
you'll have to be on your best behaviour.'

Their steaks came then and Graham suddenly realized
he was hungry. A little thought was nagging at the back of
his mind, something about that date of 7 December – but it
couldn't be important. If it had been he would have
remembered why.

Julie went to the indoor market to do Graham's shopping.
The bread was good there, cooked in revolving ovens in
sight of the counter. She liked the produce stall too, with
vegetables fresh enough to squeak, not packaged in poly-
styrene trays behind cling-film.

She was debating the respective merits of haddock and
whiting when she heard the voice in her ear. 'It is Julie,
isn't it?' She turned to see a strange face, but strange only
until she remembered the maternity hospital.

'Mary?'

'No.' The girl sounded apologetic. 'She was the blond
one. I'm . . .'

'Rose,' Julie said. 'Of course.' She remembered Rose
now, the one abortion in a ward full of new mothers. The
nurses had blamed the shortage of beds, but the rest of

their behaviour had suggested it might have been deliberate to put Rose among the dewy-eyed mums with their doting husbands.

'Fancy a coffee?' Rose said. 'My treat.' She looked as though she expected to be turned down and Julie felt instant sympathy.

'Why not?' she said.

They went into the café behind the cake-shop and slid into a narrow booth. 'What are you doing now?' Julie asked, when Rose came back with the coffees.

'Same thing,' Rose said. 'I worked in The Green Door, remember? I'm still there. What about you?'

'I've got a job,' Julie said, suddenly proud. 'It's only cleaning, well, housekeeping really . . . but I like it.' She noticed a faint blue mark on Rose's cheekbone and what appeared to be another bruise, browning slightly this time, along the length of her jaw.

'And you kept the bairn?' Rose said. She had seen the direction of Julie's stare and put up a hand to cover her chin.

'Yes,' Julie said, trying not to sound shocked that there could be any question about it. 'He's a year now. A big lad. What about you? There was a . . .' She waited for Rose to fill in the details just in case.

'A man? I'm still with him.' Rose shifted her hand a little and then smiled. She was pretty when she smiled but there were blue rings round her dark eyes and a little tremor to her lips. 'We have our ups and downs but . . . better the devil you *do* know.'

'You're dead right there,' Julie said. She felt pity stir inside her but was afraid to express it. When life was shitting on you the one thing you had was your dignity. Take that away and you were lost. She would have liked to ask about the bruises and report the sod who'd made them to the police, but it wouldn't do.

'Here,' she said, fishing in her bag. 'Take my address. You never know when it'll come in handy. You'll be welcome any time. There's only me and the bairns . . .' And a geriatric harpy and a waterlogged, deserted wife, she added under her breath.

When she parted from Rose she made her way back to

105

the fish counter and bought haddock fillet. Meeting Rose again had disturbed her. She must be thirty-five at least, and it hadn't been her first abortion. Or her last, probably.

The night Damien was born she had sat on the edge of Julie's bed, each of them drawn to the other because they had no visitors. She had told Julie about her childhood in Hull and the man who had brought her north and dumped her. Now she lived with the manager of a snooker hall, a married man who had four children. 'So a bairn wasn't on, you see,' Rose had said. She had laughed then and tossed her head. 'Just as well. I wouldn't know how to top and tail a bairn. We learned at school . . . I couldn't manage it then, so fat chance now.' But Julie had known she regretted the abortion, and had resisted the impulse to flaunt her own new baby.

Now she bought a cauliflower and some baking potatoes, and then went to get Graham's precious new loaf. He was like a bairn about his fresh bread. Easy pleased, he was, really, considering he was a solicitor. She had always thought of solicitors as old men, or at least stiff, but Graham Iley was all right. More than all right; he had a good body. There was all sorts of sports gear in the hall cupboard, and strips in the wash nearly every day.

She caught a bus to the flat and let herself in, thinking of the cup of tea she would have out of his nice china before she got down to work. She picked up her note from the hall table and carried it through to the kitchen to read while the kettle boiled.

The first item intrigued her: 'Thorough clean bedroom.' So at last she had permission to go into the inner sanctum! She had peeped in the door once and seen the rumpled double bed. Now she could take a good look. The kettle began to sing but her curiosity could not be contained. She moved across the hall and pushed at the bedroom door.

The bed was unmade, the dressing-table and drawers tidy if a trifly dusty. She moved further into the room, seeing the black towelling robe on the back of the door reflected in the mirror, moving to touch the brushes on the dressing-table, turning to the bed and seeing that the duvet cover was badly in need of a wash.

It was then that she saw the photograph. A girl laughing

into the sun – a red-haired girl looking for all the world like Fergie. A classy girl with tinted specs in her hand and a mouthful of marvellous teeth. 'Shut your mouth, you're dazzling the fish,' Julie said aloud but the quip was automatic. The photograph was beside Graham's bed, the last thing he would see at night, the first in the morning. She seized at a straw. Perhaps it was his sister? But in her heart she knew that sisters belonged in the living-room. Graham had a girl and she was important enough to be beside his bed.

'I knew it all along,' Julie told herself, wondering why indigestion was suddenly burning her gut. 'Fellers always have someone. Always.' It wasn't as if it mattered anyway. She had better things to do than worry about him.

She went back to the kitchen and switched the kettle on again, only to switch it straight off. She had gone off the idea of tea.

Yvonne caught a bus to the town centre and located the health salon almost straight away. Through the window she could see the receptionist, tall and blond with Jack-the-Ripper fingernails. They always looked like that, and it was depressing.

When Yvonne entered the foyer the girl looked up and her face spoke volumes. 'Can I help you?'

'I wanted to ask about the wrapping treatment. The one with herbs.'

'You mean Wondaslim?'

'Yes, that's it.'

'Would you want six treatments or twelve?'

'How many do you think I'd need?'

As soon as Yvonne asked the question she knew it was a mistake. The girl looked down at the appointments book but her shoulders shook slightly. Before she could look up and answer Yvonne's nerve broke.

'Do you do credit?'

The girl took a grip on the counter and lifted her head. 'I'm afraid not. You'd need to pay for the whole course in advance.' Beneath her pink nylon overall her nipples stood erect and the line of her briefs showed barely above her groin.

'She's got nothing on under that,' Yvonne thought and was shocked. Aloud she said, 'I see. Well, that'll be no problem. How much is a course?' She turned to check on the pushchair, parked outside the window, and then turned back.

'Six or twelve?' The receptionist was sounding a little desperate and Yvonne threw caution to the winds.

'Twelve . . . to start with.'

'Twelve would be £90.'

'Ninety pounds,' Yvonne said cheerfully. 'Well, that seems reasonable.'

'It's cheaper to have twelve,' the girl said. She had mastered her emotions now, and not even the sight of Yvonne's poncho falling open seemed to disconcert her. 'Six treatments is £50, so £90 for twelve is a bargain.'

'Yes,' Yvonne said. 'Well, as soon as I find out when I can get off work I'll be in touch.'

Was it her imagination or did the receptionist let out an audible sigh – whether of disappointment or relief Yvonne could not be sure. She smiled at the girl, thinking as she did so that she was not as young as she'd looked through the glass. Pushing thirty, in fact, and not so much pushing it as dragging it along behind, when you looked close. She threw her poncho across her shoulder and turned for the door.

'Thank you so much,' she said graciously, until she caught sight of herself in the mirror that bordered the door. She looked like one of those dolls you gave children, dolls as wide as they were tall. You pushed them and they swayed but righted themselves at once because they were weighted to do so.

Yvonne teetered through the door and willed herself not to grab the pushchair and run. Ninety pounds or fifty, it was still out of the question. But she would have to think of something, and quickly at that. She saw a Wimpy bar across the road and decided to invest in a coffee. It was easier to think sitting down.

*

108

A curious resignation had come over Julie by the time she got home. She had been daft lately. It didn't do to lust after the boss. It didn't do to lust, period. Lust was something that should only happen to Japanese cars. She grinned at her own joke and got up to leave the bus. She had known it all along, really . . . that Graham belonged to another world, that he would never give her a thought. But it had been lovely to dream. Now she would make a nice tea for the bairns and spend a bit of time with them. They were the important things, after all.

The men were leaving the building site as she passed, and she got the odd whistle, but she was careful not to respond. She had smiled at whistles before and they had gone on to be bloody cheeky. Now she contented herself with an extra swing of the hips as she passed, just to show them what they were missing. For a moment their chorus of approval eased her pain, but only for a moment. She felt . . . defeated, yes, that was it. Cast down. 'Bloody fool,' she told herself. Some folks never learned and she could take an A-level in it. 'He's out of your class, Julie,' she said aloud. If she let herself think of Graham again she would remind herself that it was all fantasy. That way she wouldn't get hurt.

She made a cup of tea when she got in and changed into her jeans and a T-shirt. She was pouring a second cup when Tommo's knock came at the door.

'You're back, then.' He held out a bunch of broccoli. 'I hope you still like it.'

'Ta,' Julie said, hoping the last two bunches were hidden from sight.

'How's the job going?'

She poured him tea and fetched biscuits from the unit.

'Fine. He's very nice, and the work's easy. I do a bit of shopping and clean up. And the pay's a help.' She sounded doubtful and Tommo smiled.

'Wondering where it's gone? I know the feeling. At first you think, "Get that much and I'll be rich." And you get it, and you're still scratting. But it mounts up. After a few weeks you'll begin to feel the benefit.' He was smiling reassuringly and she noticed that his teeth were white and even. He had a nice mouth, a bit sweet for a man, maybe, but that was a good fault.

'I suppose you're right. So if me money troubles are over, I've only got to worry about Yvonne and that little sod, Billy.'

'Still playing up, is he?'

'You bet! Swagging off, stealing out at night. He's not sleep-walking, so I leave the rest to your imagination.'

'Well, you'll just have to let him get on with it. You can't take everyone's worries on, you know.'

Julie leaned towards him. 'Get one thing straight, Tommo. I wouldn't care if that little swine went in for life. It's not even really Nana I lose sleep over, because she can be a pain in the arse. What worries me is my bairns. I know social workers, they go by numbers. If Number 13 goes on their list, we all go on.'

'But you're a good mother, why should you worry?'

Julie propped her chin on her hands and looked at him in wonderment. 'God, you're naïve, Tommo. In a fair set-up I wouldn't have to worry, but there's nothing fair about the way they work. I am suspect because a) I'm young, b) I'm on me own, c) I don't arse-lick . . .' She saw a look of pain cross his face at the language and tried again. 'I don't run after them and say yes sir, no sir, three bags full sir. On top of that I've had "multiple relationships" – that's what they write down. They'd like to say I was a raving nympho because it would count in court but not even they could make that stick. All the same, if Billy attracts their attention . . .'

When Tommo had gone Julie looked at the clock. Twenty minutes before Jason came out – enough time to collect Damien and sort out Yvonne.

The baby was asleep when she got upstairs and Yvonne was drinking coffee.

'I'll never get used to it without sugar.'

'That's the proper way to drink coffee, it brings out the flavour.'

Yvonne grimaced. 'If you say so.' She stood up suddenly. 'Come and see what I've done.' Julie followed her into the kitchen and looked around.

Every cupboard had a piece of Christmas sellotape across

its opening and the fridge bore a picture of two snarling Alsatians over the caption: *We live here*.

'Good,' Julie said. 'Keep it up.'

'I'll do anything you say,' Yvonne said, 'except the no-fluids diet! I can't stand that again. It makes your colon wither.'

'Colon? You haven't got a colon. There's a bottomless pit down there screaming for Mars Bars.'

'Well, at least I've got a figure,' Yvonne said, staring hard at Julie's chest. 'You take an AA bra, don't you? What does that stand for? 'Ardly anything?'

Julie ignored her. 'What will you wear when Trevor comes home?' she asked.

Yvonne folded her hands in prayer. 'Please God send me a Zandra Rhodes size 22 with matching accessories.'

'And send a little bread to pay for it, God, because Yvonne's skint,' Julie added.

Yvonne lifted her chin. 'I am weak! I am hungry! I am clothes-less, mis-shapen and without hope! I am a *victim*!'

'You're a bloody nuisance,' Julie said and turned to pick up her baby. 'Say bye-bye to Auntie Yvonne.' But Damien was chewing the front of his cardigan and Yvonne had to be content with kissing the top of his head.

Julie was about to enter her own flat when she heard a sound below. Billy was in the hall but this time he was coming in not going out. There was something bulky under his jacket but she couldn't make out what. She ought to go down and find out, but she had had enough. She went into her flat and closed the door resolutely behind her.

8

Graham had woken at intervals throughout the night, his throat dry, his head aching, a general feeling of malaise upon him. At half-past six he staggered into the kitchen and made tea, shivering uncontrollably while he waited for the kettle to boil, glad when at last he had everything he needed on a tray and could scurry back to bed.

He dozed fitfully after he had drunk the tea, waking to see how much time was left before his alarm went off. At quarter to eight he decided that going to work was out of the question. At eight-fifteen he rang Charlotte.

'God, I feel awful, Charlie.'

'What were you doing last night?'

'Nothing,' he said, wounded. 'At least, nothing to deserve this.'

'What's wrong with you?'

'I think it's 'flu. I feel foul.'

'I hope you haven't passed it on to me.' Charlotte sounded abstracted, as though she were mentally checking her medicine cabinet in search of a prophylactic.

'Thank you,' Graham said. 'Thank you so much. I didn't ring for sympathy, which is just as well as I'm not getting any.'

He expected her to melt, then, and offer consolation but all she said was: 'Why did you ring? I'm sorry to rush you but you know I've a busy day today.'

He couldn't imagine why he *had* rung her. He felt hurt and rejected, and talking at all was increasingly painful. 'Don't let me keep you!' he said bitterly. He would have liked to bang down the receiver but the uneasy suspicion that she might not call him back prevented him.

'Tut, tut,' she said, chuckling now, which only seemed to make matters worse. 'The boy does feel sorry for himself. Well, cheer up. If you're still alive tonight I'll come round and eat your grapes. Now, I must go. I told you about the flats in Channing Court, didn't I? Lie there and do some sums and think about my commission. Anyway, your Miss Thingy will be in soon. She'll probably feed you chicken soup and rub your chest with camphorated oil. If she offers, say "no", darling . . . I don't object to her rubbing you down but I want you smelling nice when I get there tonight.'

'I'll suggest she uses garlic,' Graham croaked but the thought of Charlotte coming on any terms was pleasant. 'Come as soon as you can,' he pleaded, and after he put down the phone he spent an anxious five minutes wondering whether or not he could make love if he had a temperature.

Satisfied that all would be well when the time came, he phoned his office and told his secretary he was dying. In contrast to Charlotte, she oozed sympathy, even offering to ring his doctor and collect his prescription after the doctor had called. He declined her offer but felt better for its being made.

Tottering into the bathroom, he contemplated his pale, bestubbled face. He looked rather impressive when he was haggard. He would shower before Charlotte's visit but make sure he looked suitably unkempt. Somewhere in Charlotte there was a soft streak: she kept it well in check but you could tell it was there. The sight of him in his best grey pyjamas, eyes bright with fever, cheeks concave with a day's fasting, might bring out all sorts of responses. He hopped back into bed and lay pleating the top of the sheet and listening to Brian Redhead droning on about politics, checking the clock every few minutes to wish away the time until Julie arrived to succour him.

'There you are,' Julie said, waving expansively over Yvonne's table. 'That's your day's allowance. You can eat it all now or spread it out – it's up to you.' Yvonne eyed the lettuce, the Diet Coke, the four peeled carrots and the sardines head to tail in their tin. She said nothing, merely frowned and squirmed inside her chenille dressing-gown.

'Bugs?' Julie enquired, but Yvonne was too miserable to take offence.

'I tried Epsom salts in the bath last night.'

Julie sighed. 'They won't have the slightest effect on your body weight.'

'They've had an effect on my skin. It's crinkled. When my thighs rub together it sounds like a football rattle.' Yvonne gave a final wriggle and reached for a carrot, looking at it speculatively. 'Diets are always rabbit meat, aren't they? If I keep eating like a rabbit . . . well, you know what rabbits do all the time.'

'Fat chance of you getting any nookie looking like that,' Julie said.

Yvonne's eyes filled but she firmed her lips and pulled her dressing-gown around her in an authoritative way. 'I want you to consider something, Julie. Have you ever thought you might hurt my feelings?'

'Not a chance,' Julie said. 'Your feelings are buried under layer upon layer of cellulite. I couldn't get at them with a Bren gun.'

'Oh well, then,' Yvonne said and turned to the kitchen, cracking the carrot in her teeth as she went. 'I'll make some tea.'

In the kitchen she put on the kettle and went to the fridge for milk. The Alsatians regarded her sternly and she raised her upper lip to them in a snarl before she collected the bottle.

'I can't afford to diet,' she said when she sat down. 'I'm in a Catch-22 situation, Julie. The only food I can afford is the food I shouldn't eat. What's cheap? Saveloys, black pudding, streaky bacon . . . that's for the likes of you and me. Read a diet sheet: what does it say? *"4oz of lean meat"* – there's £1.20, for a start. And fish . . . have you priced fish lately? No, I'll bet you haven't because you and your bairns never eat fish. Well, do you?'

There was an uncomfortable silence and then Yvonne continued, quieter now but more bitter. 'It's no accident we kick the bucket soonest. Read the statistics – we're D group and dropping, you and me. We'll age sooner, we'll

114

die sooner and nobody . . .' Her voice wobbled. 'Nobody . . .'

'That's enough,' Julie said suddenly. 'It's no good wallowing. You need an aim, Yvonne. Well, Trevor's coming home and you are going to look like Bo Derek when he gets here.'

Reaching for Yvonne's hand she led her into the bedroom. She opened the wardrobe door and began to rifle through the contents.

'What d'you want?' Yvonne said, intrigued.

'I want your fattest frock,' Julie said. 'The one that makes you look like a pudding.'

'Take your pick,' Yvonne said.

'No, I want the worst one . . . the *worst* one.'

Yvonne reached in and selected a wallpaper-print smock with a ruffled neck. 'This is a maternity dress. I pretended I was pregnant to get into the shop. I felt ashamed, but I was desperate.'

'Right,' Julie said, taking it from Yvonne's hand. She marched into the living-room and began to root in the sideboard drawer, producing pen and paper and drawing pins. The next moment the dress was spreadeagled across the wall, pinned out to its widest limit. Beneath it she pinned a notice: *Lest We Forget*.

'There you are, Yvonne. That's what you're leaving behind.'

'It looks like a flying elephant,' Yvonne said. 'And what will I say to the kids?'

'Nothing,' Julie said shortly. 'Just say nothing. If they ask, say it's up there to air off.'

It was a relief to get out of the house without meeting Nana or Link or someone else in need of buoying up. All the same, Yvonne was right about a proper diet costing. Sitting on the bus, Julie wondered about her children. She did her best to give them good food but sometimes there were gaps. And kids grew all the time – you couldn't tell a bone to hold on for a bit till the calcium arrived. Jason and Damien looked all right, but were they? She relaxed when she remembered she still had Tommo's order. She would spend it on some fish oil and vitamins . . . and a pair of good shoes for Jason. Good shoes were important. And there would still be something over.

She sat back in her seat, relieved; glad, too, that worrying about Yvonne this morning had stopped her from thinking about Graham Iley's girl. She'd had her food supplements all right. They had a sheen on them, girls like that; a kind of glow. She remembered the physiotherapist who had come after Damien's birth to teach her her post-natal exercises. She had been a light golden brown all over, even her boobs where they showed in the neck of her white uniform coat. Her hair had been streaked but not brassy, as though the sun really had got at it, and the edges of her fingernails had been white and powdery, as clean as clean could be. Julie looked down at her own fingers, with bitten nails and sore cuticles and brown bumps on the side of her index finger from peeling potatoes. What a fool she had been to even think about Graham Iley. She would wind up with Link, who loved her anyway, or Tommo, if she developed some sense. But never a solicitor, a professional man.

As the bus crossed the High Street and turned into a leafy road, Julie suddenly realized that she and Graham Iley lived on the opposite side of the tracks. She had never thought of that before but it was true. She turned her face to the window, staring fiercely at her own reflection, willing the tears not to come. Five minutes later she was unlocking the door of the flat and stepping inside.

'Is that you, Julie?'

Graham was propped up on pillows, looking lost and wretched in the big bed. She felt a wave of love and sympathy well up in her.

'I'm not well,' he said apologetically. He looked and sounded like a bairn, a great big bairn.

She went to his side and laid a hand on his forehead. 'You've got a temperature,' she said. 'Well, we'll soon fix that.' She knew how to cope with bairns when they were laid up, and in spite of all his fancy qualifications Graham was just like any other man, a child at heart. She went into the kitchen and began to function, allowing herself to remember the way he had smiled at the feel of her cool fingers on his brow. There couldn't be any harm in that.

Tommo glanced up at Julie's window as he got out of the van. The knickers still defied the sooty air but they were getting a bit bedraggled now. He would have to get her some proper flowers. He had seen silky geraniums some-where – she'd appreciate those. He reached back into the van for his book and pouch, and then locked the van door. It was time to come to grips with Nana Foster.

He knocked at the door and then tried the handle. 'Anybody in?'

The answer was immediate. 'No. They've emigrated.'

Nana was sitting by the fire, a cigarette dangling from her fingers, her tongue protruding between her teeth as she weighed up the merits of respective runners. 'Sit down, then,' she said, without raising her eyes.

Tommo took a chair as she let out a *tsk* of irritation and then stabbed the paper with her pen.

'So that's how you do it,' he said.

'Only when I'm foxed,' she retorted, busy with her betting slip.

'How are you going to get it on?' Tommo asked, ready to offer his services.

'Our B . . .' Nana stopped herself just in time as she remembered Tommo was thick with Julie and would undoubtedly report Billy's absence from school if she confessed it. He felt a stab of sympathy for her. She was sixty-five at least, probably more, and she had to watch herself against all comers.

'I'll manage,' she said carefully. 'There's always someone . . .'

'Well, if you change your mind, I'll lay it for you,' he said easily. 'Now, Nana, about your payments.'

'My God,' she cried, pushing aside the paper. 'I hope you haven't come to get money.'

'I was hoping,' he said, trying not to laugh aloud at her look of outrage.

'Here,' said Nana, pushing up her sleeve and offering a

scrawny forearm, 'take me blood. Go on! It's about all I've got left.'

'Now, now, Nana, there's no need to go on.' He hardened his voice. 'But I've got to have something to be going on with. You know as well as I do that if I show the office a blank book we'll have the supervisor in.' He looked down. 'Three weeks since I had anything . . . and there's the jeans to go on.'

'I never ordered them,' she said. 'Blame *her* . . . in here like the Spanish Inquisition. "Has he gone to school?" "Is he in or out?" "Has he got an arse in his trousers?" She's pitiful . . . pitiful.'

'I think you mean pitiless?' Tommo said.

'I know what I mean . . . I mean full of hell. She's down these stairs like the mother in *Psycho*, screaming and shouting. Billy does go to school . . .' Her voice wavered at the palpable untruth. 'Well, he's not one for books. They should teach him something interesting. He'd go sharp enough then.'

'Your payments, Nana?' Tommo pressed gently. He had to get money out of her today or there'd be hell to pay at the office. They had never heard the adage about blood out of a stone. He looked around the shabby room, his gorge rising at the thought of the interest she was paying on what had been an original debt of £20 or so. The sooner he was out of this the better! All the same . . . 'I want ten bob, Nana – 50p. You were making that a pound treble. I'll halve it with you . . . 50p to the bookie, 50p for my book.'

'Here,' she said, leaning forward when their business was complete. 'What d'you think about upstairs?'

'Which upstairs?' he said. 'If you mean about Yvonne's husband, it's good news.'

'Good news for us,' she said. 'Not for him, the dozy bugger. He wants his bumps read, coming back to her. But I was on about Julie and this accountant feller.'

'Solicitor,' Tommo said.

'Same thing. What's he up to, taking on a girl like that? Cleaning? I've heard it called some fancy names but never "cleaning".'

'Now, now Nana.' Tommo stood up. 'You want to watch that tongue of yours.'

'She'll need to watch more than her tongue. I hope she keeps her hand on her halfpenny, that's all . . .'

Tommo felt saliva flood his mouth. 'I'm not going to listen to muck-raking, Nana.' He was about to say something sharper when he caught sight of an object on the sideboard swathed in what looked like an old sweater. He moved closer, intrigued.

'Muck-raking? Me? Listen, *Mr* Thompson, I'm only telling you so you can do something about it before it's too late. She's a canny lass, that one, but she's wayward. You don't get two bairns by going to Sunday School. I know you've got a soft spot for her, but you won't get anywhere with your fingers in your ears.'

Tommo had lost interest in the object now, but he was anxious to change the conversation. 'What've you got here?'

'Some rubbish our Billy found. Did you hear what I said – if you want her, stop running up and down the stairs with cabbage . . .'

'Broccoli,' he corrected, blushing at the thought that he had been seen.

'Green stuff,' Nana said firmly. 'It's not greens she needs, it's a firm hand. And that sackless idiot up above her, you want to get rid of *her* before we all go down with the smit . . . or drown! Have you seen my ceiling?' She was pointing to a tiny brown patch. 'Through three floors, that was. "Is your Billy at school?" she said this morning. "No," I said, "he's out buying an aqualung!"'

Tommo couldn't help grinning. 'It's only a little leak,' he said.

'Now! Now it's a little leak.' An evil grin came over Nana's face. 'It's next time she gets a bath that's got me worried. If she lowers that backside into the water the overflow'll go clean down the street.'

By twelve o'clock Julie had managed to convince herself that the photograph on the bedside table was of no special significance. She had made tea and a soft-boiled egg with soldiers as soon as she got her coat off. Then she had swept and dusted and planned Graham a nourishing, invalid lunch. At eleven she carried in coffee.

'Where's your cup?' he asked.

She felt a little flush of pleasure but then a wave of embarrassment.

'I'm OK,' she said, but Graham would not be stayed.

'Go and get yours,' he demanded, sitting up in bed, looking too bright-eyed and coughing suddenly with exertion.

Julie fetched her cup and edged on to the dressing-table stool.

'Now,' he said, looking pleased, 'tell me about your children.'

She began to talk about the kids, relaxing as she realized he was genuinely interested and not in the least nosy. He never asked about their parentage and she never volunteered the information. She talked, feverishly at times, all the while noticing little things about him: the large wrist bones, the hair that grew on the first joints of his long fingers, the crisp hair curling in the V of his pyjamas, the strong jut of his jaw. He was lean, and all of a sudden she realized what the word 'rangy' meant.

'Well,' she said at last, standing up, 'this won't buy the bairn a new frock.'

'What else is there to do?' Graham asked a little petulantly.

She waved a hand around her. 'All sorts.'

'Can't it wait?' he said. 'I wouldn't mind a game of something. Can you play Scrabble?'

Julie had never played, but she fetched the long green box from the hall cupboard and sat on the bed where his imperious hand indicated while he dealt the letters.

'There now,' he said, looking up at her suddenly. 'This is nice.'

He was holding her eye and she smiled at him. He was right: it *was* nice. She was here with him, on his bed, close enough to smell his body. If she had been with any other man, with any other man she knew barring Tommo, they'd've had her on her back by now. She closed her eyes momentarily, thinking of Link's importunings, of Gary who had been after her from school, on and on until she was glad to give in for peace, acting the big man in the back lane and then hiding behind his mother's skirts when the damage was done. And Dave, who had taken all he could get as easily as if he'd been tasting blackberries by the roadside. She was suddenly regretful, filled with a terrible remorse that she was not new and untouched. She felt infinitely older than the man opposite her, holding his counters in his curved hand like a bairn.

She put down a letter s to add to DOOR. 'Is that all right?' she said and was inordinately pleased when he said 'yes'.

Looking up, she found the girl in the photograph regarding her, for all the world as if she knew what was on Julie's mind. She looked fresh and confident, classy . . . yes, that was the word. Had there been a back lane for her? A contemplated abortion? A labour ward with a midwife who told you this was what you got for being too free with yourself? A hundred forms to fill in just to get enough to get by?

'It's your turn,' Graham said and she looked down at her letters, blinking so that they ceased to be blurred and swam into focus. She was here, after all, and things were turning out better than she had any right to expect.

Julie stayed as long as she could, carrying in a shared lunch, laughing with him at the first episode of *Neighbours* he had seen, pretending that she had never before watched such rubbish. She stayed very silent while he watched the news, fearful he might ask her to comment. If she had been watching with Link she would have spoken out, aware of her own superiority; with Tommo she would not have feared making a mistake. But she wanted Graham Iley to think well of her, so it was best to say nothing at all.

Going home on the bus Julie thought about the future. If she and he were going to get friendly she would have to become more aware. He threw remarks so easily, about politics or world events or theatres, remarks the girl in the photograph would field effortlessly. And she would have to watch her language, too – he wouldn't appreciate a mouthful. It was going to be difficult, but she could do it. He liked her company, she knew enough about men to know that. Julie found she was smiling foolishly into the bus window and pretended to be looking for her ticket to cover her embarrassment.

She got off at her stop feeling both elated and washed out. She would make the bairns tea and then flop for a bit, and then she would make plans!

But Tommo's van was waiting at the door, and Julie's heart sank. She would have to offer him a cup of tea, and that she didn't mind. But he would be so pleased to be with her, and she didn't feel up to bearing his approval. Not now. Not after the day she'd had.

But Tommo had not come a-courting. 'I'm really sorry to bother you,' he said, getting out of the van, 'when you've got so much on your plate. But you'd only go down my neck if there was trouble . . .'

'Billy!' she said bleakly and he nodded.

'I went in to Nana's flat this morning, after money. Nana was in her usual. I got something, and I got up to go. And then I saw something on the sideboard. I didn't recognize it . . . I'd never seen anything like it, to be truthful. I said, "What is it?" and Nana said it was something Billy had found in the street.'

Julie put up a hand to lift her hair from her brow. 'Go on,' she said.

'I was in the Anchor at lunch-time – a pie and a pint. Some of the lads from the building site were there, and I could hear them on about a break-in . . .'

'I'll kill him,' Julie said, pounding her left palm with her other fist.

'It's a theodolite,' Tommo said. 'I didn't let on I might've seen it – I just said what was a theodolite like, and they described it. It's worth a bit. About £1,000. But they say the pilfering's been almost nightly, and their boss is on the warpath. He's sure they'll catch the culprits when the theodolite is fenced. It's too unusual.'

'So Billy'd be up on possession?' Julie said.

'Yes.' Tommo reached out for her bag. 'Let's get you inside. You look whacked. If you can get him to part with the theodolite, I'll take it back. I can say I came across it somewhere . . .'

'No!' Julie's tone was sharp. 'I'm not having you mixed up in this.'

She saw the flush of pleasure on his face at her defence of his reputation – saw and regretted it, but couldn't worry now. 'You've done your bit, Tommo. Thanks for telling me. Now, it's up to me . . . But I'll tell you this, that little arsehole has two choices: quick death or slow.'

She passed Nana's door without knocking. First she must reclaim her children and then she must calm down. She took her bag from Tommo in the hall. 'Thanks a bunch, Tommo, but I can manage now.'

'You won't do anything hasty, will you?'

She shook her head. 'No. I'd like to but I won't. Not now, any road.'

She wanted to reach out and touch him, even kiss his nice, kind face to show she was grateful . . . but it would only lead to trouble and she had enough of that already.

'Oh God, I'm glad to see you, Charlie,' Graham said. He had showered and changed his pyjamas and was feeling decidedly chirpier. Charlotte put down her bag and shrugged out of her coat. She had a tan sweater and skirt on, and the tiger's-eye brooch he had given her last Christmas was pinned above her left breast. 'You look . . . nice!' He bent to kiss her, being careful not to breathe on her. She was fussy about germs.

Charlotte took Marks and Spencer lasagne from the freezer and put it in the microwave, while Graham opened a bottle of Lambrusco.

'Ooh, lovely,' she said, subsiding into a chair and lifting her long legs to loop over the arm. 'I have had a foul day. We didn't get the Deneside planning permission, so the buyer's withdrawn. Bang goes my Porsche.'

'You wouldn't really drive a Porsche, would you?' Graham teased. 'Unutterably tasteless.'

'Unutterably gorgeous,' Charlotte said firmly. 'When I have the readies I'm having one. You needn't ride in it.'

The microwave pinged and she swung to her feet. 'No, don't move,' she said to his inert figure. 'I know you're feeling fragile.' She turned in the doorway to the kitchen. 'As long as you remember that later on.'

The next instant Graham was behind her, pretending to

123

pant like a dog. 'Stop it, you fool,' she said but he knew from the tone of her voice that she was in the mood to make love. He looked at himself in the mirror above the cooker. It was amazing how much better he looked.

They ate from their knees in front of the TV, seeing the Channel 4 news right through. Afterwards they drank coffee and sipped Cointreau. Charlotte moved to sit between Graham's knees, leaning her head against his leg sometimes, twisting round occasionally to argue.

At eight o'clock she looked at her watch. 'I'm going at ten, Graham. I've got to read some stuff for the morning, and I must be up at seven.' She rose to her feet and looked down at him. 'Are you sure you're up to it?' she asked, half-serious.

He stood up to take her in his arms. 'More than up to it,' he murmured against her hair.

They made love slowly, without their usual vigour. Afterwards, one arm beneath her head, the other hand resting on the mound of her body, Graham realized how comfortable he felt with her now. He moved his hand gently, tracing her navel, moving up over the rib cage, feeling the gentle swell of her breast begin. 'Know something?' he said.

Charlotte stretched slightly. 'You're ill?' she said.

'No, I wasn't going to suggest that. I was going to say that I *think* I love you.' He felt her tense slightly. 'Well?' he said, when no answer came.

'You *are* ill,' she said at last.

'I mean it,' he said, withdrawing his arm from her pillow and raising himself to look down on her. She gazed at him expectantly, as though there ought to be more, but he had said all he wanted to say. Eventually she sighed.

'I must go. You know what will happen if I stay, and I simply must get some sleep. I feel drained.' She was up and sitting on the edge of the bed, her back to him as she began to struggle into her clothes. He put out a hand and touched a single vertebra with his fingertip, moving down towards the cleft of her buttocks. She stood up sharply, reaching for her panties and stepping into them with sure movements of her long legs.

'Get some sleep,' she said, when her skirt was zipped

124

and she was running her fingers through her tousled hair. 'Ring me in the morning if you're not going in to the office.'

Graham shifted up in the bed, suddenly weary but wanting to see her to the door. 'I'll have to be up and about tomorrow. It's the do.'

Charlotte was checking her face in the dressing-table mirror, touching the corners of her mouth, smoothing an eyebrow. 'I'd forgotten about that. Have we got tickets for the draw?'

'Thousands,' he said glumly. 'They didn't exactly go like a bomb.'

'Tell me how much I owe you,' Charlotte said, looking round for her jacket. 'Actually,' she went on, 'I can see where that little tweeny of yours has been. This place is clean.'

'I told you she was good.' Graham felt a glow of satisfaction that Julie was receiving appreciation. 'She's a plucky little thing, very pleasant, very anxious to please.'

'Need I worry?' Charlotte sounded nonchalant but he sensed she was serious.

He leaned to reach out for her hand. 'You know you needn't.' She came when he tugged, feeling safer inside her clothes, and allowed herself to be pulled down on to the bed. He kissed her. 'All the same, I do like the little thing . . . she's so shabby, Charlie. Not torn or dirty shabby, just cheap. You know, shiny fabrics, frills on everything – she had this ghastly skirt on with a slit up the back with a little tear at the top . . .'

'You *have* been observant,' Charlotte said drily. She stood up. 'What size is she? You keep saying "little", "little thing", "little woman" . . . I mean, is she my size?'

He wrinkled his brow and pursed his lips. 'Ooh, I don't know . . .'

'Beast! I'm only a 12. Anyway, if she is of normal dimensions I've probably got some things she could have. You'd have to be careful, though – you don't want to sound as though you're taking junket to the poor.'

Graham swung his legs to the floor and stood up, reaching for his towelling robe to cover his nakedness. 'She wouldn't be like that. She's got too much sense to look for

125

slights. Now, kiss me and go before I get ideas. I'm still *hors de combat*, you know.'

'So you'll have to help me,' Julie said firmly. 'I'm going down there now to get it and then you've got to help me get it back into the site.'

'Me?' Yvonne said. She rolled her eyes. 'You can't be serious, Julie. My legs wouldn't carry me down the stairs, let alone into a building site. You'll have to get someone else.'

'Who?' Julie said implacably.

'Well . . .' Yvonne got sudden inspiration. 'Make Billy do it. If he got it out, he can get it back.'

'Stroll on, Yvonne. I'm trying to reform him, not give him extra practice. I can't risk him making a mess of it and getting nicked.'

'Tommo, then.'

'No, it's not fair to get him involved. He could lose his job.'

'Oh yes, we must protect Tommo. I mean, I'm just a mother of two, I don't need shielding.' Yvonne's cheeks had coloured.

'I *am* shielding you, Yvonne,' Julie said. '*And* your bairns. If Billy gets into much more trouble we'll have them round our necks. Are you so sure you're bringing your kids up OK? Suppose Hunchfront comes the day they've had onion sandwiches, like last week when you were desperate? Can't you hear the case conference? "The mother is an emotional woman, prone to breaking down, and there are criminal elements living within the house . . ."'

'Shut up,' Yvonne said, shifting uncomfortably. 'I still say I can't do it. Why not ask Link?'

'Hah!' Julie threw back her head in derision. 'He'd go in with the theodolite and come out with a dumper truck. No, Yvonne, there's only you. Wear something suitable, something to look inconspicuous, and be downstairs in half an hour. Nana'll keep an ear open for the bairns.'

Yvonne's shoulders slumped in defeat and then straightened. 'Wait a moment – you keep talking about this

126

theodolite, whatever that is. What I want to know is, is it dangerous?'

'All stolen property's dangerous.'

'You know what I mean – is it radioactive or anything like that?'

Julie made for the door. 'I'm not sure Yvonne, but if I'm glowing in the dark by the time you get down, send for the decontamination unit.'

'I'll regret this,' Yvonne said dolefully.

'If you're not downstairs sharpish you won't live to regret it,' Julie said. 'I'm going down to see Pandora and the Thieving Dutchman. You get ready.'

She barged into Nana's flat, catching the old woman with a tea-towel tucked into her neck, scooping tinned soup from a bowl. In the opposite chair Billy, minus tea-towel, was likewise engaged.

'I didn't hear you knock,' Nana said sweetly, dunking a crust into the broth and raising it carefully to her mouth.

'Cut the formalities,' Julie said, advancing to the sideboard. She pointed to the theodolite. 'What's this, Billy? And don't shrug or I'll marmalize you.'

Nana put her bowl aside and drew the tea-towel across her mouth. 'We're not in for the third degree again, are we? Because I haven't finished me tea yet, *if* you don't mind.'

Julie ignored her. 'I said, what is this, Billy?'

He had been looking uneasy, but now he decided to tough it out. 'Mind your sodding business.' He began to spoon up his soup again.

'Ooh,' Julie said, looking at Nana. 'All the charm of a football hooligan, hasn't he?'

'Did you hear the one about the pot and the kettle?' Nana said.

'I haven't come down to be charming,' Julie said. 'I came down to get you and that thieving descendant of yours out of trouble.'

Nana's expression was suddenly shrewd. 'Thieving . . . what do you mean by that?'

'This', Julie said, putting a hand on the theodolite, 'is a theodolite. Estimated worth: £1,000. Yes, you might well look shocked. I don't know what Billy told you, but the truth is that he either nicked it off the building site himself or he knows who did. More important, it is at present resting on your Queen Anne sideboard. They'll have him for larceny and you for receiving. More important still, they'll have me and Yvonne for being daft enough to live upstairs. Now, do I get co-operation?'

'Billy,' Nana said sharply, 'tell her what she wants to know.'

'I never touched it,' Billy said. 'I found it.'

'They're on to you, Billy,' Julie said. 'Or they soon will be. You've been ploating that place for weeks, haven't you, you and your buddies? Well, now they're on the warpath. I wouldn't be surprised if there's a house-to-house search.'

'Take it,' Nana said, pushing out of her chair.

'I'm going to take it, Nana, and put it back where it belongs.'

'You and whose army?' Billy said suddenly.

'Me and Yvonne,' Julie said. 'Don't be grateful, Billy, just find something to cover it up properly. We'll be down for it in a minute. You'll have to keep an ear out for the bairns while we're gone, Nana. Yvonne's as well.'

'I can't be running up and down stairs,' Nana said half-heartedly. 'There's days I can't feel my legs, let alone mount stairs.'

'Crawl up if you have to,' Julie said heartlessly. 'I'll be out there risking my good name for you.'

'No one asked you,' Billy said.

Julie moved forward and took him by the shoulders.

'Listen, you evil little toad. If I bring this off, I'll be back to sort you out. And if I can't, Link will.'

This time Billy's grin was one of genuine merriment. 'What's he, like? A hit man for Help the Aged?'

Julie struggled to keep her face straight. 'He's someone with a big mouth, Billy – if I tell him what to say. And he knows where the pollis hang out. Now, do like I said and wrap that bloody thing up. I'll be back in five minutes.'

She went upstairs, pausing to peer from the landing window. The street outside looked brilliantly lit, like an arena. Was there a dark side to the building site? She had passed it a thousand times but now she couldn't remember it. Going on into her flat, she began to get Damien ready for bed.

She had put him down in his cot and bribed Jason into bed by moving the telly into the doorway when Yvonne's knock came at the door.

'Are you there, Julie?'

When the door opened Yvonne stood there, dressed from head to foot in black . . . black tracksuit bottoms, black sweater, black gloves, a black scarf wound Arab-style around her head and neck.

'My God,' Julie said. 'What are you supposed to look like?'

'Inconspicuous,' Yvonne said, moving into the room on black rubber-soled feet. 'You said inconspicuous.'

'Give me strength,' Julie said. 'All you need is a box of chocolates in your mouth and a canyon to leap, and you're ready for the Milk Tray advert. If you walk down the street like that you'll be on TV AM in the morning. Go back upstairs and put normal clothes on . . . well, as normal as possible. We are going to walk down Grimshaw Street in full view of our neighbours carrying a stolen theodolite. I want you to look like a nice mother of two off to the Bingo. Get the picture?'

Yvonne stood still, shaking her head slowly from side to side. 'I don't know,' she said at last. 'Sometimes I feel I'm in the wrong dream . . .'

'Not the wrong dream, Yvonne,' Julie said, propelling her friend towards the door, 'we're in the wrong joke.'

They carried the theodolite down the street in a polythene bag. Yvonne had changed into her camel coat and carried her best leather handbag over her arm. She had even put on her pearl beads and earrings and tucked a chiffon scarf at her neck.

'Nice,' Julie said. 'I don't know how it'll do on the barbed-wire, but you look lovely.'

'Barbed-wire?' Yvonne said apprehensively.

'I'm joking, Yvonne. Only joking.'

They walked twice round the perimeter of the site, but found no weak spot. 'I'm going to kill Billy when I get back,' Julie said.

Yvonne's teeth had begun to chatter. 'Can't we throw it over?' she asked.

Julie snuggled further into her jacket.

'I've thought of that, but ten to one it'd smash . . . or it might fall down behind something and not be found. We need it to be there all correct when they clock in tomorrow. That's the only thing that'll take the heat off.'

'Leave it somewhere, and ring them up,' Yvonne said desperately.

But Julie had embarked upon a crusade and was not to be deflected. 'No, that'll only make them keener to ferret out the truth. I want them to think the theodolite never left there. Confuse them . . . that's what I want.'

'We'll need to wipe it for fingerprints,' Yvonne said.

Julie stopped in her tracks. 'Sometimes, Yvonne, just sometimes, a shaft of pure genius breaks through your mental fog. Take your scarf off.'

They wiped the theodolite thoroughly, and then once again for luck.

'Right,' Julie said, pausing at a place where a tree grew adjacent to the fence. 'It'll have to be here. I want you to give me a leg up into that tree. Once I'm up, I'll try and wriggle along and then drop down the other side of the barbed-wire. As soon as I'm up there, you go to the corner and keep watch.'

'If anyone comes I'll go whoop-whoop,' Yvonne said, putting a hand to her mouth Indian-fashion and letting out a war-whoop.

'No,' Julie said firmly. 'Just cough or sing "Lili Marlene". We don't want to attract the cavalry. Now, put your hands together and hoist me up.'

It had seemed easy in theory. In practice it was difficult. The bark scored Julie's hands and her toes stung where they slipped against the trunk. At last she found a resting place and the strain eased. She leaned down to see Yvonne's face, white in the darkness, staring up at her.

'Pass me the bag, Yvonne. Hurry up. Then get to the corner.'

But Yvonne's outstretched arms weren't long enough. 'You'll have to come down a bit,' she said, and Julie's heart sank. She would never make it up there again. Her arms were aching almost unbearably already.

'Julie?'

'What?'

'Even if we get it up and you get in there . . .'

'Well?'

'How will you get out?'

'Believe me, Yvonne, if I get in I'll get out. Now, let's try again.'

Down below there was feverish activity. 'Hold on. I'm coming up.'

'Don't be daft . . . you'll never do it.'

But the white blur of Yvonne's face was coming nearer. 'There . . . now . . . take it . . .' The bag came up on the end of Yvonne's arm; Julie grabbed it; there was a squeal and a thud.

'Are you all right, Yvonne?'

'I think so. Hurry up. I'm frightened down here on me own.'

It was scary up in the tree too. The branches groaned beneath Julie's weight and twigs snapped suddenly as she touched them. A broken end dug into her thigh and she winced with pain. And then she had wriggled far enough along and the yard was below her. A long way below. Was this the way Billy and his mates had come? If so they deserved a medal. She closed her eyes, gripped the bag and lowered herself the full extent of her arms. One, two, three . . . 'I must be mad,' she thought and would have gone back but the branch was bending with her weight and then she was falling and the ground was reaching up to thump the breath out of her.

She sat for a moment, gasping in air, feeling smarting pains in her legs and backside. After a moment she put out a hand and felt the theodolite. It was intact. She was pulling herself on to all fours when she heard the squeaking. Too loud for mice. Rats! She stood up, looking round, expecting to see a thousand gleaming eyes, a million gleaming teeth, but there was only one dark shape scurrying along a pile of timber.

She got to her feet and moved out into the open space at the centre of the yard. Around here were a cabin with a

stout padlock, wheelbarrows, cement-mixers – all the paraphernalia of construction. Where could a theodolite be left,
to be discovered in the nick of time and call off the heat? In
the end she left it beside a hard hat and a pair of gloves on
the window-ledge of the cabin, wiping it one more time
just in case.

Now to get out again. Barbed-wire ran right along the
fence . . . but if Billy had got in and out, so could she. She
prowled the perimeter of the yard, testing likely places,
once mounting a pile of bricks. Impossible. She went back
to the tree and then followed the line of the fence to where
the street lamp gleamed.

'Yvonne?'

There was silence and then suddenly she heard Yvonne's
voice: 'Underneath the lamplight by the barrack gate . . .'
Julie had been joking about 'Lili Marlene' – trust Yvonne to
take it seriously! Footsteps . . . male footsteps . . . were
coming towards her at a measured pace. If Yvonne was
standing there by herself, singing to a deserted street, she
would be taken away in a plain van! Julie held her breath
until the steps moved on and the song died away.

'Yvonne?'

'Julie?'

'Shut up now!'

She moved back to the tree, talking to Yvonne as she
went. 'I've got to come out this way, Yvonne.'

'You'll never do it. The branches won't take your weight
from that end.'

It was true.

'What am I going to do, then? I can't stay here till
morning. "Please mister, I was only bringing your theodolite back!"'

'Isn't there a ladder? And fetch something with you to
put over the barbed-wire. Then you can sit on it and swing
your legs over. I'll catch you when you drop.'

'OK,' Julie said, 'I'll try it.' When she got out she would
kiss Yvonne on both cheeks . . . all four, for that matter.

She found a ladder leaning against a half-built wall and a
tarpaulin folded ready in a wheelbarrow. It was hard to
haul the ladder up but she did it at last and climbed to the
top, dragging the tarpaulin behind her. She lodged it over

the wire and sat on it precariously while she pushed the ladder over until it crashed to the ground.

'Now,' Yvonne said, 'one, two, three . . .' Julie closed her eyes and jumped, seeming to fall forever until she cannoned into Yvonne and they both crashed to the ground.

'We didn't wipe the ladder for fingerprints,' Yvonne said when she got her breath back.

Julie looked at her curiously. 'Are you all right?'

'Yes,' Yvonne said, hitching her handbag on to her arm. 'Yes, I'm OK.' She paused. 'As a matter of fact I enjoyed it!'

9

Julie was tempted to tell Jason about the adventure of the previous night. She could imagine his eyes, round with appreciation of her daring. On the other hand, the less he knew about crime the better. The pack would be at him soon enough with their 'Bet you daren't nick this . . . bet you can't nick that.' She thought of Jason down at the court, head hanging, eyes wild with fear – the way she'd seen her brothers, the way Link had been in the beginning before he got cocky about the law. It frightened her, thinking like this, thinking of all the things that would . . . that were . . . ganging up on her kids.

She went through to the bedroom and moved the sheet from Jason's face. He was beautiful when he was asleep; awake he was a little sod. 'Come on, chuck, time to get up.' She left Damien for the moment sleeping on his back, both arms flung above his head, smiling the involuntary smiles of wind and dreams.

'Picky-back,' Jason said, poised on the edge of his bed. Julie took him on to her back and held both his hands in front of her throat. There was something she had to do before she made his breakfast, something she had promised to do last night. She cantered on to the landing, one hand holding his, the other supporting his bottom, and mounted half-way to Yvonne's door. 'Yvonne! *Yvonne!*'

There was the sound of a bolt being withdrawn and Yvonne's face appeared.

'I haven't heard anything yet, Yvonne?'

'That's because there hasn't been anything.' Yvonne sounded testy. She crossed her dressing-gown more firmly around her and tightened the belt. 'Now, if I can get on I might get a chance to strain a muscle or two . . . that'll make you happy.'

'It's not a question of making me happy, Yvonne.' Julie turned on the stair and began to descend. 'It's a question of making you presentable. I want to hear those floorboards groan.'

'Drop dead,' Yvonne said *sotto voce*, but Julie only grinned. A week ago tears would have been the response. Things were looking up.

As Julie went off, satisfied, Yvonne went back inside her flat.

'Can we have crispies?' John asked and Yvonne's heart sank.

'I haven't got crispies, pet.' John's face took on a martyred expression and agitation fluttered in Yvonne's breast. 'What about some nice toast?'

John shook his head but Andrea smiled comfortingly. 'I'll have toast. Can I have jam on it?'

Yvonne's agitation blossomed into full-blown panic. She had eaten the last of the jam yesterday, sandwiched between two digestives.

'I'm not having toast,' John said mutinously, and when Yvonne gave him a pleading look he shook his head firmly. 'No way.'

Andrea was turning apprehensively from mother to brother, the gap where she had lost a milk tooth making her look especially vulnerable. Yvonne reached out and patted her daughter's arm.

'There's no jam, pet, but I've got some chocolate spread.' She pulled in the belt of her dressing-gown again and faced her son. His brow was down, reminding her of Trevor when he had had one of his moods, and her heart hardened. 'As for you, John, you can go without any breakfast if you want. See if I care!' But she did care and they both knew it.

In the end he ate toast spread with chocolate, while she found money for crisps, and kissed two heads, one bristling and reluctant, one plaited and compliant.

'Bye-bye. Don't be late home. And don't fight.'

Yvonne watched them go down the first flight, proud of their sturdy frames and the confident set of John's shoulders. They weren't suffering from all the ups and downs – not obviously, anyway. She went to the banister to see them go further down. 'Eat all your school dinner,' she called. If they came home hungry she'd be in real trouble.

Andrea looked up and nodded. John kept his head down but his 'Yuck, yuck, yuck,' floated up to the landing above.

'Men!' Yvonne thought and went back inside. Now she could collapse in her chair and let the warm wash of morning telly overtake her. First, though, she had to pacify Julie. Julie meant well but she didn't understand – she was good at self-sacrifice. When she was set on something her face went pinched like a medieval saint on a charity Christmas card. But she couldn't understand that other people weren't like that.

All the same Julie had to be lived with. Yvonne set about the strategy she had worked out while she made the toast. She put an apple and a Mills and Boon on the settee and fetched the holdall packed with Trevor's hardback Westerns that she was going to sell down the market if he didn't come back. She tied a long muffler to the holdall's handles and looped it over the back of a chair and then attached it to her wrist.

She settled on the settee and kicked off her slippers, using her right toes to winkle the stool near enough to rest her feet. Bliss! On telly a cook was pouring sherry into a recipe as though it were water. They were so out of touch with real life! She opened her book and took a bite of her apple. Rodney was about to ravish Fiona, or as near to ravishment as Mills and Boon could go.

Comfortably settled, she began jerking her wrist to raise the holdall and then letting it drop again, emitting a satisfying thud. Tomorrow she would diet; by next week she would be able to touch her toes. Somehow she would pay for a course of Wondaslim and emerge like Venus. In the mean time she was in the mood for a good read.

Still, though she took in the words on the page, her mind kept wandering. It had been exciting last night, out in the dark, up to something. Julie couldn't have managed without her! And knowing Billy, it would be bound to happen again.

She let the book fall to her lap and watched Mad Lizzie leap around the TV screen. Her left arm was tired of jerking the holdall – perhaps a little bit of the real thing would be in order? But when she stood up and began to swing her arms her ears sang and her breakfast tea lifted uneasily in her stomach. She looked at the clock. In a moment Julie would be up with Damien. She hoisted the holdall into the bedroom and threw herself on the settee, panting slightly to simulate exhaustion. If only she could lay her hands on £50. It didn't seem much. Last night they had handled something quite small worth £1,000 – enough for twenty Wondaslims. If she had kept the theodolite and sold it, she could have been down to seven stone! Life was so unfair.

In the end she fetched Trevor's letter from the mantelpiece and read it through again. *'I think of you often, you and the kids and the good times.'* Had there been good times? Once, perhaps, when they were young, before the kids. Before stretch-marks and nappie buckets and the mortgage going up. Before that two weeks in Spain that had changed the whole course of their lives.

Yvonne was getting ready to cry when she heard Julie's step on the stair, and then Damien was in her arms, still warm from his bed, and the feel of him, little and chunky and dependent, drove every other thought from her mind.

'You were OK last night,' Julie said. Yvonne was aware it was a big and rare compliment but it seemed not to matter. She had a baby in her arms again and nothing else, not even Trevor, seemed important.

Julie let herself into Graham's flat with a feeling of delicious anticipation. She had enjoyed yesterday, making a fuss of him, playing a game she had never played before but in which she had held her own. Today he would probably be up and about but still groggy. They could sit either side of the fireplace and play Scrabble again, sipping coffee and swopping anecdotes. There were heaps of things she hadn't yet told him, and he seemed so interested in her life.

But Graham was not up and about, and when she knocked and pushed open the bedroom door he was not in bed either. He had gone to work, she could tell that from the evidence of his hasty departure – clothes scattered about, in the bathroom toothpaste uncapped and razor soapy and discarded on the shelf. In the kitchen his note said: *'No dinner tonight.'* That was all; no message.

Julie went back into the living-room and shrugged off her coat. She was disappointed but it didn't last for long. There would be other days. Besides, she liked being here on her own, in this quiet place, with dozens of things yet to explore without being nosy. Records and tapes and books, piles of them on tables and shelves. A lot of them were sports books, and sport left Julie cold, but there were other books which she had dipped into: Spike Milligan and David Bellamy and Kingsley Amis, who must be good because he'd had something on the telly. Most of the names were strange to her but she'd bottom them all, given time. Graham paid her for three hours but she was there for four or more, scrupulously careful to read or explore only in her own time.

She went into the bedroom, deciding to strip the bed. Beds were always grotty when you'd been bad. She had her arms full of dirty linen, ready to take it to the washer, when she saw the penguin suit hanging out on the ward-robe-door. Black with silk lapels, and a cummerbund. A white shirt with a pleated front was hanging beside it, but there were faint stains on its front and a grey line around the collar. She lifted it down and added it to the bedlinen. It would be washed and dried in an hour.

While she loaded the washer she pictured Graham all togged up tonight, maybe with a carnation or great big cuff-links, and a black dickey bow like Robin Day. You had to have style to get away with a dickey bow. She pictured the men of her acquaintance in evening dress. Link would look ridiculous . . . except that she had seen Rod Stewart in a monkey suit once and he had looked surprisingly good. Maybe Link would look OK. Tommo would look like the bloke at the Majestic cinema, the one that stood in the doorway to throw out agitators. As for Gary or Dave . . . Gary would have looked uncomfortable, and Dave would have taken to it as to the manner born, the bloody swine! Julie thought of his face when she had told him she had

138

fallen wrong, that funny little sly look that had said, 'You can't pin this on me.' She shoved in detergent and turned the knob to D. It had taken a while to understand the automatic washer but she had the hang of it now, and operating it made her feel like a Concorde pilot.

She washed the breakfast dishes and then put on the kettle. She would have her coffee after she'd dusted and hoovered. She had meant to look for something healthy in Graham's freezer and cook it nicely, to build him up after his 'flu. Now there was no need.

While she drank her coffee she thought about the evening suit and where Graham could be going. Men dressed up like that for boxing dinners, or they did if they wanted to swank. She wanted to believe it was a boxing dinner but in her heart she knew it would not be. *She* would be there, the girl in the photograph, done up like a dog's dinner with daft strappy little shoes on.

Julie felt a surge of jealousy. She had never been to a proper dance and only once to a disco with Dave when he had been getting on her good side. There had been dances at school, but the lasses had stood on one side and the lads on the other and both sides had hurled insults or scoffed at anyone who dared to get up with a partner of the opposite sex. Sometimes she had got up with another girl and jogged about. She had liked it, and had looked forward to the day when she would do it properly, in a club with a feller. And then there had been Gary, and soon afterwards Jason. Why had she let it all happen? They had offered her an abortion; pressed it on her even. But she had remembered Evelyn Box from the next street who had got a council house and a giro for getting a bairn, and she had made up her mind to do the same.

Even then she might have changed her mind if her dad hadn't been so bloody. 'I've just got you lot up . . . I'm not going through it again,' he had said, and Julie had seen how she could get away from him forever. Away from him deciding everything, dictating which channel on the telly, which station on the radio, demanding a piece of beef every Sunday when no one else could stand it, making fun if she changed her hair or did a bit dance to music; away from him belching over his food or coming in plastered at

139

weekends; most of all, away from him hanging over the whole house like a big black cloud. Her mother might be willing to stand it but there was no need for her, Julie, to put up with it any more. She was pregnant and had status and a right to get away.

It had all seemed so rosy. A baby in a pram with a quilted coverlet. People treating her with respect. No more school. And most important of all, an income! Money of her own. No one had told her the money wouldn't ever be enough, that the baby would cry and pap all the time, and be sick on the quilted coverlet so that it was never out of the wash. No one had told her that wringing out terry nappies knackered your hands, but that disposables cost the earth, and that your belly went all shrivelled and then was covered with silver marks. No one had told her what it was like to be alone with a baby, an animate object that couldn't respond so that you never got a decent conversation.

'Someone should have told me it would be like that,' Julie thought. Instead they had given her milk tokens and vitamins, and promised her a key. She had lain in bed in the room she shared with her sisters and planned that first house down to the last detail: carpets, cushions, curtains, garden, the lot. But when her name had come up they'd given her a house up the Cut that no one else would take because it was manky. She had left Belgate, then, and come into the town, where rooms could be rented. She had lived in two bedsits before Jason was born, and then they had found her the flat in Grimshaw Street, three rooms, kitchen and bath.

Julie looked round Graham's sitting-room, relishing the space, the pale colours, the matching of everything. Someone had planned this room, gone out and shopped for it, not knocked it together from what came to hand. She leaned against the music centre, imagining the room as it might have been if she had planned it. She had always wanted an off-white carpet: it would speak money and luxury because only the very rich could afford to be so impractical. She would have glass tables scattered about everywhere, or maybe tables topped with mirror tiles with great big bowls of flowers reflected in them, and embossed velvet curtains hanging in swathes down the walls.

She closed her eyes momentarily, half expecting to see it all when she opened them again. What she saw was someone else's nice, tasteful room. She would never have a room like this – and all because of a couple of mad moments up against a wall in a cold back street, with Gary promising to love and cherish her for ever and ever as long as she stopped saying 'no'. But no good blaming Gary – it had been her choice. And even after that she hadn't learned her lesson but had fallen again for someone even less genuine in his affection than Gary had been. 'I've never been loved,' Julie thought. 'I've never even been courted.'

Tonight Graham would drive up to that girl's house and ring her bell and help her down the steps and into the car, just like *Dynasty*. They never had a hair out of place in soaps. They never went to the lavvy either, but something had to be left to the imagination.

Julie finished her coffee and carried the cup to the draining-board. A sudden flurry of rain drummed against the window and she wondered if it would rain tonight and ruin Graham's evening. No, that was just spite, and spite didn't get you anywhere. She would just have to take her life in hand, that was all. She would get all those things she had missed; it was just a question of being patient and working hard. She had a job now, after all, and that had come out of the blue. The one thing you could count on in life was the unexpected. That, and determination – and she had plenty of that. Julie felt quite cheered up as she went to take the pleated shirt from the washer and put it in the tumble drier.

Yvonne sat in the park until the cold seat struck through to her bum and she had to move. She didn't want piles, thank you, not with Trevor coming back. She gripped the handles of Damien's pushchair and broke into a brisk trot. She was bound to lose weight now that she had charge of a toddler. She was forever fetching and carrying, running after him. An uneasy vision intruded of the rusks she finished off, the milky drinks that she made for Damien and just tasted first, but she put it away. She had the diet in hand now, and there was always the Wondaslim. She had looked in the window today as she passed the salon and everyone there had been slender.

'Everyone there wasn't greedy,' said the voice in her head, in tones suspiciously like Julie's. It wasn't a question of greed, though: it was a question of money. Easy enough to look good if you could afford it. She had taken all that for granted when she was married – the cosy afternoons in the hairdresser's, under the dryer with a cup of coffee and *Woman and Home* – once she had had her nails done for Trevor's Works dance. And, afterwards, home to the nice semi with the bull's-eye glass in the door and the ruched blinds. She still had the blinds, tucked away ready for better days, but the last time she had gone to look at the house the bull's-eye-glass door was gone, replaced by oak with brass trimmings.

If Trevor came back . . . when he came back . . . they could start again. He was still a trained draughtsman, and, besides, he could turn his hand to anything. Bit by bit they could get it all back. Unless he took one look at her and went back to Spain. Yvonne began to run with the push-chair towards the park gates.

She was within sight of the house when she saw the van, its bumper tied on with string, parked outside Number 13. Link was leaning on the bonnet, his Walkman glued to his ears, his eyes vague as he jogged about in time to the music only he could hear. She expected him to be waiting for Julie but his face lit up at the sight of her.

'I've got it, Yvonne!' He was going to the back of the van and unlocking the doors to take out a bicycle without wheels. 'The exercise bike. It's brand new.' He set it on the pavement and shut the van doors, rapping smartly on the coachwork when he was done. The van wheezed and shuddered, and then swayed into the middle of the road and went off.

'Who was that?' Yvonne said.

'A mate.'

Link had hoisted the bike to his shoulder and was tickling Damien under the chin. 'Come on then,' he said to Yvonne, 'the sooner you start the better.' A brown paper parcel was protruding from his jacket, and now he tapped it. 'I've brought something else, an' all. Let's get inside and I'll show you.'

'You'll be OK with this, Yvonne,' Link said as she preceded him up the stairs. She could hear the bike catching the stairs and the sound of rasping metal on paint made her grit her teeth. She would never to able to use it – she'd never been able to ride a proper bike. If they left her alone to try it, cautiously, until she got the hang of it . . . but she knew those two. It would be, 'Get on, Yvonne,' 'What are you waiting for?' and 'I could be half round the block by now,' from Cleverclogs. She opened the door and went through with the baby in her arms. 'Mind my paintwork,' she warned Link, just a fraction too late.

'It'll buff,' he said cheerfully, looking at the jagged weal in the painted door. 'Don't worry about little things, Yvonne. There'll be worse to come.'

Yvonne felt a sudden crazy desire to bash in Link's face, but controlled herself. He meant well, she must hang on to that.

She made tea and then sat down at the kitchen table.

'How old do you think I am, Link?'

This was not a question Link wanted to answer and it showed in his face but Yvonne waited.

'Thirty?' he said at last.

'I'm pushing forty! Do you know . . . well, can you imagine . . . what it's like to be forty, Link? To be abandoned, dumped, cast up like flotsam and jetsam? I was a good wife, at least I think I was. I kept the house nice. I looked after the kids.'

Link nodded glumly as though she was painting a familiar picture. 'What did he do?'

'Earned. Arranged the odd family outing. Expected his meals cooked and . . .' She coloured. 'Well, his other needs met.' She frowned slightly as if considering the phrase. 'Anyway, there was no stimulation, Link. No meeting of minds.'

Link's eyes were glazing slightly and he looked at the clock. 'You want to lose weight,' he said helpfully, his eyes straying to the bike, perched between two chairs at the ready.

'No,' Yvonne said firmly. 'I don't want to lose weight, I want to eat, eat, eat. Chocolate, beef dripping, vanilla slices, chopped pork . . . icing sugar! That's what I *want*, Link. You're talking about what I need – what I need to do to get out of Grimshaw Street and back into the rat-race.'

She seized the bicycle's handlebars and put her right foot on the pedal, then she turned to Link again. 'This may kill me, and if it does I'm coming back as a bird . . . so that I can poop on every bastard that's pooped on me!' She sounded magnificent but the accompanying gesture was less so. She lifted her left foot from the floor so that her weight was on the right foot. The pedal went down suddenly and precipitated her forward into Link's arms.

'Nice,' Julie said from the doorway.

Link was at pains to put Yvonne away. 'I'm only here with the bike, Julie. You know, I promised.'

Julie armed him aside and regarded the bike. As she looked at it the pedal that had borne Yvonne's weight trembled and fell to the floor. 'I take back what I said about it being nicked,' Julie commented. 'They must've paid you to take it away.'

Link bent to replace the pedal. 'It's OK. It goes, that's the main thing.'

Yvonne was trying to mount, wincing as the seat cut into her backside. She wobbled slightly and clutched at Julie.

'Oh God,' Julie said, struggling to right her friend and the bike, 'it's like trying to change the engine of a 707 in mid-flight.'

'I'm trying,' Yvonne said. 'You're so impatient!'

'All right,' Julie said. 'Take it at your own pace. But start pedalling.' Obediently Yvonne began to turn the pedals.

'I brought something else,' Link said. He produced the brown paper parcel from his jacket and unwrapped it to reveal a pair of pink plastic sweat-pants. 'Our Isobel used these. You can use them if you want, Yvonne.'

'How much?' Julie said, 'and don't say "cheep".'

Link was hurt. 'They're not for sale. They're a loan.'

'Oh, I do beg your pardon.'

'It's OK,' he said, turning back to Yvonne who had fallen into a reverie over the handlebars.

'Yvonne!' Julie said. Yvonne jumped and began to pedal again furiously. 'Stop,' Julie said and moved nearer the bike to inspect the mileometer. 'Oh, you've done .001 miles.'

Yvonne was impressed. 'I can feel it in my thighs.'

Julie looked at her in despair. 'Yvonne, .001 of a mile is nothing. You haven't moved that bike from the chair to the sideboard!'

'You're not supposed to move it,' Link said and Julie smote her forehead with her hand.

'Give me strength! Let's forget the bike for a moment.' She held up the sweat-pants. 'Get into these.'

'What are they?' Yvonne said, peering close. 'I haven't got a bladder problem.'

'They're not incontinence pants, Yvonne.' Julie turned them around to demonstrate. 'They're sweat-pants. Every ounce of effort you make with these on is doubled. Go in the bedroom and put them on.'

Yvonne took the sweat-pants into the bedroom but reappeared immediately. 'Are you sure it's hygienic . . . other people's knickers?'

'They've been boiled,' Link said, 'and anyway our Isobel's very clean.'

'And fat!' Yvonne said. 'Your Isobel's still fat.'

'She didn't persevere,' Julie said. 'I keep telling you you've got to persevere. Now get on with it.'

A moment later Yvonne reappeared wearing the pants and walking like a robot.

'I feel like the Tin Man.' Her voice rose. 'We're off to see the Wizard . . .'

Julie was running a finger round the legs and found them tight enough. 'That's good. They ought to help.'

'They won't help,' Yvonne said bitterly. 'Nothing helps. I've got no food, I've got no money, I can't buy a paper and read me horoscope to see if me luck's turned. Now I'm locked inside this plastic chastity tent . . .' She raised her leg in a gesture of protest and there was an ominous rending sound. Yvonne turned to stone and Julie went round the back to inspect the damage.

'Well, you've done it now.'

'What am I going to tell our Isobel?' Link asked.

145

Julie's answer was swift.
'A lie!'

Julie had bought fish fingers for tea, cooking them with mashed potato and some of Tommo's broccoli. She was spooning it into Damien's mouth and urging Jason to extras when Tommo's knock came at the door.

'I'm just on me way home. I thought I'd look in.'

Julie put out a bare foot and linked the rung of a chair to pull it out from the table.

'Park yourself. I've got the kettle on.'

'I don't want to interrupt,' Tommo said but he sat down just the same.

'Here,' Julie said, pushing the dish towards him, 'you feed the bairn, I'll get the cuppa.'

He took the spoon gingerly and fished for a lump of potato. 'There now,' he said, as Damien's mouth opened obligingly and he banged the tray of his high chair for more. 'There now, who's a clever lad?'

From the cooker, where she waited for the kettle to boil, Julie regarded man and baby fondly.

'How's things, then?' she asked when she was reseated.

'Fine.' Tommo was still intent on clearing Damien's dish. 'You know that bit of business I was mentioning?' Julie nodded. 'Well, it looks like it's going ahead.'

'What *exactly* are you going to do?' Julie asked, pushing his cup towards him.

'Well,' Tommo said, flushing with pleasure at her interest, 'you know how many mail-order catalogues there are now? Dozens of them – hundreds probably. They come out twice a year, spring/summer and autumn/winter. At the end of each season they have stock left over – good stuff, unsold. If it's not a seasonal line and they've got plenty of it they might advertise it again in the next catalogue . . . but if it's seasonal, or if they've only got a few left, it doesn't pay them to do that.'

'Why not?' Julie asked.

'Wasted space. Printing isn't cheap, so every inch of a brochure has to earn its keep. If they've only got two, say, of a gents' suit there's no point in puffing it. So they get rid.'

'And that's where you come in?'

'Right,' Tommo said. 'I take all their surplus stock for a very reasonable price. They don't want hassle, they just want rid. So I can sell really cheap and still make money.'

'Nice,' Julie said approvingly.

'It could be,' Tommo said carefully. 'We'll have to wait and see.' He spooned the last morsel into Damien's mouth and laid down the spoon.

'Have you signed off yet?'

'Signed off?' Julie was shocked. 'What d'you mean?'

'Well . . . come off benefit, now you're working?'

'I can't afford to give up me giro, Tommo. We were just existing on benefit. Not living . . . existing. What I'm bringing in will make all the difference but I couldn't live on it.' She challenged him. 'Could you live on £45 a week, and feed three mouths?'

He shook his head. 'No, I couldn't. I just thought, well, if you want to keep yourself right . . .'

'I'd *like* to keep myself right, Tommo. I don't want trouble. But I've got no option – it's law-break or starve. I might be prepared to starve meself to keep on the right side; I won't starve my bairns. And don't go po-faced on me, Tommo. It's not me who's to blame, it's society.'

Tommo frowned. 'Is that all he pays you, £45?'

'It's the going rate.' Julie didn't like Graham being criticized. 'And the job's easy. I'm me own boss, I come and go when I like.'

'Well,' Tommo said carefully, 'it's your business. How's Yvonne?'

Julie grinned. 'About half-way to Redcar by now, I hope.' Tommo's brows rose. 'She's using an exercise bike that Link got her. You should see her face – agony!'

'Is Trevor really coming back to her?' Tommo asked.

'I doubt it. He wrote to ease his conscience, but I don't think he'll actually come back here. Why should he? He's out there bathing in sangria, no responsibilities. He'd be a fool if he gave all that up.'

'What about his wife and kids?'

'What about them? They're on Social, they won't starve.

They won't *live* but they won't starve. Trevor'll come back when he's older and greyer and can't pull the Spanish birds any longer. When arthritis strikes and he needs specs he'll suddenly remember he's got a dear little wife and kiddy-winks. By then Yvonne'll've got a home together, all ready for the Prodigal Son.'

'And she'd kill the fatted calf for him,' Tommo said. 'Typical woman.'

'You wouldn't leave your wife, would you?' Julie asked.

'No,' Tommo said simply. 'If I made a commitment I'd keep it. And if I had kids . . . well, there's no way I'd leave any kid of mine.'

'No,' Julie said thoughtfully. 'I don't think you would.' She lifted the pot to refill his cup. 'Now, don't you want to hear about the theodolite?'

The band was good. 'Super for dancing,' Charlotte said. They moved around the floor in a pleasant alcoholic haze, arms linked around necks and waists, feet just clearing the floor in time to the music.

'Love me?' Graham asked.

'Partially,' Charlotte answered and nibbled his ear. Occasionally other revellers seated at tables around the floor threw streamers in an effort to entrap the dancers. Others blew gold cardboard kazoos or tweeters with feathered ends.

'It's a bloody good night,' someone said as he and his partner loomed past.

'Bloody good,' Graham agreed. He had drunk plenty, but there was room for more and a car laid on for home time. What more could a man ask? Charlie was coming back with him and they would tumble into bed together and touch limbs briefly before exhaustion overwhelmed them. 'Rather like being married,' he thought, finding the idea mildly pleasing.

'Graham!' Someone was tugging at his sleeve.

'Sod off, Mike,' he said amiably, but the treasurer was not to be put off.

'It's time for the draw. The Newcastle people are leaving at midnight, and it takes a good half-hour.'

'Go on,' Charlotte said, withdrawing. 'Do your duty. I'll be waiting with an open bottle . . . just make sure I win oodles of prizes.'

Graham had never won a thing, not in any of the draws, winter or summer. But this time the second ticket out was his . . . a lady's wristwatch.

'I'm not going to be a gentleman,' he called out to cries of 'Fiddle!' and 'Sack the organizer!' 'I bloody paid for those tickets. It's for my lady!'

There were hoots of derision, and Charlotte was flashing across the floor to hold out her wrist.

Graham felt really elated as he drew out the rest of the tickets. It was nice to win something. He'd spent £25 on tickets, but the watch was worth £50 at least so he'd made a profit.

The penultimate prize was a weekend at Crathie Castle Health Farm. 'All celery and celibacy,' Mike shouted, 'and the lucky winner is . . . Simon Farjeon!' There was drumming of feet for the team captain and more cries of 'Fix!'

Now the draw for the final prize – the Paris weekend.

'I don't believe it,' Mike said, leaning to the microphone as he read the name on the ticket. 'Don't blame me, I wuz a good boy once . . . the Paris weekend goes to Graham Iley, the lucky sod. B and B for two up the Champs.'

This time there were whistles and hootings and cries of 'Dirty weekend,' and 'Ooh-la-la!'

'We've done awfully well,' Charlotte said when Graham got back to the table. 'It won't be a top-flight hotel . . . still, perhaps we can pay a supplement and go upmarket?'

Graham filled his glass and held it, squinting, to the light. 'I am a deeply, profoundly, unutterably, indelibly, incredulously lucky man . . .'

'Incredulous? That's the plonk talking,' Charlotte said. Above the pink silk of her strapless dress her breasts were round and fuzzed slightly, like peaches.

'Marry me, Charlie?' Graham said.

'Now?'

'Now. Immediate consummation.'

'Time to go home,' Charlotte answered, and relieved him of his empty glass.

They were all pulling his leg as he and Charlotte wove

149

their way towards the door, and Graham felt a great warmth for them . . . his friends.

'Well, will you or won't you?' he said to Charlotte.

'Won't I what?'

There was an eagerness in her tone that suddenly sobered him. 'Careful, Iley,' he thought and shook his head, as though bemused.

'Won't I what?' Charlotte repeated.

'Can't remember,' Graham said, shivering as the night air struck him. 'Was it something obscene?'

'Shut up, darling,' Charlotte said, holding up a hand to signal the car. 'You'll frighten the horses if you're not careful.'

She spoke lightly but even through his alcoholic haze he could tell she was cross.

Julie kept watch until midnight, fearful that Billy might not have learned his lesson. At eleven Link appeared in the hall, hands in pockets, a muffler wound round and round his neck like a sick giraffe. She leaned over the banister. 'Don't bother coming up, Link, because the answer's no.'

'I came to see Yvonne,' he said but they both knew he lied.

'Yvonne went to bed at half-past seven, Link, totally knackered. At least that bike keeps her quiet. Now, go home like a good boy.'

He went without argument, and Julie was glad. Though she would never let him in her bed again, she didn't want to hurt him. She had done a lot of thinking up there on the landing, hearing Grimshaw Street crack and settle around her, hearing the wail of a police siren far off on the main road, the howl of a cat out on the tiles, the faint far-off chiming of the church clock on the quarter-hour till nine, and thereafter on the hour only.

Somewhere Graham Iley was dancing, cheek to cheek probably. Anyway proper dancing, hand in the small of the back and everything. She had read in a book once that men used to wear gloves at dances and then she had seen a pair in a junk shop – white kid with pearl buttons. It must've been nice. Times had changed, but there was still a bit of grandeur left, if you were lucky. She shifted her position, trying to escape the draught that came up the stairs from somewhere in the Arctic.

She had loved the feel of that evening suit . . . silk lapels and little buttons all over, some of them on stalks. They had to handstitch buttons like that. Most things you bought nowadays were sewn on with one long nylon thread and when one went they all went. Everything of Graham Iley's was good quality. Viyella pyjamas, lovely to feel, lovely to wash. She took pride in his laundry. In time he would come to rely on her.

Julie put out a hand to tuck her skirt tighter around her knees. Her fingers looked chewed and she was suddenly ashamed. All very well to tell Yvonne to buck up, but she hadn't taken herself in hand for years. Well, never really, except for daft things at school like stealing paint from art class for eyeshadow and Vilene from sewing to pad your bra. She could do with some Vilene now. Since Damien her boobs had been noticeable for their absence and not even a £6.99 Stoppem Floppem had helped. Still, things were getting better: she worked, and that was something. It was probably as near to the good life as she would get.

She heard the first sonorous note of midnight strike. Billy wouldn't go out now. Perhaps he had learned his lesson? And perhaps Jesus was a closet meteorologist! She got to her feet and went into her flat, shooting home the bolts and switching out the lights, already planning what she would do tomorrow to improve her appearance, broaden her knowledge, and change the course of her life.

10

Yvonne's face lit up as always at the sight of Damien. 'Come on to Auntie Yvonne, pet,' she said and held out her arms.

'Got any tea made?' Julie asked, already feeling the pot. It was hot and she went in search of a mug while Yvonne settled Damien on the floor in a circle of protective chairs and stools. 'Play with these,' she said, handing him a box of cars, 'instead of chewing your jumper.'

'Have you heard anything from the building site?' Yvonne asked nervously when they had exchanged news. 'Sometimes when I think about the other night I come out in a sweat.'

'It'll be OK,' Julie said. 'As long as Billy keeps his gob shut.'

For a second Yvonne looked scared then she shook her head. 'He never speaks at all, Julie – let alone talk to the police.'

'He can talk when it suits him; don't you believe anything else. Now, before I go . . .' Julie stood up, 'aren't we forgetting something?'

'What?' Yvonne asked innocently but her eyes flickered.

'Hup, two, three, four?' Julie suggested.

'I'm not doing any exercises,' Yvonne said flatly. 'I read in an article that it takes seventy miles of walking to lose one pound of body weight.' She sighed. 'Do you think Trevor *will* come back, Julie?'

'Yes. I do. He'll come back, take one look at you and be on the next jet to Marbella. And don't say I'm cruel, Yvonne, because kindness only breeds weakness. If you want Trevor back, get off your backside and work for it.'

Nana was waiting in the hall. 'Been up there again, have you? She needs more attention than a pint of milk on a gas-ring. What's she like today?'

'Never mind about Yvonne,' Julie said. 'Billy gone to school?'

'Yes,' Nana said, complacently. 'Up and out, no trouble. I think he got a bit of a shock the other night when you told him what that troglodyle was worth.'

'Theodolite,' Julie said. 'Well, I'm glad he's taken notice of something.' She was preparing to turn away when a shadow loomed on the other side of the glass in the front door and someone knocked.

'Who's this?' Nana said, pulling her cardigan across to cover her nightie. 'I'm not in . . .'

Julie gave her a withering look. 'What are you going to be when you grow up, Nana? Where'm I going to say you are, this early?'

'I can't see anyone. You know I don't like facing people, not even when I'm dressed.'

There was a second knock at the front door. 'Well, get inside,' Julie said. 'But if it's trouble, I'm showing them straight in.'

The figure on the door step was a small, elderly man with a cherubic face.

'Does Mrs Foster live here?' he asked courteously.

'Yes,' Julie said. 'She's not in just now. She's shopping. But she lives here.'

He was smiling. 'Good. I've been to some trouble to track her down.'

'Track her down?' Julie asked. His face was weather-beaten but the eyes were startlingly blue amid the wrinkles.

'I was a friend of her late husband's, in the Merchant Navy. Went through the war together. I knew Edie years ago, when I lived in Sheffield. I've moved up north to live with my son now. I knew Edie lived in this area, or used to . . . she's taken a bit of tracing. Still . . . if you'll tell her I called. Sammy Winterbottom. I'll come back.' He turned away then back again. 'She's well, I hope?'

Julie smiled and nodded as he continued.

'And the little feller . . . she had her grandbairn with her, didn't she?'

'Yes, the little feller's fine as well,' Julie answered through gritted teeth.

'He'll be a comfort to her,' Sammy said, with a departing wave.

'He's a comfort to us all,' Julie said. 'I can't find words to describe it.'

She closed the door and turned to see Nana's left eye in the crack of the door. 'You heard that?'

'Chilly Bum Bum,' Nana said wonderingly. 'I thought he'd snuffed it years ago.'

'Chilly Bum Bum?' Julie said.

Nana nodded. 'That was what the lads called him. He was a mate of my hubby, a good mate. I heard his wife died not long after he left the Navy. She was all right but she was a southerner – mouth full of marbles and big ideas. You know what they're like. Anyway, like I said, she snuffed it.'

'Well, he hasn't. He looks as fit as a flea and he's coming back, so get this dump cleaned up.'

'I beg your pardon?'

'Get your clothes on and sort this room. At least clear a chair for him to put his chilly bum on. And tell him to watch his pockets if your little grandbairn comes in while he's here.'

'God, you've got a gob on you, Julie Baxter,' Nana said but she was already shedding her cardigan.

There was the smell of frying bacon when Julie let herself into Graham Iley's flat.

'Is that you, Julie?' Graham was seated at the kitchen table, his big newspaper propped against the milk jug. 'I've just made coffee, pull up a chair.'

'You're not poorly again, are you?' Julie asked.

'Hung over . . . otherwise fine. We had our annual dinner dance last night at the rugby club. I got in *très* late and rather the worse for wear.' She thought he blushed suddenly but couldn't be sure. 'Anyway, I'd arranged to go in to the office late today, so everything's fine.' He stood up suddenly. 'There's something I forgot . . .' He vanished into the bedroom and she heard him moving around.

154

'He's tidying up,' she thought and smiled indulgently. 'Don't worry about anything in there,' she called. 'I'll see to that once I start.'

Graham was indeed tidying up, making sure there was no sign of Charlotte's occupation of his bed the night before. Half-way through he straightened up and frowned. Why was he doing this – as though Julie was his mother? Ye gods, she had two illegitimate kids, so she was hardly green. All the same . . . he retrieved a cerise silky stocking from the dressing-stool, scuffed a fan of talcum into the pile of the carpet, and smoothed one side of the bed.

'I was just looking for a file,' he said when he returned to the kitchen. 'But it must be at the office after all.' He sat down again. 'I had a stroke of luck last night. Two, actually. I won a watch in a raffle and – ' He paused for effect. 'A weekend in Paris! Have you been to Paris?'

He could see from Julie's round eyes that she had never been out of the country.

'No,' she said. 'I've seen it on the telly but I've never been. Is it nice?'

'Expensive. But it's got something – you know, the capital thing: the smells, the bustle, the elegant women . . . and the architecture, of course. That's spectacular.'

'I had an Eiffel Tower once, in a snowstorm. You know, one of those little domes you shake up and it snows. Me brother smashed it to see what was inside.'

Graham speared a mushroom. 'How many brothers have you got?'

'Three, and two sisters. I'm the second youngest.'

'Do they live near you?' Graham was genuinely curious about Julie's circumstances and once more she was surprised by his interest.

'No, they're in Belgate. In the county. That's where I was born. Me brothers are in the pit like me dad, and I've got one sister married to a miner. The other one lives in Slough. Her man's an electrician. I don't see any of them much.' Julie wondered if she should explain about the family feuds, the rivalries, the bickering over everything under the sun, the four months she had spent in care once when her mother went off, but she decided against it. Graham seemed to have his own life in such good nick that she felt ashamed to own up to less.

They talked about Paris and exchange rates and what he would do with two days there. Julie loved the way French names rolled off his tongue. She had had two French lessons once, with a teacher who had really tried but hadn't stayed. They had learned to say *bonjour* and *merci beaucoup* and *un deux trois quatre* but that was all. She had fancied herself speaking French and had said *merci beaucoup* to everyone till some cow in a cloakroom had told her it was naff and the proper thing to say was *merci bien*. She had never felt the same about it after that, after being made to look foolish.

'Did you like French?' Graham asked as he drained his cup, as though he was sure she had done it properly, year after year.

'Not much,' she said and pulled a face. 'It always seemed a bit daft to me.'

He grinned but Julie wished the words unsaid because they made her sound thick. Still, too late to get them back.

After he'd gone she cleared up the bedroom, brushing the silk-lapelled jacket, which was covered with face-powder on the front, and putting the pleated shirt in the dirty washing. She cleaned up the kitchen and got a piece of beef out of the freezer, ready to cook later. He had showed her how to defrost things in the microwave but she still distrusted it. She put the meat on 55 and set it for thirty minutes, then she put on her coat and went out to do the shopping.

She had collected the fresh loaf and some onion rye bread when she heard Link's voice. 'Wait on, Julie man!'

He looked morose, his hands thrust into his jacket pockets, a frown on his face.

'What are you doing here?' Julie said.

Link's eyes rolled heavenwards. 'I've been down the Restart place.'

Guiltily Julie remembered that today had been his compulsory interview at the Job Centre. So much seemed to have happened lately that it had slipped her mind. 'How did it go?' she asked, and when his eyes rolled again, this

156

time in anguish, she slipped her hand into the crook of his arm. 'Come on, I'll buy you a coffee in the caff.'

They settled on either side of the narrow table with two coffees and a packet of crisps. 'What happened, then?' she said. 'Have they found you a job?'

Link shook his head. 'I've got two weeks. If I haven't got something by then I'll lose me benefit. They say I've got to go on a course . . . something about rehabilitation . . . with being off work for such a long time.'

'You've never worked,' she said, without rancour and biting on a crisp.

'I have,' he retorted but his eyes didn't meet hers. Six weeks in one job and four in another did not constitute a sound working background, and they both knew it. 'Anyway,' he said, rallying, 'I've had a bit of trouble finding what I wanted.'

Julie nodded. 'You know that book I got out, *Understanding the Human Mind* – as far as I can make out from that, you're suffering from Role Confusion, Negative Identity and Self-absorption.'

Link looked suitably impressed for a moment and then doubt began to dawn. 'I think some books are rubbish,' he said. He was twisting the small button at the neck of his jacket and now it came away in his hand.

'Give it here,' Julie said. 'I'll sew it on for you after.'

'I can sew it on meself,' he said.

Julie shook her head. 'Link, when I'm on "Desert Island Discs" and I've got to take an object of no practical use, I'll take you.'

'There you go,' he said, 'just like Nana says, always sniping. I'll stitch me own button on.' He closed his hands firmly around the button and lifted his coffee cup. 'Anyway, I'm going to get a job. I'm not going on any courses.'

'What d'you fancy?' she asked, and then, as inspiration struck, 'You could go on ET. You only get ten quid on top of your giro but you can train for something. And don't turn your nose up at the word "training" – it's not like school. It's working but learning at the same time. I know loads of people who've been on it and a lot of them got jobs at the end.'

She waited for Link to respond but he was fiddling with his ear.

'Now what?' she asked.

'It's the button,' Link said. 'It's gone in me ear.'

Julie jumped up and tried to retrieve it, but the more she touched it the further it disappeared into the labyrinth of the ear.

'It won't go through me eardrum, Julie, will it? I need me hearing for me drums.'

'You'll have to go to Casualty.' Julie was looking at the clock on the café wall. 'I can't come with you but you'll be all right . . .' She shepherded him out of the café and in the direction of the Infirmary. 'You'll be all right' she said again and, when he still hesitated, gave him a push.

She was late now, as well as full of remorse about Link, and she began to run towards the market where she bought Graham's fruit and veg. She had finished her purchases and was hurrying for home again when she saw Rose. This time her lip was puffed out on one side and a small cut straddled a bruise above her cheekbone.

'Him?' Julie said straight out, when they came face to face. Rose shrugged an answer but her lip trembled. 'Well, what are you doing about it?' Julie insisted. She would have liked to take Rose somewhere where they could sit down and talk but there wasn't time. 'Look,' she said desperately, 'I can't stop now or I won't be back for the bairns.'

Rose's eyes filled. 'Yes . . . you look after your bairns. I wish I still had mine.' She was not talking of the aborted baby, Julie thought, but of the two little boys she had left behind with her husband and who had later been taken into care.

'Will you come round my place?' Julie said. 'No. 13, Grimshaw Street . . . a No. 11 bus, get off at Union Street. Come, Rose, you can stop with me if you need to. You can't let him treat you like a punch bag.'

Rose put up a finger and probed her lip. 'I've had worse than this.' She moved the collar of her shirt and Julie saw that the skin above her breast was patterned pink and blue and fading yellow, not from one beating but from one after another.

158

'Come,' she repeated urgently. 'No. 13, Grimshaw Street,' but even as she hurried away she knew it was unlikely that Rose would show up. She had seen other women like that, locked in to a regime of beating and reconciliation, unable to break away until there was an ending of some sort – the unmourned death of the beater or the violent retaliation of the victim.

Miss Hays leaned forward in her chair. 'It must be difficult for you sometimes, Mrs Foster.'

'No,' Nana said. 'I manage.'

'But surely . . . I'm not suggesting that you're not a very active, healthy woman, but wouldn't you like to think you were in sheltered accommodation? With someone to watch over you?'

'Watch for me dropping off me perch? No thank you. I've heard about them – they have their hand in your pocket before you've snuffed it, and when you're gone they ploat your things. No thank you. I've got Billy . . . I can manage.'

'Yes,' Miss Hays said, 'Billy . . . but you won't always have him, will you?'

Nana's heart started to thump uncomfortably. If only Julie were here – she always felt better when Julie was around, for all her cheek. She thought of Billy, hidden in the bedroom. If he was hearing this he might take flight and do something daft.

'What d'you mean?'

'Well,' Miss Hays' eyes roamed the room, 'it's hardly suitable for a growing child, is it? And he must be too much for you sometimes.' She was wheedling now, pretending sympathy so that Nana would give way. A cough formed in Nana's chest but she daren't let it out. You couldn't show weakness in front of this lot or they'd have you in the Geriatrics soon as look at you. Besides, if they thought she couldn't take care of Billy . . . she straightened up in her chair.

'Is that the time? I'll have to be getting on. I've got . . .' She sought for an excuse and suddenly remembered Julie's

159

lies of the previous week. 'I've got a class tonight. Wood-work. They don't like you to be late.'

Miss Hays' eyes were on her, filled with disbelief. 'Woodwork?'

'Yes. Didn't I tell you? I'm making a . . .' She sought desperately for inspiration and suddenly remembered her father in the days when he had used hammer and adze. 'A pipe-rack.'

As she saw Hunchfront through the door Nana couldn't resist a dig. 'It's surprising you keep so much weight, running about like you do, in here, in there.' Her eyes roved over Hunchfront's ample bosom. 'Still, as long as you're healthy . . .' She was about to say, 'you can put up with anything else,' when she saw that a deep blush had already mantled the social worker's cheeks. That would teach her!

As the front door shut behind Hunchfront, Julie appeared from under the stairs, where she had been crouching. 'I thought she'd never go. What did she want? I hope your Billy wasn't dolling off?'

'No,' Nana said, hoping Billy would have the sense to lie low a bit longer. 'He's at school, where he should be. He'll be back any minute. How's your day gone?'

'All right,' Julie said. 'Are you *sure* she was just calling? I don't trust her.'

'Yes,' Nana said. 'I saw her off.'

'Good.' Julie turned on the stair. 'I bumped into Link this afternoon. He got a button stuck in his ear.'

'It should've been his windpipe,' Nana said and went back into her own room.

Yvonne stood outside the health salon, her eyes glued to the price-list. *'Wondaslim. £50.'* It might as well have been £150 for all the chance she had of paying it. And yet it was her only chance – they just wrapped you up and when they unwrapped you your weight was gone. She'd had enough of starving, especially at the moment, when her nerves were on edge. She had never wanted food so much in the whole of her life as she did now. Yesterday Julie had made her a salad so threadbare that she could see the

160

picture on the plate through the contents. She clasped her hands together inside her poncho, willing herself not to think of food. Six treatments for £50.

For a moment she contemplated bank robbery or prostitution but she didn't have the necessary nerve for either. She could take a lodger, though; that was possible.

Feeling a hand on her shoulder, she swung round. 'Link! What are you doing here?'

They fell into step side by side and shared their troubles.

'. . . so they put this little hook in . . . he had a thing on his head just like a miner's lamp. He fiddled on, and then out it came.' Link rubbed his ear, and fished in his pocket to produce a folded tissue. 'They gave it back for a souvenir.'

'Nice,' Yvonne said. 'Well, as long as you're all right . . . I just came into town to see about some slimming treatments.'

'Are you still using the bike?'

'Now and again,' Yvonne said, 'but I need something more drastic, Link. They've got a thing there called Wondaslim. They swathe you in bandages soaked in herbs and you sort of melt away.'

Link was nodding. 'I've read about that. It's called holistic.'

'No, it's Wondaslim,' Yvonne said.

'Yeah.' Link was nodding. 'But herbs is holistic, and you can get acupuncture and aromatherapy. I'm going to try that. It's good for relaxing.' Everyone knew he was highly strung and needed to relax. 'Well,' he said, 'when do you start?'

Yvonne sniffed and fished for a hanky. 'I can't afford it. If I had it I could save it, on what I didn't eat. But that would take time, so I go on eating and I can't get it.' They had both slowed their step, trying to untangle the logic of what she had just said.

'How much did you say?' Link asked, abandoning semantics in favour of straight mathematics.

'Fifty pounds,' Yvonne said hopelessly.

'I've got the football sweep money,' Link said. 'Fifty-three pounds so far. I could lend you that, then you wouldn't eat, and you'd save it, and we'd put the money back.'

'What if someone won in the mean time?' Yvonne said but already her eyes were shining.

'No one'll win in the next few weeks,' Link answered, 'and if they do I'll think of something.'

Julie parked the pram beside the large-print books and set Jason free in the junior section. She loved the time she spent in the library – or she used to love it. Since she had been at Graham Iley's she had begun to wonder. There was so much she didn't know, so much you couldn't get from books. Now he was going to Paris and he talked about it as though it was just next door. She moved between the racks, past the London section to Foreign, and searched along the row until she found a book on Paris.

It had a picture of the Eiffel Tower on the front, brooding over a misty city. She dipped inside: *'All roads lead to Paris, the reigning queen of France . . .'*

Putting it under her arm, she looked further along the row. *Paris France. Personal recollections*, by Gertrude Stein. She opened it at random. *'And so France cannot change . . . it can always have its fashions but it cannot change.'* It was big print and looked easy to read. She would have that too, and a book about Josephine and Napoleon. She knew a bit about them already, but there would surely be more to their relationship than 'Not tonight, Josephine.'

She finished off with a leaflet entitled *Thinking of Starting a Business*? which might be of use to Tommo.

'Come on,' she said to Jason. 'Time to go home.'

'So you see we can't go to Paris after all,' Charlotte said cheerfully. 'It's an utter bind that it's the same date as Alison's wedding, but it can't be helped.'

Graham moved towards her and stooped to kiss her neck beneath the heavy hair. 'Perhaps I could persuade the travel agency to change the Paris date? I doubt it, because it was a cancelled booking they had, but it's worth a try. Then we would still get away.'

'I couldn't go before the wedding,' Charlotte said. 'It's going to be a dreadful rush – weddings take so much

162

work to arrange. I can't imagine why Ally wants it so soon.'

'Afterwards, then. I can just imagine being with you in Paris – the shutters opened on the street, an accordion playing somewhere . . .'

'The stench wafting gently from the sewers, and the hookers congregating under the window. Very romantic!' Charlotte said.

'Sometimes,' Graham said, turning her to face him and grasping her waist in both hands, 'sometimes you are a shade too practical for my liking.'

'One of us has to be.'

'I'm practical.' As if to prove it he moved to the bench and began to assemble the tray for coffee.

'I'd rather have a drink,' Charlotte said. They were eating out but not until nine-thirty.

'Wine?'

'Something special . . . to drink to Ally and Hugh.'

He opened a bottle of Montrachet and they sank on to the hearth-rug, the bottle balanced on the hearth.

'To us,' Charlotte said when the first toast had been drunk.

'To us,' Graham said and raised his glass. Charlotte's eyes were on him and he knew she was waiting for something else. 'What made Ally decide to tie the knot?' he asked, to change the subject.

'Love, I suppose,' Charlotte said but suddenly her eyes were wary.

He took a drink. 'They could have lived together without marrying,' he said.

'They could have,' Charlotte said. 'Not that I would. I can't see the point of living together without a commitment, can you?'

'No,' Graham said, but even to his own ears he sounded less than convincing.

'*If* I ever moved in with anyone,' Charlotte said carefully, 'I'd want the works – like Alison. Laura Ashley, Venetian honeymoon, nice *maison* . . . everything.'

'Yes,' Graham answered, equally carefully, 'it does tend to be a package.'

'Could you bear it?' she asked.

163

He reached for the bottle.

'I think so. When the time comes I think I could.' He raised his glass and drank. 'Did I just propose?'

'No,' Charlotte said. 'We were simply tossing the proposition around.'

'A Green Paper?'

'Precisely.'

'Ah,' he said, 'I see.' He had talked a bit too much but at least he hadn't completely committed himself. He was glad about that.

Tommo knew he was in for trouble when he saw the unlaid table.

'Good day?' he asked and bent to kiss his mother's cheek before it was snatched away. Inside him the little boy who had trembled at a tongue-lashing still trembled.

'As if you cared.' He saw a vein throb suddenly in her temple, below the careful iron-grey hair.

'Now, you know I care. I couldn't get home at dinner-time. I had business.'

His mother was reaching for a pinafore, tying it round her waist with small, smooth hands. 'That's as may be.'

'I did have business, mother.' Tommo moved to the sideboard and began to fetch out the cutlery, wondering as he did if he should tell her about the premises and the job lots and the whole exciting project. But he knew she wouldn't approve. She would think it a terrible risk, and he would feel the weight of her disapproval for that much longer. Better wait until it could no longer be kept secret.

He looked around the room, suddenly disliking the terrible neatness of it all. 'It looks as though no one lives here,' he thought and felt somehow diminished. The room was no different from the way it had always been. It was he who was changing . . . because of Julie, probably – or maybe thirty was a turning-point. But the order, the regimentation of life with his mother was starting to oppress him, and that was a fact.

She was bending to the oven, her hands protected by oven-gloves. Her every movement was precise and controlled, and he thought of Julie, so disorganized, so different. If he ever . . . if he and Julie . . . he couldn't get his tongue around the concept . . . whatever happened, his mother would never accept it. They had been together, the two of them alone, for too long. When he was a child she had seemed a big woman. Now he could see that she was less than average weight, but there was power in the small, firm body and resolution in the set of her head.

He would never let her down. That was one of the reasons he wanted to go into business for himself: he could never support two homes on his earnings. He was well paid if you counted his commission, but it wouldn't stretch to two life-styles. He couldn't ask his mother to draw in her horns, and if he ever took responsibility for Julie and her children he wanted to do right by them.

His mother was spooning out casseroled beef with a face like a thunderclap: he was in for a bumpy evening. In his childhood he and his mother had never laughed together, or romped. They had never had rows either, like Julie and Jason, or cuddled as those two did. But she had been good to him in her own way.

Tommo carried the cruet from sideboard to table and pulled out his mother's chair. 'How did your day go?' he asked again, but she merely sniffed and sighed as if to imply his continuing indifference. He had a sudden wild desire to do something drastic to precipitate a scene. There had never been a scene in this house; even when his father went he had gone quietly, bending to kiss his son's head, picking up the leather-bound cardboard suitcase, letting himself out of the door like a wraith. His mother had watched her husband go without a word, and then she had turned to her six-year-old son. 'The nights are drawing in now,' she had said, and Tommo had never forgotten her words.

'Would you like some music?' he asked now.

'If you want it we'll have to have it, won't we?'

The total unfairness of her remark enraged him. They both knew her word was law: it always had been. But things could change. Usually Tommo gave way for the sake of peace. Tonight he went to his music centre and took out his *Phantom* LP. He selected his favourite track

165

and went to sit at the table as 'Point of No Return' crashed out into the room.

Julie had been reading for an hour now and her eyes were tired but she turned one more page.

It showed a map of the Parisian suburbs, and gave details of the Arc de Triomphe, erected to honour the French armies. Graham had mentioned it, and Julie had always thought Napoleon was buried there, but in fact it was an unknown soldier from World War 1. According to the book, twelve avenues radiated from it, their names like water-music.

She felt her eyes grow heavier and leaned back against the pillows. Arc de Triomphe. She had seen it on telly, but up close it would be different. Everything always was. Arc de Triomphe . . . Champs-Elysées . . . Les Invalides . . . Her tongue kept touching her teeth as she mouthed the words. She could learn French at night-classes. 'Champs-Elysées'. If Graham couldn't find anyone to go with him, might he ask her? She could get a passport from the post office, and Yvonne would have the bairns.

Not that it would be a mucky weekend: Graham wasn't like that. It would just be sightseeing and nice meals and a look at the shops. She closed the book and set it aside, then put out a hand to the lamp. On the other hand he might expect . . . you could never be sure with men. And she would, if he wanted.

In the darkness she turned on her side. She would if he wanted because she always did. Because it was easier than saying no. Because it was expected. Because they got so upset if you turned them down. Because she had been brought up to believe it was owed. She squeezed her eyelids together, trying to summon it all up, trying to remember if she had ever enjoyed it.

'Did I ever do it for me?' she thought. Perhaps once or twice . . . but if it had been meaningful, why couldn't she remember? She put a hand down to her belly, flat and taut beneath the flimsy nightie but seamed with silver stretch-marks just the same. Would Graham think she was second-hand if they ever got around to anything? He had never flickered when she mentioned the bairns, but men were different about sex when it had an end product. That made it holy, somehow. Sanctified. As if they thought you could pay for it screaming your head off in a labour ward. Just punishment! She threw off the covers suddenly and half-ran to the children's bedroom.

They were both asleep, both smiling the satisfied smiles of the young. They were all right. It was all right. She returned to her bedroom for her big sweater and then went through to the radio. It was early for the midnight DJs, but there would still be music somewhere.

11

Yvonne seemed quite content when Julie arrived to deposit Damien. 'You're in a good mood,' Julie said, but Yvonne just smiled and Julie decided it wasn't worth pursuing. 'Done your exercises?' she asked, knowing full well there had been no sound from the tortured floorboards. This time Yvonne simply looked enigmatic. 'Oh well,' Julie said, 'it's no business of mine.' This brought forth another cherubic smile from Yvonne and Julie left, discomfited.

Nana did not look enigmatic when Julie looked in on her but she did look distinctly tidier and her face had been washed. Much of the disorder had gone from the flat and there was no sign of Billy. 'Well, well,' Julie said 'things are looking up.'

'What do you mean by that?' Nana asked, for all the world, as though she generally portrayed a *Good Housekeeping* image.

'Never mind,' Julie said, 'just keep it up. If Hunchfront doesn't come today she could come tomorrow.'

'I didn't do it for her,' Nana said scornfully, and then, remembering she mustn't admit to improvement, 'I don't know what you're on about. It's going upstairs so much, it's addled your brain.'

But Julie had suddenly grasped the truth. 'It's him you're out to impress, is it? Walter Winterbottom?'

'Sammy,' Nana corrected, 'and the answer's "no". Anyway . . . you haven't asked your usual question.'

'What's that?' Julie feigned ignorance.

'Where our little Billy is? Poor bairn! He can't do right, by you.'

'You're on to a winner there,' Julie said cheerfully. 'He's

168

incapable of doing right, that one. When he dies they won't bury him, they'll screw him into the ground.'

'My God,' Nana said devoutly. 'If your tongue doesn't stick to the roof of your mouth one day, madam, there's no justice.'

'Of course there's no justice,' Julie said, turning to the door. 'Just retribution, which is what'll fall on you and him if I find out he's dolling off. Now . . .' She moved closer and seized Nana by the shoulders. 'Givvus a kiss while you're reasonably sterile and keep that bedroom door shut. If Sammy catches sight of your po-po it'll damp his ardour no end.'

For once Nana was lost for words and a blush spread over her crumpled cheeks. 'My God,' Julie said. 'The Aurora Borealis. And I didn't think it was possible.'

She was laughing as she went out into the street but on the bus she started thinking. Sammy had had an aura of respectability about him. Maybe he was just what Nana needed!

'You've got a nice place here, Yvonne,' Link said, sipping coffee from his teaspoon and gazing around him. 'It seems bigger than Julie's. There're three bedrooms.'

'If you count an attic,' Yvonne said. 'I couldn't put my children up there. Not now. Not when they've got no father.' She sighed. 'It's all floored out and there's a funny little dormer, but it wouldn't do for my kids.'

'Maybe later on,' Link said kindly, and realized his mistake too late.

'I won't be here much longer,' Yvonne said fiercely, tears starting up in her eyes.

'No,' Link said, 'I don't expect you will. Now, I've brought the sweep money . . .' He counted out £50 in tens and fives and pound coins. 'There's no one near a win,' he said confidently. 'Spurs are on four and Middlesborough on five. It'll be three weeks before we have to pay out.'

They put Damien into his padded catsuit and Link carried him downstairs and strapped him in his pushchair. 'I might as well come with you,' he said amicably. 'I'm at a bit of a loose end.'

'OK,' Yvonne said, too grateful to ponder what they looked like as they took turns to run with the pushchair. 'You can keep Damien while I go in and book.'

Link did look after Damien, holding firmly to the pushchair while his nose was pressed up against the plate-glass window of the health salon.

'I want to book for Wondaslim,' Yvonne said firmly, conscious of Link's encouraging stare through the glass. The receptionist gazed suddenly at an imaginary spot on her flawless white coat and scratched at it with a long coral fingernail.

'Six treatments or twelve?' she said at last, still intent on spot eradication.

'Six,' Yvonne said, proffering the £50. 'As a start.' She leaned forward. 'How many does it take, usually?'

The receptionist's eye roved from the crown of Yvonne's head to the spot where she vanished behind the counter and then from right to left of her poncho and back again.

'It all depends,' she said at last, and then, with a weary sigh, opened the appointments book. 'We can fit you in next week . . .' She pursed her lips. 'Friday?'

'What about tomorrow?' Yvonne asked desperately. In her eagerness she had seized the edge of the counter and was rearing up towards the receptionist.

'Impossible,' the girl said imperiously but Yvonne had spotted a white space on the page.

'There,' she said triumphantly, trying to point to it. Her poncho got in the way and she threw it back with a flourish. 'There, you've got a vacancy there.'

A supercilious smile had come to the porcelain features of the receptionist. 'If that's what you want, madam. It's the hair transplant clinic.'

Yvonne's discomfiture seemed to mollify her. 'Could you make nine a.m. tomorrow?' she asked, looking at the page again.

Yvonne thought of having to leave home at an ungodly hour, of the hassle of getting the kids out, of the way Julie's face would twist when she found she couldn't go to work on time. None of these things mattered. 'Yes, I can make nine a.m.,' she said, and accepted the deckle-edged appointment card.

'OK?' Link asked when Yvonne emerged. She was walking with head held high.

'Yes,' she said. 'It's all fixed up.' Slenderness, it seemed to her now, was only a bandage away.

Julie had decided to bottom Graham Iley's bedroom, pulling furniture away from walls to dust the skirting boards, using a nozzle to get into the edges of the carpet and do the ledges above door and windows. She polished each surface and set its contents back in place, buffing items where necessary, hah-ing on the glass of his bedside photograph in order to bring a gleam to the picture.

The girl looked back at her as she polished the frame, confident and smiling.

Perhaps she lived far away, and that was why she never came here? Or perhaps she did come? Right now the drawers could be filled with her lacy underwear, even other, more personal things. Julie stood with the photograph clasped to her chest and gazed at the double bed. Perhaps they did it there, and the girl would get pregnant and find out the hard way. Except that Graham would not go off and leave her to face it alone.

She sat down on the edge of the bed, painful thoughts crowding into her head. There were two sorts of women, the valued and the valueless, but by the time you realized the difference you had passed irrevocably into one camp or another. And sometimes it was decided for you in advance.

She set the photograph back in place and got to her feet. She felt sad suddenly and filled with a longing to get away, never to see Graham Iley or his flat or his fucking photo again. He didn't matter – or rather he mattered as little as someone from outer space. Let him go to Paris with the girl from the bedside table . . . who would have a big bum, judging by the size of her shoulders. She would never say *merci beaucoup* and show herself up. It would be all *excusey moi* and *reen ne vaploo*.

Julie went into the kitchen and ran the tap with its ever-present supply of hot water. In the end she would show everybody, Mr High and Mighty Iley included. She showered washing-up liquid into the bowl until the bubbles rose

171

up in pillows of foam, then she took the washing-up brush and thrashed the water with it, just to show who was boss.

Her anger lasted until she let herself in at the front door of No. 13 Grimshaw Street and laid her shopper and shoulder-bag on the bottom stair. If Nana was still in an upbeat mood it would be nice: she could do with cheering up. For the first time she had been glad when it was time to quit Graham Iley's flat, and now she was flat and miserable. She turned the handle and opened Nana's door to find a scene of domestic bliss.

Nana was sitting at one side of the fire, Sammy Winter-bottom the other, except that he had slipped from the chair to the floor and was holding out a half tea-cake on a fork to the roaring fire. From the look of her Nana had just finished toasting the other half. Her face was glowing and wisps of hair fell over her heated brow. She was ladling butter on to the tea-cake and pushing it on to her companion's plate.

'Excuse me,' Julie said, as they both looked up and saw her. 'I just looked in. I won't bother you now.' Sammy smiled but Nana's eyes were flashing messages, 'Get lost' prominent among them.

'Don't let me stop you,' Sammy said, but Nana put out a restraining hand and as Julie closed the door she heard her speak.

'Let her go, Sammy. She'll only be down here with her troubles again. Sometimes I think my mind won't take any more, her upstairs and that other one two floors up, only worse. I have my work cut out, I can tell you . . .'

The rest was silenced by the closing door, but not before Julie had let out an indignant gasp. Nana as a prop for the rest of the tenants! Indignation gave way to laughter as she went upstairs. The old faggot deserved to get on, with a side on her like that!

She deposited her bags and then went on up to collect the kids. She half expected to find Yvonne distracted with the extra chore of collecting and caring for Jason, but instead she still seemed to be in the serene mood of the morning. 'Something's up,' Julie thought. Two instant conversions in one house just wasn't on.

An explanation was soon forthcoming. 'I've booked my treatments,' Yvonne said. 'Six Wondaslims.' She said it as though she was announcing a breakthrough in the Common Agricultural Policy. 'I start tomorrow morning, so you'll have to go to work later.'

'You've booked them?' Julie said. 'I thought you had to pay?'

'I did pay,' Yvonne said, at first defiant and then sheepish. She would have gone to the bedroom but Julie was ahead of her, arms outstretched.

'What with?' she said. And then, firming her lips, 'I want an answer, Yvonne. Where did you get £50? Not honestly, that's for sure.'

Yvonne looked right and left for inspiration and then gave way. 'I borrowed it.'

'Who off?'

Again Yvonne looked for escape but there was none. 'Well, if you must know, Link loaned it to me . . . out of the sweep money.'

'He did what?' For once Julie was lost for words, subsiding into a chair to contemplate the ceiling. 'Well, that's it,' she said at last. 'S. N. T. B.'

'What does that mean?' Yvonne asked.

'Situation normal: totally buggered,' Julie said. She lowered her gaze to fix Yvonne. 'How could you, Yvonne? You, a mature woman who knows the facts of life . . . the *real* facts of life which are entirely financial. How could you ask a boy to commit a crime? Because, mark my words, Yvonne, when that sweep comes up and he can't pay out, he'll be lynched!'

'I didn't ask him,' Yvonne said uneasily. 'He offered.'

'And that makes it all right, I suppose. God, when I think of it . . . fifty quid down the drain. You won't lose weight, Yvonne, unless it's through running half across the county when the winner finds out where his money's gone.'

'I'm going to pay it back,' Yvonne said tearfully. 'If I get a boost to my morale, a bite won't pass my lips. I'll save a bomb, Julie – you know that. I'll have the money back long before it's needed.'

'Well, if we're depending on you stopping eating, Yvonne, I'm off to buy running-shoes too. Ye Gods, I thought things couldn't get worse . . . but wrong again, Julie, wrong again.'

She levered herself to her feet, picked up Damien and she and Jason went out to the stairs.

When Julie had gone Yvonne carried a mug of tea into the bedroom and opened her wardrobe door. She needed the appropriate wear for a health salon, something casual and comfy and easily removed. She thought of lying there, herbally wrapped and shrinking visibly. They could hardly charge that kind of money without showing results, whatever Julie might say.

All her trousers had gone at the crutch as her weight had ballooned, but a skirt didn't seem right somehow. She pictured herself in a tracksuit, turquoise blue with white trim: that's what she would like, but beggars couldn't be choosers. She picked out the least torn trousers and carried them to her armchair to mend.

She was biting off the cotton when she heard a tap at the door. Who could it be at this time?

The woman on the landing was well-groomed and pretty and carried a briefcase. She flashed an identity card at Yvonne and smiled warmly. 'I hope you don't mind my calling on you. A young lad let me in downstairs. I'm from Cassandra, Britain's leading mail-order catalogue.' She unfastened her briefcase. 'I've got a catalogue here. You get ten per cent off everything you buy and everything you sell to friends. Twenty weeks to pay, and thirty-eight in some cases.'

'Do you have tracksuits?' Yvonne asked.

The woman nodded. 'Pages and pages of them.'

'In my size?' Yvonne said and when the woman nodded again, 'You'd better come in.'

Charlotte came out of the door, throwing a last-minute instruction over her shoulder, fastening her briefcase as she went. She slid into the front seat of Graham's Sierra and threw her bags on to the back seat. 'What a day! I hope you've got an evening of unalloyed pleasure planned because I am quite fed up.' She leaned back in her seat, putting up a hand to adjust the head rest, sinking lower so that her skirt rode up to reveal rounded silk-clad knees.

'I thought we'd have a drink first and then eat afterwards,' Graham said. They were going to see *Presumed Innocent* and the performance began at seven forty-five.

'OK. Make it the Rosemount.' She put out a hand to rest on his thigh. 'I'm famished, but I suppose I can hang on. I heard from Ally today. Fatal news.'

Graham glanced sideways. There was a note in Charlotte's voice but it wasn't doom, more a wry amusement. 'They haven't called it off?'

'Definitely not. In fact they're planning a double celebration. Wedding in December, christening in April. The parents are livid.'

'Well!' Graham said inadequately. Alison pregnant, goody-goody Alison. He changed gear for the Rosemount entrance and let his breath out in a small whistle of astonishment.

'Quite,' Charlotte said. 'However, we shall have to make the best of it. Mother is pretending it isn't happening. Daddy is looking for his horsewhip. Metaphorically, that is. He's taking it quite well, everything considered. He doesn't think wind should blow on his daughters, let alone the breath of scandal.'

'God,' Graham said and pulled into a vacant parking-bay. 'Hasn't anyone told him we're in the 1990s?'

'Thousands of times,' Charlotte said airily, 'but he ploughs on regardless.'

Graham climbed out and went round to open her door, admiring the way she swung her legs out of the car, the effortless style with which she got out herself. Her perfume, wafting across his nostrils, created the same pleasurable sensation it had done the first time he smelled it.

'By the way,' he said, as they moved together across the car-park. 'I tried to change the Paris weekend but it's not on. It *was* a cancellation, so we have to take it then or not at all.'

'Tough,' Charlotte said. 'Perhaps someone will buy it?'

'We couldn't sell it,' Graham responded uneasily. 'We got it for nothing, after all.'

'We bought thousands of tickets,' Charlotte said, 'that's

175

how we got it! All the same, you're right. Raffle it again, that's probably the best idea . . . but you'll have to get a move on.'

As they walked into the crowded lounge Graham saw heads turn, male heads in admiration, female in envy, and the familiar sense of pride filled him. He really was a lucky man. And, unlike her sister, Charlotte was scrupulous about her pill. At least he bloody well hoped she was!

'Anyone in?' Tommo's head came round the door and Julie smiled a welcome. Damien was asleep on her lap, his mouth ringed with orange, his hands still sticky from his tea, laid out like starfish, palms uppermost.

'Someone looks worn out,' Tommo said, looking down at mother and baby. He felt emotion rise up in him for both of them, so that he had to clear his throat before he could continue. 'I just looked in on my way home, to see if you were all OK?'

'Find a seat,' Julie said. 'I can't get up but there's tea in the pot and some cheese on toast, if you don't mind it clay cold.'

He sat down at the table and poured lukewarm yellow tea. 'Do you want a top-up?' he asked and refilled the mug she held out to him.

'Well,' he said, when he had bitten into a slice of toast and chewed enough to let him speak. 'I've burned me boats.'

'You've signed the lease?' Julie said, eyes twinkling.

'On the dotted line. The building's mine for three years, rent to come off the purchase price if I go ahead and buy later. Not only have I signed, I've ordered fittings and commissioned a sign.'

She grinned. 'What've you called it? "W. Thompson", I bet.'

But his grin told a different story. 'No, Miss Cleversides, as Nana would say. I've called it "Tommo's". Well, it's what everyone calls me, so why not?' His mother would have a stroke when she found out but 'so what' to that too.

'It's been a funny day today,' Julie said, easing Damien to her other arm. 'Nana's doing a singing nun act . . .

you'll have to see it to believe it. I'm in a mood, if I'm truthful. You know, unsettled. But Yvonne, she's gone berserk, her and Link. She's booked those slimming treatments – my God! – and guess what she's used for money?'

'Don't tell me,' Tommo said.

'Link's sweep,' Julie said dramatically. 'People's money that they've given him to keep. And he blows it on wet parsley. I mean, I know *he* has no brains but her . . . she must be witless.'

'Desperate,' Tommo said, taking out his hanky to wipe his mouth as he finished the cheese. 'She loves Trevor, that's what's at the bottom of it.'

'She doesn't love him enough to knock off the biscuits,' Julie said bitterly.

'There'll be hell on if someone wins the sweep,' Tommo said suddenly. 'How many has Link got on the book? I bet there's a few rough types.'

'I hope there is,' Julie said. She was about to lick her lips at the thought of Link and Yvonne getting their just deserts when the door opened and Link appeared. He scowled at the sight of Tommo ensconced at the table but Julie's outburst changed his look from disapproval to terror.

'Don't show your face in here, Link Jefferson. I've heard what you've done, and of all the sackless, witless things I've seen you do, this takes the biscuit.'

'What's she on about?' he said to Tommo, anxious for an ally, no matter who.

'Don't ask me,' Tommo said. 'I'm out of it.'

'You know what I'm on about, Link – I'm on about embezzlement. Stealing. Putting a hand in the till. Has the penny dropped? No? I'll try again. Fat Yvonne gets mummified down the health club, you get marmalized down the back street when you can't pay out. Does *that* ring a bell?'

Link drew himself up. 'I only came in to tell you about me job, not to get a gobful. Seeing as you've got company, I'll go.' He turned in the doorway. 'Anyway, I don't see what it's got to do with you – I'm the one with the responsibility. I'm not up to much, Julie . . .' A note of pathos had come into his voice. 'I don't think a lot about myself – that's an inferiority complex – but I stick by me friends.'

'You don't think you're up to much?' Julie asked sweetly.

'No,' Link said, holding his head up proudly, waiting for her to contradict his low opinion of himself.

'That's not an inferiority complex, Link,' Julie said. 'That, my son, is a moment of truth.'

It took a moment for him to work out what she meant but it dawned at last.

'Get stuffed, Julie,' he said and clattered off down the stairs.

They heard him halt in mid-flight and clatter upstairs again. He opened the door and looked bitterly at Tommo. 'You want to watch yourself, mate,' he said. 'You're a bit long in the tooth to stand up to her. She eats pensioners for breakfast.' He turned to Julie. 'I've got a job anyway: I'm going to be a street artist. Kosher. But you won't care.' He glared at Tommo and left.

'Take no notice,' Julie said when he had finally gone.

'I don't,' Tommo said ruefully. 'You learn to take a bit of lip in my trade. Now, can I lend you a hand with anything?'

He went upstairs to collect Jason from Yvonne and carried him down on his shoulders. He gathered Damien from her lap then, leaving her free to top and tail Jason ready for bed and then they swopped, she carrying the sleeping child to the kitchen sink to sponge his face and hands, he taking Jason to his bed and submitting to a reading session with Jason correcting him whenever he muddled the text.

'He's off,' Tommo said when he came back. 'I don't think he'll wake up.' She had changed Damien into his Ninja Turtle sleeping suit and now she carried him, rosy and clean, to his bed. 'You're a good little mother,' Tommo said, watching from the doorway.

'I wish you were right,' Julie answered, tiptoeing from the room and closing the door against her hand for fear of a click. 'But I'm a bad mother in a lot of ways. I spoil them sometimes, I give in for a quiet life, I don't always see to their needs . . . not properly . . . and I deprived them of the one thing they need. A father.'

178

She was being too honest for Tommo to dissemble. 'Yes,' he said, 'boys do need a man when they're growing up.'

'Not only boys,' Julie said, resuming her seat by the fire. 'Girls need a father, just as much – maybe more.' She smiled at Tommo's slight frown of incomprehension. 'Your dad's your first lover, Tommo. Not in any mucky way, I don't mean that. But it's him telling you you're special, pretty, valuable that makes you demand respect. Expect it. If your dad treats you like horse-shit . . .' She shrugged. 'Don't get me on a soap-box, not tonight.'

'I won't,' Tommo said, seeing the unnatural sparkle of her eyes. 'I'll tell you what I am going to do. I'm going down the Tandoori for Kashmiri chicken, poppadums, double pilau and a Bindi Bajhi. How does that strike you?'

'Double pilau?' she asked.

'Treble, if you want it. I feel like splashing out.'

'You're on,' Julie said. 'I'll warm the plates.'

They ate in a companionable haze of firelight and muted telly, sharing the cartons around, licking their fingers with gusto, oohing and aahing over especially succulent bits. Tommo had bought a bottle of Spanish white wine and they drank it from tumblers, at first in a mad-cap celebration of friendship and then to dull the pain of the moment when it must come to an end.

'I'll have to go,' he said at last. 'Mother'll have the police out by now.'

Julie moved to lay her hand on his arm. 'Ta, Tommo', she said. 'I needed that tonight.'

'We should do it again,' he said thickly. He wanted to reach out and hold the funny, thin little body, soothe the tousled hair, take the weight of responsibility off her, if only for a while. But he didn't dare.

'I'll pay you back one day,' she said as he left.

'My pleasure,' he answered and raised his hand in farewell.

When he'd gone Julie went to get washed, cleaning her teeth so that the tastes of the Orient gave way to peppermint. Once in her nightie she gathered her library books and curled up in a chair. She was reading Gertrude Stein's personal recollections, and they were heavy going.

'*Paris, France is exciting and peaceful.*' Suddenly she

couldn't read on because the pictures in her head were too vivid, of Graham and the photograph girl together under the Arch of Triumph, ascending the Eiffel Tower, laughing and talking and drinking wine. The pictures became painful, and Julie turned to the end of the book. Some words jumped out at her, from the final page: *'to live as they please is pleasanter than to be told.'* There it was again, more talk of choice: *'To live as they please'*. But who could do that? Who was free?

She closed the book and put her head on her arms, trying to blot out the feeling that life was carrying her remorselessly onward, leaving her no choice at all.

'What time is this, then?' Tommo's mother's face was impassive but the line of her lips was straight as a ruler.

'It's late,' Tommo said apologetically. 'I know, it's late.'

'There's a good meal gone on the back of the fire. I'm glad we can afford it. But that's not what cuts me, William: it's the deceit, the double-dealing. You're in with the wrong set, I can see that. After all I did to set you on the right road.'

'I had to work late,' he said, despising himself for the lie. 'I knew I couldn't get home, so I got a take-away.'

His mother came closer to him and inhaled. 'You've been drinking.'

'Just a glass of wine.'

But she was lifting an imperious hand. 'Hush. Don't go on. It's none of my business, after all – that's what I must accept now. I'm dispensable. You're a man. I can pray you keep out of trouble but that's about all. I'm going to bed. See to the lights.'

Tommo felt all the joy of the evening ebb away in that moment. 'I'm sorry,' he said again. And then 'Good night, mother. God bless.'

12

Yvonne sat in the lotus-pink waiting-room, knees neatly together under her gaberdine skirt, her handbag balanced under her outstretched hands. Her tracksuit hadn't arrived yet but she still felt good. The woman next to her was definitely fatter. She was gazing at a Monet print on the opposite wall and Yvonne ventured a thumb and forefinger to gauge the width of her upper arm and then applied the finger-span to her own. Her face sank. The other woman was thinner!

Suddenly a tiny woman in a starched white dress appeared. The dress finished above bony knees and scrawny legs that ended in white leather clogs. She had the face of a malevolent pixie and muscles in her arms to rival those of Geoff Capes.

'Are you next?' she asked. Yvonne looked at the other client but she was still intent on the Monet. Yvonne stood up on suddenly shaky legs.

'Come along, then,' the pixie said and led the way into a tiled antechamber. There was a terrible chill about the place and an odour of mixed disinfectant and stale water. Yvonne shivered. Somehow she had expected a more luxurious ambience.

'Been here before?' the pixie asked.

'No,' Yvonne said.

'Down to bra and pants then, while we get you measured.' She was looping an old tape-measure around her neck and rolling up her sleeves. 'I'll make a start on your dossier.'

Yvonne's eyes rolled a little. She had heard the word 'dossier' before, mostly in films about the Gestapo. She began to climb out of her poncho with movements that were suddenly reluctant.

'Age?' the pixie said.

'Thirty-seven.'

'Sex?' the woman said absently, writing even as she spoke.

'Not lately,' Yvonne said, but not a trace of a smile crossed the pixie face as she wrote F for Female in the appropriate column.

'Address?'

'13 Grimshaw Street.'

'Occupation?'

'Wife and mother,' Yvonne said proudly.

'Weight?' There was a moment's hesitation and then Yvonne spoke.

'Ten stone five.'

The pixie put down her pencil and reached for Yvonne's now bare arm. She urged her towards the scales and tipped the indicator along the bar until they were in balance. 'Eleven stone nine,' she said and went back to the dossier.

'Height?'

'Five foot six,' Yvonne declared firmly.

The pixie looked at the crown of Yvonne's head and then at her feet. 'Five four and a half,' she said and wrote it down.

Now it was time for the measuring. She drew the tape from her neck and advanced on Yvonne. The pixie's legs reminded Yvonne of bendable drinking straws, wrinkled at the knees, but her face resembled nothing but stone.

She began with the upper arm, drawing the tape round but keeping a finger inside so that the recorded measurement was a generous one. She reeled off the figures as she went, moving to write each one down.

'Awful, isn't it?' Yvonne said sheepishly as the figures mounted. The pixie shook her head as though to express despair and then turned on her heel and went out. Inside Yvonne a desire blossomed and expanded, a pure white desire to go home. She glanced at the chair which held her garments . . . was there time?

'Right,' the pixie said, reappearing with an armful of much-used crêpe bandages and a bucket of evil-smelling liquid. She looked at Yvonne. 'It's not going to be easy. Still, stand up, arms out, legs apart.'

Yvonne moved forward and obeyed. The pixie plunged the first bandage into the bucket and held it there until it was soaked through, then she lifted it, dripping, and placed one end against Yvonne's midriff.

'Ooh,' Yvonne said, wincing as the cold bandage struck her still-warm skin. The pixie's head only came to the level of her bust. She looked down on the tightly curled black hair and shivered until she realized that the pixie's other arm couldn't reach round her to retrieve the wet bandage and bring it round again. The tiny figure heaved and stretched but all in vain.

After a moment she stopped trying and stood back to ponder. The next moment she reached for Yvonne's hand and placed it firmly on the end of the bandage. 'Hold that there.' She took the rolled bandage and moved around Yvonne's immobile figure until she came to the front again and the first circle was complete. She moved again, faster and faster, like someone circling a maypole. When the first bandage ran out she doused a second and carried on and then a third and a fourth. Icy rivers of fluid ran down Yvonne's legs, puddling around her bare feet so that she shifted uncomfortably on the tiled floor, until the mummification became so total as to render movement impossible.

'Couldn't it be warm?' she begged through chattering teeth.

'No,' the pixie said, not pausing in her circumambulation except to thread the bandage in and out of Yvonne's legs. 'That would destroy the enzymes.'

'I thought it was herbal?'

'Herbal is enzymes,' the pixie said firmly.

'What do enzymes do?' Yvonne asked.

'They penetrate the tissues and shrink them.'

'I like the sound of that, but I don't . . . think I can . . . stand much more.'

There was no reply. Instead the pixie tucked in the end of the last bandage and reached for the bucket, tilting it to throw the last of the liquid over Yvonne's mummified figure.

'Thank God,' Yvonne thought. 'Nearly done.'

The pixie disappeared and then returned, holding a black wet suit. She held it up and squinted, measuring it against Yvonne. It failed to measure up and she disappeared again to find a larger suit, man-sized. She held out the suit to Yvonne, opening it at the waist. 'Step in,' she said. But Yvonne could not lift her bandaged leg high enough and began to totter dangerously. The pixie shot out a muscular arm to steady her. 'Step in,' she said again, and threaded a black latex leg over Yvonne's foot.

At last it was on and the zip could be pulled up with both hands while Yvonne pushed in swathes of bandaged bust and midriff. Looking like a Michelin man, she was propelled into the next room where other black-clad figures were lying on plastic sunbeds, covered by Indian-type blankets in garish colours. The pixie pointed to an empty bed but however hard she tried Yvonne could not flex hips or knees to lie down. The pixie sighed heavily then she hauled Yvonne into position and pushed her so that she fell lengthwise on the bed.

'Oh, my God,' Yvonne shrieked as she went, and then, when she had landed, 'Can I have a blanket? I'm so-oo cold.'

The pixie lofted a blanket into place. 'This won't warm you up . . . it's to keep the cold in. We don't want you drying out.' She turned and walked away, letting her shoulders sag and her stomach bulge as though to indicate she had just finished a gargantuan task.

'How long?' Yvonne wailed but it was too late.

On the adjoining bed a black-clad figure stirred and Yvonne turned her head to see how big she was.

'First time?' the other woman asked, catching her eye.

'Yes,' Yvonne said, through chattering teeth.

'I thought so,' the woman said. 'We all make comparisons the first time.'

'I was just wondering how far on everyone was,' Yvonne said defensively.

'How far gone, you mean. By the time you get here, you're in trouble. Has she told you about the enzymes?' Yvonne nodded. '*I* don't think it works, you know,' the woman continued.

'Why do you come, then?' Yvonne asked.

184

'Spite,' the woman said smugly. 'My old man pays for this lot. I like to see the look of pain on his face when he writes the cheques.'

Suddenly the pixie returned, bypassing Yvonne to move to another recumbent figure.

'Right, Miss Hays,' she said. 'We'll have you in the sauna now.' Yvonne's eyes widened as Hunchfront reared to her feet and tottered past, the pixie in her wake. Wait till she told Julie!

Jason had played Julie up on the way to school, stepping in and out of the gutter while she shrieked at him about traffic. She was glad when at last he vanished into the maw of the schoolyard and she could turn for home. It would be eleven at least before Yvonne came back from the salon and she could go to work. Two hours! How had she filled her morning before she had had a job?

She parked the pushchair and gathered Damien into her arms as Nana's door opened. 'It's you, is it? Given your job up?'

'No, Nana. We don't all give up before we've started. I'm going in late today because Yvonne's got a bit of business on.'

'What?' Nana said, suddenly interested.

'Business,' Julie said. 'I don't know what.' She tried to change the subject. 'Have you heard about Link's new job?'

'Painting, you mean?'

'That's right,' Julie said, relieved. If Nana found out about the Wondaslim she might find out about the sweep money, and that would never do.

'What's he going to paint?' Nana asked. 'I don't like modern artists. They paint scribble.'

'It's not scribble, it's abstract.'

'It's abso-bloody rubbish, I know that much. I've often thought I'd take it up meself if I got stuck. A few wavy lines and a black dot and you're in the National Gallery nowadays. Anyway, to come back to the point . . . where's the hoover-maniac gone?'

'Out,' Julie said. 'I think she's gone after a job.'

'Job?' Nana cackled. '*She* couldn't hold down a job . . .

she couldn't thread cotton through a hula-hoop.' She moved closer and peered at Julie. 'Something's up, isn't it?'

'No,' Julie said firmly. 'And I'll have you know that Yvonne worked in a bank.'

'How long ago was that?' Nana said scornfully. 'The last time that one worked, Robin Hood pinched her wages on the way home. Anyway, she's turned sackless since she got married. It takes some women like that.'

'You won't be doing it again, then?' Julie asked, beginning to ascend the stairs. Nana was looking noticeably tidier and her cardigan had not a single spot upon it.

'Me?' Nana said now, eyes widening in an impression of innocence.

'Yes, you. You and your gentleman caller.'

'Sammy?' Nana said nonchalantly. 'I should co-co. If I ever married again it'd be to a real man. Besides . . .' Her face fell slightly. 'Our Billy wouldn't like it.'

'I shouldn't let that stop you,' Julie said. 'In fact, if I can have that in writing I'll even be a bridesmaid. I'm all for thwarting your Billy, bless his little cotton socks.'

She ran upstairs laughing as Nana defended Billy and railed against his detractors.

It seemed to Yvonne that an eternity had passed as she lay squelching gently inside the cold wet suit. Underneath her the bed groaned with every movement, making her wonder if it was going to collapse. One by one the black-clad figures were collected and ushered through the door but it seemed that her turn never came. At last the pixie reappeared.

'Right,' she said. 'There's no one in the sauna so we can get you in now.' She held out a hand to help Yvonne to her feet but the client's frozen limbs failed to respond. The pixie tugged and pulled, and then let go. She went round to the other side and began to push from behind until she had managed to raise Yvonne to a sitting position, then ran round the bed again and grabbed her, just as she threatened to fall back. 'Right,' she said and heaved. Yvonne came upright and began to totter towards the doorway and the blissful warmth of the sauna.

'Not yet,' the pixie said, and turned her back into the antechamber. It took five minutes of their combined efforts to remove the wet-suit. It had been cold inside it but suddenly, as the air reached the bandages, the chill increased.

'Oh God,' Yvonne moaned, setting her jaw to stop it dithering. The pixie pulled out the end of the bandage and began to run the maypole in reverse, revealing Yvonne in wet bra and knickers, her flesh marked by the lines where the bandages had bitten into her flesh.

But Yvonne was past caring now. She wanted warmth, wonderful, searing heat that would bring life back to her frozen limbs. She curled up on the warm, dry bench of the sauna with a purr of pleasure. Perhaps it had all been worth it after all?

The pixie threw a pan of water on the coals and moved back from the hissing steam. 'Right you are, then. Just relax.' A blissful smile had come to Yvonne's face. She felt slimmer, lighter, almost ethereal . . . and the worst was over. She closed her eyes.

Suddenly the door swung open again. 'Right, that's your two minutes.' The pixie hauled Yvonne to her feet and dragged her to a nearby shower. Once she was inside needles of ice-cold water assaulted her flesh. Outside the pixie stood looking at the large watch on her bony wrist. 'OK – back in the sauna.'

Yvonne reeled back to the heat. 'What happens now?' she asked weakly.

'Five minutes in the sauna, one minute in the shower.'

'For how long?'

'Half an hour.' Yvonne made no protest. Protest was useless. There was only one thought on her mind: escape. There was a warm dry world out there and she wanted to be part of it. She sat back. Five minutes this time. It would be enough.

As soon as the pixie disappeared she got to her feet and crept from the sauna, moving cautiously along the wall. Excitement gripped her, and she thought of the night she and Julie had replaced the theodolite. She had managed then, she could manage now. She reached the corner of the wall and peered round.

187

At the bottom of the corridor the pixie was leaning against the wall, drawing on a cigarette and blowing the smoke in the direction of an open window. Yvonne backed away and sought another exit. She needed the locker room. She tried two doors before she found another corridor. Three rapid steps and the lockers were in front of her.

At first she tried to dress properly but time was ticking away. She pulled her poncho over her half-naked body, grabbed the rest of her clothes and made for the door. She was half-way through when she remembered the dossier. If they had her address they might come and drag her back. She darted to the other door, her shoes clacking from her still wet feet. There was the desk and there was the document. She snatched it up and ran, not stopping till she was out in the street and could pause to hitch her shoes up over her heels.

The journey home on the bus was a nightmare as draughts found the loopholes in Yvonne's clothing and the euphoria of escape gave way to the cold chill of embarrassment. She hammered on Julie's door as she passed and then hurried on up the stairs to her own flat.

Ten minutes later, wrapped in her dressing-gown and clutching a steaming mug, she continued to pour out her tale. '. . . and I'm not kidding, Julie, she looked like a poison dwarf.'

'At least you've learned your lesson,' Julie said smugly. 'How many times have I told you there's only one way to lose weight? Sacrifice, that's the answer. S – A – C – . . .'

'What d'you think about the social worker being there?' Yvonne interrupted, anxious to divert her.

'I try not to think about her, and neither should you. Think about £50 up the Swannee!'

'Don't,' Yvonne said. 'I must've been mad.'

'Well,' Julie said magnanimously, 'we won't dwell on it. Let's get you back on a strict diet-and-exercise regime . . .'

'I won't be strong enough to exercise if I'm not getting anything to eat.'

Julie made for the door. 'What was the name of the salon? I'm sure they'd like to know the whereabouts of their missing customer.'

In one bound Yvonne was clear of the chairs and leaping vigorously to a beat of four.

Julie had almost caught up on her chores at Graham's flat by two o'clock. She could still be home in time for Jason – and even if she wasn't, Yvonne had offered to look out for him. Julie smiled, thinking of Yvonne and the health salon. There was a sucker born every minute and Yvonne was four of them. She finished polishing the steel draining-board and lifted the kettle. There was plenty of water to scald a tea-bag. She pressed home the switch and reached for a mug as the front door opened and closed. A second later Graham was in the kitchen.

'It's only me! I forgot my squash gear.' Julie wanted to put up a hand and check her hair and face, but he might notice.

'Want a cuppa?' she asked and put the kettle to the tap when he nodded his head.

'How are the kids?' he asked when they had settled at the kitchen table.

'Fine,' she said. 'Bl – right little nuisances, you know, but fine really.' She pushed the biscuits towards him, faintly embarrassed at offering him his own hospitality. 'All set for your Paris trip?'

'Can't go,' Graham said mournfully, accepting a petit beurre. 'There's something on . . . a family wedding.' He was aware that he was editing Charlotte out of his story and for the life of him he couldn't understand why. 'It's a shame, but I'll probably sell the trip or raffle it for charity. It won't be wasted.'

'I've been reading about Paris,' Julie said. 'A book by Gertrude Stein.' Graham looked impressed so she carried on. 'It was good. It danced about a bit. I mean, she didn't stick to a story or anything like that, but in the end I liked it.'

'Wasn't she the Alice B. Toklas lady?' Graham said, but didn't wait for an answer. 'You like reading, don't you? I've got quite a few books here. You can borrow any you like. Browse around a bit and help yourself.' It felt good encouraging Julie to read, reminding him of his days in the

189

sixth form when he had been indulgent to the sprogs and they had all looked up to him. 'Who d'you like reading? I'm into le Carré myself . . . and Desmond Bagley. And I like biographies.'

Julie had looked a bit overcome but now her face cleared. 'I always get a book from the biography section. I had Robin Day last week. It was good. He's a bit cocky, but that's just him. And he talked really nicely about his mam and dad.'

It was a new aspect of the great Sir Robin, and Graham smiled. 'He's a one-off, isn't he? Good job, probably.'

This morning Julie had on a blue jumper and jeans, both of which had seen better days. But her hair was tied back with a blue-and-white ribbon and her eyelashes came half-way down her cheeks.

'Are you doing OK with cash?' he said carefully. 'I mean, bus fares not taking too much out of your pay or that sort of thing?'

'I'm fine,' Julie answered, but he noticed that her hands tightened around her mug. 'Honestly. It's made a big difference, actually – getting a wage and everything.'

Graham knew he should collect his things and go, but he didn't want to. He wanted to stay here and talk . . . or, rather, encourage Julie to talk. It was pleasant to bring her out of her shell. It really did make him feel good. And it couldn't do any harm.

'Tell you what,' he said. 'I don't have to hurry back. I'll give you a quick game of Scrabble. Loser washes up.'

When Julie smiled she looked all of fourteen. He leaned back in his chair while she went for the Scrabble, feeling at peace with the world.

Julie had looked forward to reclaiming her children but when she arrived at Yvonne's flat she found all three of them down on the floor playing 'Wolf'. Jason was squealing with delight as Yvonne snorted and pounced or lay in wait behind chairs. Damien rocked backwards and forwards on his bottom, gurgling with pleasure at the goings-on.

'Don't take them home yet,' Yvonne begged. 'My nerves are on edge, Julie, I need the kids.'

Through the bedroom door Julie could see John intent on his homework. Presumably Andrea, too, was working in the bedroom that she shared with her mother. Julie was tempted to say, 'Play with your own children. I want mine,' but children were not toys, something to be picked up and used. Her children were happy where they were. She promised to come back again in half an hour, and left.

Downstairs she felt oddly unsettled. Here was what she craved – peace and quiet, a chance to do the hundred and one things that usually got left undone. But instead of doing them she wandered to the window and stood looking out at the view. 'Grimshaw Street': it was a bloody awful name, that was certain. She tried to envisage the local worthy who had been its namesake, but nothing would come. If she got up a petition they might agree to change its name to Floral Avenue or Rainbow Way. Except that every brick, every concrete paving-stone cried out, 'Grimshaw'. 'It suits,' she thought, and turned away.

It was a relief to hear someone at the door, even when the someone turned out to be Link.

'Oh God,' Julie said, 'what do you want?' but she pulled out a chair at the table for him and went to put on the kettle. Link looked alert for once and positively cheerful.

'It's dead good, this painting job,' he said. 'I've seen the feller. Canny guy, big ideas. We're going to do a mural, twenty-three feet high. Twenty-three, Julie!'

'So?' Julie said, as though twenty-three-foot murals were an everyday occurrence. Straight away she regretted it. Here was Link getting enthusiastic about work, and she was putting a damper on it. 'Sounds good,' she said, spooning instant coffee into mugs. 'Where are you doing it?'

'Shields Road, on that gable end. It'll be hard work,' Link said, obviously seeking praise.

'So it should be,' Julie said. 'Hard work's good for you. That's what's been missing in your life, Link. Graft. Elbow grease. Getting a sweat on.'

'All right,' he said uneasily, 'don't go on. I'm not afraid of work. I'd've had a job years ago if the right thing'd come up.' He supped his coffee. 'I've got ambitions. And he says I can have a free hand.' His eyes shone but Julie had a sudden sinking feeling. Letting Link loose on a twenty-three-foot wall could be a mega-mistake.

'I can see it, Julie. Green for the earth, that's on the bottom and then a kind of blue-white fading away into space and then the galaxies spinning in . . . pow, pow, pow!' The music from *The Year 2000* hung in the air as he spoke.

'Galaxies, Link? In Shields Road? Why not a nice garden with flowers and a path.'

'No, man. You want to make people sit up. I might do a jungle scene . . .' He snarled and clawed the air.

Julie put down her mug and leaned forward. 'I hate to bring you down to earth, my son, but don't you want to hear where your sweep money's wound up?'

'Is she thinner?' Link asked, his face lighting up.

'No,' Julie said. 'She's a fugitive, in hiding from a poison dwarf with a slop bucket as far as I can make out. Don't bother with *Twin Peaks* or *Nightmare on Elm Street*. Just come round to Grimshaw Street, No. 13: "All human life is here".'

Long after Link had gone upstairs to commiserate with Yvonne, Julie sat on at the table. He had taken the news of the wasted £50 without a tremor. Some people would have moaned and gone on about it, but not Link. 'I love him,' she thought, 'and I want him to get on.' Perhaps the mural would be the start of something? She could only hope.

She turned to contemplation of her afternoon with Graham Iley. He liked her! He could have come and gone this afternoon, no sweat, but instead he had chosen to stay. Julie felt a fatuous smile engulf her face and was glad Link was not there to see it. She was living in exciting times now, no doubt about it. She pushed back her chair and got to her feet to find the biography of Josephine and Napoleon she had been reading last night, turning again to the beginning, to a letter Napoleon had sent to Josephine which had impressed her no end, so that she had read it over and over until she fell asleep, the book still open in her hand.

'. . . *what a bizarre effect you have upon my heart . . . I drink a burning flame from your lips . . . meanwhile,* mio dolce amor,

192

a thousand kisses; but do not give me any for they set my blood on fire.'

What would it be like to be kissed by Graham Iley? Julie sat down at the table and closed her eyes in contemplation.

13

Julie struggled up from sleep, unsure whether or not the knocking at the door was a dream. It was still half-dark. Furthermore it was Saturday. She was sure of that. She reached for sweater and jeans and stumbled towards the door.

'OK, keep it down,' she hissed. Any minute Damien would wail and then there would be no more peace. She drew back the bolt and opened the door. Link stood there burdened under a pile of musical instruments, a snare drum, a guitar, a bass guitar, a clutch of microphones, a keyboard, a spaghetti of leads, and a long-necked object with strings.

'Let's in, Julie.' He was looking harassed and Julie smelled trouble.

'Not on your life. What's this lot?'

'Gear.'

'I can see it's gear, Link. What is it doing on my landing?' She drew in her breath and pointed to the long-necked instrument. 'And what in God's name is that?'

'A sitar.' Suddenly proud, Link freed a hand and drew his fingers across the string. The sound died away and he collected himself. 'Let's off the landing, man. This lot's heavy.'

'Are you sure you don't mean "hot"?' Julie asked.

Link said, hurt, 'If you mean, is it nicked, no it's not. It's the group's, if you must know. And the sitar's mine.' He looked suddenly sheepish. 'We're a bit behind with the payments and the guy's getting heavy. So if I can leave it here till he cools off . . .'

'No,' Julie said. 'No, no and no. The one thing I don't

want in my life at the moment is a repossession merchant. Hop it, Link, and take the sodding sitar with you.' She looked at the inlaid handle. 'How much did you pay for that? Correction: how much should you have paid for it?'

But Link was not about to tell her. He was trying to scrabble everything together and failing. As she watched he slumped to the floor and lifted the sitar on to his lap. 'Stop,' Julie said. 'Forget I asked about it. Get up and get out of it, before I throw the sitar and all the rest of the paraphernalia over the banisters.'

Link struck an indignant chord. 'Wait,' he said dramatically. 'Wait till you're in *shtuck*.' He struck another chord. 'Friends? They don't act like friends when you need them. "She'll help us out," I told the lads, "she's a good sort." Now you're going to toss the gear downstairs. Nice!' The last reverberation of the sitar died away but Julie didn't answer. She simply seized the guitar and raised it to the balustrade.

'All right, all right,' Link said. 'Don't get physical. This lot's valuable, you know.' He was about to strum the sitar once more but she seized his arm.

'You wake my bairn, and you'll never strum another note – because I'll bite off your finger ends.'

Link looked pathetic, sitting there in his parka, the sitar neck projecting a foot above his head. Pathetic and funny, so that Julie had to turn away to hide her smile as he scrambled to his feet. In the end she helped him get the gear down into the hall and held the door as he hefted it over the step.

'How will you get it away?' she asked.

He shrugged. 'I dunno. The van's gone.'

'Because you thought I'd be soft enough to let it in my flat?'

'No,' he said. 'Well . . .'

Julie pursed her lips. 'You can put it under the stairs while you fetch the van back. Ten minutes. Ten minutes, Link, or it goes on the pavement. And you know who lives in there.' She pointed to Nana's door. 'Little Billy Lightfinger. If he gets his thieving hands on it you won't have as much as the key of F left to play.'

She saw the warning had gone home by the speed of Link's exit and, satisfied, she went back upstairs.

It was cold now, winter cold. Julie thought of the way the fuel bills would rise and then shut her mind to it. She would cope. And this year she had a job to help out.

'Julie!' The whisper came from above as she reached her landing.

'What?'

'Who was that?' Yvonne sounded in the grip of fear.

'Link.'

'Are you sure?'

'I think so, Yvonne. I think I recognized someone I was in the Infants with.'

Yvonne's contrite face appeared over the banister. 'I'm sorry. I thought it might have been somebody from the health club.'

Julie moved further out so she could look up without arching her neck. 'Yvonne, be realistic. They've got your money and they won't be giving it back. They're hardly likely to come after your body, pet. They'll let you keep that . . . all of it!' Suddenly she peered closer. 'What have you got on, Yvonne?'

Yvonne looked down at the collection of T-shirts and cardigans that covered her frame. Her cheeks coloured a little and then her chin came up defiantly. 'There's only one good thing about not having a man, Julie. It means you can go to bed comfy.'

'I know,' Julie said with feeling. 'I know what you mean.'

They were about to go their separate ways when they heard a sound below. Julie looked down, expecting to see Link returning, but it was Nana who stood there, rubbing sleep from her eyes.

'What the hell's going on up there? It's the middle of the night.'

There was the sound of Yvonne's door closing above.

'Nothing's wrong, Nana. Go back to bed and get your beauty sleep.' Julie was alarmed to see that Nana was fully dressed and had obviously been asleep in the chair all night.

'I won't sleep now. I'm wide awake. It was her, I suppose

196

. . . the hoover-maniac. What's she done now? Had I better wake our Billy and evacuate?'

Julie thought of the gear stowed under the stairs. 'Leave your Billy where he is, Nana. And it wasn't Yvonne.' She thought quickly. Mustn't mention Link. 'It was the postman. A recorded delivery.'

A smile touched Nana's face. 'In trouble, are you? I know what one of them means.'

'No, Nana. No trouble. And I'm not telling you what it was, either, so stop fishing.' She decided to go on the offensive. 'Have you been to bed? You look like a haystack. What if Sammy Winterbottom turns up?'

'It wouldn't matter,' Nana said. 'He's known me since I was a lass, anyway. No point in putting on a show for him.'

There was a disconsolate note in her voice. Perhaps she feared Sammy wouldn't come again? Behind her, in the doorway, Billy had appeared dressed in the old T-shirt and underpants that served him as pyjamas.

'He'll probably turn up today,' Julie said. Nana shrugged and tried to look dead-pan but Billy's brows came down in a scowl.

'He's jealous,' Julie thought, and, as if he read her mind, he suddenly put a thumb up to his nose in a gesture of derision. 'You want to get bucked up, Nana,' Julie said aloud. 'It's Saturday . . . anyone could come.'

'But not Hunchfront,' she thought as she went back into her own flat. That was the really glorious thing about weekends – you were free from official interference.

'Want any breakfast?' Graham raised himself on his elbow as he spoke and tidied Charlotte's hair from her eyes.

'Like what?' she said, opening one eye.

'Bacon, sausage, eggs, mushrooms . . . My *chef de cabinet* keeps me well stocked up.'

'Women can't be chefs,' Charlotte said, turning to face him. 'It's one more province men hog to themselves. Not that I mind. I loathe cooking.'

'What will you do when you're married?' The moment Graham asked the question he regretted it but mercifully

Charlotte didn't take it up. Instead she rolled on to her face, muttering, 'Breakfast, slave!' as she did so.

Her hair was a curious mix of red and gold. Graham could see the paler hairs shining among the red mass on the pillow. She would have blue-eyed, red-haired children like Fergie. He pictured himself with a Princess Beatrice in his arms. Could he cope? He leaned back against the headboard and pondered, and gradually his eyes grew heavy until he almost slept again.

Eventually Charlotte groaned and turned over. 'I thought you were making breakfast?'

'I am,' he murmured equably but didn't move.

'What are you thinking about?' she asked. 'Your eyes have glazed.'

'I wasn't thinking about anything,' he said. 'But about that Paris trip . . . it would be a pity to waste it. The question is: what do we do with it? There isn't time to raffle it, not to get in a decent sum. I thought I might give it away.' The idea had just entered his head but the more he thought about it the better he liked it. 'As a matter of fact, I thought I might give it to Julie. She's never been out of the country. Never. Think of that.'

Charlotte was raising herself upon the pillow. 'Julie? Totty Julie? She's a char, darling; she wouldn't know what to do with Paris. It's not that I begrudge it, it's just that I think you're being unfair to her. She'd be out of her depth.'

Graham put out a hand but she shook it away. 'And stop that, darling. For God's sake, it's eleven o'clock. I want to get up, if you don't.' He couldn't quite make out why but she was clearly annoyed.

Julie was standing at the window looking out at a still-grey sky when she saw Tommo's van draw up and then the obligatory broccoli precede him from the driving-seat. She would be careful what she mentioned liking in future. She moved towards the door, separating Jason and Damien as she went.

'He started it,' Jason said, scowling.

'He's only a baby,' Julie answered.

'Well, he still started it!' She always admired the way

Jason could stick to his guns in the face of logic. He ought to go far. All the same, the prospect of an unbroken day in his company was chilling. She liked going out to work now. At first it had been an act of defiance, an object lesson for Yvonne. Then it had become a welcome means of making money. Now it was an essential part of her life, the most exciting, stimulating part of it, if she was truthful.

'You're glad to have a day off, I suppose?' Tommo said, when he arrived. He looked down at Damien, sucking on a wooden block and picking bits of its coloured-paper covering from his mouth. Jason had taken refuge in a chair drawn up to the TV set and looked far from happy. 'What about going out for an hour?' Tommo continued. 'We could go to the funfair.' He raised his voice. 'You'd like that, wouldn't you, Jason?'

Jason was still sulking. His eyes gleamed interest but he simply shrugged his shoulders. 'Tell you what,' Tommo said. 'You get ready . . . I'll pop off and do one or two errands, and I'll pick you up in half an hour. We could go to McDonald's for some dinner.'

'You've said the magic word,' Julie said as Jason raced for his coat. 'That's where he wants his ashes scattered . . . McDonald's. It's his favourite place.' She had taken him once, on his birthday, and he had loved it. No need to coax him to eat, there. Ever since then he had watched for the TV adverts and begged to be taken again, but she had always had to say no for lack of money. A wave of gratitude swept over her. Tommo was good . . . the best. 'Only if I pay me share,' she said, and tried not to let her smile split her face.

Yvonne watched her children go off after lunch with mixed feelings. She was glad they had friends and somewhere to go on a Saturday. On the other hand, the day stretched ahead of her like a desert, lonely and unbroken by landmarks. John had gone to play football. That meant he would be home at six, bruised and famished, cheerful if his team had won, unbearable if they hadn't. Andrea was going into town with her best friend and her parents,

199

which meant she would come back with big ideas Yvonne couldn't even bear to contemplate.

She was about to go and lie down when she heard a tap on the door, and then Link's voice. 'Are you in, Yvonne? It's me.' She was glad to hear a human voice but embarrassed that it should be Link. What if he wanted his money?

He looked anxious when she admitted him. 'Put the telly on . . . someone's just said Liverpool have scored three in the first ten minutes.'

Fear clutched Yvonne's heart. She didn't understand sweeps but she knew goal-scoring was involved. 'What does that mean?' she said, holding on to a chair as Link switched on the TV.

'Trouble,' Link said. 'If they score twice more I have to pay out.'

'But you haven't got the money,' Yvonne said.

'Give that woman a Kewpie doll,' Link said. 'I haven't got the money.'

'What will they do to you?' Yvonne asked, the tears already starting.

'To us, Yvonne. What will *she* do to us? I can face the winner! It's Kenny Pallitt who's got Liverpool, and he'll be reasonable. It's Julie . . . she'll have my eyeballs for earrings. You know what she's like.'

'It's none of Julie's business,' Yvonne said half-heartedly, but Link had ceased to listen. Instead he was moving closer to the screen where the tiny ball was being booted with unerring accuracy towards the other goal.

'Jesus,' he said as a roar went up. He clapped a hand to his eyes as the ball hit the cross-bar, bounced back, was handled, dropped, and kicked into play. As it sped back again goalwards he sank to his knees, his hand still to his eyes with fingers just wide enough apart to see.

'Eeek,' Yvonne said, and then 'Eeek,' again. She put a hand to her chest and then, in the absence of anything better to do, she too sank slowly to her knees in a position of prayer.

McDonald's had lived up to its promise, providing boxed 'Happy Meals' for the children and huge cartons of hot coffee and hamburgers for Julie and Tommo. But it began to rain as they entered the funfair, icy rain blown by an east wind from the sea. They went from ride to ride, Tommo carrying the baby, Jason running eagerly ahead, but the cold gradually defeated them.

'You haven't got enough on,' Tommo said as Julie's teeth began to chatter. 'I'm OK,' she said, but the area between knees and skirt hem was gradually turning numb and the wind was penetrating between skirt top and T-shirt.

They gave in after the Dodgems and splashed across the mud to the car. Even Jason seemed to accept it was time to go home. 'There now,' Tommo said when they were safe in the car, the rain and wind locked out to pluck impotently at the windows. 'We'll soon have you home in the warm.' He had banked up the fire before they left and covered it with ash from the grate so that it would not burn away too soon.

Julie felt herself relax in the seat. Someone else had taken care of something for once. It was a nice feeling. She watched the rain-lashed streets from the car window and thought how pleasant it was not to be going home without adult company.

'What a day,' Nana said from her doorway as they ran, whooping, into the hall. Julie had the baby and Tommo carried Jason easily, in spite of his bulk. Jason was too heavy for Julie now and it was good to see him carried again, kept clear of the rain and the mud in a man's arms.

'This house's never cooled while you've been gallivanting,' Nana said. 'That boy-friend of yours, the light-in-the-head one, is upstairs . . . that's a bad combination. She's as cracked as he is, mark my words. The noise that's come out of that flat, the crying and cheering . . . And I've had two men round selling fish and a feller from the LSD party wanting to know if I had any housing complaints. "Have you got a week?" I said. He says she should be ejaculated after that water business.'

'LSD party?' Tommo asked.

'Yes,' Nana said impatiently. 'The green vegetables or whatever they're called now.'

'Salads,' Julie said, starting to mount the stairs.

201

'Don't be funny,' Nana said. 'David Steel's lot, that's who I mean. The LSDs.'

Tommo and Julie exchanged glances. 'Well, they do get some weird ideas,' he said. 'Maybe Nana's right.'

'Of course I'm right,' the old lady said. 'And when he comes back, you tell him about upstairs. It was bad enough when she was on her own. If she gets pally with that Link . . .'

'He's all right,' Tommo said, setting Jason to the ground. 'Just a bit young.'

'Too young for her,' Nana said scathingly, 'unless she wants a toy-boy now. I hope he's had survival training.' She moved closer to Tommo. 'Do you know . . .'

'Not the paintings again, Nana, please,' Julie said. 'I don't think you're entitled to criticize.'

'Go on, I don't care,' Nana said as they moved up and out of earshot. 'If you're getting at me, it means you're leaving my poor little Billy alone. He's got his head down to his homework . . . bite on that!'

'Homework?' Tommo said as Julie opened her door. 'Does that sound like the Billy we know and love?'

'He'll be doing maths,' Julie said, straight-faced. 'He's keen on the metric system.'

Tommo tried to get the joke he knew was in there but couldn't. 'Tell,' he said.

'He studies meters,' Julie said. 'Not how to measure them . . . how to break into them.'

There was nothing Jason wanted to watch on TV so they got out his Mousetrap game, Jason competing with Tommo and Julie competing for Damien, so he didn't feel left out. Once or twice, Julie looked up to find Tommo's eyes on her. She smiled at him, enjoying the answering warmth in his smile, thinking how nice it was for the kids to be like a proper family for a little while.

They watched TV after that, and then had a crazy half-hour that lasted an hour and a quarter, leaping around like mad things till they were all worn out.

They got the tired children to bed with the minimum of fuss, then she and Tommo settled in front of the TV with cups of packet soup and thick, soft, corned-beef sarnies.

'Nice,' Tommo said. Julie had put thin sliced onion in his

and peppered and salted it to add taste. Her own sandwich oozed tomato sauce. Link had looked in on his way down from Yvonne's and been offered a share, but had declined with disapproval and clattered off, hands in pockets.

'You ought to get out more, Julie,' Tommo said. 'You've got a bit of colour in your cheeks tonight. It suits you.'

'I was that cold when we got in,' she said. 'I feel lovely now. You did a good job with the fire. And don't worry about me getting out: you can't have bairns and a social life, I know that.'

'Do you ever have regrets?' Tommo asked.

Julie sipped her soup for a moment, pondering her answer.

'Not really. I mean, I couldn't regret either of the bairns. I love them. So, no, I don't regret.' She sipped again. 'I wouldn't like to see it happen to someone else, though.'

'It does,' Tommo said, 'all the time now. If I counted up the one-parent families on my books it'd be sixty per cent, easy. And they don't all cope like you do.'

'You think it's wrong, don't you,' she said. It was a statement, not a question.

'I don't sit in judgement.' Tommo wasn't backing down, and she liked him for it. 'But I can't say I think bairns coming into the world without a dad's a good thing, because I don't.'

'It isn't,' Julie agreed. 'It's not fair on the kids . . . or on the mothers, but *they've* asked for it.'

'That's a bit hard,' Tommo countered.

'Yeah, it is,' Julie said, 'because we don't get much help. I don't mean only now, I mean before, when it matters. When it could make a difference.'

'Sex education, you mean,' Tommo said. She saw him go faintly pink but at least he could speak about it now. What sort of life had he had to be so shy at thirty?

'We got sex education at school,' she said. 'The mechanics of it and contraception. But nothing about the long-term, nothing about a baby being for life, or needing a proper home. They never said we should use our brains about it. Most of the teachers let you know you shouldn't sleep around, but we had this one who was there just to teach it. She went round all the school: "See me after if you're having a relationship," she said. So I stayed behind and I told her about Gary and me. She gave me some leaflets about contraception, and she talked about maturity and sexuality. I didn't know half what she was on about, but she seemed to think it was OK, me and Gary. I think I wanted her to say it wasn't OK. I'm not sure we'd've stopped . . . well, he wouldn't, but I might have . . . but I think I wanted her to say, "No way."' She looked up at Tommo. 'Does that sound daft?'

'No,' he said. 'No. I know what you mean. You wanted to know there were fences.'

'Yeah,' she said. 'That's it exactly. I felt as though I was in a bloody great prairie with no lines, no fences. I wanted someone to say, "You can't go here," and "You can't go there." But she just said, "Be careful," and I thought that meant, "Go ahead." As though she thought I should do it.'

'It's difficult,' Tommo said. 'Where do you draw the line between repression and licence? I don't know.'

'Neither do I,' Julie said. 'But if someone had worked it out I might have been grateful. On the other hand, I might not. I love Jason.'

'Of course you do,' Tommo said and smiled approval.

'Would you do different, if you could go back?' she asked.

He brooded for a moment. 'Yes and no,' he said at last. 'I like tallying, so I'd still do that . . . you meet people, you give them what they want and see their faces light up – that part's all right. But I wouldn't work with this firm, they're rip-off artists. Between them and me mam coming on like the wrath of God I'm about sick.'

'Drink your soup,' Julie said soothingly. 'Your mam'll come round in the end. And you'll soon be working for yourself. Don't let a few rows get you down, they form your character.'

Tommo nodded. 'They make you like Quasimodo – ' he grimaced like a gargoyle and inclined his head to one side – 'all bitter and twisted. Still, here's to more days like today,' and he clinked his chicken and sweetcorn with her minestrone.

14

Yvonne was playing the tragedy queen again when Julie went up to leave Damien. 'I've had a weekend and a half here. Worry, worry, nothing to cheer up about, no joint for Sunday. That's the bitter end for me, not being able to have meat in a piece. If I ever get out of this I'll never use the word mince again. Never.'

'What sort of "worry"?' Julie asked but Yvonne was suddenly reticent. 'And what was Link doing here on Saturday? I forgot to ask you yesterday, but Nana was on about the pair of you whooping and hollering . . . and Link has been conspicuous by his absence this weekend.'

But Yvonne was telling nothing. 'Say bye-bye to mammy,' she said to Damien and then, when Julie looked as though she might persist, 'Tommo's never been away from your place, has he? If I didn't know better . . .'

'It'll keep,' Julie thought as she kissed Damien and waved through the banister. Neither Link nor Yvonne was capable of keeping quiet for long; sooner or later she'd have it out of them. It couldn't be anything to do with the £50 because the sweep hadn't been won on Saturday.

She decided not to call on Nana as she left – she was early this morning and didn't want anything to spoil it. Besides, it looked like rain and although she'd put on her red mac she didn't want to get caught.

Fate had different plans. Sammy Winterbottom was raising a hand to the knocker when Julie opened the street door. His face looked pinched inside his muffler and the old blue eyes that had been so bright now looked distinctly watery. *Chilly* Bum Bum was about right, Julie thought, and hid a smile.

'Edie in?' he asked, and Julie ushered him into the hall as Nana's door opened and Billy appeared, shrugging into his denim jacket. Nana was behind him looking her usual unkempt self. When she saw Sammy she came over coy and put up one hand to clutch her cardigan together, the other picking at her hair, still flattened from a night in the chair.

Billy's habitual scowl deepened at the sight of the old man. He hesitated, almost as though he would turn back, but Julie was too quick for him. 'Off to school, William? What a good lad.' His arm tensed under her hand but he allowed himself to be dragged through the doorway and propelled towards the street.

'I'm not too early, am I, Edie?' Sammy said anxiously. 'To be truthful, I was glad to get out of that house. I'm not popular there, I'm afraid.'

Nana was making polite noises of sympathy but making no move to go back inside.

'It's a tip in there,' Julie thought. 'Or the jerry's on show.' She abandoned hopes of an early start at work and dived to the rescue.

'Mr Winterbottom,' she said confidingly, putting a hand on his arm, 'while Nana . . . Edie . . . puts the kettle on, I wonder if you could give me the benefit of your advice. There's nothing like a man's opinion, is there? That's what we're short of in this house . . . among other things.'

Burning gratitude sprang up briefly in Nana's eyes. 'I'll put the kettle on,' she said to Sammy. 'You see what Julie wants.' She sighed heavily to indicate that Julie's importunings were an everyday occurrence, and smiled wearily to show she would be grateful for someone to share the load.

Julie drew Sammy towards the cavity under the stairs, which Link's gear had occupied until the day before. 'It's under here,' she said. 'I know it's a bit dark, but I had a feeling I could smell dry rot.' From Nana's flat came the sound of mad activity and Julie rattled the pushchair out into the passageway to cover the noise.

Sammy spent a satisfying five minutes tapping the plasterboard and testing the woodwork with his penknife.

'It looks all right to me,' he said at last. 'Tell you what, though . . . I'll bring a torch along next time and we'll have a good dekko.' He looked his old self now that he had something useful to do. 'Don't you give it another moment's thought. I'll make sure it's all right.'

Nana appeared in the doorway then, looking less dishevelled if a little out of breath. 'Ready for your tea?' she said sweetly, and then, to Julie, 'You really mustn't bother Mr Winterbottom with your problems, Julie. He's only come on a visit.'

Julie would have cheerfully throttled Nana, but at that moment Yvonne appeared on the stair with Damien. She was dressed like Julie in a red nylon mac. Nana looked from one to the other. 'Going to a Noah's Ark party?' she said and vanished into her flat.

Julie helped the pushchair over the doorstep and fell into step beside Yvonne. 'I'm going down the surgery for some valium,' Yvonne said as they trudged towards the school. Her words died on her lips as they both suddenly saw Hunchfront's yellow car parked a hundred yards ahead. But it was not the car itself or the spectre of its owner that had chilled the blood: it was the sight of Billy crouched by the rear wheel in the act of letting the air out of the last of the four tyres.

'Oh, my God,' Yvonne said, 'is that car whose I think it is . . .'

'Yes,' Julie said through clenched teeth. 'That is Hunchfront's car and that little assassin with the valve caps in his hand lives in our house.'

'What shall we do?' Yvonne said.

The door of the house at whose kerb the yellow car was parked opened suddenly and Hunchfront appeared, talking to the householder nineteen to the dozen and fussing with her briefcase.

'What shall we *do*?' Yvonne said again as Billy straightened up and darted out of sight around the car.

Julie gripped the handle of the pushchair and turned it around. 'Run,' she said, 'and the last one back home gets the case conference.'

Yvonne took a shaking fit and threatened to flee with the kids to her cousin in Glasgow before Hunchfront's vengeance descended, and it took Julie half an hour and a pot of tea to convince her that Hunchfront's victims formed a long list and blame would be hard to apportion. 'I'm paranoid, Yvonne, but not even I think she'll automatically blame us. Not unless she's got eyes in the back of her head and she saw Billy.'

'She's got eyes in her arse, that one,' Yvonne said with uncharacteristic coarseness. 'We're getting to her,' Julie thought sadly. 'Another year and you'll never know she was a lady once.'

Julie would have given Nana an earful about Billy as she left for work but when she put her ear to the door she could hear the hum of conversation and she didn't want to interrupt a tête-à-tête. For some reason she liked Chilly Bum Bum. He was good for Nana, which was one reason. Billy hated him, which was two *and* three. And there was something about the innocent gaze of the old man that warmed Julie's heart. 'He's like a grandpa,' she thought as she set off for the bus. 'At least, he's like a grandpa should be.'

She made coffee as soon as she reached Graham's flat and then sat down to study the list he had left. '*Peel potatoes for two, and top and tail beans in bottom drawer of fridge. Ninja Turtles book on hall table is for Jason. I found it in the office.*'

She ran her eye over the rest of the instructions and then went back to the first one: '*Peel potatoes for two.*' So he was entertaining. So what? He probably had people in all the time. Men were different nowadays; they liked entertaining. Well, professional men did. For a wild moment she even wondered if he might appear and invite her to stay for supper, but she dispelled this fantasy by getting on with her work, which was what she was paid to come here for, after all.

She was in the middle of making the bed, lofting the duvet high in the air, when she heard the key in the lock. She dropped the duvet and turned to the dressing-table mirror to check that she didn't look too bad. She would do. She felt a smile blossom and moved to the bedroom door, but the smile faded when she saw that it was not Graham who stood there, putting the key back into a tan suede clutch-bag. It was the girl from the photograph on the bedside table.

'Hallo,' the girl said, throwing back the heavy red hair.

'You must be Julie. I'm Charlotte Conway, a friend of Graham's.' Was it Julie's imagination or did she flourish the key for a second before dropping it into her bag? 'I've come to pick up some things of mine,' she went on sweetly, moving past Julie into the bedroom.

A mad impulse to bar the way or at least ask for identification came and went in Julie. 'Would you like a coffee?' she said instead and, when Charlotte accepted, she went through to fix kettle and mugs.

Charlotte settled herself at the kitchen table. There was no sign of anything she had collected from the bedroom, and Julie moved across to the vegetable rack so that she could squint into the hall. Nothing there either. 'She's come to check me out,' she thought and felt nerves numb her brain.

She stuck to the sink, peeling potatoes, trimming beans, and sipping her coffee in between answering Charlotte's questions. They were posed in the friendliest manner, and when Julie went over them in her mind afterwards they were harmless enough. 'And I answered like a nerd,' she thought and could have kicked herself.

'Have you always done this kind of work?' Charlotte asked, as she finished her coffee and dabbed her lipsticked mouth with a tissue.

'Yes,' Julie said. 'Well, no . . . at least . . .'

'But you like it?' Charlotte finished for her. 'Who looks after your children?'

'They go to school. I mean, Jason goes to school. Damien stops with my neighbour.' Was she mistaken in thinking Charlotte looked disapproving. 'She's very good with him,' she added defensively.

'I'm sure,' Charlotte said, standing up. 'Well, I must go.' She tightened the suede belt around her waist and checked her seams. 'It's been nice meeting you. Graham is hugely pleased with you, no worries there. Don't let him be too slobby. Come to me if he gives you trouble.'

It was a joke but Julie found the other girl's proprietary tone far from funny.

'He's nice to work for,' she said stiffly. She'd have liked to say, 'We play Scrabble on the bed and he teases me and he really cares about my kids,' but she didn't want to cause trouble for Graham. Besides, she felt at a disadvantage. Charlotte was so polished, so shiny, so fucking sure of herself. She was smiling at Julie now, and fiddling with her expensive belt again to show off her nice figure.

'I'm glad to hear he's nice to you,' Charlotte said. 'So he should be. You've relieved him of all the grotty housework. I think you're a brick to do a job like this. God knows, my job is interesting and yet I know how fed up I get, so what it must be like for you . . . still, I suppose it's different if you're doing it for someone else.' She moved to the refrigerator and opened it, scanning the shelves. 'I must say you've improved this. He never had anything in it but *fromage frais* in the old days . . . and mouldy cheese. I used to warn him about salmonella, but you know Graham – in one ear and out of the other.'

Julie was consumed with indignation. If she had a man like Graham she wouldn't run him down . . . not to anyone, and certainly not to someone who worked for him. Charlotte was throwing back her heavy hair, still regarding the fridge with a speculative eye.

'I think he's very good about his food,' Julie said stiffly. 'He's no trouble to feed, I know that much.'

Charlotte's eyes narrowed as she shut the refrigerator door and turned.

'You're too soft on him, Julie. I admire loyalty, but don't get carried away.' It was a warning and they both knew it.

Julie turned on the tap and began to wipe down the draining-board and clean the sink while her tormentor gathered up her things. She dried her hands to show Charlotte off the premises, and then leaned her forehead against the closed door. She didn't feel sad or angry or defeated, just flat. She could walk under a duck now without scratching its belly, and *that* was a fact!

'Julie!' She turned as she got off the bus to see Tommo waving from the van. 'I've been watching for you,' he said.

She walked towards him, smiling, trying to shrug off her misery. Why inflict it on Tommo?

'Get in, you look perished,' he said, reaching across her to close the door. 'Have you got five minutes?' He looked at his watch. 'It's twenty minutes to school-time: I can have you back there by then.' He wanted her to see his new acquisition, the shop in Rosamond Street. The keys lay on the dashboard, tagged with the estate agent's label.

'OK,' Julie said. 'As long as I'm back for Jason.'

The shop smelled musty and airless, and the door wheezed as Tommo pushed it open, but it was roomy and lined with decent shelves. Behind lay a spacious back shop with a large barred window and a tiny toilet off it. 'What do you think?' he said, sounding all of fifteen.

'I think it's smashing, Tommo. Really good. And after I've cleaned it up it'll be even better.'

'I can't ask you to do that,' Tommo said but Julie could tell he was pleased.

'You can't stop me. I can't wait to get my hands on this place. A good clean, some pine disinfectant . . . a bit of paint and some light-shades. There's something about a naked bulb that puts you off.'

'I'm going to have strip lights,' he said. 'Pine woodwork, and striplighting, and a T-logo here and there. For "Tommo", you know.'

'Will you stock *everything*?' she asked, and saw his face light up.

'Everything! Every bloody thing you can put a name to, excuse the language. Electricals down that side, soft goods there, fashion and shoes at the bottom end – male *and* female. Kids' stuff near the door, so they can keep an eye on the prams.'

'You've got it all worked out,' Julie said admiringly.

Suddenly Tommo's arm came round her shoulders and she turned to see his face almost on a level with her own.

'You're a good friend, Julie. No, a good ally, d'you know that?'

Julie felt pleased but uneasy. 'I suppose I have me moments,' she said, moving away as gently as she could so as not to hurt his feelings. 'Anyroad, I'm in here as soon as you like, and don't you forget it. And now, let me tell you about this morning: the only thing that'll stop me from cleaning up this place is if I'm in Durham for GBH on Billy

211

or Nana or both. Wait till you hear what that evil little swine's done now.'

'We could pawn something,' Link said. He and Yvonne were sitting either side of the fire discussing the void in their lives that resembled £50.

'What?' Yvonne said. 'I've parted with every decent thing I had. What I've got now wouldn't fetch 50p.'

'I've got me drums,' Link said gloomily, 'but I might need them if a gig crops up. I've got a few other musical things, too, but I need to keep me practice up.'

'Still,' Yvonne said, 'it'd be better than trouble.' She didn't mention Julie's name but it hung in the air between them.

'Could you get anything out of the Social?' Link asked.

Yvonne shook her head. 'I never have much success there. Not that I've tried much. I feel too ashamed.'

Link stopped miming his triplets and paradiddles, and puffed out his chest. 'That's the wrong attitude, Yvonne. You've got rights. This is a Welfare State, in spite of Maggie Thatcher. No one starves in Britain. We've all got a right to take out of the kitty.'

'But who's putting in, Link? No one in this house. How many in yours actually contribute?' Link did a mental calculation and then dropped his head.

Yvonne shook her head. 'Trevor used to pay his stamp and his taxes, but he was up to every dodge for a rebate. I mean, no one wants to pay, not even when they've got it, do they? They say save the National Health, pay the teachers . . . but when it comes to a penny on income tax it's sod the kidney-machines, close the day nurseries. It's a selfish world, Link.' She was launched on a tirade now. 'Don't think what you can do for Britain. Don't think about your wife and children or your white-haired granny . . . just take, take, take. Take off, in Trevor's case.'

She brooded for a moment and then inspiration struck.

'We could ask Tommo for a loan.'

'Nah,' Link said without hesitation. 'I don't want any favours off him. Besides, we've got no collat.'

'Collat?' Yvonne asked.

'Collateral,' Link said. 'I don't know exactly what it

means but you can't get a loan without it. Even if I had it, and I could get a loan, I wouldn't get one off him, though.'

'I could,' Yvonne said. 'At least I think I could . . . and it's me who owes the money, after all.'

'We're not asking him,' Link said stubbornly. 'He's too well in here as it is.'

'Well, we've got to do something, before the weekend,' Yvonne said. 'Liverpool's sure to score.'

'You could go and ask for your money back,' Link said, cheering up. 'You only had one treatment.' He wrinkled his brow in an agony of arithmetic. 'That makes . . .'

'. . . no sense,' Yvonne finished for him. 'I couldn't go back there, Link. I would sooner . . .' She drew herself up dramatically. '. . . sell my body on the street than face that hell-hole again.'

'You haven't seen Julie when she's really roused,' Link said, 'and if Arsenal scores, and Jinty McGregor comes braying your door for his money . . .'

'I wish I was dead,' Yvonne said bitterly.

'It might come to that, an' all,' Link said and he was only half joking.

Yvonne saw him off from the landing without either of them finding a solution. She had hardly shut the door when someone knocked and she opened it again, expecting to see Link returned. But it was a woman who stood there, her face half-shrouded in a head-scarf.

'I'm sorry to bother you.' The woman spoke slowly as though it was painful to talk. 'I wondered if Julie Baxter was here?'

'No,' Yvonne said. 'She's out, I think. Anyway, she's not here.' Was she mistaken or did the woman slump at her words?

She was already turning away. 'I'll call again. Sorry I bothered you.'

'Wait,' Yvonne said. The woman turned back, and Yvonne saw that the left side of her face was beaten almost to a pulp. As if she feared Yvonne's gaze she averted her face and Yvonne saw she was swaying slightly. 'I think you'd better come in,' she said, and stretched out a hand.

*

'I've decided what you should do with Paris,' Charlotte said as they drove towards the theatre.

'Yes?' Graham said, turning into the car-park and negotiating his way between a Land Rover and an Audi. They were going to see a nondescript thriller with two former soap stars in the lead parts, and he didn't envisage a sparkling evening ahead. Besides, he had almost decided the Paris weekend was going to Julie, if she wanted it. 'Well?' he said, as they climbed out.

'You *should* give it to your cleaner,' Charlotte said decisively. 'I called in today to see if I'd left my diary. I hadn't, but I've found it now. Anyway, we had a talk and I've decided I like her. She won't be needed while you're in Cheshire with me, ergo she should go to Paris. It can be her Christmas present. And I'm going to look out some clothes for her. She's awfully undersized, but I'm sure to have something. Have you got the tickets? We might have time for a drink before the first act, if we hurry.'

They entered the ornate foyer of the theatre, Graham feeling rather pleased with life in general as he took Charlotte's elbow and steered her towards the circle bar. People looked at her admiringly. She would be an asset, no doubt about that – and in the end she had been OK about Julie. Funny little Julie and her wide-eyed interest in anything French. She was a bit like Edith Piaf, actually, now that he thought about it. A little sparrow from the streets.

He bought chocolates for Charlotte, and a stiff souvenir programme filled with lots and lots about nothing at all, and when the lights went down he reached for her hand and held it until the interval.

'And then he stands up . . . with Hunchfront only a few feet away . . . and walks off, calm as you please, with the car practically flat on its chassis and me and Yvonne and the bairn slap-bang in the middle of it,' Julie said.

'So?' Nana said airily. 'He didn't get caught, did he? She can't pin it on him.'

'She can't. I can,' Julie said. 'When he crawls out from

whichsoever stone he's hiding under, I'm going to have his arse tanned for a lampshade.'

'The Germans did that in the war,' Nana said. 'Made things of human skin. Everyone thought that went out with the Iron Curtain, but they didn't know about the Social.' She chuckled suddenly. 'He should've let them tits of hers down while he was on – there'd be more gas in them than in the North Sea.'

Julie had a sudden picture of Hunchfront leaping about like a deflating balloon, making rude noises all the while, but she didn't permit herself a smile. This wasn't funny. And she mustn't let on about Hunchfront and the Wonda-slim – Nana had a mouth like a cross-Channel car-ferry.

'What are you going to do about it, Nana? It may suit you that Billy did for Hunchfront, but the fact remains he could get his collar felt for today's little episode. Dozens of people must've seen him – what if one of them sneaks? What if the police knock on that door in a moment and say they've come for him? It'll be a different tale then; it'll be "beam me up, Scotty" and let Julie get me out of it. I keep telling you, Billy's not a little kid any more. Yes, I used to take Mars Bars back to Woolies, and I persuaded No.20 not to tell the Council about their windows. But this is grown-up stuff he's into now, Nana – no one's laughing any more. No one but you, and you have a chance to have the smile wiped off your face before long. And before you speak, don't say I'd like that, because I wouldn't actually.'

'All right,' Nana said, capitulating suddenly. 'I'll give him a good telling off when he comes in. I'll fettle him, don't worry.'

'Good,' Julie said, mollified. 'How's lover-boy, then?'

'I don't know who you mean,' Nana said airily. 'I've more than one string to my bow, you know.'

'I beg your pardon,' Julie said. 'I meant the distinguished elderly gentleman who goes by the name of Samuel Winterbottom.'

'Well,' said Nana darkly, 'if you'll shut up a minute, I'll tell you all about poor Sammy. He's having a life with that daughter-in-law of his! "Don't sit there, don't step there, don't speak till you're spoken to." She wants his board, but she doesn't want him, if you ask me.'

'What's Sammy's son doing about it?'

'Taking the line of least resistance . . . what men always do when they're between a rock and a hard place. It's only women ever settle anything, really, whatever men may say.'

'You're right there,' Julie said feelingly.

'Sammy had a little business after he left the Navy,' Nana said. 'He sold it to come up here, so he's got a few bob. It was an off-licence, and he got a fair price. His daughter-in-law would like him to snuff it so she could get her hands on the loot, but I've told Sammy to look after himself. "Keep her waiting," I said. "Let her tongue hang out."'

'I should think so,' Julie said. 'Hard bitch!' For once she and Nana parted on a note of sweet accord and Julie went upstairs to bath her kids feeling reasonably at peace with the world.

When her evening chores were done she took Josephine to bed with her. She sat up against the pillows, shrouded in all the woollies from her jumper drawer, putting her free hand between her thighs to warm it and then swopping it with the one that had frozen to a claw from holding the book. She had forgotten that Napoleon too was the subject of the story, for Josephine was beginning to obsess her. She could identify with Josephine in several respects. Josephine had given birth to two children – by an absolute bloody swine, if the book was to be believed. Napoleon was not on the scene yet, but the guillotine was looming. All Josephine cared about, though, was her children's safety, another aspect that endeared her to Julie.

On the day the Tuileries were mobbed Josephine had rushed from the Boulevard St Germain to be with her child in the convent where it was being educated. Julie paused, thinking she might send Damien to a church school now she had seen what the local Infants had done to Jason. Tonight he had said 'Sod off,' when she had mentioned bed-time and she had to clip his legs to get obedience.

She read on, hoping she hadn't been too hard on Jason in order to get at her book. That would be selfish, and not at all like Josephine who was now determined to get both the children to safety following the King's execution. Unfortunately their father, who had never bothered with

216

them up to now, put in an appearance and foiled the escape plan.

A sudden terror seized Julie. What if Gary ever came back and demanded Jason? Worse still, if Dave wanted access to Damien? She could deal with Gary if she had to, but Dave was fly. 'Sharp enough to cut himself,' according to Nana, and she could be clever when she wanted.

'I wouldn't give them up,' Julie thought, trying to concentrate on Josephine. It was no good. She had to pad through to the children's room and check that they were safe and breathing. When she came back to bed she shivered for a while, turning the pages and trying to empathize with Josephine again. It was useless: reading of Josephine's plight only emphasized her own. But she must read something. She had taken Gertrude Stein back to the library on the grounds that she talked a lot about nothing. That only left the Paris guide with the misty Eiffel Tower on the cover. She opened it at random, lighting upon Les Invalides, the burial place of Napoleon.

Six coffins shroud him, hidden under the majestic sarcophagus in dark red porphyry stone designed by Visconti. The crypt also shelters the tombs of great generals of the French Army, and that of Napoleon's young son, who was called the King of Rome.

So Napoleon had come from the back streets of Corsica and made his son the King of Rome! Where would her sons wind up? Not like Billy or Link, please God. That's what it would be though, if she wasn't careful. Julie felt tears prick her eyes, tears she had repressed ever since Charlotte's visit to the flat. It was all very well saying you would take on the world, setting your lip up to anyone and everyone that stood in your way. In the end though, you were a worm – or less than a worm: a leaf that would be blown wherever Fate decided.

She wriggled down in the bed, letting the Eiffel Tower fall from her hand, thinking of the golden girl striding into the flat, key in hand, demonstrating power. She felt terror grip her, but it was too cold to get out of bed and she was too tired to dance. She put out the lamp and turned into her pillow, trying to think of Les Invalides and the red porphyry tomb of Napoleon whom Josephine had loved.

15

For the first time in days there was a hazy sunshine for the walk to school. They went by a different route so they could look in the grounds of the Catholic church to see if the crib had been set up yet. 'It's far too early yet,' Julie had insisted but Jason was adamant. The Christmas toy adverts were on the telly, therefore Santa Claus would be in the shop, and the crib would be in the churchyard. 'OK OK,' Julie had said, when mutiny threatened. 'It's not even December, but you won't be told.'

Privately she railed against toy-manufacturers as they walked uphill. The summer was hardly out before they started brain-washing kids, drenching the little girls with sickly-sweet dolly ads, zapping little lads with weaponry. If Jason got everything lethal he'd asked for so far, they could stand down the three Services and leave Jason to cope on his own.

'There,' she said, when they found the grotto bare except for the usual statue of Virgin and Child, 'now will you believe me?' She wondered if she should explain that Baby Jesus was still there, even if he wasn't in a crib with wise men in attendance. In the end she said nothing, not out of disbelief but because the whole subject was so vast that she couldn't cope – not at quarter to nine in the morning, anyway.

As they breasted the rise and began to move down towards school again she looked across towards Shields Road. The gable end stood out, still red brick and bare but garlanded now with scaffolding and, right at the bottom, a few feet of green paint. She hoped they would make a success of the mural. Link needed a good achievement. If he didn't get something solid in his life soon he would probably waffle on forever. She looked at Jason, moving ahead of her now, his navy-corduroy-covered legs pumping steadily on towards school. He was her anchor, he and Damien. Sometimes they felt like millstones, but really they made a focus for her life. 'I couldn't live without them,' she thought. 'Or I wouldn't want to,' which was the same thing.

Jason was turning. 'Come on,' he said bossily. 'Why did we come this way?' He didn't say, 'It's all your fault,' but it was there in his eyes. For a moment Julie wanted to tell him whose idea it had been, expletives undeleted. In the end she just quickened her pace. Mothers were there to be blamed, after all, especially for your own actions when they went wrong.

Nana was lurking in the hall when she got back. 'I've had an idea,' she said.

Julie let out a theatrical groan.

'Now, shut up,' Nana said. 'You'll like it when you hear it.' She looked spruce again and Julie could've sworn there were spots of rouge on her cheekbones.

'I'm going to have a party,' Nana declared, folding her hands over her stomach while the effect of her words went home.

'Acid House or Tupperware?' Julie said, but Nana just looked mildly irritated.

'I'm going to give a party,' she repeated. 'You can come, and her upstairs – £2.50 each.'

'Ha!' Julie said. 'I knew your Billy was behind this somewhere.'

'It's got nothing to do with our Billy,' Nana said. 'He doesn't even know about it. You're the first one I've told. We'll have ten people – she won't come for less than fifteen quid, and there's the food to pay for. I'll get the others. There's plenty of them. She'll only have women, but that's all right . . .'

'She?' Julie asked. 'Who's she?'

Nana's tongue tsked against her teeth. 'I've just told you, her from Rosamond Street. The medium – clair . . . fancy something. She tells you what's going to happen in the future. They say she's uncanny.'

'I'd've said she was very canny at fifteen quid a night for telling lies.'

'She doesn't tell lies,' Nana said patiently. 'Ask anyone. She takes something belonging to you . . .'

'Two pound fifty,' Julie said.

'Be serious,' Nana insisted. 'She takes your watch or your ring or something, and then she tells you everything that's going to happen. If *you* don't want to know about your life there's plenty will. Anyroad . . .' She turned and leered. 'I'd've thought you'd need to know, the way you're carrying on. Tallymen in and out all hours of the night, half-wits hanging round, fancy men paying for your services . . . oh yes, if anyone's in need of a few tips, you are.'

From the corner of her eye Julie had watched Billy come nearer and nearer to the door, drawn by his interest in what his grandmother was saying. Now Julie pounced, flinging back the door to grab his arm.

'Who have we here, then? Let any good tyres down lately, Billy? Well, don't stand here listening to your Nana. She's got another bee in her bonnet, but it needn't concern you because I can see your future all too clearly and I don't need a crystal ball. A nice long custodial, that's what you'll get.'

Nana had managed to collect herself. 'What are you doing here, Billy? I thought you went off long enough ago. Now, off you go like a good lad. And stick in.'

Julie expected an argument but for once Billy seemed happy enough to obey. He shot the cuffs of his shirt from the sleeves of his denim bomber-jacket, flicked up his jacket collar and slid between them to the door.

'He's up to something,' Julie thought, narrowing her eyes, but Nana gazed after him fondly.

'He's broadening out, isn't he? I see it every day. He's turning into a man.' The depth of affectionate satisfaction in her voice defeated Julie.

'I've got to get on,' she said, lifting Damien from the pushchair.

'Tell her upstairs,' Nana said. 'Two pound fifty. It's not much to find out whether your man's coming back or not.'

'I'll tell Yvonne,' Julie said, 'but I was under the impression you couldn't stand the sight of her?'

'I can't,' Nana said, 'but I need the numbers, don't I? Besides, you can't help feeling sorry for her. No backbone, and a face like the north end of a southbound cow. She's hardly been lucky up to now.'

Yvonne's eyes grew round as Julie relayed the invitation. 'A fortune-teller? Will she be any good?'

'No,' Julie said. 'She'll tell you what she thinks you want to hear and take your money, that's all.'

'How will she know what I want to hear?' Yvonne countered.

'Well, it won't be easy,' Julie said, 'seeing as I don't think you know what you want yourself. You say you want Trevor back but you do nothing about it. I see you've taken the dress down. You don't like to be reminded, do you? Well, carry on as you are. It'll end in tears, though, mark my words.'

'Everything ends in tears,' Yvonne said bitterly. 'That's the one thing I *am* sure of.' She leaned forward. 'Still, I'm not the only one with troubles.'

'What d'you mean?' Julie said, interested now.

'I had a visitor last night.' Yvonne paused for dramatic effect. 'Your friend Rose. Her face was like a pudding, Julie. You've never seen the like of it.'

'Him again!' Julie said angrily.

'She didn't say, but I knew it was a man. I mean, you don't walk into lamp-posts, do you?'

'Is that what she said?'

'Yes. Said she heard somebody call her name and it distracted her. I made her a cup of tea and I said to wait for you, but she had to go. Poor girl.'

Julie had no doubt that Yvonne did pity Rose, but there was another note in her voice as well – a slight smugness at hearing of someone worse off than herself.

By the time she got to work Julie had put Rose to the back of her mind and was having second thoughts about Nana's party. It still sounded like a load of rubbish, but what harm could it do? They would have a laugh and a night out and a reason to dress up. Nana would have to be civil to Yvonne, and that might improve the atmosphere all round. Besides, you never knew about psychics . . . sometimes they did have a gift. And it would be nice to see into the future. At least, it might be. Julie made herself a vow to believe it if it was good and dismiss it if it wasn't.

When she had hoovered and polished and cleaned she took down the oilskin bag with the Martini logo and went out with Graham's shopping list.

She caught sight of Rose as she was leaving the bread stall. Her face was as bad as Yvonne had said, and she was as pale as death, with dark rings around her eyes. On the spur of the moment Julie issued an invitation.

'Listen, Rose. Fancy a night out? The woman under me's having a fortune party – £2.50 and you get to hear your fate.' They both laughed then, certain that they knew the most life had in store for them.

'Will your neighbour be there, the one upstairs? Did she tell you I called round?'

'Yes,' Julie said. 'Yvonne mentioned it, and she'll be there.'

'Oh well,' Rose said, 'it's a night out, isn't it?'

'Girls only,' Julie said.

Some people couldn't stand hen parties but Rose smiled wanly. 'That clinches it. If I never see a man again it'll be too soon for me.'

'You're still with him, though?' Julie asked and Rose nodded.

'I haven't the guts to move out, if that's what you mean. Anyroad, now I've got this he'll lay off. It won't last, but it's nice while it does.' She scribbled her address so Julie could let her know the date of the party and they parted on a wave of Rose's perfume.

'Not cheap,' Julie thought – and Rose's clothes were good, too. All the same she certainly paid for them.

Julie was putting away the shopping in Graham's kitchen when the phone rang. 'Julie?' It was Graham, and her heart began to thump. Had she done something wrong? Or had Charlotte put the block on things?

'Look,' he said, 'I've been thinking. That Paris trip . . .' She felt the room revolve. He was going to ask her to go

223

with him. Dreams did come true! She had always known it. She heard her own voice, small and stilted.

'The one you won?'

'Yes, that's it. The thing is . . . I can't go.'

She felt a sudden tremendous relief that ruled out the possibility of disappointment. She couldn't have coped, anyway: he would have found her out.

'And I want you to have it. We . . . that is, I think it would be a good opportunity for you. You've never been abroad . . . now's your chance.'

Julie tried hard to keep her head. 'How much is it?'

'It's nothing, knucklehead. I won it . . . it's a gift to you. And if you're worried about spending-money, I can advance your wages. It's for two, so you could take a friend. Jason's probably too young . . .'

'Yes,' Julie said, trying to analyse her feelings. 'Yes, Jason couldn't go.'

'The woman in the upstairs flat, then?' Graham said. 'The one you worry about?'

'Yvonne. Yes, Yvonne might come with me.'

'I must go now, I'm due in court . . . but we'll talk about it tomorrow.'

Julie put down the phone and walked through to the kitchen. She wasn't going to France with Graham Iley. On the other hand half a loaf . . . she moved to the kettle and filled it, then poured half the water away before she switched it on. For once in her life she was nonplussed, and a cup of coffee would help.

By the time she got home she had wound herself up into a state of wild excitement. 'I'm going to Paris,' she told Nana. 'Paris, Paris, Paris!'

'Send my congratulations to Rome and Berlin,' Nana said tartly, and leaned closer. 'I've had Sammy round again. Poor Sammy.'

'Did you hear what I said?' Julie asked. 'I said I'm going to Paris.'

'I heard the first time,' Nana said. 'It'll be another of your hare-brained schemes, no doubt. And who'll have your kids, 'cos don't look at me and our Billy . . .'

'Leave my kids with your Billy?' Julie said. 'I'd sooner trust them to a crocodile.'

Nana smiled serenely. 'Sticks and stones, Julie Baxter, sticks and stones. Sammy thinks my Billy's a fine lad.'

From within the room came the sound of violent retching. 'Billy sounds pleased about that,' Julie said sweetly.

'He'll come round,' Nana said. 'Now less the talk about Paris and listen about this party. I've booked the wife from Rosamond Street . . .'

'. . . and I've asked a friend of mine – Rose, they call her, I don't know her second name. But she's coming.'

'She knows it's £2.50, doesn't she?' Nana said.

'Yes,' Julie said, climbing the stairs. 'We all know it's £2.50. Just don't put your Billy on the door. Although . . .' She paused and looked down. 'If she's so clever with the crystal ball she'll have him pegged before she gets here.'

She took the news about Paris to the top floor. 'Want to come?' she asked Yvonne. 'It's all paid for, bar spending-money.'

'I couldn't,' Yvonne said firmly. 'I'm never going out of this country again, it only leads to trouble. I haven't got over Spain. A £350 package, and it ruined my life. You want to watch yourself if you go to Paris . . . you could pay a bitter price for it.'

'You know, Yvonne,' Julie said, 'if you're not very careful you're going to turn into a bore. It's all misery with you. Moan, moan, moan.'

'What have I got to be happy about?' Yvonne was stung. 'I talk misery because it's all I've got to talk about. In case you haven't noticed, I'm in debt – heavily in debt. If I don't find £50 by the weekend Link has a chance to get his legs broken. Where's the sunshine in that? If you can find any, let me know!'

'I know you've got it tough,' Julie said, scooping up Damien's things and reaching to pick him up too. 'But you want to go in for some positive thinking.'

Yvonne nodded. 'Positive thinking? You're right. I'll start right now. I positively think that if you're not out of this flat in one minute flat I am positively likely to do you harm.'

'There you are,' Julie said. 'That's what I like to hear.' And then, as Yvonne looked around for a weapon, 'All right, all right, I'm going.'

225

She had collected Jason from school and was running home with him on the step of the pushchair when Tommo pulled alongside them. 'I don't need a lift,' Julie said. 'I'm enjoying the walk. But I'll have the kettle on as soon as I get in, if you want a cuppa.'

'I'll go with Tommo,' Jason said, trying to get between her legs to the van. She watched Tommo fold him in and then set off briskly. Tommo would keep an eye on things while she was in Paris. Not just the kids . . . Yvonne was reliable enough in that direction. No, it was the house in general she would worry about while she was gone. Anything could happen in two days – anything!

'Are you sure you should go?' Tommo said dubiously when she told him. 'It's a big city. I mean, a girl on her own . . .'

'I won't be going on me own,' Julie said, shocked. 'I wouldn't dare do that. No, I'll take someone. I asked Yvonne, but she can't. And I don't think she would if she could.'

'I think she's not too keen on Europe,' Tommo said, grinning. Julie was about to say, 'What about you?' but the ticket was for a double room. She tried to imagine sharing a bed with Tommo. He would smell nice and feel nice . . . she imagined his face above flannel pyjamas and found the prospect pleasing. But it wouldn't be fair. Instead she said, 'I could ask Rose. She's a woman I know who's had it rough. A break would do her good.'

But even as she spoke, Julie knew Rose wouldn't come: she was like a moth to a flame, hating the burn but unable to fly from danger. She would probably wind up taking Link, although he was enough of a liability on his own home ground, let alone in a foreign capital.

'What about spending-money?' Tommo asked as they drank their tea.

'Funny you should say that,' Julie said, trying not to grin. 'What am I good for?'

He pursed his lips. 'Well, you're a good payer.'

'So I should be,' she said. 'I've been juggling debt since I learned me two times table. I shouldn't really take out any more, but what option have I got? I'm not passing up a chance like this for a few quid spending-money. And I'll

226

need something to wear – nothing much, just some nice trousers and a top . . . and maybe a pair of shoes.'

Tommo groaned. 'We're talking mortgages here. Still, I think we can arrange something. Not on the books, not at their rate of interest. I'll loan you out of me own pocket . . .'

Julie began to protest but he held up a hand. 'No, listen. I'm going to rely on you when I get this business off the ground. You've got ideas, and that's not my strong point. I'll get me money back, with interest, only it'll be in kind.'

Julie couldn't resist the impulse then to lean forward and kiss his cheek. It smelled nice, as she knew it would. 'I'll help you, Tommo. You'll be a bloody entrepreneur by the time I'm finished.'

'There,' Charlotte said, unzipping the holdall. 'They ought to fit, and they're good quality. What she had on the other day was tat. I had heaps of shoes too but she's nowhere near a size six.'

'Good,' Graham said, trying to pretend an enthusiasm he didn't feel. He could hardly say, 'Here's a pile of second-hand clothes,' without it sounding insulting. And lately he had thought Julie looked quite nice . . . a bit showy, perhaps, and cheap material, but the way she dressed suited her.

He lifted the holdall on to a chair and went to get glasses and a corkscrew.

'Hmm,' Charlotte said, 'nice wine. French?'

'Marks and Sparks,' Graham said. 'Now, what's this about Ally's wedding?'

'She's having the most terrible trouble, because of it being done in such a hurry. Photographers and cars and things like that are booked yonks ahead nowadays. And she's being really childish about it. "Face facts," I told her when she rang today. "This is a shotgun wedding and that's no one's fault but your own."'

'I thought they were getting married anyway?'

'They were, but no one could understand the haste. Now we know why – Ally slipped up.'

'Surely Michael had something to do with it?' Graham said.

'No,' Charlotte replied firmly. 'She was on the pill and Michael trusted her to do it efficiently.'

'That's all very well,' Graham said, feeling a desperate sympathy for Ally, the black sheep of the family. 'But accidents do happen . . .'

'Not if you're careful,' Charlotte said. 'If I ever tell you I'm pregnant you can be quite sure I intended to be.'

'You wouldn't do that to me?' he asked in mock-anguish, trying to divert Charlotte from her soap-box.

'I might,' she said teasingly. 'If I couldn't bring you to the brink any other way.'

'Schemer,' he said. 'By the way, I told Julie she could have the Paris trip.'

'Have you seen her today?' Charlotte asked sharply.

'No, I rang her. She was . . . well, a bit taken aback, I think.'

'So she bloody well should be, darling. In the job five minutes and she gets a two or three-hundred-pound bonus.'

'Hardly that.'

'Well, three figures anyway. Who's she taking with her?'

'I didn't go into details. She's probably got a boyfriend.'

'With her track record that's more than likely,' Charlotte said, stretching her arms above her head so that her breasts thrust forward against her sweater. She looked good when she did it, almost feline, but Graham could never quite convince himself that it was an unconscious gesture.

'I don't really think she's very . . . well, sexy, for want of a better word,' Graham said.

'What is she, then?' Charlotte was amused now. 'Chaste? Virginal? You're not claiming immaculate conceptions, are you?'

'I'm not claiming anything,' Graham said. 'Anyway, why are we talking about Julie when . . .' He reached for her and pulled her against him . . . 'there are more important things to discuss?'

'Like what?' she said, swinging her legs up on to the settee and snuggling closer.

'Like what I wear to this wedding. I want to make a good

228

impression.' He dipped his middle finger in his wine and dabbed behind his ears. 'I fancy pink, myself. It's my colour!'

Julie had wrung out Jason's socks for the morning and hung them above the fire when she heard Yvonne at the door. 'Julie, are you there?'

'Where else would I be, Yvonne?'

'Don't be sarky. Not now. I think we've got a problem. I saw Billy go out of the back door – I was in my kitchen, and I could see him in the light from the street lamp.'

'So he's out again,' Julie said. 'I've given up on that. He's a bloody little escape artist and there's nothing I can do about it.'

'I know,' Yvonne said. 'But he's just come back again, carrying something.' She paused. 'And he's hidden it in the old WC.' There was an ancient outside lavatory in the yard, relic of an earlier occupation and unused nowadays except in emergencies. 'He was in there for ages.'

'Not another theodolite, please God,' Julie said. 'Where is he now?'

'I think he's gone back into the flat . . . I'm not sure.'

'We better go down and have a look,' Julie said. 'And then we can tackle him with the evidence.'

They let themselves out into the dark yard, the light from the street lamps brilliant above the wall, a well of darkness below.

'Wait for me,' Yvonne said and took a firm grip of the back waist of Julie's jeans. They opened the wooden door of the outhouse, trying to set it back as silently as possible. 'Pooh,' Yvonne said, 'this place stinks.'

A paper-wrapped bundle lay in the far corner, and Julie stirred it with her foot. She sniffed. And then sniffed again.

'Stand out of the light, Yvonne.'

Yvonne moved obediently aside and Julie bent to unwrap the bundle, sniffing as she did so. 'Sweet and sour, egg-fried rice, prawn curry . . .' The empty cartons lay on the greaseproof wrappings. Yvonne was also sniffing the air.

'Someone's been sick in here.'

'I'm not surprised,' Julie said. 'There's five cartons here, and two of them are curry sauce. Even he couldn't finish them all.' She sounded abstracted and Yvonne knew something was coming.

'What I want to know,' Julie said at last, 'is where he got five quid, because that's what this little lot must have cost. Five quid and not a penny less.'

Yvonne sighed, and then smiled up into the lamplight. 'Well, at least there's nothing to put back this time. Not that I didn't enjoy the enterprise, but once was quite enough.'

Julie looked up the yard towards Nana's curtained window. 'He's been up to something, Yvonne, and I'll find out what if I have to kill him in the process.'

16

Julie had slept intermittently, dreaming of Chinese take-aways and *The Sweeney*, and waking once in a sweat because a policewoman was pulling packet after packet of Christian Dior stockings from Yvonne's double oven. She was glad when she could get out of bed and spend her usual five minutes looking out on the still-sleeping Grimshaw Street. She was just sitting down with her tea when she heard a tapping on the door. Yvonne again with more forensic, no doubt.

But it was Link who stood there, a Dr Who muffler around his neck, a flask and bait-can under his arm. 'I'm on me way to work, Julie, so I can't stop.'

'Good,' she said, returning to her tea.

'I've come about this party,' he said, sitting down across the table from her. 'I'm coming. I'll have me £2.50 all ready.'

'You can't come, it's women only,' Julie said.

'You're joking. I mean, I need to come.'

'Well you can't. Unless you have a sex-change by tonight.'

Link leaned forward. 'I *need* to know my future, Julie. I've got plans.'

'If you've got plans, you don't need to know . . . or rather you do know because you've already decided.' She put her head on one side and considered. 'Don't try to work that out, Link, because I don't know what it means meself. Anyway, you can't come to the party so forget it. However,' she paused for dramatic effect, 'if you behave yourself you might . . . just might . . . be going somewhere better.'

'Where?' Link asked sceptically.

231

'Paris.'

He got to his feet. 'Yeah, I know. How am I going? Concorde?' He turned in the doorway. 'One of these days you'll stop taking the piss out of me, Julie.'

'I don't think so, Link. It's the only pleasure I've got.'

Yvonne caught Tommo at the end of Rosamond Street. 'Mr Thompson!' He knew she was after a loan as soon as he looked at her. He had seen nice women before with twin spots of colour in their cheeks as they begged for temporary respite from their troubles.

'You're formal this morning, Yvonne.'

'Well, actually, it was business I wanted to see you about.'

'Fire away then – unless you want me to call round your place?'

'No.' She shifted her grip on the pushchair. 'No, here'll be fine. The thing is . . .'

Tommo saw her agony and felt sympathy. She wasn't used to this. 'How much, Yvonne?'

'Fifty pounds,' she blurted. 'The thing is, I need it by Saturday.'

'Are you sure you need it?' he said gently. 'Loans don't come cheap, you know. If you want to buy something, you'd be better off getting an account.'

'I can't get credit,' she said. 'I have no status, you see. I'm just relying on you knowing me . . . knowing I won't let you down. And anyway, it's money I need – I owe someone.'

'It's not gambling, is it?' Tommo asked, alarmed. Women could get into terrible trouble if they got the itch.

'No,' Yvonne said, 'nothing like that. And it won't happen again, I can promise you that.'

'OK,' he said, suddenly remembering the money she had borrowed from Link for the slimming treatment. 'We'll see what can be done. I'll come round later on and do the paperwork. You going to this fortune-telling party tonight?'

'I am if I get the £50,' Yvonne said.

'Bad as that?' Tommo said, as he prepared to get back into the van.

'Worse,' Yvonne answered, grasping the pushchair. 'Still, I might get good news tonight about the future. You never know.'

'I'm expecting to hear all the gen, mind . . . all the millionaires and sudden windfalls and unexpected visitors from the past.' He was making jokes but Yvonne thought he looked strained.

'Is everything all right . . . with you, I mean?' she asked.

'Yeah, I'm OK. I've got to talk to my mother tonight . . . about a bit of business, and everything. I don't want her to hear from someone else.'

'Mebbe she'll be pleased?' Yvonne said.

He shook his head. 'I doubt it. Still, it's got to be faced.' He turned on the engine and she knew he didn't want to talk about his mother any more.

'Well, I hope it goes well,' she said and moved off.

In the van Tommo opened up his account book. Yvonne had been the only person in Grimshaw Street not on his books – now she too had fallen. He looked up at the sky and shook his head. Tick was the twentieth-century disease, and no one was even working on a cure.

Throughout the day Julie's attitude towards the evening at Nana's had vacillated. On the one hand, it was a change, a bit of variety. On the other, she had so much to think about, so many plans to make, that she almost begrudged leaving her flat. By half-past five, however, she had to become whole-hearted.

'Get yourself down here,' Nana called up the stair-well. 'I can't do everything on me own.' There was bread to slice and spread with butter, pickles to open, tomatoes to quarter and corned beef to slice. 'I've got sly-cake for afters,' Nana said, 'and there's plenty tea and sugar.'

Billy was sitting in the fireside chair, his face half-shielded by a lurid comic.

'You don't look good,' Julie said to him solicitously. 'Had a heavy supper last night, did you?'

His eyes flicked up, and back to the comic.

'Curry sauce?' Julie said. 'Spare ribs Peking-style? Egg-

233

fried rice, swimming in fat? Yes, that's got to you, hasn't it?' Billy's lip attempted a snarl, and then wobbled.

'There were five quid's worth of empties, Billy. Five quid's worth down the outside lav. But never mind about that . . . just tell me where you got the money to buy them.'

'Get lost!' Billy was gaining confidence again and Julie knew she had to be quick or lose the advantage.

'I'll get lost as soon as you tell me, and your Nana, where you got five quid.'

'I don't know what she's on about.' Billy addressed Nana.

'See,' Nana said. 'You've misjudged him again.'

'My God, he may be an evil little sod but he's clever,' Julie said. 'The one consolation is he'll come to a sticky end one day.'

'He probably will, with you ill-wishing him all the time.'

Julie's eyes rolled heavenwards. 'From your lips to God's ear, Nana!'

'Where's my stuff?' Jason asked when she went back upstairs.

'What stuff?'

'Trifle and things.' He had his Arthur-Scargill I-want-my-rights-look and Julie tried not to smile.

'There's no trifle. It's not a party like that . . . it's just bread and meat and things.'

Outrage crossed Jason's face, closely followed by his Help-me-I'm-deprived look.

'You know what you are?' Julie asked. 'A ruddy little manipulator.'

If he understood what she said, he didn't show it. 'I want some party food,' he said and set his jaw.

She gave him two tinned frankfurters and a munchmallow, and promised herself she would regulate his diet tomorrow. He looked OK but you could never be sure.

He went to bed easily enough, and Damien went out like a light. 'You know where I'm going to be,' Julie told Jason. 'Down Nana's. I'll leave the doors open and the lights on, and John and Andrea are upstairs as well, so you'll be OK.'

He nodded, his eyes already droopy with sleep. Julie

went into the bathroom and was back-combing her hair when she heard Link on the landing.

'I thought she might've changed her mind,' he said. 'I've got me £2.50.'

'She hasn't, so buzz off,' Julie said.

'Anything to eat?' he asked hopefully. She put down her comb while she spread him bread and Marmite and scalded a coffee. 'Now off you go,' she said, when he had wolfed the lot. 'Nana won't change her mind; there's no way you'll get in; no one will crack; you've had your chips; so don't spoil my night by haunting the place. Just give up and go home, Link, then we can all enjoy ourselves.'

He shook his head as though in wonderment. 'You've turned hard, Julie. I don't know why I bother sometimes.' Before she could retaliate he went on. 'But you'll be sorry before long – when you see what I'm prepared to do for you.'

'You're buying me a Porsche,' Julie said.

'No, I'm doing something better than that. Something special. You'll be sorry . . . you'll regret . . .' His reproaches echoed up the stair-well as she pushed him downwards.

Julie looked in on the kids, removing Jason's Turtle figure from his sleeping fingers and tucking in his bedclothes. Now for the future! In spite of all her reservations she couldn't help feeling excited as she went downstairs.

'She hasn't come yet,' Nana said.

'Who?' Julie asked, surveying the empty room.

'Madame Zohree.'

Julie's eyes widened. 'Madame who?'

'Zohree. Zoe-ree. None of you kids can hear straight. It's those diskets . . . you've got no eardrums left.'

'I thought it was the wife from Rosamond Street?'

'It is . . . that's her, Madame Zohree. They say she's wonderful. She went to Effie Taylor's and looked into her hand. "I see the sea rising," she says. So Effie looks down the runners at Sandown and there it is: Ocean Swell. Willie Carson up, ten to one. Effie puts the gas money on and it romps home.' Nana looked triumphant for a moment and then her face fell. 'I hope she's not coming to an empty house here. I told her ten people. Where's Yvonne?'

'Upstairs, I expect.'

'Well, go and get her. Not that I like her, mind – she could make trouble in an empty house, that one – but . . .'

'. . . you need her £2.50,' Julie finished. She went up the stairs and opened Yvonne's door. Several parcels were scattered around the room and Yvonne stood in the middle trying to zip up a striped dress. Julie looked at the parcels.

'What's this lot?'

'Just a few odds and ends . . . from a catalogue.'

Julie reached out and tugged at the striped dress. 'Well, I can see it's odd but I can't see the end.'

'Now don't start, Julie.'

'I'm not saying a word . . . except that you don't fit that dress.'

'Do you wonder! Trevor hasn't paid for two weeks, and the giro's gone to the gas, so we've been living on fritters.'

'What kind of fritters?' Julie asked.

'Anything you can dip in batter . . . onion, potato, cornflake packet. The kids are playing war.' Yvonne managed to pull up the zip and gasped. 'There now . . . what d'you think?' She twirled around and there was a long pause before Julie spoke.

'Why are you buying on tick?'

'I haven't got ready money.'

'You mean you've frittered it away,' Julie said, and then, as Yvonne failed to smile, 'Sorry.' She put out a consoling hand. 'Come on down quickly, and cheer up. You might get some good news tonight.'

There were four more people in the room when Julie got back to Nana's flat, three elderly women whom she recognized from around the doors . . . and Link.

'What's *he* doing here?' she demanded.

'We're running short,' Nana said firmly.

'You said no men,' Julie insisted.

'Well, Link's all right then because he's still coming and going. Now, where's the . . .'

There was a knock at the door and Madame Zohree appeared. She was a tall, handsome woman wearing a black throw and large drop earrings. She carried a holdall emblazoned with *Fly British Airways* and a table lamp with a red shade.

'You've arrived,' Nana said, looking pleased. Julie eyed the bag.

'You've come by British Airways. I thought you'd've come on a broom stick.'

Nana gasped but Madame Zohree merely narrowed her eyes at Julie, obviously marking her down as a trouble-maker.

'Is this the room?' she said, looking around her. 'I need to soak in atmosphere.' She put down the lamp and holdall and put a hand to her head, as though in pain. 'I'll let you know when I'm ready. Do they know about the fee?'

'Oh yes,' Nana said. 'You won't have any trouble there.'

Madame Zohree sat down and used a long fingernail to unearth a scrap of food from her teeth. She looked at it for a moment and then popped it back into her mouth. Suddenly she spoke again. 'I need a small dish for the contributions. I don't like handling money . . . not when I'm on a higher plane.'

'We're back to British Airways,' Julie said, *sotto voce*.

Madame Zohree looked at her. 'You don't live here,' she said, frowning. 'At least, not in this room. I see stairs . . . and there's a child . . . no, two children. One dark, one fair.' She peered at Julie. 'Surely not yours, you're not old enough. And yet I see them . . .'

In spite of herself Julie was impressed. 'See?' Nana hissed in her ear.

'Can I go down to the end of the room?' Madame Zohree asked, taking the dish Nana proffered. 'I need my lamp and a little space . . . then I'll be ready to give.' She sighed deeply as Nana and Julie carried the table to a corner and plugged in the lamp.

At that moment Yvonne entered the room, a vision of brown and white stripes, a clean hanky clutched in either hand. One of the elderly women leaned forward to Julie.

'You'll be well satisfied when she does you. She's always good. It's a gift.'

'I thought it was £2.50,' Julie said but she was beginning to wonder. After all the woman had never seen her before, and yet she'd been spot on about the kids.

'Right,' Madame Zohree said. 'I think I'm ready. Can we have the main light off, please, and the first one here?'

The three elderly women leaped forward like greyhounds from the trap, but she put up an imperious finger and summoned the middle one forward. Nana put out the light and the pair at the table went into a huddle, the medium's voice droning on. Julie sat down beside Yvonne.

'What do you think?' Yvonne whispered.

'I don't know what I think,' Julie said. 'Half an hour ago I thought it was a load of rubbish, but now . . . she just looked me in the eye and out it came, Yvonne. The kids and everything. So I'm keeping an open mind.'

'So you've been done?' Yvonne said.

'No, that was just a taster. I've still got it to come.'

Yvonne shifted uneasily. 'I'm not sure I can stand it.'

'Well, lie down to it, Yvonne, because you're needed to make up numbers.'

The elderly woman was leaving the table and another was taking her place. 'Dynamic,' the first one said. 'That's all I can say . . . dynamic. "You've suffered," she said just like that. She got my gallstone and my dad's military medal and she says I'm going abroad.'

Billy emerged from the bedroom and crossed to whisper in his Nana's ear. She reached up to the mantelpiece for money and pressed it in his hand. 'There you are,' she said. 'And watch the road.'

'Sod you,' he said smoothly and once again Julie felt doubts. Billy was too bloody happy at the moment, too happy by half.

The other old lady took her turn. 'You're next, Yvonne,' Julie said.

'I can't, Julie. Me nerve's gone.'

'You're going, Yvonne.'

'I'm not,' Yvonne said, firming her lips.

'It's Wednesday today,' Julie said. 'I only allow mutinies on Tuesdays and Thursdays.'

'Well, you'll have to come with me,' Yvonne said. Julie stood up.

'All right . . . let's get it over.'

Madame Zohree motioned them to chairs and pushed the saucer forward. Yvonne put in £2.50 and her eyes brimmed. Madame reached for her hand.

'I see water.'

'She's spot on there, Yvonne,' Julie said.

Madame gazed closer at Yvonne's palm. 'There's separation here.'

'Oh God,' Yvonne said.

'It's gone on a long time.'

'Oh God,' Yvonne said again.

'It's going on a lot longer,' the medium said. This time it was Julie's turn to moan.

'Oh God,' she said. 'Oh God!'

'Well?' Charlotte said, pirouetting in front of Graham. The red velvet frock with its petticoats swirled around her legs, the low neck stood away from the curve of her breasts and showed off her long, firm throat.

'It's lovely,' Graham said. Charlotte twirled again and looked down at herself.

'It feels nice . . . ceremonial. I wouldn't be seen dead in it ordinarily, but it's what Ally's always wanted. And when we get the shoes and stockings and the gloves and head-dress . . . I can bear it for one day.' Her long bare legs were still brown, and her navy tights lay where she had discarded them. She looked special in the red velvet dress, like someone from a Gainsborough picture. Graham moved to her and took her in his arms.

'Be careful,' she said. 'Watch the frock, you monster.'

'I'm not interested in the frock,' Graham said. Charlotte smelled good – flowery and fresh – and her flesh under his hands was firm to his touch.

'I'd better take it off then,' she said demurely. They moved to the bedroom and started to undress in a leisurely fashion. 'I can't stay too long,' she said as they climbed into bed. 'Mummy is ringing tonight to finalize one or two things. Besides . . .' she sighed as she moved into his arms. 'I haven't done my list.'

'List?' he queried.

'Yes. Things to be done. You know, everyone has one. I tick mine off every night but today, shopping for the dress, it all got away from me.'

'So,' he said, his hand moving from her waist to her ribs to her breast.

'So everything,' she said. 'You have to keep on top of things. I'm very organized, darling. I like things to be right.'

Suddenly Graham wished she would stop talking. While she was waffling he could feel desire slipping away. Fear consumed him, the fear of not being able to perform, the one unmentionable, the thing you couldn't acknowledge even to yourself. He buried his face in her scented neck, trying to think of all the wicked things that come unbidden to the mind but refuse to surface on demand.

They all made a pretence of eating the party food but their ears were cocked for the slightest whisper from the corner where Madame Zohree was conducting her tête-à-têtes. 'Your turn now, Julie,' Nana said and stood back to let Julie get by.

A lot of what Madame Zohree said was predictable: handsome men, and money in abundance, an illness in someone close which would pass. But then came the nub: 'You'll go abroad, I can see it here. A capital city. But you want to get away from here, right away. There's nothing for you here, nothing but trouble and strife.'

'That figures,' Julie said but Madame ignored her.

'Go while you can, before it's too late,' she said. Then briskly, 'Right, I think that's you done.'

There was a knock at the door as Julie stood up, and then it opened.

'Rose!' Yvonne said, suddenly sounding cheerful. Rose was paler than ever but her bruises were well covered with make-up and she looked smart in a black dress with bugle-beading on the bodice.

'This is Rose, Nana,' Julie said and Nana graciously inclined her head.

'Pleased to meet you,' Rose murmured.

Nana looked pointedly at Rose's bare ring-finger and then nodded towards Madame Zohree. 'You go next. She might cheer you up.'

Rose sat close to Madame Zohree, who went straight into her spiel once the £2.50 was safely secured.

'Poor thing,' Yvonne said, looking at Rose. Again there was that note, almost of jubilation in her voice.

'Poor stupid thing,' Julie said. 'She wants to give that man the heave-ho.'

Yvonne sprang to Rose's defence. 'You make it sound so easy, Julie, but then you've never had a relationship to break up, so you can't understand. It's not all black and white.'

'No,' Julie said sweetly. 'It's black and blue, Yvonne, up with which no woman should have to put!'

At that moment Rose stood up and came to rejoin them, and Link almost knocked over the table in his eagerness to be next.

'What did she tell you, Rose?'

Rose smiled ruefully. 'Nothing I didn't know. She got a lot of things wrong but a few things right. She said I should leave Ray . . . well, we all know that.'

Nana had come to their side. She leered at Yvonne. 'She told *her* her man wasn't coming back. He's run off to Spain.'

A blush mantled Yvonne's cheeks. 'I wouldn't say he's run off. He's gone to look for work.'

'He's buggered off,' Nana said, her old self now that Yvonne's £2.50 was safely in the bag. 'And if and when he comes back, you want to tell him to go rattle his castanets.'

'Coarse,' Yvonne said. 'Coarse.'

Link came back, jerking and shaking as though to music audible only to him. 'She knew I was a musician.'

'Well, it was either that or St Vitus's Dance,' Nana said and went to take his place opposite the clairvoyant. During the long, hushed conversation that followed, Nana seemed to droop. 'I'd love to know what's going on up there,' Julie said *sotto voce* as she watched them, but just then Nana stood up and began to potter on with the dining-table, moving food from one plate to another in an aimless fashion.

At the other end of the room Madame Zohree was gathering up her money and the three elderly ladies were starting to twitter.

'We ought to be going now, Edie. It's cracking on and

241

we don't like corners at night. Thanks for the food and the opportunity.'

The second lady leaned forward. 'We could have a weegie board next time, and explore the unconscious.'

'Start with Link,' Julie said. 'He's half-way there already. Still, he'll see you home.'

'I wasn't going yet,' Link said, looking at the table where there was still bread and butter and a solitary piece of sly-cake.

'You were,' Julie said. 'It just hadn't emerged from your unconscious.' She reached for the sly-cake and bunged it in his mouth, cutting off further protest. 'Come round tomorrow and I'll tell your fortune for you.'

Nana was seeing Madame Zohree out, the two of them talking and nodding. 'I'll have to go, too,' Rose said. She stood up, wincing as she did so and putting a hand to her side.

'Are you OK?' Julie asked, but Rose just smiled. 'Well,' Julie went on, 'you know where I live. You're welcome any time.'

'I'll remember that,' Rose said. Suddenly she bent to kiss Julie's cheek and then Yvonne's, and went without another word.

'Who is it she lives with?' Yvonne asked. 'Fancy hitting a nice woman like that.'

'He's an effing monster, in my book,' Julie said. 'She'd be far better off without him.'

'Well,' Yvonne said, reluctantly, 'I suppose you're right. But what about the emptiness, Julie? What about the lack of conversation? What about . . .' She hesitated. 'Well, all the things you go without?'

'Sex?' Julie enquired.

'Money,' Yvonne said feelingly. 'Money!'

'Cheer up,' Julie said. 'You'll get your middle-class status back one day, Yvonne. Trevor'll come back when he gets tired of the Costa Plenty.'

'Trevor isn't coming back, Julie – Madame Zohree said it and she's right. I've known it all along, really. She says I should leave here, and start again.'

'She told me that, too,' Julie said. 'Get out while the

going's good . . . or words to that effect. And she knew I was going to Paris. Well, a capital city.'

Nana joined them. 'Did she tell you to emigrate, Nana?' Nana shook her head.

'No. But she said I shouldn't change things. She said there was someone come into my life to cause trouble.'

'Well, it's not me,'Yvonne said, startled.

Nana tsk-tsked, as though to suggest that Yvonne was a fly persecuting an elephant. 'She said beware of grey-haired men.'

'Chilly Bum Bum?' Julie said.

'Yes,' Nana said. 'It makes you think.'

'Well,' Julie said gloomily, as she guided Yvonne upstairs. 'That was a cheerful night and no mistake.'

'She said you were going to Paris,' Yvonne said, sniffing. 'That's cheerful.'

'I suppose so,' Julie said. 'But she's flattened you and Nana, and she didn't do much for Rose.'

'Link seemed happy enough.' They had paused on the landing and Julie put a hand on Yvonne's shoulder.

'Yvonne, my love, Link is always happy, even when he's moaning. That's because he is a simple man, in every sense of the word.'

'He's lucky,' Yvonne said. 'I've had about enough of being sensitive. That's what intelligence does for you . . . it lays you open and then you get people like Nana making digs.'

'Take no notice, Yvonne. She doesn't mean it.'

'But it's hurtful, Julie. And I've got enough to bear.'

It took ten minutes of sympathy and exhortation to persuade Yvonne into her own flat. When she got back downstairs Julie felt drained. Perhaps Madame Zohree had a point . . . if she left Grimshaw Street she'd only have herself to worry about.

She had checked on the children and was getting into her night things when she heard the knock on the door.

'Go away, Link,' she said.

'It's not Link. It's me.' Julie drew back the bolt, and her irritation turned to astonishment.

243

'*Tommo*? Is something wrong?' As he walked past her she smelled drink, lots of it. 'I'll get you a coffee,' she said hastily.

He was sunk in a chair when she came back with the mug, his tie loosened at his neck, his normally sleek dark hair tousled above a slightly stubbled face. It made him look younger, less formal . . . even quite attractive.

'Trouble with your mother?' Julie asked.

He nodded. 'World War Three. I'm doomed, she's doomed, the business is doomed – and I haven't even started it. I've got no gratitude, no sense, no right to do anything but drive around in me van flogging flannelette sheets.'

He sipped his coffee. 'Anyroad, enough of me. How did you get on tonight?' His words were slurring and his eyelids heavy. 'I should've been there, I know what she'd've said to me: "You're not married but there's a tie . . . a cord." I'd've said, "Yes, there is. Only it's a noose." I can't get free, Julie – not that I want to dump my mother. I love her. But she's eating me up, I'm being devoured, smothered. That's not mother-love.'

'Will she be worried about you now?'

'Probably. I told her I was off to pick up a woman.'

'That *will* worry her,' Julie said.

'Only if she thinks I'm enjoying it. It's pleasure my mother can't stand.' Tommo's face changed suddenly. 'I didn't mean you! You don't think . . .'

'No,' Julie said firmly. 'No offence meant and none taken.'

He went quiet then, hardly moving except to rub his eyes as though they were tired. She got up and switched on the lamp and then put out the centre light. As she did it she wondered if he might take it the wrong way, but then she remembered it was Tommo, who could be trusted.

It was peaceful now, the ticking of the clock suddenly noticeable. Tommo sighed. 'I ought to go but I don't . . .' He seemed to be searching for words. 'My God, I've supped some beer tonight.'

'I can see that,' Julie said drily. She was intrigued by this new aspect of her friend. So he was like other men, after all. He could crack.

Tommo burped suddenly and gave a feeble grin by way of apology. His eyes were closing and gradually a smile of pure contentment formed on his lips. Any minute now he would snore, Julie thought, remembering her father – and the next moment Tommo's lips trembled and a gentle snore emerged.

In the end Julie took the mug from his unresisting hand and fetched a blanket to cover him. Poor Tommo, he didn't deserve what he was getting out of life. But who did?

She got into bed trying to concentrate on Paris, but not even Josephine could help her tonight.

17

Julie woke before daylight and switched on her bedside lamp. She was in a quandary about Tommo. Did she go in and wake him, or let him sleep off the indulgence of the night before? If it had been Link she'd have gone in with a cold flannel and doused him awake, but Tommo was different. She could understand what pressures had driven him to drink too much. What could she say now to make him feel better?

In the end Tommo himself solved the problem, tapping gently on her door. 'I saw your light go on. I've made some tea . . .'

'Ta,' Julie said and reached for her sweater. It was a treat to sit up in bed sipping tea. Tommo had retreated as soon as she took the cup from him, and she had a few precious minutes to herself to sip the perfect liquid, hot and strong and sugared just right, and work out what she was going to say to him. But again he forestalled her, coming back with a second cup and lingering at the foot of the bed.

'I'm really sorry, Julie. I don't know what came over me.'

'Newcastle Brown?' she suggested, trying to make light of it.

'I should be ashamed,' he said. 'No, I *am* ashamed. I had good reason to drink too much, but no excuse at all to inflict it on you. I'll get out in a minute, quietly, before anyone's about.'

Julie was about to tell him that her reputation was already shot when she thought better of it. If he had any illusions left, let him keep them. He had never seen Link in her flat except in the day-time . . . besides, he wasn't a man to think badly of anyone. There was a strong stubble on his

246

chin now and a hang-dog air about him that she found moving.

'You look awful,' she said mildly and was glad to see him smile. 'What will you tell your mother?'

'God knows,' he answered. 'I'll think of something, I suppose – if I can get a word in. Anyway, I'll probably see you later. Thanks for the couch. Do I remember correctly, or did you tell me you'd had a good night at Nana's?'

Julie shook her head. 'Bleeding disastrous. According to Madame Zohree . . . yes, you may well goggle . . . according to her, Trevor isn't coming back, Nana's Chilly Bum Bum's a wrong'un, and I ought to emigrate. Poor Nana, she only had the party in the hope she'd hear about orange-blossom. Instead she's been told to give lover-boy the heave-ho.'

'Waterworks all round?' Tommo said.

'Yvonne's crying enough for the lot of us.' Julie shook her head. 'I know most of it was rubbish, but Madame Zohree did come out with some funny things. I mean, she knew about my kids. She knew I lived upstairs . . . well, in this house. She even knew I was going to Paris – a capital city, she called it. Now how often have I been anywhere, Tommo, let alone a capital city? Yet she picks it up at once.'

'You probably gave it away,' Tommo said. 'That's how they pick things up, body language and little remarks . . . they've got it all off. Anyway, I've got to go. I'll sneak out . . . and I won't tell anyone.'

Julie drained her cup, straining to hear his exit, but Tommo was true to his word and she never heard a thing. 'There goes an honourable man,' she thought, and felt somehow cherished. She had gone to bed last night without fearing she might wake to find him groping in the night. Anyone else . . . and it wasn't because he didn't have it in him. Julie suspected he could be virile enough given the right moment.

'Let him meet someone nice,' she thought. 'And God help her if I find her letting him down.'

She was up and dressed and fixing Jason's breakfast when Link arrived, still waxing enthusiastic about Madame Zohree. 'Only you shouldn't have sent me off with them three. I was all round the houses getting them home.'

'Well, tough,' Julie said. 'Chivalry'll never be dead while you're alive. Anyroad, stop moaning and listen. I've got a free holiday in Paris, well, a weekend break. I need someone to go with, so as I don't waste the other half . . . and you can go if you want. And if you behave yourself!'

'Paris?' Link looked as though Julie had said Mars or Uranus.

'Yes, Paris. Paris, France. *Oui oui* and *merci beaucoup* and shut your mouth, Link, before a fly gets in.'

He left on a cloud of good intentions. He would care for her, guard her, interpret, translate and bring her safely home. 'Very nice,' Julie said. 'Make sure you do.' But she knew she would have to care for him from start to finish, and she suspected he knew it too. 'Poor Link,' she thought and went to wake the bairns.

She could hear Yvonne arguing with her kids as she went out on to the landing and Nana looked glum as she stood in the hall to see Billy off to school. 'I've never slept a wink,' she said, shaking her head. 'But I've come to my senses. I hope you got your money's worth; I certainly did.'

There was a note of steely resolution in her voice which boded ill for Sammy. It would be a shame, Julie reflected, if Chilly Bum Bum got the bum's rush. He had half-civilized Nana. For a moment she wondered if she should remonstrate with the old lady, point out that last night had been an evening's daftness, no more. But Jason was tugging at her skirt, wailing about being late, and she let it go. Billy moved ahead of her out of the doorway, looking sleek and presentable for once and remarkably like the Cheshire Cat.

'He looks pleased with himself,' she said to Nana.

'And why not?' Nana said. 'Don't you start – I had enough of the SS yesterday.'

'Hunchfront?' Julie asked, alarmed.

'Yes, her.' She mimicked Miss Hays' voice. ' "Tut, tut, Mrs Foster, our school attendance . . . we're still a little short of perfect, aren't we?" "*You* might be," I said, "but I'm not. I've been left fifty years." "I mean your Billy," she says. "Well, why don't you say so, silly cow?" . . . well, I didn't say that last bit. Anyroad, I told her he hadn't been

248

off since the last time she was here, but she just keeps on about school records. "Are you saying I'm a liar?" I said.'

'He *has* been going to school, I suppose?' Julie asked.

'Would I lie?'

'Anywhere but in bed,' Julie said.

Nana waved fondly as Billy turned the corner, then looked at Julie. 'Stop worrying, man. I've told you . . . our Billy isn't putting a foot wrong. I don't expect the social worker'll be back, she'll have found someone else to persecute.'

'She'll be back!' Julie said. 'When I got up this morning I thought, "This is a nice day: Now watch some bastard spoil it." And they have.'

'A young girl like you shouldn't swear,' Nana said smugly.

'I know. I don't want to swear, it's a sign of a limited vocabulary. Unfortunately when I'm around you I find myself lost for words.'

'Well, you can just forget about Hunchfront.' Nana grinned ruefully. 'My God, she does have a big chest, though.'

'She's smart,' Julie said, arming the pushchair over the step. 'I'd like to know where she gets her clothes.'

'I know where she gets her bras made,' Nana said as the door closed. 'Harland and Woolf.'

Jason decided to give Julie one of his rare kisses before he went into school and she felt a pang. Would he be OK while she was in Paris? Was she right to go? She would talk to him about it tonight and if he seemed in the least upset she would call it off. She had never really believed it, anyway, not from the first moment it had been mentioned. Nice things like that only happened in books. She would be stuck in 13 Grimshaw Street for the rest of her life, with the Geriatric Delinquent downstairs and the Incredible Weeping Woman up. And if she did go, there was the question of the money. You couldn't go to Paris without some spends.

Graham had stayed late especially to deal with Julie. She needed the travel agent's folder, now with her name

249

inscribed, and he needed to offer her money again. It would be nice if she said no – it would demonstrate a fine independence, and there'd be no hassle about getting it back later – but he had to offer. There was also Charlotte's holdall of clothes. He had been embarrassed about them at first but now he realized he had been foolish. They were expensive clothes, hardly worn. Julie could probably put them to good use and if they didn't fit she could sell them. Charlie was making a nice gesture, and the least he could do was pass it on.

If he had wanted a reward to his generosity he got it from Julie's face when he handed over the tickets.

'I told you you were getting it,' he said, surprised at her incredulity.

'Are you sure?' she asked, for the umpteenth time. She looked pleased about the clothes too. She didn't root through the bag, which showed breeding; she just thanked him, and turned down his offer of money in a tone that brooked no argument.

Graham lent her his Paris guide, and smiled when she rabbitted on about Napoleon and Josephine and the Arc de Triomphe. 'You won't see everything in two days,' he said 'but you can make a start.' The first time he had gone to Paris was with his grandmother when he was eight. He had been back dozens of times since and still never made Les Invalides. 'I've eaten in some good restaurants, though,' he told Julie, his voice tailing off as he remembered the bills.

He had to tear himself away eventually. There was something very moving in the way she hung on his every word, her lips slightly parted as though in wonderment, her face crinkling with laughter at his feeblest joke.

'I really do hope I see you again before you go. I'm away that weekend . . . from the Thursday to the following Tuesday actually . . . but I'll ring to find out how it went.'

'I'm not on the phone,' Julie said and Graham cursed his own bland assumption that everyone had everything that made life easy. 'I could give you a number, though. A number where you could get me, if you said when.'

'Brilliant,' he said. 'Leave a note of it and I'll ring you . . . you get in on Sunday. I'll ring you at 5 o'clock Monday,

250

tea-time . . . how will that do? Then you can tell me you had a marvellous time.'

Graham felt wonderful as he waited for a break in the traffic so that he could ease his car into the flow. He had made someone very very happy. It was a nice feeling. If Julie stuck by him he would do it again. There would be lots of opportunities. He pushed his Vivaldi tape home in the tape-deck and hummed along to the magic music all the way to his partner's place in the car-park.

Julie read the travel documents from cover to cover in her coffee break. They were weird-looking things on flimsy paper, but she supposed they would be all right. If anything was wrong with them she would make her mouth go at the airport until they let her through anyway. You had to stick up for yourself. She made a mental note to walk up to the phone box tomorrow: they could go that way round to school. She would leave that number for Graham, and would be there at five on the Monday. He really wanted to know how she'd got on . . . which meant he did care about her a little bit, whether he knew it or not.

It was her day for doing his washing and she lifted the things from the linen basket, liking the smell of sweat and soap and indefinable masculine odours that might or might not be tobacco and alcohol. She had never washed for a man before – only Jason and Damien, and sometimes a woolly for Link because his mother shrank everything she got her hands on.

Washing for Graham Iley was different. Julie carried the clothes through to the washer and then, on an impulse, buried her face in their folds, inhaling the essence of the man.

Nana was lurking in the hall when Julie got back, anxious to tell of Yvonne's misdeeds now that last night's truce was over. 'Do you want the good news or the bad news?'

'The good news,' Julie said. 'Only the good news.'

Nana ignored her plea. 'The bad news is Yvonne's still here. The worse news is she's gone stone mad with that catalogue: the parcels's been coming through here like peas going to Birds Eye. The postman's fed up . . .' Nana moved her hands to illustrate sizes . . . 'big ones, little ones, she thinks that bloody flat's elastic. And that's not all . . .'

Julie clumped upstairs while Nana's suggestions that she leave Billy alone and worry about Yvonne's debts floated past her.

She knew Yvonne was up to something from the feverish rustle of paper and the too-nonchalant welcome, but in any case the catalogue parcels lay on open view. Whatever Yvonne was hiding, it wasn't them.

'All right?' Julie asked.

'Fine,' Yvonne answered, draping herself across a chair as far as she was physically capable of draping.

'Fine?' Julie said. 'Good.' She leaned forward. 'You know, Yvonne, you could've been an actress. You've got talent.'

'You don't need talent nowadays,' Yvonne said. 'You just have to walk around with your hand full of coffee beans.'

'Wit-ty!' Julie said. 'Now, what are you up to?'

'Me?' Yvonne said, all wide-eyed innocence. But her eyes flicked towards the kitchen and away, and Julie leaped for the door.

A plastic bag stood on the draining-board, filled and spilling over with groceries.

Julie moved closer: Ardennes pâté, pink salmon, Eccles cakes, drinking chocolate, packets and packets of biscuits, a slab of puff pastry, a box of rum truffles.

'Rum truffles?' Julie said. '*Rum truffles*! Have you gone mad?'

Yvonne's eyes blazed. 'Yes. Yes! Yes, I have! I got a £50 loan, Julie, from Tommo – for Link, I knew what I should do with it, but instead I bought some shopping. Proper shopping, not bashed tins and cheapex biscuits and chopped pork and weak tea. I bought what I used to buy, what my kids were used to . . . and I'm not sorry, Julie. Not if I drop down dead for it.'

'You will if someone gets that sweep up this Saturday,' Julie said. But she was shaken by Yvonne's fervour and by the little voice in her head that said, 'Me too. I understand.' Aloud she said, 'Well, it's done now. Just don't eat it all at once.'

'Do you know who I've been thinking about all day?' Yvonne asked. She had gathered one of the velvet cushions from the settee and was clutching it to her as though for comfort.

'Who?'

'That Rose. I can't get her out of my mind. How does she stand it, Julie? I will say this for Trevor, he never laid a finger on me, or the bairns. Not that I'd've let him. Still, there's a principle.'

'Don't ask me to explain it, Yvonne, because I can't. I'd only be hit once and I'd be gone. But some women seem to come to terms with it.'

Yvonne clutched her cushion tighter and shook her head. There was a funny look on her face, a mixture of pity and a kind of satisfaction. 'Of course, she's not married,' she said. 'That won't help.'

Julie was about to point out that her single status left Rose free to make changes, but just in time she realized that for once Yvonne had something to feel superior about, and it was almost making her cheerful.

'No,' she said slowly. 'No, I don't suppose it does help.' She got to her feet and looked at Damien, asleep on the settee. 'I'd better get him down. It's nearly school-time.' She gathered Damien into her arms and made for the door.

'I'll get the rest of the £50,' Yvonne said contritely. 'I only spent £18.'

'OK,' Julie said. 'Do your best.'

She settled Jason in front of the telly when they got in and laid the still-sleeping Damien in his cot, then she carried the bag of clothes Graham had given her through to the bedroom. She was about to try them on when she heard Link in the living-room, and she stuck her head round the door.

'Keep the noise down, Link. Our Damien's asleep.'

He winced and put up his hands in apology. She came back to the stove, scalded tea and set out two mugs and some biscuits. 'Have you been at work today?'

He looked hurt. 'You know I have. You saw me go this morning.'

'I didn't see you go to work.'

'Well, I did. I like going to work now.' His eyes gleamed. 'You'll be pleased as well before long.'

'If you keep a job longer than a fortnight, Link, I'll be over the moon.'

Link sighed. 'You've never understood, Julie. I've been caught in a trap . . .'

'You've been caught in a Mickey Mouse time-warp, my son. That's been your trouble.'

Link scowled and began to play his imaginary drums, whistling softly under his breath as he did so.

'What are you doing?' she asked.

His head came up proudly. 'I'm playing "Toccata for Drums".'

'Oh,' Julie said. 'I thought you were building a shed. Anyway, pay attention. We've got to make plans for Paris.'

'How are we going to pay for it?' he said, miming the drums again in his anxiety.

'We'll have to see Tonto's friend, won't we.' Link looked blank and she smiled. 'The Loan Arranger.'

'I'll get me own money,' Link said. 'I'm not borrowing off Tommo, no way!'

'That's up to you,' Julie said. 'Now go, because I'm busy.'

'I could stop,' he said. 'I could help you. We could have a good time.' He gave her what he hoped was a sultry look. 'You know what I mean.'

Julie's smile was weary. 'I know what you mean, Link. I've seen it often enough on the telly. The waves come thundering on to the shore and when the tide goes out you're in trouble. Stop thinking mucky thoughts and go home.'

Once more he was wounded and driven to retaliate. 'You know Shirley Thomas . . . blond, sexy, works down the coffee bar?'

'Married to Jakie Thomas? Him that trains with weights?' Julie asked.

'Yeah . . . they don't get on. I'm taking her out on Saturday. We're going Dutch.'

'That's good,' Julie said. 'Holland'll be the best place to be when Jakie finds out.'

'Come on, Julie man, don't keep giving the needle.'

'Go home, then,' Julie said ruthlessly.

'I've got nothing to go home for . . . and don't say that's my fault. Blame the government for me still being at home. You can't set up on your own if there's no work. I belong to a deprived generation.'

'Life's always been the same, Link . . . tough! Always has been, always will be.'

'How d'you make that out?' He was disbelieving.

'It's true . . . look at history.'

Link looked blank and she tried to come down to his level. 'Take your nursery rhymes, then. What's the old woman who lived in a shoe? A one-parent family with a housing problem. The cow that jumped over the moon? A milk producer without visible means of support! See what I mean.'

But Link had had enough. 'See you tomorrow,' he said and went home.

Julie sat on Jason's bed before he went to sleep and told him about Paris.

'Will you be all right with Auntie Yvonne?'

Jason pondered. 'I expect so,' he said at last. And then, 'You get plenty crisps and biscuits with her.'

Julie sighed inwardly, thinking of rickets, but he couldn't come to harm in forty-eight hours.

'I love you,' she said. 'You're my big boy.'

Jason was swift to take advantage. 'Can I have a jam sandwich?'

'Little bleeder,' she said, but they both grinned. 'I *do* love you,' she said and would have kissed him but he shrugged her off.

When she had filled his needs she went back to her own bedroom to try on Charlotte's clothes. They were lovely material and Julie was impressed by the width of the seams, but they hung on her, especially across the chest. Standing before the mirror, she wondered how Charlotte could be so well endowed when she, the mother of two children, had nothing to show for it? In the end she changed into her nightie and sweater, and felt better straight away. She carried the travel documents and Josephine to bed and read until she fell asleep.

18

Julie had arranged to go for her passport after nine o'clock, when the post office opened. Link was to go at four-thirty when he knocked off work but at nine-fifteen he was tapping at her door.

'Why aren't you at work?' Julie asked.

Link looked both sheepish and relieved – and there was an extra quality there, a kind of suppressed excitement. 'I thought I might as well come with you,' he said.

'But what about work? You're dolling off on Friday afternoon anyway . . . you'll get the sack.'

'No,' he said. 'It'll be all right.'

Julie sighed, but she knew Link in this mood. She'd seen it before, and she could hardly drag him to work by force.

'OK,' she said. 'But I hope you know what you're doing.'

They took turns in the photo-booth, ribbing each other through the curtain, waiting expectantly for the damp facsimiles to ooze from the slot. After that they queued at the post office counter, Julie a little surprised that Link could produce the necessary documentation. So he could be organized when he chose! She'd remember that.

'I've never had a passport before,' he said, looking down at his new one with satisfaction.

'It's only a visitor's passport,' Julie said and was instantly ashamed of diminishing his triumph.

She knocked on Nana's door when they got back. Billy was sitting by the fire, looking smugger than ever.

'Before you start,' Nana said, 'he's off poorly. It's his chest.'

'Serious?' Julie said hopefully but received no reply.

Nana looked unkempt and downcast. 'Seen Sammy?' Julie asked her.

'Yes,' Nana said. 'Seen him and seen him off. He won't be back.'

There was something about the set of Billy's lips that put Julie's teeth on edge. 'That's nice,' she said. 'You have so many old friends you can afford to dispense with the odd one. Just don't come for me when you're lonely.'

'I won't do that,' Nana said tartly. 'You don't get blood from a stone. Anyway, I don't want to talk about him any more.'

Julie stood her ground. 'This is bloody madness, you know. I'm not saying Sammy's a good'un or a bad'un, but writing him off because of a two-pound consultation with a wife from Rosamond Street is lunacy.'

'It's not just that,' Nana said. She nodded towards Billy, who was apparently engrossed in a war comic. 'He never liked him. That's enough for me.'

'It's enough for me, and all,' Julie said, thinking Billy's disapproval an automatic recommendation, but before she could continue Tommo called from the hall.

'Julie!' He looked flushed and happy and her heart warmed to him. 'I've got the keys for the premises.' They were big and black, a fearsome bunch, and Julie had to hide her smile at the way he had said 'premises', as though he had leased the Albert Hall.

'Got any time later on . . . just for a look?' he asked.

She moved towards him. 'I've already looked, but I'll come round with me sweeping brush. Four o'clock do?' Tommo demurred, but she could see he was grateful.

When he'd gone Nana went into the attack. 'So you're going in on his hare-brained scheme? He'll lose his job, that'll be the end of it. One more in the dole queue.' Billy started to chuckle and Nana picked up on it. 'Our Billy says Link's got the chop. I'm not surprised. Billy says he's ruined that wall.'

'Lies,' Julie said firmly. 'He's doing very well.'

'That's a joke,' Billy said. 'He only moves the ladders for them.'

'It speaks, does it? It actually speaks,' Julie said, for once at a loss.

*

Graham looked at the tailor's boxes stacked on a side chair. It was a hell of an expense . . . still, the suit would last forever as long as he didn't put on weight, and he didn't intend to do that. He had seen other men when they gave up rugger: they went to fat, bay-window style. Of course beer had something to do with it but it was the sudden cessation of activity that was really to blame. He wouldn't give up overnight. He'd scale down, coach the Junior XV, use a gym.

Graham suddenly realized that he would mind terribly when he no longer merited a place in the first team. It had been a good . . . no, the best . . . time of his life. Except that no one else seemed to mind when it happened to them. Blokes joked, and stood on the sidelines, and stayed active in the club. They had compensations: wives and kids. If he and Charlie ever had kids they'd be athletic: her brother was a hockey blue and her father had played for Somerset. She had a good pedigree. Not that that counted . . . well, not too much. On the other hand, parenthood was a serious business. Charlotte would make him the right kind of wife, no doubt about it, but in a funny way he found that certainty rather off-putting.

If they married, he would be able to chart the progress of their lives for the next twenty years. Charlotte would keep on working until she was pregnant. She'd stop for a while, and then go back and immediately get pregnant again. He'd seen it happen a dozen times. She'd get fatter and go at the waist and wear comfortable shoes and talk about food processors and mothproof carpets all the time. And he would have to ring home if he was going to be late, and he'd only get one night a week with the boys and that would be monitored. All in all, it was not a pretty picture.

If only she were more like Julie. A little, well, wild . . . But even as Graham thought it he knew it was foolish. He liked Julie, admired her in some ways . . . but there were limits. She was, not to put too fine a point upon it, common. No, if there had to be a wife at some time in the far, far distant future, it would have to be Charlotte . . . or someone very like her.

He looked around for some work with which to divert himself, but his in-tray was empty and there was no point in disinterring the McLaren file – not in the middle of the afternoon. He was about to stand up and look out of the window when the phone rang.

'Darling? It's me.' Graham wondered if Charlotte knew he had been thinking of her but they had never discussed telepathy. 'You know we're staying on after the wedding? Well, mummy is planning a big family dinner on the Monday, as all the aunts will be around, and she'll be relying on you and me to ferry people to the airport and that sort of thing. Also she wants them to really get to know you.'

Graham promised to be pleasant to the entire family and checked his diary as soon as he put down the phone. There was a Round Table Committee meeting on the Monday evening, but he could skip that. He thought about the family dinner: he would be there on approval, no doubt about that – as his sisters' husbands had once been, at their table. He felt suddenly morose and for no reason that he could explain he picked up the phone and dialled his own number. Julie would probably be gone, it was half-past three – but he could still try.

She was there, her voice on the phone as child-like as ever. 'I came in late,' she said by way of explanation. 'I got me passport this morning.'

She sounded excited and very young, and Graham had a twinge of doubt about sending her off to Paris. 'I hope you're going to be all right. Who's going with you?' He was reassured to hear she was taking a schoolfriend. 'All the same, be careful. Two girls alone in a city.' He thought of what it would be like to show Paris to two wide-eyed girls who had never before seen it. More fun than a wedding . . . top hat and morning suit and a collar like a vice. 'Well,' he said reluctantly, 'I'd better let you get on. Have a wonderful time. I may see you before you go, but if not I'll ring you at five o'clock Monday. Don't forget to leave the number.'

He walked to the window then and looked down on the town centre. He had been here for eight years, four as a partner. He would probably be here for at least another thirty years, growing affluent and cautious like Henry and Martin . . . or else like Philip who was in disgrace for groping a secretary! Graham had a sudden terrible sense of tramlines stretching away into infinity, as remorseless as any prison bars. If only he could throw it all up and go to Paris!

He turned back into the room and took out the grey topper, putting it on at a rakish angle in front of the mirror above the fireplace. To his surprise he looked quite handsome. He was only twenty-eight, after all. There was heaps of living still to do.

Yvonne had held the sleeping Damien in her arms for more than an hour. Now, her legs beginning to stiffen, she levered herself to her feet and went to lay him on the settee. His face, where it had rested against her breast, was flushed and his eyelashes lay on his cheek like moths. She had put him down successfully and was slowly withdrawing her arm from beneath his head when she heard the knocking below. It was someone at Julie's door. Who could it be at this time in the afternoon? She made sure the sleeping child was safe and tiptoed on to the landing.

The woman was neatly dressed in a grey tailored coat and a grey felt hat with a grey-and-white striped ribbon. She had navy cotton gloves on her hands, hands which clasped a navy handbag except when one of them was raised to rap on Julie's door.

'She's not in,' Yvonne called down helpfully. The woman looked up.

'Who are you?'

Yvonne was a little taken aback. 'I'm her neighbour.'

The woman's lips firmed in irritation. '*Whose* neighbour? Who lives here?'

'Julie Baxter,' Yvonne said, wondering why anyone would knock on an unknown door.

'Is she young and blond with two children?'

Yvonne blinked a little but nodded as the woman stepped back to get a better view.

'And no husband?'

This time Yvonne had had enough. 'Who are you?' she said, trying to sound haughty.

'My name's Thompson.' The woman craned her neck

further back, obviously expecting a reaction. Yvonne just kept on staring until the woman spoke again. 'I'm William Thompson's mother.'

It took a moment and then Yvonne twigged. 'Tommo's mother?'

The woman seemed loath to accept the nickname, giving the merest nod of the head. 'Where is she . . . this Julie?' She jerked her head towards Julie's door.

Something in the gesture and the woman's tone annoyed Yvonne. She felt a faint tremor of her knees but her chin came up. 'Do you mean my friend Julie Baxter?'

'I don't know her name . . . she's blond . . .' There was a pause and a sniff. 'Apparently.'

'Apparently?' Yvonne heard her own voice of outrage and couldn't quite believe it. 'Apparently? Just what d'you mean by that?'

The woman didn't flinch, merely stuck out her chin before answering. 'I've never seen her. I'm told she's a bottle-blonde and has two children who have no father. Or fathers? No one seems sure. But she's making a fool of my son . . .'

All the years of tuition in being 'nice' rose up in Yvonne. 'Don't be rude', 'Be polite', 'Smile', 'Don't point', 'Don't shout', 'Never ever use bad words'. They rose up . . . and quailed before the force of her fury.

'Out!' she said, moving towards the head of the stairs. 'Out you go. Out! Out!' She brushed the air with her hand as though dismissing a fly.

The woman stood her ground for a moment and then, as Yvonne kept on coming, tossed her head and turned away. Yvonne watched her go, hanging over the banister till she reached the hall. A sense of gratification welled up in her, a feeling she had righted a lifetime's injustice in one moment. 'And bugger off!' she said with gusto as the door closed, spoiling her triumph by bursting into tears.

She had dried her eyes and was making tea when a knock came at her door and immediately Yvonne's blood ran cold. She had faced the woman once but she couldn't do it again. She went to the door, wondering whether or not to answer. The knock came again but there was a hesitant quality in it that aroused Yvonne's curiosity. She opened the door and braced herself for whatever might come.

'Hallo.' Rose was standing there, dressed in a belted mac, her collar turned up around her face. 'I'm not being a nuisance, am I? It's just that Julie's out and I remembered what you said about "any time".'

Yvonne was already drawing her over the threshold. 'I was just making a cuppa and I hate to drink alone. Besides . . .' For a moment her voice faltered and she wondered whether or not she could trust Rose with the news of Tommo's mother and her onslaught on Julie. She only hesitated for a moment. Rose had her back to the wall just like they did and could therefore be trusted. 'I've never been so upset in my life as I am now. It'll be a relief to tell someone.'

Rose's tired, battered face perked up at the prospect of news. 'We're all the same,' Yvonne thought and went to fetch an extra cup.

Rose was sympathetic about Yvonne's ordeal and Yvonne felt herself relaxing as the afternoon wore on. Once or twice she saw Rose glance at the clock and her heart sank at the thought of her leaving. It wasn't that she talked much; hardly at all, really. But she *listened*. 'It's ages since someone minded what I said,' Yvonne thought and felt herself visibly taller.

Eventually there was a sound from the flat below. 'That's Julie,' Yvonne said. 'No, don't move. I'll nip down and fetch her. I want to see her about Mrs Thompson anyway. You finish your tea.' She moved the wine table closer to Rose's chair and topped up her cup. 'There now, I'll only be a minute.'

She felt excited going downstairs with a story to tell. 'It was awful, Julie,' she said and launched into the details.

'What did she want?' Julie said. Tommo's mother! What *could* she want? But in her heart she knew. She was going to get the blame . . . for everything.

'Don't ask me,' Yvonne said, round-eyed. 'But she wasn't pleasant.'

'What do you mean? Who did she want?'

'You. But she didn't say why.'

'What does she look like?' Julie asked. She was collecting

cleaning tools as she spoke, everything she might need for her trip to Tommo's new shop.

'Old,' Yvonne said. 'I mean, old-fashioned. Well-dressed but a bit like a . . . well, a prison visitor. Gloves and laced-up shoes and everything.

'How many prison visitors do you know?' Julie enquired.

'Don't be sarky,' Yvonne said. 'I stuck up for you.' Too late she realized her error and winced.

'What d'you mean, stuck up?' Julie turned and put down the bucket she was carrying.

'Well, I don't mean that exactly,' Yvonne said. 'She was just hoity-toity so in the end I told her to scram.'

'I bet!' Julie said.

'I did.' Yvonne was hurt. To be brave and not be believed! 'Off you go', I said. Out! And she went.' She paused and leaned closer. 'Are you going to tell Tommo?'

'Of course I am,' Julie said. 'She might've wanted him . . . it could be important.'

'But why should she think he's with you?' Yvonne asked.

Julie gathered up her tools. 'I don't know, Yvonne, and I'm not going to worry about it now. Take care of the kids, and I'll see you when I get back.'

'I've got Rose upstairs,' Yvonne said. 'She's having a cup of tea, poor thing.'

'He hasn't been at it again, has he?' Julie asked, alarmed.

'No, nothing like that. She just fancied a chat . . . and I did say come round.'

'So she doesn't want me?'

'No,' Yvonne said. 'No. You get off with Tommo and you can see her later. She's all right with me.'

Julie clattered down the stairs with her assortment of brushes and bottles in the pail. 'Your mam's been round apparently,' she said when Tommo appeared in the door-way, uncertain how else to approach it if not directly. He was holding open the van door and reaching for her burdens, and she saw his welcoming smile fade.

'*My* mother?' he said, his initial astonishment quickly giving way to misery. 'What did she want?' It was barely a question because he seemed to know the answer already. He shut the van door and moved to the passenger side to settle Julie in. 'Watch your legs. That's it.' He closed the door and walked round to climb behind the wheel.

'Yvonne saw her, not me,' Julie said. 'I don't think much was said. Anyway, you'll probably find out when you get home.'

Tommo concentrated on starting the engine and manoeuvring away from the kerb before he spoke. 'Why your place? I didn't think she knew the address.'

'Don't ask me.' The road ahead was busy, and Julie saw him frown.

'Well,' Tommo said, changing gear with a grind, 'I've done it now, haven't I?'

Julie smiled but lapsed into silence. What did he mean, and what could his mother have wanted? Nothing nice, that was for sure.

He helped her out of the van outside the shop and they stood gazing up at the shop door. 'It's not bad,' Julie said, looking at the mosaic that bordered the glazed window.

'The door needs painting.'

'Yes,' Julie said. 'Brown and orange to pick up the tiles. And a reeded blind behind the glass. They always look smart.' Tommo opened the door and the smell of musty air overwhelmed them as it had done last time. 'Leave it open,' Julie said. 'It'll give it a good airing while we're here.' She looked around, seeing the dust, the broken woodwork, the discarded packaging, the debris of its former ownership. The first time she had seen it, the shop had looked spacious. Now it looked derelict. 'Right,' she said. 'Let me at it.'

For the next two hours they swept and wiped and polished, clearing rubbish from corners and shelves, feeling fresh air flow through the door.

At one point Tommo leaned on his brush. 'What are we doing this for, Julie? The whole place has to be done up, and they'll mess everything up again.'

'Maybe,' Julie said, not ceasing her movements. 'But you can't work out how you want it while it's a dump. If you ask me, it doesn't need that much doing. Not at first, not as long as it's clean. When you get your stock in folks'll hardly see the structure. You don't want to spend too much to begin with.'

Tommo grinned. 'You've got a good head on you, Julie. You could be right.' He looked around. 'Tell you what, if I don't do much to it, how's about I spend what I save on a slap-up night out for two?'

'Done,' Julie said. She couldn't cut him down today, when he was getting a bit of pleasure out of life . . . and when his mother was probably waiting for him at home with a rolling-pin in her hand. Besides, what harm could a night out do? If he got his business off the ground he would mix with different people and make a better life for himself, and that would very likely solve the problem for her.

'I'll miss you while you're away,' Tommo said. 'Still, it'll do you good.' When she had told him she was taking Link she had seen him wince but he had made no fuss about it. Now she tried to reassure him.

'I'm looking forward to it, Tommo. I want to see everything . . . well, as much as you can in two days. I'd've gone on me own but it would've been a sin to waste the other half. If you hadn't had so much on you could've come. Still, Link hasn't had much in the way of treats!' She wielded her mop, seeking the right words. 'I palled up with Link in the Infants, you know, that awful first day. He's been a brother to me since then, more than me real brothers if I'm honest. But that's all it is . . . brother and sister.'

It wasn't a lie, she thought when Tommo seemed noticeably more cheery. It might have been once but it wasn't now and wouldn't be in the future. No more monkey business, for Link's sake as much as her own. It was time for him to grow up.

Link was sitting by her fire when she and Tommo got back. He was hunched into his parka, his hands thrust into his pockets, his brows down.

'What's Old Father Time doing here?' he asked, hardly dropping his voice and nodding towards Tommo as he went to stow the buckets and brushes. 'Where does he get his Phyllosan? Age Concern?'

Julie cut him short with a freezing look and fingers on his arm that caused him to wince. 'He's going in a moment, when he's had a cup of tea, so shut up.'

Now Link lowered his voice further. 'Can I stop tonight?' He allowed himself to drop back into the chair and swing his legs over the arm.

'No,' Julie said, gazing out on Grimshaw Street as she filled the kettle.

'Aw, Julie man . . .'

'You can stop on Tuesday,' Julie said. Link's eyes lit up. 'Tuesday, July the 4th, 1998.'

It took a minute for the penny to drop. 'I'll be past it by then,' he said.

Julie smiled. 'Don't worry . . . you can always get some Phyllosan from Age Concern.'

Tommo, having finished stowing his brushes, came into the kitchen. He gave Link's slumped figure a jaundiced look. 'Settled in for the night?'

'I might be,' Link said, defiantly. He turned to Julie. 'I could bring me video round.'

'I'm not in the mood for horror films,' she said.

'I've got other things but horror.'

'*Mickey Mouse*?' Tommo said. '*The Famous Five go Fishing*?' There was a new note in his voice and Julie realized stags were locking horns.

'Very funny,' Link said. He yawned to express his contempt but Tommo was not deterred.

'Tired?' he said. 'Oh, of course, I forgot you were working for a change.' He looked at Julie as if to say, 'He's an idiot, isn't he?' but she couldn't desert Link. Not now. 'Yes, I know how keen you are on your job,' Tommo repeated.

'OK, OK,' Link said. 'I've been a casualty of the Thatcher-induced recession . . . but it's different now.'

'Huh!' Tommo's snort was a masterpiece, but Julie had had enough.

'Oi,' she said loudly. 'Can we have a truce? I've had a hard day. I'd like some peace.' She looked pointedly from Link to the door but it was Tommo who cracked first.

'I can't stop for tea. Thanks for your help, Julie. It's much appreciated.'

'Don't mention it,' she said, pulling Link to his feet and propelling him to the door as well. She saw them both over the threshold and sat down with a fresh cup of tea.

'Julie?' Link was back again.

'I thought you'd gone with Tommo,' she said brutally.

'I sneaked up,' Link said proudly. 'I thought you might want company.'

'How considerate.' Julie's tone was silky. 'Now you've got thirty seconds to reach the front door.'

'Or?' Link asked, but Julie never got a chance to answer. Jason came through the door and walked past them to switch on the TV.

'Hallo, my darling son. What a lovely greeting for your mother.' He ignored her, switching channels till he found the desired programme.

'Where's Auntie Yvonne?'

'Upstairs with Rose.' Jason smiled. 'Yak, yak, yak!' Then he hunched his shoulders to show conversation was over.

'You know that medium woman, Madame Zohree . . .' Link said.

'Fortune-teller,' Julie said flatly. 'Mediums work with spirit guides. She did it all with waffle.'

'I thought she was good,' Link said. 'She said I'd wind up with you. She seems to have upset Nana, though; she's properly off her feed.'

'God,' Julie said. 'I thought Nana was a pain when she was full of hell, but this is worse. I couldn't get two words out of her just now.'

'Why's she so down?' Link asked.

'Because of a man, my son,' Julie replied.

'Nana?' Link's eyes were round.

'Yes, Nana. Why not Nana? It doesn't drop off once you're thirty, you know. She was soft on Chilly Bum Bum . . . Mr Winterbottom to you.'

'So?' Link said.

'So she got rid of him because of what the fortune-teller said. That he was after a soft sitting-down.' Link was looking mystified and she explained: 'He lives with his son and daughter-in-law, and the daughter-in-law's a shit. Madame Zero said he only wanted to move in with Nana so he could get away from his daughter-in-law.'

Link grinned. 'Out of the frying pan into the fire. Nana'd give him lug-ache.'

'We know that, but does Sammy?' Julie asked.

267

'He seems a canny old chap,' Link said, edging further into a seat. Julie knew what he was doing, trying to keep her mind off his presence so that he could inveigle his way in for the night, but she couldn't be bothered to argue. Something else was preoccupying her.

'I've never been very happy about that party.'

'It was all right,' Link said. 'Eats and everything for £2.50.'

'Madame Zero knew all about me,' Julie mused. '*And* Yvonne and you and Nana. But when it came to the others, the outsiders, you might say, she wasn't so clever.'

'She got Rose being battered.'

'A blind man could've got that,' Julie said. 'No, it smells.'

'So?' Link said vaguely.

'So where did she get her information?'

'From her crystal ball?' Link offered.

'She didn't have a crystal ball,' Julie said thoughtfully. 'But she might have had a nark.' The next moment she was up and out of the flat and down in Nana's living-room.

'Where's your Billy?' she asked a startled Nana.

'Why?' Nana said and then, seeing Julie's air of excitement, 'He's out.'

Link had followed Julie down, and now Billy appeared from the bedroom. 'Well, isn't that clever?' Julie said. 'He's out but he's in.' She turned to Nana. 'Did Billy go round Madame Zohree's?'

'Yes,' Nana said after a moment's thought. 'He went to book her. I give him a note.'

'Well, Billy?' Julie said.

Billy didn't reply until Link moved forward and took him by the lapels.

'Get off,' Billy said contemptuously. 'Who's scared of you?'

Link shook him but Billy's eyes still glared.

'Where did you get that Chinese food?' Julie demanded of Billy. 'The stuff you threw up in the outside lav?'

'Give,' Link said, his voice taking on a tinge of Jimmy Cagney. 'Where did you get it?'

Billy wrenched himself free. 'Off Wha-U-Won,' he said.

'Oh, very nice,' Julie said. 'He's running the Barnes Road branch of Save the Children, is he? Feeding the poor?'

'I paid for it.'

'You paid for it. Well, that's good. That makes me feel a whole lot better. What with?'

'Money,' Billy said sullenly.

'You never got it off me,' Nana said.

Link let go of Billy and raised a clenched fist. Billy smirked at this and made a suggestive gesture with his index and middle fingers, causing Link to raise his hand, palm inward towards Billy's face as though to strike him.

'Don't hurt him,' Nana murmured. 'He's only a bairn . . .'

'I'll do more than hurt him,' Julie said. 'Now, tell us where you got money for five Chinese take-aways.'

'I sold something,' Billy said trying to wriggle free.

'Oh, my God, me candlesticks!' Nana rushed for the bedroom. Link and Julie waited open-mouthed till she returned. 'They're still there!'

'OK,' Link said, 'if it wasn't your Nana, who did you rob?'

'No one. I only sold something . . . something I knew . . . me own business.'

Julie looked from face to face. 'I'll tell you what he sold: it was us, down the river.' She turned to Nana. 'He told Madame Zohree all the things she told us: Yvonne's Trevor, my trip to Paris – *and* what to say to you about Sammy Winterbottom!'

'You little sod!' Nana said, but Billy was past her and out of the door. Nana followed him, shouting. 'I'll bray the daylights out of you when I get you.'

'I hope you've learned your lesson?' Julie said. 'After this, no more fortune-telling, no more gambling, no more *Sporting Life* . . .'

'Can I still spit?' Nana said.

'That's about all I want you to do. I want a bit of peace.'

269

19

Julie parked the pushchair in the library porch and lifted Damien out. Some mothers left their kids outside but that was dangerous. Besides, it was winter now, and cold enough to kill. She shivered as the wind penetrated her jacket. When she'd paid for the kids' Christmas presents she was going to get herself some warmer clothes. There were times lately when her legs had felt numb. Still, perhaps it would be warmer in Paris. She tried not to smile idiotically into space at the thought of Paris as she shepherded Jason up to the counter to return his books.

She put the book about Josephine and Napoleon on the counter, along with *Understanding the Human Mind* which had turned out to be rubbish! Josephine lay along the cover, draped in gauze, looking enigmatic. What a woman she had been! Even the King of Rome, Napoleon's son by the other woman, had said so. Julie had the quote off by heart: '*If Josephine had been my mother, my father would never have been sent to St Helena and I would not be wasting away here in Vienna.*' Poor King of Rome, who'd turned out to be king of nothing in the end. Julie took Jason's books from his upstretched arms and put them alongside her own.

The librarian came to the counter. 'Can I have this one out again, please?' Julie said firmly, pulling Josephine back towards her. While Jason browsed Julie collected a clutch of forms about further education that were displayed in the centre of the library. You never knew when things like that could come in handy. She might even interest Link in some of them. Something was going on in his head – it was finding out what that was difficult.

She helped Jason choose his books with care, anxious to

keep him happy while she was away. 'Look,' he said suddenly, discarding everything he had chosen so far and pointing to a piled display in a corner. 'Santa!'

They were all there . . . *The Little Snowman, Santa goes to Toyland, Rudolph and the Red Cave* and a clutch of Bethlehem stories. No *Santa and the Ninja Turtles* but that would come, no doubt.

'We'll see the crib on the way home,' Jason said confidently, as she got his choice of books stamped.

'We might,' she answered cautiously, 'but it's still early December.' And when they trudged up the hill in the cold darkness there were only the usual statues in the grotto.

'It's no good taking a strunt,' she said reasonably, when Jason expressed his opinion by kicking at the gatepost. 'We'll come back soon. It's got to be there before Christmas.'

But as they walked home, fear entered into Julie. Jason wanted the crib so much, had remembered it from last year – and if her experience was anything to go by, wanting something was a sure way of being disappointed. This could be the year the church decided that there'd be no crib, and if they did there wasn't a blind thing she could do to save Jason from pain.

As always, the feeling of being unable to protect her children filled Julie with anxiety. To exorcize it she switched her thoughts to Graham Iley and the note she had left him, giving the phone number and reminding him she'd be there at five pm prompt on Monday.

Monday! By then she'd have flown to Paris and back. It was unbelievable. Josephine's Paris! She put out her hand to the book perched on the pushchair, just to make sure it was there, relaxing as she felt its smooth bulk.

'What are you smiling for?' Jason asked and Julie had to make up an excuse. She could hardly say she was turned on by long-dead lovers, but the story of the Emperor and his true love had affected her. *'To live in a Josephine is to live in Elysium. A kiss on your mouth, your eyes, your shoulder, your breast, everywhere, everywhere.'* That's what he had written . . . but it hadn't stopped the sod leaving Josephine when it suited him. Men! They were less use than alligators. At least you could make those into handbags!

271

They were passing the end of Rosamond Street when she saw Link, hunched into his parka, a haversack on his back.

'Where've you been?' he asked, looking up the hill, and then, without waiting for a reply, 'Did you see my wall?'

Julie had looked across at the top of the hill and seen the pale blur of the painted wall as they walked but it had been too dark to see detail. Now she looked at Link's expectant face and couldn't disappoint him.

'Yes,' she said, 'I saw it. Very nice. Now, have you asked for Friday afternoon off?'

Link said 'yes' but she knew he was lying. 'Well, just don't mess me about, Link,' she said balefully. 'This is my one chance to see a bit of the world and if you screw it up I'll slaughter you. We're getting a lift to the airport off Tommo and I want you there at two-thirty sharp, with everything. *Everything*, Link, especially your passport.'

'OK, OK,' he said, hoisting his haversack higher. 'Don't lose your wool. I'll be there and we'll get to Paris. And we'll have the readies an' all: I've seen to that.'

Julie shuddered a little, wondering just what he'd done to get cash, but this was neither the time nor the place to discuss it.

After they parted she lifted Jason on to the step of the pushchair and began to run. It felt like rain and she didn't want to get wet.

Yvonne had promised to lend Julie two flight bags, and these were waiting in Yvonne's living-room, still with their Spanish labels. 'I hope they bring you more luck than they brought me,' Yvonne said, in doom-laden tones. She was already in nightdress and chenille dressing-gown, her toe peeping through a hole in her velour slipper. 'Nice, isn't it?' she said, twisting her foot left and right. 'That's the story of my life . . . a hole in the bucket.'

'You take a big size,' Julie said, 'but I wouldn't've called them buckets.'

'Very funny,' Yvonne said wearily. 'You're young, Julie, but soon you'll realize there are some things too bad for jokes.'

'I'll bring you back some pong,' Julie said. 'Nothing like French perfume.'

272

Yvonne's eyes sparkled briefly but then she lapsed into lethargy again.

Nana was no more cheerful when Julie went down there. 'God,' Julie sighed, 'I'm glad I'm getting out of this house, even if it's only for two days.'

'That's right,' Nana said darkly, 'go off and enjoy yourself. Leave me here, lonely.'

'If you're lonely, Nana, you've only got yourself to blame. If you want Sammy back, make an effort.'

'I've ruined it now,' Nana said. 'He won't come back.'

'He might,' Julie offered, 'if you ask him nicely.'

'You didn't hear what I said to him,' Nana said, wincing at the memory.

'Knowing you, I bet it was subtle. Bugger off?'

'Worse,' Nana said, shaking her head.

'Say you had a brainstorm,' Julie suggested. 'Sammy'll be pleased to hear you've got a brain, stormy or not. Send your Billy round with a note. He caused the trouble; let him get you out of it.'

'What would I say?' Nana asked. And then, squaring up, 'I've got my pride, you know.'

'Yes,' Julie said, 'that's all you've got. No one to have toasted tea-cake with, no one to witty-watty with, no one for a bit of how's-your-father on Saturday nights . . .'

'You've got a wicked mind,' Nana said. 'Got any note-paper upstairs?'

Julie packed her things, zipped the bags, and then checked the list she'd made out for Yvonne: menus, suggestions for outings, the whereabouts of anything and everything Jason or Damien might need over the weekend. Should she be going off and leaving them? The question had tormented her for days now . . . still, in seventy-two hours she'd be home again.

The forms she had brought from the library lay on the table and she leafed through them in case she got a chance to mention them to Link while they were away. According to the forms, anybody could study anything. Languages, GCSEs and A levels, even homeopathy – but there was nothing that would especially appeal to Link. Julie lingered

273

over details of the Business Studies course. If she hadn't already got a job she could've taken that, and then helped Tommo build up his business. She had no doubt he would succeed. There was something about him, a certain quiet determination, that convinced her. For a brief moment she imagined herself in a business suit, briefcase in hand, parking her Porsche in front of Tommo's latest warehouse. Then she remembered Paris, and Paris was so real and so imminent that it drove every other thought from her mind.

When she put out the milk bottles she looked up at the night sky. She would see the same stars in Paris; it wasn't that far away. And the bairns would be all right with Yvonne, and Tommo to back her up. She had given Tommo her spare keys, just in case.

She was about to go back into the house when she saw Link come round the corner, hunched against the wind but making for her door. Julie held up her index fingers, forming them into a cross.

'Back, Dracula,' she said. And then, as Link halted, nonplussed, 'Go home, Link, and dream about the Champs-Elysées. That's what I'm going to do. Alone!'

But it was not the Champs-Elysées that occupied her dreams. It was the phone box on the hill above the town, from where Graham Iley would ring her on Monday so she could tell him that, like Josephine, she had been to Paris and conquered.

20

The male aircrew on the Air France plane wore wedding rings and looked like Sacha Distel. The hostesses had lacquered faces and bare legs. One was very elegant and wore a rope of knotted pearls that made Julie salivate. They gave out free newspapers and looked after everyone with an almost contemptuous, world-weary air but Julie had to admit they had X-factor. She looked at their faces, wondering if Josephine had been like that, a cut above the ordinary . . .

The bus from the airport was small and basic, and the Gare de l'Est, where it decanted them, smelled to high heaven. 'This place stinks,' Link said and Julie, unwilling to admit it, kicked his shin and said, 'Don't start!'

The taxi they got into was grubby and the driver black. He insisted on putting their bags in the boot and charged them extra for it. 'Highway robbery,' Link said, and received another kick on the shins from Julie. In the darkness the streets of Paris seemed shabby, almost derelict – but then suddenly, in front of them, they saw the Arc de Triomphe, bigger and infinitely more ornate than it appeared in pictures, brilliantly lit from what seemed like every angle.

It was still there, peeping round the corner, as they paid off the taxi. Julie had never in her wildest dreams thought they would be staying right in the centre of Paris, but here they were. Link pushed open the heavy doors and she saw a tiled lobby lined with ferns in large pots. It was dark and claustrophobic, but the Oriental man behind the desk spoke perfect English.

'Is he Chinese?' Link whispered. There was a note almost of terror in his voice.

'Vietnamese,' Julie whispered back, trying to sound confident, and saw a gleam of approval in the slanted eyes.

They signed in as Mr and Mrs Baxter, the name on the vouchers, and the Vietnamese man carried their bags to a room on the third floor.

'Thank you,' Julie said when they were safe inside. The man seemed to hesitate, then he smiled, gave a little bow and went out, closing the door behind him.

'It smells funny in here,' Link said, sniffing.

'It's just stuffy,' Julie said. 'I hope you're not going to moan the whole time we're here.' She felt suddenly flat and filled with a longing for Grimshaw Street, but it wouldn't do to show it. She went to the window and fiddled with the net curtain and unfamiliar catch until it was open and she could push it wider. The trees outside had lost their leaves but a single conker clung here and there.

'Horse chestnuts,' she said, suddenly remembering Paris was famous for them. But Link had turned on the telly and was a picture of consternation. 'Julie,' he said, a sob in his voice, 'this telly's in *French*.'

They went out straight away and found themselves in the avenue Victor Hugo. A girl in a yellow jacket was standing on the corner.

'She's on the game,' Link said confidently.

'Get away,' Julie said. The girl was beautiful and perfectly dressed, and had the haughty air of a lady.

'She is,' Link insisted, tapping his nose. 'I can tell.'

Julie was about to pour scorn on him when a car drew up at the kerb and the girl approached the side window. There was a rapid conversation and then she climbed into the front seat with a flash of long, silk-clad legs.

'We've got to buy some water,' Julie said, her heart thumping uncomfortably at the sight of the car driving away. What if the girl was murdered? And what about Aids?

'Do you have to pay for water in Paris?' Link said, his eyes widening. Graham had cautioned Julie about the inadvisability of drinking French tap-water and she meant to obey, but if she wasn't careful Link would imagine he had everything short of beri-beri.

'No,' she said patiently, 'you don't *have* to pay for water. But you can't rely on tap-water like you can at home. So you buy bottled water to drink.'

'Fizzy?' Link said hopefully.

'Yeah,' Julie said, 'if you like.'

She had a sudden sense of what it would be like to be here alone, to be free to soak up the grace of this city without someone to take care of all the time. And yet there would be no chance of her being free, not for years and years – the bairns would see to that, she thought resentfully. Then just as suddenly she felt guilty. They loved her and she loved them. 'But they're still millstones,' said a voice in her head.

They bought a bottle of water and some apples in an over-stocked shop and then sat down at a pavement café. A waiter in a wide white apron swept up, his book at the ready. 'Two coffees,' Julie said firmly.

'Any beer?' Link said hopefully. The waiter looked wearily from one to another.

'Un beer, un coffee,' Julie said.

'Toot sweet,' Link said and then, to Julie, 'that means "bloody quick".'

'Well,' she said surprised. 'Culture!'

Link smiled seraphically. 'I'm not going to take any notice if you're sarky, Julie, not while we're here. I made my mind up right at the beginning. Two days in Paris, I thought – no arguments. Besides . . .' He hitched his chair closer. 'I want to talk to you while we're here.'

Julie's heart sank at the intimate note in his voice. There was still the night ahead, the night when she must tell him that the bed was strictly for sleeping in, nothing more. She had felt funny lately, a bit churned up, but one thing was becoming crystal clear. She was tired of sex . . . of sex as it had been, anyway.

A table's width away two lovers sat, hands entwined, their eyes sparking from one another. Julie felt her own eyes prick, and looked away.

'About you and me,' Link said. 'I was thinking it would be a good idea if I moved in with you. We get on . . .' He

277

paused. 'I think I love you, Julie. I must do or I couldn't put up with you. Anyroad, I could look after you and the bairns. I understand them. I . . .'

Julie cut him short. 'You're not moving in with me, Link. Not ever. And while I'm on the subject, this weekend is for sight-seeing not nookie, so get that into your head. Toot bloody sweet!'

Nana licked the envelope and pressed it closed. It had once held a birthday card from Julie. Now she crossed out the 'Nana' written on it and substituted, 'S. Winterbottom, Esq.' She raised her voice. 'Billy! Get out here!'

He came sullenly but he came. Since the business of Madame Zohree he had been treading carefully and Nana was enjoying her new-found power over him. She pushed the envelope towards him. 'Take this round to Sammy's. 18 Eglinton Street. It's for him, and only him.'

'What if he's not in?'

'Wait for him,' Nana said. 'Hang round his place like you hang round that bus shelter.'

Billy wanted to defy her but he didn't dare. Not yet. Nana knew it wouldn't last: it was in the nature of things that young'uns defied you sooner or later. She'd been through it with his mam, and she knew. For the time being, though, she was in control, thanks to Julie.

She thought of Julie in Paris now with that half-witted lad – they would come to no good end, those two. On the other hand she had Julie to thank for her new supremacy . . . and Sammy might be back, once he got the note. She offered up a prayer for a wonderful weekend for Julie and a return to find her bairns safe and sound, then she went into the bedroom to struggle into her brassière, in case Sammy came straight round.

Tommo switched off the lights in the back shop and refurled his measure. It was going to be all right. He knew what was needed now, and he had the money. Most important of all, his resolve had hardened since his mother's visit to Grimshaw Street. He had told her never to do it again and she had stood, stony-faced, neither agreeing nor disagreeing. He was thirty: nearly half-way through his life if you believed the Bible. What did his mother want for him? What did she want from him?

He started to gather up his jacket and the odd tools he had brought with him. Lately he had spent a lot of time trying to remember his childhood. He hadn't thought of it much before but at present it obsessed him. Had his mother always been the way she was now, dried up and bitter? Or had she once been a happy young mother like Julie?

Tommo thought about Julie as he waited to catch the barmaid's eye in the Lamb and Flag. She would be in Paris now, living it up with Link. They would laugh and drink and then go to bed together. He made himself face it once more: Julie went to bed with men as easily as some women shelled peas. And yet there was also an innocence about her, an untouched quality, an utter lack of greed or malice or manipulation. He carried his drink to the corner, slipping out of his coat before he sat down.

He thought of Julie again, laughing as she swept up the shop, biting her lip over Nana or Yvonne. Could he make her happy? Sometimes he knew he could, knew it with certainty; at other times he looked at the various gulfs between them and knew it could not be. But it wasn't up to his mother to decide, by God it wasn't. He drained his glass and got up to get a refill.

He was collecting his change when a man spoke behind him. 'Bill? It is Bill Thompson, isn't it?' Ages since someone had called him anything but Tommo, except his mother of course. Swinging round, Tommo recognized the man, or the boy he had been at school. A bit of a braggart! They exchanged news of jobs, and then the man said, 'Got a family? I've got three. Smashing kids.'

'No,' Tommo said.

'Not married?' Was there an implied sneer in the question?

'Not yet,' Tommo said, sipping carefully. 'But there is someone, so you never know.'

When the other man had gone Tommo ordered another drink. 'Make it a double,' he said.

He left going home as late as he could, and he knew he

279

shouldn't be driving. Parking the van at the kerb, he climbed out, unable to work out why he was being such a fool. He needed his licence more at this juncture than he had ever needed it, and he'd been in real danger of throwing it away.

A light was on in his mother's room. She was still up, but unlikely to come down in her nightclothes. The row would start tomorrow, at the breakfast table – except that it wouldn't be a row, just an icy confrontation. Tommo began to fish for his keys, feeling an unaccustomed lack of dexterity and not liking it much. Mustn't throw everything away now, when life was so full of opportunities. He had told that bloke in the pub that he might be going to marry Julie. It was possible. You never knew what you could achieve until you tried.

It took several attempts to get the key home and he knew he had scratched the lock. His mother would see the marks when she polished it as she did every second day; would see them and draw her own conclusions. Tommo pushed open the door and stepped into the antiseptic hall, knowing perfectly well the reason for his condition: it was to dull the pain of knowing Julie was in Paris with another man.

It was too quiet in the house with Julie absent. Yvonne put Jason and Damien to bed in her own children's room and then conducted John and Andrea down to Julie's flat where they would sleep. She had explained that this was because they were quite grown-up while Jason and Damien were not and needed to be close to her, and they had accepted it in good part.

Now she settled Andrea in Julie's bedroom and John in Jason's room. 'No carry-on, mind. You can watch the telly if you don't fight, and go to bed when you're tired. I'll leave the doors unlocked so you can come and get me if you need to and I'll be popping up and down.' This last was said in a warning voice. She knew what they could be like if she wasn't on top of them.

She went back upstairs and checked on the younger children. They were fast asleep and no wonder, the carry-on they'd had with John. She felt a warm glow at the thought of her house being full, but it faded with no children around her to fan the flame and she wandered into the kitchen.

Julie would be in Paris now, eating frogs' legs and wonderful gooey cheese. Yvonne cut herself a slice of Edam and nibbled morosely. If she could only get into her clothes again she might cheer up. Clothes did have an effect on you. As soon as they had got to Spain Trevor had cast his vest, and look at the consequences of that!

It had been too much to hope for, a fairy-tale ending, with Trevor coming back to her. People like her didn't get fairy-tale endings; they got screwed. She wanted to say 'fucked-up' like they said in American movies, but she didn't dare. Once you resorted to language like that . . . it was like casting your vest. You were never the same again.

She went back to the living-room to clear up the mess the kids had left. Andrea's reading book lay open at the tale of the princess who went to bed with the frog and woke up with a prince. 'If I did that', Yvonne thought, 'I'd wake up by myself covered in water-weed.' She was trying to decide whether to laugh or cry when she heard a knock and then Rose's voice, 'It's only me, Yvonne!'

This time one of Rose's eyes was half-closed, but the set of her chin was resolute and she was carrying a holdall. 'I've walked out.'

'Thank God,' Yvonne said fervently. 'I think he'd've killed you in the end. Why did he do it?'

'I forgot his mother's birthday,' Rose said simply. 'I should've sent her a card.'

'You can stay here,' Yvonne said, 'until you find somewhere. There's the couch – or you can have John's bed temporarily. We'll manage.'

'I thought I could maybe use Julie's bed . . . till she gets back?' Rose said tentatively. 'That'd give me time to turn round.'

'No.' Yvonne spoke sharply. 'No, you mustn't be on your own down there. He might turn up. You stay up here with me.' She braced her shoulders. 'I'll give him birthday card if he shows his face.'

She helped Rose out of her mac and put a cushion behind her head when she sat down. 'You rest there while

281

I make some tea. It's going to be all right, you see if it's not.'

Traffic went here and there around the Arc de Triomphe seemingly without a pattern, and the pavements were thronged with purposeful young people going somewhere. Link and Julie stood for a moment watching a faint search-light sweep the sky.

'She's there again,' Link said suddenly, and Julie followed his finger to see the girl in the yellow jacket. She was moving towards another car which was slowing at the kerb. A brief negotiation, and the girl got in again, before the car accelerated away into the night.

'I bet she makes a packet,' Link said morosely.

'I bet she gets her throat cut one day,' Julie retorted.

They agreed they couldn't afford a pavement café again and walked back to the hotel. Link reached for her hand but Julie tugged it away. She didn't want another confrontation at bed-time.

She couldn't understand her own feelings at the moment. On the one hand she felt happier, more elated, than she had ever felt in her life – but she felt tearful, too. As though she were badly done to. Why should she feel like that now, on the most exciting weekend of her life? And why did it hurt to think of Graham, off somewhere in the country? And why did the Parisian girl in the yellow jacket keep intruding into her thoughts?

She was glad to get back to the quiet room with its rose-pink velvet curtains. Outside the horse-chestnut tree shivered in the wind that had blown up suddenly and Julie could hear accordion music somewhere . . . 'The Long and Winding Road'.

'That's a disco,' Link said. 'We could go if you like.'

He was moving up on her and Julie put up her hands to ward him off. 'Get off my neck, Link. You know what I think about lovebites. No one puts their mark on me.' He persisted with his nuzzling. 'Give up, Link, I'm knackered! I want to sleep.'

She went into the flower-sprigged bathroom, the Lennon/McCartney music ringing in her head. Often she

282

didn't understand their lyrics, but Beatles songs always stirred you. She felt tears prick her eyes and tried to decide why she wanted to cry like this. She wasn't lonely. She would only have to call his name and Link would be there, taking her in his arms. But that was the last thing she wanted. She could hear him moving about, rooting in the bags in the bottom of the wardrobe, and then there was silence except for his whistling along with the music outside, which had changed to 'La Vie en Rose'. She picked up the soft pink towel and began to dry her face.

'Julie.' Link's whisper was hoarse against the door. 'Are you there?'

She was tempted to pretend she was in the bath but instead she braced herself for an argument. 'No. What d'you want?'

'Come and have a look.' There was such a note of elation in his voice that she couldn't resist opening the door a crack.

'What d'you think?' he said, pleasure in his voice. She looked at him. He had taken her heated tongs from her toilet bag and experimented with his hair. Now his face was crowned with a mass of blond sausage curls.

Julie stood in the doorway, trying not to laugh. 'Well, rock on, Vera Duckworth,' she said at last and went back to the washbasin.

Yvonne watched Ida Lupino walk out into the rain and then wiped her eyes. On the settee Rose slept the unbroken sleep of exhaustion and pills. It was after midnight and Damien would wake at six but still Yvonne sat on for the late-night headlines. There was no earthquake in Spain or France and no threat of insurrection here at home. She could go to bed. She checked on Julie's children: soundly asleep. She let herself on to the landing. She never went to bed without checking on her own children and tonight was no exception.

She was about to descend the stairs when she heard the whispering below. It was Nana and the old man, Sammy Winterbottom, saying good-night in the hall. Yvonne peered cautiously down. Nana's face, upturned, looked almost girlish in the dim lighting. Sammy's downbent head, white-edged and shining pink in the centre, was both pathetic and protective of the woman he stood so close to.

As she watched them come together Yvonne's knees wobbled and she sank on to the stair until she could look through the banisters. She saw Nana's hand come up round his neck, her broad wedding-ring gleaming in the light, her old hand, at a distance, looking white and vulnerable.

At last they drew apart and he went out into the night with whispered words. Nana stood until the door closed behind him and then turned back into her own flat.

But Yvonne sat on on the stairs thinking that for everyone in the world there was someone, except for her. And then she remembered Rose. Rose would need a lot of help, no doubt about that; and if she, Yvonne, was going to do right by everyone she'd better get her sleep.

21

After breakfast they went out to the huge roundabout surrounding the Arc de Triomphe, walking through a wide subway and then coming out into the sunlight again within the monument, seeing that the creamy stone was tinged with apricot, and the roof covered with carved flowers and an archway presided over by cherubs.

'He's got a willy,' Link said gleefully, pointing to one Cupid.

Julie sighed. 'If that's going to be the level of your conversation while we're here . . .' she said threateningly. He wandered off then and she sat down on a stone bench to contemplate the wonder of it all.

There were names carved on the walls – Jaffa, Peschiera, Roveredo . . . names she recognized from her book about Josephine and Napoleon. Underneath were the names of men who must have been Napoleon's heroes: Moreau and Lafayette, Bernadotte and Ney, and below him a MacDonald. What was a Scotsman doing there? She vaguely remembered some kind of tie-up between the French and the Scots, and made a mental vow to look it up when she got home.

She recited the battles to herself as her eye ranged over them: Ypres, Luxembourg, Breslaw, Saragosse, Austerlitz, Jena . . . 'Want a coke?' Link said, handing her a can. He opened his and began to drink, but immediately a man in uniform was there, shaking an admonitory finger.

'What's he on about?' Link said, round-eyed.

'No drinking,' Julie said. 'Not in here, anyway.' They stashed the half-empty can in her shoulder bag and moved on. Suddenly an old man confronted them. He had medals on his chest and a cap on his head. 'I love English,' he said and lifted his stick like a machine-gun. 'Boom-boom-boom,' he said and beamed.

'Let's get out of here,' Link whispered. 'They're all barmy,' but Julie stood for a minute, eyes closed, saying a little prayer for the lone MacDonald dying so far away from home, and for the men of her grandfather's generation who also had fought for a free France.

'Look,' Link said, nudging her awake. ''*Allo*, '*Allo*.' Three gendarmes stood in a group, caped and kepied. 'Gad moaning,' Link said and then, delighted at his own talent, 'Gad moaning.'

They walked back through the subway, seeing only one piece of graffiti: '*You don't need permission for anything*' it said in English.

'See,' Link grinned. 'The French have the right idea.'

Graham struggled with the unfamiliar collar, swearing quietly under his breath. The dressing-table stood in the bay window of his bedroom and down below in the garden he could see some of the comings and goings. The flowers had just been delivered, colourful and exotic on baker's trays, seeming to be enough for an army of bridesmaids and VIP guests.

Once he saw Charlotte's father come out into the open air and look up at the sky as though fearing rain. It must be hell to be father of the bride. Perhaps it would happen to him one day? Unless he had only sons. Boys were easier – nice uncomplicated creatures who got train-sets for Christmas. And you didn't have to pay for their weddings!

A car drew up at the gate and a tiny bridesmaid, shrouded in what looked like white fur, was helped out. There seemed to be dozens of bridesmaids. He felt the collar click into place and straightened up in relief. Now for the stock.

While he was fiddling with the grey silk necktie he thought of Julie in Paris. Please God, she would be having a good time. He found he was smiling foolishly, thinking of her there with her girlfriend, the two of them wide-eyed in the Place de la Concorde, watching the voracious fish in

286

the Tuileries Gardens jumping for scraps until they made the water boil. She would use her little bits of French to order at pavement cafés and buy tickets in the Métro . . . when she had said *'merci bien'* to show him she could do it her eyes had widened in apprehension in case she got it wrong. That was the day he had noticed the fragility of the wrists above the little red hands, which always looked chapped but were soft enough when you accidentally brushed them with your own.

'Darling?' Charlotte was easing into the room, her face glowing above the red velvet dress. 'Don't talk too loudly,' she said, a finger to her lips. 'Mother doesn't approve of meetings in bedrooms.'

'Not even at eleven o'clock in the morning?' Graham stage-whispered.

'Not even then.' She moved closer and put up her hands to his neck-tie. 'Let me.' A few deft turns and it was fastened. 'There.'

'You've done this before,' he accused.

'Only for daddy.'

He put his arms around her, feeling the unfamiliar velvet over her familiar flesh. She felt good in his arms, quite solid but still slender. 'Shall we run away together?' he said, his lips against her hair.

'Elope?'

'No,' he said. 'I wasn't exactly thinking of doing the honourable thing. I was thinking more of a motel, a tent, the back seat of a car.'

Charlotte was gently detaching herself. 'I've got to go, darling. There are aeons of jobs and the aunts mustn't get to the Moët . . . not just yet.'

He pulled a face. 'Don't you want to take care of *me*?'

She came briefly into his arms again. 'I will, I promise you. Tonight, when they're all flaked out and sleeping like logs, I'll come at midnight. Leave me a light in the window.' Around her neck the thin row of pearls was less lustrous than her skin and her eyes were clear and green above the downy cheeks.

'You look like a peach,' Graham said, and smiled. 'Have a lovely wedding.'

She was halfway to the door. 'I only hope Ally doesn't

go into premature labour at the altar. Wouldn't it be a hoot . . . especially with the Archdeacon here. *Quelle horreur!*' She ran back again and kissed him. 'I love you. Get dressed and come down quickly, *tout de suite.*'

'*Tout de suite,*' he agreed and stood smiling until the door closed behind her. It had just shut when he remembered he needed to check on his duties as usher. Charlotte had outlined them more than once, but he felt the need of recapping. He opened the bedroom door and went on to the landing, thinking he would catch her on the stairs. She had already reached the hall, however, and he was about to call her name when he heard her mother's voice below, out of sight of the landing.

'I've been looking everywhere for you, Charlotte. Aunt Bea is being her usual helpful self and I couldn't find you anywhere?' There was an interrogatory note in her voice.

'I was in the loo.' So Charlotte was serious about her mother's disapproval of bedroom visits!

'Yes, darling, I didn't mean to hound you . . . it's just that I do worry. This business of Alison . . .'

Charlotte was murmuring soothingly as her mother continued. 'It doesn't do to get a name. I know it's the 1990s, so don't point it out, but people . . . especially parents . . . don't like to think a girl has been, well, too free. If you have hopes of Graham . . .' They were moving away and he strained in vain to hear what followed, before moving back into his room, feeling suddenly overwhelmed by the thought of the day ahead.

Yvonne let herself into the hall, the plastic carrier weighing heavily in her other hand. Rose had given her a £10 note to do shopping – 'just to get odds and ends' – and she had just spent the happiest half-hour she had had in a long time. She was about to mount the stairs when Nana's door opened.

'Hold on, there!'

Yvonne turned. Nana had folded her arms across her chest and was looking distinctly hostile.

'Yes?' Yvonne said, trying to sound detached.

'Have you read your rent book, madam? The back page?

No sub-lets, that's what it says. What'd this house be like if we all took in Tom, Dick and Harry?'

'If you mean Rose . . .' Yvonne said.

'Rose?' Nana cackled. 'She's more like an autumn crocus, that one. Still, to come back to the point, this house's not elastic, I've told you that. You'll have it down on top of us if I don't watch it.'

A look of grim satisfaction had suffused Nana's face and Yvonne rebelled. She moved forward, transferring the bag to her other hand so that she could shake an admonitory finger in the old woman's face.

'You . . .' she said. 'You . . . are a faggot. And a bully. And . . .' She sought for something really vicious. 'And a pain in the arse. Now, mind your own business.' She mounted the stairs in silence, for Nana was too shocked to reply.

They bought tickets for the Métro and got out at Concorde. A tall obelisk stood across the way but they used the map and turned into the Tuileries Gardens. A man was leading donkeys with gaily coloured saddles on them and Julie thought of Jason. He would love a donkey ride. One day she would bring both boys here. They sat on a stone bench and watched some Japanese tourists feed the fish, whose open mouths appeared above the parapet gasping and snatching for food. 'They look like Yvonne when she's got a hunger pang,' Link said.

When it grew too cold to sit they walked up on to a shopping street, past men playing bowls in a sand-pit. The sound of bowl clacking on bowl was soothing. 'That's *boules*,' Julie said. Link looked superior.

'I know that,' he said. 'I saw it on telly once.'

They walked along past shops full of smart clothes at what looked like astronomical prices. 'They have good gear for guys,' Link said longingly, his nose almost pressed against the window. But Julie was looking into the alley-ways that ran between the shops and led to little court-yards, shadowed and filled with tubs of greenery, even this late in the year.

'This is the rue de Rivoli,' Link said, when they came to

289

the corner. He looked at her for approval of his pronunciation and then repeated it for his own pleasure. 'Rue de Rivoli.'

They sat at another pavement table and drank Coke. 'Have you thought about what I said?' Link asked. 'About you and me? We could get married . . . I wouldn't mind.'

Julie knew what was going through his mind and she was anxious to put him straight.

'That isn't why I said "no" last night, Link. I'm not holding out for a commitment, if that's what you think. I'm not into getting married or shacking up. I don't want a relationship . . .' But even as she spoke she remembered playing Scrabble with Graham, putting the counters on the board. You could send messages that way: 'I LOVE YOU.' She shook her head slightly, as though trying to dispel foolish notions and looked at Link again. 'Do you understand?'

'OK. No sweat,' Link said but she could see he didn't understand, which was fair enough when she didn't understand herself. She tried to think of something pleasant, imagining herself with a courtyard and a balcony overlooking the flowers. Even then an image intruded to spoil things, a vision of the prostitute she had seen last night, flaunting herself in her yellow jacket. That was the only way she would ever get a courtyard: by paying for it on her back.

'I hope you're not getting daft ideas,' Link said. Julie was alarmed. Surely he couldn't read her mind?

'What d'you mean?'

'Well,' Link said uneasily, 'that Tommo's always hanging round . . . like Old Father Time.'

'He's thirty, Link,' she said. 'Our generation. Well, mine.' Link was about to remind her they were the same age when the penny dropped. He contented himself with a weak riposte.

'Well, he's nearly old enough to be my father.'

Julie sighed. 'He's had a lot to try him, Link, but mercifully God's spared him that.'

'You know something?' Link was leaning forward, eyes suddenly indignant. 'The women round here are arrogant.' Julie looked at the women moving along the pavement. It was true that they walked like queens, or rather like kings who bowed to no one. They were brown and taut with shining knotted hair and the twinkle of gold jewelry everywhere.

'One of them turned you down?' she asked sympathetically.

'They don't even bloody look,' he said indignantly. 'Hard-faced bitches!'

A violinist was playing Jewish music when they went back into the Métro, and Link showered loose change into his open violin-case. 'Keep it up, man,' he said encouragingly but the musician played on as though he had not heard. They travelled to Trocadéro and saw the Eiffel Tower before them, like something out of Disney. There were statues all around, handmaidens, some of them naked. 'They like their bare buff in France,' Link said ruminatively.

'God,' Julie said, 'I've heard of one-track minds . . .'

Her eyes were fixed on the golden Palais de Chaillot, which she recognized from the picture in Graham's guide-book. She stood still for a moment to drink in its splendour, and then moved slowly on.

A black man was dancing on the terrace in time with music from a ghetto-blaster. He wore black-and-white tap shoes and another man, white and clearly deranged, was capering in imitation. Another black man in a black-and-white striped suit and black top hat walked by. 'Cool, my man,' Link said admiringly. 'Cool.'

Fountains were playing as they walked towards the Eiffel Tower, and golden animals reared up around them. Crossing the bridge over the Seine, between rows of paintings for sale as originals but all looking suspiciously alike, they halted in the middle.

'I think this is the best day of my life,' Julie thought. Below the bridge a pleasure-boat sailed by.

'Want to go on one?' Link asked.

She shook her head. 'We can't afford it, Link. The money's running out. I'd've liked to go up the Eiffel Tower, an' all, but we can't afford that either.'

Link grinned and fished in his back pocket for a roll of currency.

'Where did you get that?' Julie said, ready to give him a lecture.

'Sold something, didn't I?'

'What?'

'Me sitar . . . well, I couldn't get away with learning it. Besides, I'm going in for keyboards when we get back.'

They walked down to the quayside and paid their thirty-five francs for the boat trip, which Julie decided was preferable to going up the Tower at forty-seven francs.

'Ta,' Julie said, when they were aboard, and squeezed Link's hand.

'I would do anything for you, Julie,' he said and for once he sounded quite grown-up. 'I've got to keep some back for the sweep, but the rest is yours.'

They got end seats on the boat so that they could look out at the bank, seeing the ancient buildings. A guide described each one and filled in the history, but soon Julie was too rapt to listen. She had a strange feeling of being two people. One of them was a tiny, minuscule figure in the face of so much history. As they passed under the bridges she could see that they were the original stones: she could reach out and almost touch history. Perhaps Josephine had sailed here just as she was doing now? But on the other hand her mind felt as though it were suddenly expanding, as though she was growing almost visibly as the excitement of her surroundings gripped her.

She looked at Link to see if he too was being affected but he was miming his drums. She sighed, remembering him at school. He practically failed plasticine, so what else could you expect?

It was getting dark by the time the boat trip ended, and a new moon showed above them. Suddenly the Eiffel Tower was lit up and it was breathtaking. The boats were lighted too, a huge armada of brilliance sailing up and down the river.

'We can come again tomorrow,' Link offered as they tore themselves away, but Julie knew there wouldn't be time.

They chose to come out of the Métro by l'avenue de la Grande Armée because Julie remembered that when they had done it in the morning the Arc de Triomphe had been framed in the entrance and they had risen towards it in wonder. The second time around it was even more breath-taking, the lighting illuminating it now against the night sky.

Entering the hotel, she consigned her worries to the back of her mind as Link whispered in her ear: 'He's on again, that Chink. He never sleeps.' The Vietnamese man was in the bar during the day; he had delivered their coffee and rolls that morning; now he was behind the reception desk.

'Perhaps he's a twin?' Link went on. 'That would explain it.'

They went out to a pavement café to eat sausages and tiny chips and giggle over the menu, but they were both tired. Back in their hotel room, an American war film was showing, and Link sat up in bed, exulting over hearing his native tongue.

Julie thought of all the things she had seen since she came to Paris: the fish in the Tuileries, the tap-dancer at Trocadéro, the tower and the statues and the gold animals by the fountains. But the images that remained were of the girl in the yellow jacket and the name of the solitary Scotsman in the Roll of Honour of Napoleon's men. MacDonald. Had he died in France and had they carried him back to his native hills? Or was he lying here, lonely? 'I'm lonely,' she thought and turned on her side so Link would not see. She had looked for the yellow-jacketed prostitute as they came home and felt a pang that she was not there and might be in danger.

Eventually Link slept, lying on his back breathing gently, looking for all the world like one of the cherubs from the Arc de Triomphe. As the thought struck her Julie knew she had to go there, just once more . . . and alone. She dressed swiftly, one eye on the bed, but Link never stirred, not even when she took the key from the dressing-table and went out on to the landing. She passed the Vietnamese in the lobby and muttered something about 'fresh air', but he only smiled and went about his business.

It felt strange to be out on the streets by herself, but Julie negotiated the crossings and only knew fear when she came to the subway, deserted at this time of night. Dare she go through it on her own? She took a deep breath and started to run, not stopping until she emerged within the monument, an echoing island in the sea of light that was Paris by night.

She touched the carved walls and spoke one or two of the names aloud . . . Moreau and Lafayette, Bruix and Bernadotte. She said another prayer for MacDonald and then, eyes still closed, she made a vow to come back one day and bring her children to see the richness that was here. She was returning to the subway when she remembered Josephine, whom Napoleon had never stopped loving even though he cast her so cruelly aside. 'And God bless Josephine,' she said out loud, 'and her children.' And then, as another afterthought, she added the little King of Rome.

Link was still sleeping when she got back and did not stir when she slipped into the bed beside him.

It was Yvonne who went down to answer the heavy knocking on the outer door, which they had locked at eleven. Rose stayed cowering on the landing; Nana peeped from her own door. Only Yvonne had the courage to pull back the bolts and open the door on the chain.

'Is Rose here?' He had a black moustache and looked a bit like Alan Whicker. The collar of his camel coat was turned up around his face and he was smoking a thin black cigarillo. 'Common,' Yvonne thought, and was instantly fortified.

'No,' she said firmly.

'Come on,' he said impatiently. 'We both know she's here. Fetch her.'

'Now, look . . .' Yvonne said, but Rose was already beside ber.

'I'm not coming back, Ray. I've had enough.'

'Don't be silly, Rose.' He dropped the cigarillo and stamped on it. 'Come home and we'll talk it over.' His tone became more wheedling. 'You know I didn't mean it. Come on back and we'll have a few drinks. We can work it out.'

Yvonne could sense that Rose was weakening. She cleared her throat. 'Is that what you said last time? And the time before?'

Ray ignored her. 'Come on, Rose. Don't hang about.'

Yvonne heard Rose sigh and reached out to take her arm. 'Remember, Rose! Remember last time.'

There was a pause and then, without speaking, Rose turned and began slowly to climb the stairs.

'Rose!' Ray was shouting now and Yvonne heard Nana's 'tsk tsk' in the background.

'He'll wake my Billy . . .'

'Sod your Billy,' Yvonne said and would have closed the door except for Ray's suede shoe wedged in the opening.

'She'll come back,' he said. 'Interfere as much as you like, she knows where she's well off!'

Yvonne sought for words and, finding none, lifted her foot and stamped hard on his shoe where it stuck out into the hall. She felt her heel go home on his shoe and would have done it again if he had not yelped and withdrawn it. She slammed the door and shot home the bolts.

'My God,' Nana said, appearing in the hall behind her, 'I never knew you had it in you.'

Charlotte came at one o'clock creeping along the landing, opening Graham's door, crossing the space to his bed gingerly in the lamplight. He hesitated only briefly, then folded her in as soon as she slipped out of her dressing-gown, feeling the silk of her nightdress, running his hand over the curve of her hip, the firm slope of her thigh. 'Comfy?' he asked.

'Very. I must be out of here before everyone wakes up,' Charlotte murmured, and Graham squeezed her to reassure. 'Wasn't it a lovely wedding?' she said and he squeezed her again, this time in agreement.

While he had lain there waiting for her he had been filled with lust. Now, suddenly, he simply felt comfortable. He thought of Charlotte in the church that morning. She had played her part perfectly, lifting the train, taking the bouquet, shooing the little attendants into place.

Her father had talked in his speech of 'my lovely girls' and Charlotte had looked at Graham and pulled a little face of embarrassment.

'Love me?' she asked now.

'Well,' he said, 'I'm not sure . . .' Her hands were on

him then, tickling, seeking his vulnerable places. If she kept that up it would start and he didn't want it to, not yet. He was aware of a nice amount of champagne swimming in his veins; he felt warm and safe and sentimental, not really lustful at all. Suddenly he remembered one of Julie's terrible jokes. He had spelled out LUST on the Scrabble board and she had said, 'Lust? That's what happens to Japanese cars.'

He chuckled and felt Charlotte's lips against his neck. 'What are you laughing at?'

He put his hand on her breast, feeling it just too full for his hand. A perfect size. 'Nothing,' he said. 'Nothing important anyway,' and moved his hand to the safety of her waist.

'Don't you want to?' Charlotte whispered.

Graham cuddled her closer. 'Not yet. Shall we get some sleep first?'

She sighed a little but it was more exhaustion than disappointment. 'OK. But I've got to be out of here before morning.'

'Go to sleep.'

'Love me?'

'Of course I do,' he said and heard her breathing slow and deepen. Did he love her? He certainly wasn't averse to her, that was for sure. He felt sleep overtaking him and postponed worrying about anything until the morning.

22

Julie woke early, at once sad that there were only a few hours of Paris left and elated that soon she would see her children. Beside her Link slept like a baby, the yellow curls with their heat-crinkled edges tousled now.

Beside him, on the bedside table lay the remains of his sitar money. Not a lot of it left because he had bought souvenirs for everyone. Julie wanted him to grow up but please God he wouldn't lose his enthusiasm or his generosity while he was doing it. She moved cautiously, but he didn't stir, and at last she was free of the bed and could pad softly to the window and throw it open on to the Paris street.

She wanted to see Sacré-Coeur today, and the Pompidou building . . . this last because Graham had said she must. And maybe the Arc de MacDonald . . . for so it would now always be to her. But above all she must come back to Paris. That was the most important thing of all.

Link's eyes opened. 'Last day,' he said cheerfully. 'What d'you want to do?'

Julie decided to be generous. 'What do you want?'

'Let's go to the Moulin Rouge,' he said. 'Or the Folies Bergères.'

Julie sighed. If that was the height of his ambition . . .! She thought of his home life, the rows, the strife, his two elder sisters both with kids and still at home so that he'd been glad to get out. He hadn't had a chance really. Not yet.

'We'll see,' she said. 'We might get to one of them if you behave.'

*

When Graham awoke he thought he was dreaming. The duvet was up around his face, and he gasped and paddled for air. And then he heard what had awoken him: the raised voices on the landing.

'How could you, Charlotte! How could you . . . when we've had all this trouble with Alison?'

'You've got it all wrong, mummy,' Charlotte said desperately.

'I couldn't bear another scandal.' Her mother was wailing, and then there was whispering and the sound of another bedroom door opening and closing.

They had been caught . . . *flagrante* ruddy well *delicto*! Graham groaned and slid beneath the duvet again until Charlotte appeared, a finger to her lips, to pull the cover away.

'It's all right,' she said kindly. 'They won't horsewhip you. I've told them we are engaged.'

Tommo broke eggs into the pan with abandon. The rule was one, but today he felt like six and if he felt like six he was ruddy well going to have . . . three! He was beating in butter and milk and watching his toast when his mother came into the kitchen. His head was throbbing unmercifully but this time his heartbeat was steady.

'Mother! You can sit down, it's nearly ready.'

'I just want tea.'

'Please yourself.' It was not the answer she expected. Normally he would have offered variations, begged her to try at least a piece of toast. Now he decanted his own eggs on to buttered toast and carried them to the table, together with tea-pot and milk and sugar.

'I enjoyed that,' he said, when he was done, wiping his mouth with a smack. His mother supped her tea and he could almost smell the tension emanating from her.

'Now,' he said, pushing back the chair the better to relax. 'It's cards-on-the-table time. I'm going into business. I may fail and lose everything, but I'm eighty per cent sure I won't. I know my trade . . . or I know what it used to be, what it ought to be. I think I'll make money, and if I do you'll share in it.' He paused to wipe his mouth again.

'Funnily enough, I love you, mother. You've done everything in your power to stop me but it hasn't worked. I love you and I care for you, and I always will. What I won't do is let you ruin my life, or even interfere. Because if I let you, and if you succeed in spoiling things for me . . . and we both know what I'm talking about . . . I'll come to hate you and I'll go, right out of your life! So for your sake as much as mine, I'm going to run my own life from now on. And if I can get Julie to share it I'll be a lucky man.'

He waited for a burst of venom but it never came. For a moment the silence panicked him but then he remembered his new resolution. 'More tea?' he said and picked up the pot.

They took the Porte de la Chapelle line as far as Pigalle and emerged into the bustle of the boulevard de Clichy just as the guidebook said they would. Julie had expected glamour in the street of the Moulin Rouge, but instead there was a dirty crowded avenue with pigeons fighting over crusty bread in the gutter.

The Moulin Rouge itself was a disappointment. The Red Windmill was small and tawdry, and the foyer was what you might see in any English cinema . . . pictures of glamour girls in feathers. No naughtiness other than a bared breast here and there. 'Lovely pair of tits,' Link said ruminatively, 'but the parks is better.'

A Japanese man was posing for a camera under the mock Toulouse-Lautrec murals. Julie had seen them before in a book in the library and recognized the man with the pointed chin. A black man appeared in front of her, dressed in colourful robes and jangling bracelets for sale. 'Nice,' he said, teeth gleaming. 'Nice?'

'Let's get out of here.' Julie was beginning to wish they had gone back to the Tuileries. But then they turned up a side street and the magic began – an assault of smell and colour and sensual delight. Fish and meat were temptingly displayed, and fruit that was out of a dream in its perfection. Peaches and melons and grapes, and much that was wonderful that she had never seen before.

Cooked food in shells was mixed up with raw meat –

that was unhygienic, but no one seemed to care – with filled avocados with swirls of mayonnaise, and brawns and pâtés, and wonderful kinds of bread everywhere. 'I'm famished,' Link said and fished for his money. While he patronized *charcuterie* and *boulangerie*, Julie looked at the tiny windows towering above and around. More people must live to the square inch in Montmartre than anywhere else in the world.

'Not more than in China,' Link said when she told him. 'That's why their favourite sport's ping-pong. They don't have any room for anything else.'

'That's not their favourite sport,' Julie said.

'What is then?' he said truculently.

'They've got a population of 900,000,000, Link. Work it out for yourself.'

They ate their purchases on the terrace in front of the Sacré-Coeur, looking out on a hazy Paris of tower blocks and spires and domes like St Paul's. Everywhere black men in polka dots and stripes were selling everything under the sun, and the only way to escape them was to go into the dimness of the church where candles spluttered at the feet of the Virgin and there were red gladioli on the altar.

'It's not as big as Durham Cathedral,' Link said proudly and received a glare from the pew in front.

Somewhere a child was crying, and Julie had a sudden longing to have Jason on her knee. Most of the people in the prayer section were men, and some of them had children with them. 'I *will* bring Jason here,' she thought and prayed for strength to keep the vow.

Out in the sunlight again a group of Chinese were playing guitars and cameras flashed but the music was American pop which somehow spoiled the effect.

They didn't talk much on the way back to the hotel. Julie noticed that there was very little graffiti and hardly any litter, and it made her feel ashamed. And they hadn't got to the Pompidou building, which was a pity. She wondered if she should lie to Graham when they spoke but decided against it. She would simply promise not to miss it next time.

The Vietnamese man was hovering in the hall. 'He does everything here,' Link said. 'If we said we wanted entertainment he'd be through that door straight away with a banjo. He's exploited.' Julie was thinking that there were twenty-two bridges in Paris and she had seen only a handful. But she had seen the Arc and the statue in the Tuileries gardens, a man and woman naked but beautiful with it. Her head fitted on his shoulder, his penis was limp and their arms loosely entwined. Julie had looked at it and thought, 'That's what being serene means.' And then they had moved on to see a white-faced Chaplin figure do his robot dance, and she had given all her small change to some children to put in his box. 'I'll remember it all,' she thought . . . but remembering would not be enough.

She had bought a little painting for Graham, a water-colour of the pond with all the toy sailboats on it. She wouldn't tell him about it when he rang her. She would keep it for a surprise.

Yvonne had gone down to lay Julie's fire but someone had been before her. It crackled gently in the grate and there was a new loaf on the table, a bunch of broccoli, some groceries in a plastic carrier and a bunch of scarlet artificial geraniums. 'Tommo,' Yvonne thought. It wouldn't be that old faggot downstairs – she was more likely to take than give. For a moment Yvonne felt a stab of jealousy. Why should Julie get so much attention? But when she went upstairs Rose had a cup of tea ready and Yvonne felt a flood of gratitude.

'I've been thinking,' Rose said when they were seated comfortably, mugs in hand. 'I can't impose on you forever. I only came because I had nowhere else to go. I don't really know Julie that well and she might not want me hanging around when she's just off a plane.'

'No,' Yvonne said cautiously, aware that Julie might come back entwined with Link or with a French onion-seller in tow.

'I'm going to get a job,' Rose said. 'I've got good bar experience, and when I get rid of these bruises I'll get something soon enough.'

'Yes,' Yvonne said wistfully. 'The first time I saw you I thought you were smart.'

301

'I trained as a hairdresser,' Rose said. 'Years ago. I should've stuck at it. I might have, if it hadn't been for Ray.' She looked at Yvonne's hair. 'I could do yours for you, if you'd like? You're not bad-looking yourself, Yvonne. You just need a few tips.'

Yvonne put down her mug, trying not to look too keen. 'I've been thinking too, Rose. There's another bedroom here, an attic. It's warm and dry . . . only a dormer window, but the hot tank's there, so it's cosy.' She moved to the trap door and pulled down the extending ladder. 'I would've put John up there but I wanted them both beside me when I moved in.'

Rose was looking up into the attic like a hunted fox looking at sanctuary. 'If you're sure it wouldn't be imposing?' she said. 'It'd be ideal up there . . .' She suddenly touched Yvonne's arm . . . 'with you down here to stick up for me.'

'Not at all.' Yvonne felt better than she had felt for weeks. Being a deserted wife was bad but being a battered common-law wife was infinitely worse. At last she had some status!

'Sit down, Graham.' Charlotte's father indicated a straight-backed chair and Graham sank on to it, feeling as though his wedding tackle was three feet long and growing. No one had prepared him for a situation like this. What did you say to a wronged father? If he ever got out of this he would never take risks again.

'Well, this is unexpected,' Mr Conway said. He cleared his throat. 'My wife is . . . understandably . . .' He cleared his throat again and stood up. 'I think we'll have a drink.'

They both felt better with wide squat tumblers of whisky in their hands. 'Now, about this wedding . . .' Mr Conway said. 'We'd have preferred to wait awhile, but that's what we said to Alison and look what happened there.' He drank deeply. 'Charlotte tells me you're a solicitor.'

It was Graham's turn to clear his throat. 'Yes, sir. I'm a partner in quite a large practice. Litigation mostly.' He hadn't contemplated marriage. Not yet. Not without a period of adjustment. He was about to murmur something about a long engagement when he heard a creak from the hall. So Charlotte's mother was lurking out there. He might have expected that. He could face it out man to man, but Charlotte's mother was something else.

'Of course I want to do whatever will make Charlotte happy, sir. We've known one another for more than a year and I'm sure she'll make a very fine wife.' Even as he said it he thought it sounded less than fraught with feeling but Mr Conway seemed not to notice.

'Shall we say May?'

'Why not, sir. May will be fine. You and Mrs Conway must meet my parents. They'll be delighted when they hear.' Graham held out his glass for a refill and let the last tiny sliver of resistance ebb away. When they finished the whisky Mr Conway called in his wife and daughter and opened a bottle of Moët.

'To Graham.' Charlotte's mother lifted her glass in a gesture of reconciliation.

'And Charlotte,' he said in return, smiling knowingly at his fiancée and ingratiatingly at her mother, wondering why Charlotte looked so composed when she ought to be as taken aback as he was.

'You'll need to see the vicar in plenty of time,' Mrs Conway said. 'And you want to work out who your bridesmaids will be.'

'Cars and photographer,' Mr Conway said gloomily, 'that was Alison's biggest problem.'

'This wedding won't be like Alison's,' Mrs Conway said icily. 'Not at all alike.' Graham tried to catch Charlotte's eye and, failing, felt for her foot with his own but when he found it the gesture was repulsed and when he met her eye she gave a small frown of reproof.

'We trust you, Graham,' Mrs Conway said. 'I'm sure we've had quite enough upset for one family. Quite enough.'

Mr Conway nodded solemnly and so did Charlotte.

'Don't worry, mummy,' she said. 'You have nothing at all to worry about.' Above her head Graham could see an invisible neon sign light up: NO MORE NOOKIE.

'Oh well,' he thought. 'It isn't that long till May.' And only another thirty-six hours before they would be leaving.

303

He looked at his watch. Julie would be in the air now, a Paris weekend behind her. He mustn't forget to ring her tomorrow at five sharp.

Nana looked at the clock. 'I wonder where our Billy is?'

In the chair opposite Sammy folded his hands in his lap. 'Don't worry, Edie. He's only young. He'll be off somewhere larking about.'

'He doesn't lark, he vultures,' Nana said. It was a relief to have someone who was fair about Billy, even gave him the benefit of the doubt, but it made it all the easier for her to see him as he really was, and what she saw she didn't like.

'What are his friends like?' Sammy asked.

'Reggie Kray, mostly,' Nana said. 'I don't know, I'm about at the end of my tether.'

Sammy removed his pipe from his mouth and pointed the stem at her. 'You relax, Edie, and stop worrying. Leave the lad to me. There's a nice music programme on about now. Let's sit back and enjoy it.'

'But you don't understand, Sammy.' Nana felt a duty to explain, to prepare him for the worst. 'I've got to be honest, Billy's not an easy boy. I defend him . . . well, he is me own flesh and blood . . . but he's a handful.'

'In what way?'

She thought for a moment before she replied. 'If he'd been born with a silver spoon in his mouth, he'd've nicked it out of the midwife's saucer.'

'Bad as that?' Sammy said, seeming unperturbed.

Nana felt increasingly desperate. 'And he's got a gob on him.'

'They mostly have nowadays,' Sammy said mildly. 'It doesn't mean all that much. They were bred by an "afraid to say no" generation. What else can you expect? We deny them nothing, except our attention. Watch the telly, clap your earphones on, go and spend some money . . . but don't bother me. It's not how we were reared, Edie, is it?'

She shook her head as he went on.

'On top of that they get conflicting messages. Trendy vicars are the worst. It doesn't matter what you do, as long

304

as you care about it. Break the law, as long as it's in a good cause. Cut a fence, throw a brick . . . as long as you mean well, it's OK. Then the bobby comes along and says, "Right lad, you're nicked." No wonder they're confused.'

Nana tried to find words but couldn't. In the end she sat back and listened to the brass band, her foot tapping to the music, her hand beating time until Sammy reached out and imprisoned it in his own.

When Billy came in Sammy stood up. 'Come by the fire, lad, and get warm. You look perished. I've just been talking to your grandma. We need some advice, about our plans and that sort of thing . . .'

A scowl started up on Billy's face, tried to change midway into a leer, and lapsed into a weak smile. Sammy was presiding over the kettle. 'I'll make us all a nice cup of tea and then we'll see what you have to say.'

Nana turned away and looked into the fire. The little sod would win in the end but if she got five minutes' peace in the meantime she wasn't going to grumble.

'Have you finished?' Link asked, regarding her tray eagerly. Julie nodded and switched it with his empty one. He finished off her fromage frais and her cream cake and the rest of her red wine, and stowed all the unopened sachets in his pockets. When the air hostess came back both trays were bare.

'Not long now,' he said.

'Are you glad to be going home?' Julie asked.

'Yeah,' Link answered. 'I've missed the telly, and the beer was crap. The franks were nice, though, and the crusty bread, and all the bare-buff statues.'

'What will you remember most?' she asked.

He pondered. 'That Vietnamese,' he said at last. 'If he wasn't twins I'll eat my hat. I give him all me spare change when we left and he said "We, mercy." So there must be two of them.'

'Oui, merci,' Julie said. 'Yes, thank you – that's what he said. They were ten-franc pieces you had left. No wonder he was pleased.'

They had bought as much booze and cigs duty-free as

they could afford. 'We shouldn't give Nana fags,' Julie said but bought them just the same. They trundled their trolley through the green channel and walked towards the entrance.

'A taxi'll cost a bomb,' Link said. 'I'll just have to use the sweep money.'

'We'll go shares,' Julie said. And then Tommo was there, smiling, taking her bags, and all Link's cracks about Old Father Time didn't matter because she was really home.

23

When Julie first woke up she half expected to hear the sounds of Paris but there was only the sound of Damien cooing in his cot. She got out of bed, pulling on her jersey, and went through to collect him before he woke Jason. It was too late. 'I'm not going to school today,' Jason said.

'Oh no?' Julie responded. She held Damien in her arms and shepherded Jason through to the fire. 'Why not?'

'I'm poorly,' he said.

Her resolutions about patience were beginning to melt already.

'Where? Does your head hurt?'

'No, me leg.'

She examined him carefully for trauma but his legs looked as sturdy and unblemished as ever.

'Was Auntie Yvonne kind to you?' She wanted a 'yes' but only a qualified one – no enthusiasm.

'She has runny jam,' Jason said. 'And syrup. And her bed bounces. I'm going back next week. And Auntie Rose is getting a video next week.'

'Nice,' Julie said. 'But now you're going to school.'

They were having the brown-bread wrangle when Tommo arrived.

'I put the geraniums in the box,' Julie said, gesturing towards the window where the plastic blooms defied the winter sky. She had removed the knickeranii but the pants were ruined, got at by the weather. She had put them in a plastic bag and consigned them gently to the pedal bin. They had served her well while they lasted.

'I thought you might be a bit pushed your first morning back so I've come to give you a lift.'

Tommo held Damien while she washed and dressed Jason, and quelled Jason's grumbles about going to school when one of Julie's bags was still unopened.

'You've got all you're getting, chum,' Julie said. 'A set of boules and a jigsaw. You're a lucky boy.'

Tommo fumbled in his coat pocket. 'How about a Twix? Would that do?'

Jason accompanied them, munching contentedly, and they all sat in the van until the school bell rang. 'There now,' Tommo said. 'That one's off your back.' He chucked Damien under the chin. 'And you won't give any trouble, will you?'

'Anything happened while I was away?' Julie asked. She had had a garbled version of events from Yvonne and seen Rose briefly, but you could never be sure Yvonne had the right end of the stick.

'I've got things straight with mother,' Tommo said. 'She won't bother you again. All the same . . .' He had started the van but now he switched it off again. 'Julie, I've been doing some thinking . . .'

Julie's heart sank and she hurried to stem his flow.

'I've got to get back, Tommo. I've got a lot to do.'

'You're not going into work today, though?'

'No, but I've got to meet someone at five o'clock. And I'll have to sort Rose out before I go.'

He started the engine again without demur, and when Julie looked at his face she thought he seemed relieved.

She let herself into the house and looked at Nana's door. If Billy was dolling off . . . As if on cue the door opened.

'Before you ask, he's gone to school. Come in and search . . . don't forget behind the pictures and inside the toilet rolls. I suppose she's been on, her upstairs with the lodger and the loose mouth . . .'

'. . . it's better than a loose wire,' Julie said. 'I worry about what'll happen when you start growing up.'

'Well, stop worrying,' Nana said smugly. 'I'm doing all right.' She held out her left hand. A gold signet ring fitted snugly above her wedding ring. 'Take a look at that, and eat your heart out, Zsa Zsa Gabor!'

She looked at Julie, who was agog. 'Nice to see you strapped for words for a change.' She folded her arms.

'While we're on, I might as well tell you I'm having a party tonight, an engagement party. We're having . . .' she narrowed her eyes and adopted a sing-song voice, '. . .fish-achips. I've ordered them off Wha-U-Won and he'll have them ready for half-past eight. Our Billy's going to collect them. You're all invited − that half-wit you went away with, and the two merry widows upstairs. You wouldn't believe what's gone on here while your back was turned. And Tommo's invited too. It's not my idea, it's Sammy's. Him and our Billy thought it up.'

'Who's paying?' Julie asked faintly.

'Me,' Nana said. 'I put all me money on Paris Shenanigans at Sandown on Saturday, on account of your dirty weekend, and it romped home.'

Julie ignored the innuendo. 'How much did you give your Billy?'

'Not a penny, as God's my witness. Anyroad, I couldn't − I'll need it all for the fishachips. Chinkies doing battered cod, that's what we've come down to. Still, his chips are lovely.'

'So they should be, the price they are,' Julie said. 'It's since they put VAT on.'

'Is that what it is?' Nana said. 'I thought they tasted funny.'

Julie had a cup of coffee to fortify herself and then went upstairs to be greeted by a radiant Yvonne. 'Now come in and sit down. Rose and I were just saying you must be worn out.'

Rose was installed in a chair by the fire, looking quite at home and smiling, which made a change.

'You're asked to a party,' Julie said. 'To celebrate Nana and Sammy getting engaged. Fishachips from the Chinky at eight o'clock. We'd better all bring a bottle, or something.'

'I'm glad about the news,' Yvonne said. 'I could make some of my dip. It's luscious with crisps.'

'And I can get booze wholesale,' Rose said, 'if no one'll take offence.'

'Don't let that stop you,' Julie said. 'Yes, the dip'll be lovely, Yvonne. Don't dip into it beforehand. It'll be a nice start to the meal.'

Yvonne had launched on a grumble. 'She's going senile down there. She won £60 from the bookie – £60!' Her eyes glazed as she thought what she could do with £60. 'And it's all going down the drain.'

'Well, it's better spent on a party than frittered away.'

'Don't mention fritters,' Yvonne said.

'Should we buy a joint present?' Rose asked.

'We could send them a kissogram,' Julie suggested.

'More like a smack-in-the-kissergram,' Yvonne said. 'She tortured me while you were away.'

Julie saw Tommo again as she went to the shop. 'You're asked to a party,' she said. 'Nana and Sammy are engaged.'

Tommo beamed and Julie smiled. 'You look happy,' she said.

'I am. I'm glad for Nana, she needs someone to look after her . . . and I don't often get asked to parties. I don't make friends easily. I'm all right when I'm working, I mean, you've got the patter to hide behind then, haven't you? It's different in private lives.'

'You're all right with me,' Julie said.

'You make it easy.'

She knew what he meant but chose to ignore it. 'Yeah, I like talking to men. When I was in care I liked the men in the home best, but you were never allowed to be alone with them . . . not for long. As far as the world's concerned, all women are Florence Nightingale and all men are child-molesters. And it's just not true. Take Hunch-front.'

'No thanks,' Tommo said, grinning as he drove away.

Julie parked the pushchair outside the shop and carried Damien inside. Ali's face lit up at the sight of her, bringing a burst of their native tongue from his wife, ensconced in her usual place behind the till.

'So you're back,' he said to Julie, chucking Damien under the chin. 'How is Paris? Very French?' He grinned at his own joke.

'Very,' Julie said. There was a sudden eruption behind the till but he didn't turn his head. Julie moved away in an attempt to defuse trouble but he followed her. An elderly

310

customer came in at the door and his wife called 'Shop' in stentorian tones. He didn't turn his head but leaned even closer to Julie.

'Shop yourself,' he said, winking at her. He inclined his head towards the shelves she was examining, pretending to help her choose. 'My wife is cross,' he said. 'She is not a trusting woman. I am a father of five, I tell her. I am respectable.' He shrugged. 'She does not listen.' He took his hand and mimed a mouth with his fingers. 'Yak, yak, yak.' He would have moved closer if a bundle of gardening raffia had not whizzed past his head.

'Hoi!' he shouted, his eyes popping. 'This is not a ruddy cricket pitch.'

'Cricket,' his wife said. 'Ruddy cricket!' She lapsed into her own tongue again, eyes flashing, words erupting like machine-gun bullets.

'What's she saying?' the elderly customer whispered to Julie.

'I think she's pulling his stumps,' Julie said and left to try her luck at the Co-op.

Yvonne and Rose had agreed terms – very favourable terms, Yvonne thought, but Rose seemed satisfied.

'If I had a bottle of champagne I'd open it,' Yvonne said.

'Let's have another cuppa,' Rose said and moved to the kettle. She was carrying the tray to the coffee table when they heard Link's voice on the landing, and a moment later he was through the door. There was a bulge under his jacket and Yvonne eyed it curiously.

'What's that?' she said.

He shifted uneasily inside his anorak. 'You won't tell Julie, will you? She'll play war!' He reached in his coat. 'Look at that!' It was a puppy, golden-brown with eyes like goldfish bowls. As they looked at it, it cowered.

'God,' Rose said. 'Give it here.'

'Where did you get it?' Yvonne said, as Link handed it over. 'It doesn't look old enough to be away from its mother.'

'I took it off some boys,' Link said. 'They were using it for a footie game, so I chased them. Me mam says it can't

311

stop at home on account of our Tracy's baby and me dad's whippets, but I'm not dumping it.'

The dog had buried its head in Rose's bosom and she was stroking it with a controlled intensity.

'They should be shot,' Yvonne said, reaching to ruffle its fur. Rose looked up and their eyes met. 'It can stop here,' Yvonne said.

'Good,' Link said. 'I thought you'd cr . . .' He bit back the word but Yvonne was ahead of him.

'You thought I'd crack? Cheeky monkey.'

'I'll look after it,' Rose said. 'It won't be any trouble.'

There was terror in her voice and Yvonne patted her arm. 'It's stopping, Rose. What's one more mouth to feed?'

'Are you going to live here?' Link asked Rose when Yvonne had given out tea all round.

'Yes,' Yvonne said. 'She's having my attic, we're going to get some furniture and give it a good clean out . . .'

'I can get you some furniture,' Link said. 'Good stuff, an' all.'

'It's not hot, is it?' Yvonne asked, remembering Julie's warnings.

Link looked hurt. 'No, it's not. I don't do that now, it's kid's stuff. If I want something I get HP.'

'Do you pay?' Yvonne said.

He shifted again.

'Usually. Anyway, like I said, I can get you some good second-hand stuff. Nipping clean and dirt cheap.'

A slight frown had furrowed Yvonne's brow. 'Shouldn't you be at work?'

Now Link looked extremely uneasy. 'Well,' he said, 'as a matter of fact . . .'

'He's done it now,' Yvonne said dramatically as Julie came in from her shopping. Julie put the pushchair under the stairs as Yvonne descended to tell her news.

'Who's done what?'

'Link. He's got the sack again.'

'You're joking,' Julie said.

'Absenteeism!' Yvonne said dramatically. 'He stopped

312

off to go to Paris. He asked, and they said no, so he went anyway. So this morning they sacked him.'

'Oh God,' Julie said. 'I wish I'd never asked him to go now.'

'He'd've lost the job anyway,' Yvonne said. 'You can't blame yourself.' She leaned forward. 'You haven't heard everything yet, either.'

'Not more,' Julie almost wailed. 'What else has he done?'

'Go and see,' Yvonne said. 'Go and see his wall. I'm saying nothing. And, anyway, Rose is waiting for me.'

Julie put Damien back in the pushchair and half-ran to Shields Road, causing Damien to squeal with delight when the pushchair bowled along like a chariot. She found Link standing on the bank, looking down on the wall.

'Yvonne says you've lost your job!'

'Yeah,' he said. 'It looks like it.'

'You have or you haven't,' Julie retorted. And then, despairing, 'You said you were enjoying it.'

'I was,' Link said. 'Still, I've done what I wanted to do, so it's OK. I did it for you, Julie.'

'For me?' she said wearily. 'What do you mean "for me"?'

Link raised his arm and pointed at the wall.

'What do you think of that?' he asked proudly, and she looked at the wall.

It had been painted white all over and then the first nine or ten courses of brick had been painted green to represent the earth. Above that there were trees, and then patches of blue fading into infinity, an infinity of stars and moons and satellites. A universe. And across it all, somewhere between the Milky Way and Ursa Minor, in letters a foot high, *Link loves Julie* was sprawled in vermilion paint.

'My God!'

'I think it looks good,' Link said defiantly, and Julie saw that he believed it – believed that she should be up there among the galaxies, emblazoned on the wall for everyone to see.

'What did they say?' she asked.

There was a moment's hesitation. 'About that?' he asked. 'I dunno.'

'You don't know? What happened, Link? Exactly?'

313

'I turned up this morning,' he said. 'For work. And he said, "Bugger off". So I finished the wall off.'

'When did you do it?' Julie asked faintly. She wanted to be angry with him but it wasn't easy.

'Lunch-time,' he said. 'When they went off to the pub. It was there, wasn't it, all that stellar space. Ages ago I wondered, what else does it need? That's when I decided. But I would've waited, if he hadn't finished me.' Link thrust his hands further into his parka. 'I think it looks good.'

'I've got to go,' Julie said faintly. 'I've got someone to meet at five o'clock. We'll talk about it later on.'

She would rather have gone to the phone box by herself, leaving the kids to be cossetted and fussed over by Rose and Yvonne, but Jason wanted to go with her and having seen so little of him in the last few days Julie was unwilling to refuse. So she took them both.

The light was already fading, almost gone, but when they reached the phone box at the top of the hill she could just see Link's wall, earth and space and stars and moons and galaxies spinning on forever. And across them all 'Link loves Julie'.

Tomorrow they would have to talk. She would work out something for him, a proper job with a chance to meet new people. That was what he needed. She lifted Damien from the pushchair and shepherded both children into the telephone box. It was four fifty-five by the church clock; only five minutes to go. Damien was sucking his anorak again and she let him carry on. Anything, as long as it kept him quiet for the next few minutes.

Graham intended to use the extension in the hall to ring Julie but as he came down from his room he was seized by Mrs Conway.

'It's so fortunate. The vicar's called to say what a lovely wedding Alison's was, and we've told him your good news.' She was propelling him towards the drawing-room, and he tried to resist.

'I've just got to make a phone call.'

'Not now,' she said, shocked at his reluctance. 'It can wait till the vicar's gone, surely?'

Charlotte appeared, pink-cheeked and girlish. 'Hurry up, darling.'

'I've got to phone Julie,' he hissed. 'Remember? I promised.'

'Do it later.'

'She's waiting in a phone box,' Graham said desperately. 'We arranged it.'

Mrs Conway had preceded them into the room and was holding open the door, and Graham had a sudden terrible feeling that when he entered that door would clang shut behind him. Forever!

'Don't be silly, darling,' Charlotte said soothingly. 'She's probably not there. Girls like her forget. You can find out all her news on Tuesday.'

Graham hesitated, looking back at the phone. It *had* been a long time ago that they'd made the arrangement. And there *was* always tomorrow. He put up a hand to straighten his tie and went in to meet the vicar.

Julie stayed in the phone box for forty minutes, shifting Damien from one arm to another when he refused to sit on the ledge, pacifying Jason when he whined to go home, pretending to search the directory when anyone passed.

In her heart she had always known Graham would not phone . . . but that had not stopped her from watching the handset, waiting every second for the comforting sound of its ring. At last she knew it was hopeless and, besides, the needs of her children could no longer be denied. 'Come on,' she said. 'Time to go home.' She felt a sudden sense of relief that it was over, that she knew where she stood. Now she could put away the fantasy and get on with making the reality better.

Damien was falling asleep and she lowered him gently into the pushchair, wincing as blood returned to her leaden arm. He was putting on weight, and no mistake. When she straightened up she looked over the dark town, seeing the pubs well lit and the roads like highways of light, going

315

everywhere and nowhere. 'Like me,' Julie thought, her resignation turning to despair.

'We're going to see the crib on the way home,' Jason said. It was a statement and Julie did not argue.

In the darkness the painted mural glimmered faintly. Tomorrow they would paint out Link's declaration of love and she would set him free, once and for all, to grow up. She had a funny feeling that Link would make something of himself one day, in Parkhurst or Parliament, or maybe both. And Tommo would thrive and prosper, and marry a nice woman and live happily ever after. She felt a little tremor of unease at that. She would have to be a *very* nice woman or she, Julie, would have something to say.

She was walking towards the church when she heard Tommo's van behind her. It drew level and stopped, and he opened his door. 'Get in. I'll get the bairns.'

'I can't, Tommo. We're going to the church to see the crib. I promised Jason.' Did he know she had waited three-quarters of an hour in a cold phone box for a call that never came? She hoped not.

He stepped out of the van and moved towards her, reaching to ruffle Jason's hair where it appeared from his hood. Jason grinned up at him but pulled at his mother's hand, impatient to go. Tommo looked down at his feet, cleared his throat and spoke.

'I'll come straight out with it, Julie, because . . . well, if I don't I'll lose me nerve. I don't have much to offer, not at this stage, but I care about you and your kids and I've got big ideas . . .'

Julie put out a hand. 'Tommo, before you go on. I like you very much. In fact, I'd even say . . . well, I was very fond of you. But I've got some sorting out to do before I decide anything.'

'So you're not saying "no"?' he said.

'You haven't asked me anything,' she answered. And then, to change the subject, 'There's the party tonight. Nana's engagement.'

He nodded. 'I know,' he said impatiently. 'But listen, Julie, I don't give up easily. Not when it's something I want.'

316

'I know,' Julie answered, feeling Jason's impatient tugging at her jacket.

'Well,' Tommo said, suddenly deflated. 'I'll see you tonight, then.'

'Yes,' she repeated, 'I'll see you tonight.'

Tommo got back into the van and shut the door. Julie was about to turn away when he wound down the window. 'I meant what I said, Julie. I won't give up.'

'Good,' she said and saw him smile.

She moved away then, impelled by Jason's desperate urge to see the crib. 'He's like me,' she thought, 'always thinking his dream's around the corner.' The thought of all the disillusion that lay ahead of her son overwhelmed her . . . until they turned in at the church gates and the crib was there, the stable lit by the star, the patient beasts, the shepherds, and the Magi and Joseph, watching over mother and son.

'See,' Jason said, his eyes sparkling. 'I told you it would be here, didn't I?'

As they walked home, Julie thought about the Virgin. In pictures She looked serene but in reality She had probably worried about her baby, about draughts and diseases in the stable and the long journey ahead.

Women were born for worry, Julie realized. There was no escape from it – not for virgins or Parisian whores or even empresses like Josephine, who had died, according to the book, *'killed by her own anxious heart'*.

'I mustn't drift,' Julie thought, tightening her grip on the handle of the pushchair. If she was ever to find happiness it would be through her own efforts. There was no other way. She thought of the forms she had brought from the library for Link, promising an education, making it seem easy, within everyone's grasp. Could she do it? Could she learn and grow? If she worked part-time for Tommo she could go to night-school. She could learn bookkeeping and proper English and enough French to manage when she went back to Paris. If Nana turned respectable, and Rose rescued Yvonne, there would be no shortage of baby-minders, only a bloody argument over who got to do it!

In the darkness Julie smiled, thinking of working along-side Tommo, helping him prosper, seeing him get what he deserved. She would work out her notice at Graham's until he found someone else, but that chapter was over. She allowed herself to picture him one last time but the image was blurred. She would always be grateful to him, though, for helping her to glimpse the amazing world outside.

She was impatient for Jason to see Paris, to have a nice home and plenty of books and no more holes in his trainers. And she could do it if she tried. She might even sign off, if it all came right.

They were half-way down the road now, the hill falling sharply away. 'I liked the crib,' Jason said. 'It was good.' He pursed his lips, reflecting. 'I want a space-suit for Christmas,' he said at last. 'What do you want, mam?'

Julie started to run, the wind catching her breath so that she had to shout for her reply to be heard. 'What do I want, darling? I want . . . everything! And toot bloody sweet!'